ONE HUNDRED BOTTLES

UNIVERSITY OF TEXAS PRESS   AUSTIN

ONE  Hundred BOTTLES

CIEN BOTELLAS EN UNA PARED

By Ena Lucía Portela

TRANSLATED BY ACHY OBEJAS

This publication received support from the National Endowment for the Arts.

**NATIONAL
ENDOWMENT
FOR THE ARTS**

LIBRARY OF CONGRESS CATALOGING-IN-PUBLICATION DATA

Portela, Ena Lucía, 1972–
  [Cien botellas en una pared. English]
  One hundred bottles = Cien botellas en una pared / by Ena Lucía Portela ; translated
by Achy Obejas. — 1st English ed.
    p.   cm.
ISBN 978-0-292-72332-0 (pbk. : alk. paper)

  1. Cuba—Fiction.   I. Obejas, Achy, 1956–   II. Title.   III. Title: 100 bottles.
PQ7390.P64C5413   2010
863'.7—dc22
                                                   2010006344

TRANSLATOR'S ACKNOWLEDGMENTS

Mil, mil gracias a Megan Bayles, my indefatigable proofer, and to Casey Kittrell of UT Press, whose patience is golden.

Something small has decided to live.
ANNA AJMATOVA

Chapter 1

At least one blow

IF THERE WAS ANYTHING THAT GREATLY IRRITATED HIM, THAT PRE-disposed him to violence and murder, it was when somebody tried to make him believe. Ha! His face would turn red, fiery red, a steely red, with vibrant flames, and there would be Moisés in the middle, crazy with horns and tail, a furious serpent, a basilisk, a dragon, a devil in his inferno. A heck of a scene. It got so you wondered if he'd die, just like that, from spontaneous combustion.

He didn't hide the absurd and even ridiculous side of his anger. He knew that none of those miscreants, wretches, imbeciles, or fucking bastards would ever make him swallow even the tiniest of their tall tales. They lacked shrewdness, spark, street smarts. They had no class. They lacked everything he had in surplus, stuff he didn't even need. What were they thinking, huh? That he was born yesterday? That he was some kid, a brat from the day care center? That they could fool him just like that? Pretty bold of them, those jerks . . . the obvious lies, so stupid, designed for weak minds—they made him even angrier than the more sophisticated efforts. The clumsier the fib, the greater the disrespect to his intelligence.

In any case, controlling himself was a huge effort. He'd already been cited various times for creating a public nuisance, for hitting a transit officer, for beating three black guys from Los Muchos tenement to a bloody pulp, for throwing a bench at a mirror in a bar, for breaking a bottle over the redneck who ran the pharmacy, and for trying to burn down a little hotel. He was subversive to the max, to the point that some folks called him The Anarchist, The Terrorist, The Bomber. Sometimes he'd be held overnight, and since he was always waiting for the next hearing, his police record was frequently indistinguishable from the New York phone directory. The only thing that kept him out of jail was his psychiatric history, which included the prodigious testimony of one Dr. Hermenegildo Frumento, who added that Moisés was not, fundamentally, bad. In other words, that his capacity for trouble was no greater than that of a typical citizen, an average man submitted to many challenges, and to all the malevolence of the tropics: the unnerving and humid heat, a persistent drizzle, mud, stickiness, the smell of rot, mosquitoes, fruit flies, bureaucratic incompetence, etc. On more than one occasion, he'd tried to strangle his therapist, but without much success. Luckily, he'd never thought of carrying firearms. He satisfied himself with dreaming about a rifle, and a National Rifle Association of which he'd be president and number-one lunatic. Those guys—those brazen jerks—wouldn't leave him alone. They insisted, reiterated, persisted ad infinitum with a disgusting cool. And still they dared to give him mocking looks, those smug sonzabitches with their cynical squints.

He knew, since he was so sagacious, that those rotten preachers didn't believe a word of their own lies. How could they possibly believe? People who believe—he asserted this as he shrieked and pounded on the table—people who *really* believe, never try to convince anybody else. They don't need a consensus. They don't think they're some kind of apostle. They believe they're happy when they direct themselves toward what they believe they love (I love this phrase) and the rest is bullshit. You have to be really insecure, really screwed up, really in a bad way, to climb up on a podium and lecture, beg for someone else's consent, and then go out hunting for proselytes. So when they tried to deceive Moisés, what they were really doing was deceiving themselves, adjusting, rounding out, perfecting the story in the same way somebody might introduce improvements to the comfort of their own apartment. Incapable of living freely, they lived in a greenish and foul bubble of fallacy. They needed his troubled faith to feed their own famished one. But instead of appeasing him, this thought only made him more indignant. So they were trying to use him, eh? Pigs, monsters, loathsome jerks, assholes. How infuriating. Oh, how he hated them!

It was during a pleasant fall evening, the equinox, with little birds chirping and tiny frogs in the ponds, that I dared suggest he shouldn't pay attention to them, that he should just shrug it off.

"Forget about them, boo," I whispered in his ear. "Just go on your way. No more fighting the enemy and getting all worked up and bent out of shape. Isn't your point that they can't and won't ever be able to convince you? So then, sweetie"—I kissed his neck—"why suffer over something that's obviously not worth it? What do you gain from getting like that, my love? If you don't take care of yourself, one of these days you're going to have a mad breakdown, a stroke, some kind of attack. You'll be left all stiff, just like that, a veg. And I haven't the faintest idea how to take care of disabled people." I unbuttoned his shirt very slowly. "You have to get out of that vicious cycle, boo, c'mon . . . You're too tense, too tight"—he really was. "Look at yourself. Why don't you try to relax? Like, yoga. 'Yoga' means tranquility, equanimity, great calm, very little anxiety, spiritual peace or something like that, I don't remember . . ." I rubbed his chest. "The most important thing is your health. Look, when they see that you're indifferent to them, that their opinions don't matter one bit to you, they'll leave you in peace. That's how it always goes. You pay them no mind and they move along, to dick with somebody else who'll pay attention to them. Just play dumb, baby, and you'll see how it goes. You'll see, I swear." I kissed him on the mouth.

To be perfectly honest, I didn't have the vaguest idea who "they" were. It's just that it occurred to me that, in a situation that desperate, it might be best to stay on the sidelines. Pay no mind. Laisser-faire, laisser-passer.

But, as it turned out, he didn't listen to me. Worse, he looked at me with horror.

"Get off of me!" he screamed, and shook me off as if I were a hairy spider. Next thing I knew he threw a fist in my belly and the other at my eye so I wouldn't be such a wuss. Oh, women! Always with their ignorance, their nonsense, always with their frivolous plots. Women were the very height of retardedness. Who could have come up with them? They were so stupid, women. They couldn't begin to understand the essence of things, the world as a place of will and representation. Did he have to explain everything to me? Was I such a cretin? If he didn't pay attention to them—now at the height of a lycanthropic episode, Moisés bared his teeth and growled like a ferocious wolf while I crawled on the floor and tried to get out of reach, just in case he decided to kick me—those ruffians, those charming thugs, would feel it their right to believe that he believed what they wanted him to believe (the nausea and pain didn't really allow me to capture the intricacy of such an interesting idea), because in his silence he'd have given his permission, and they would act accordingly. Yes, he knew them well. So well, like the back of his hand. How could he not? They swarmed every corner. Everywhere he looked, there was always at least one of them . . . (I looked around, just in case, but none had managed to get into the room.) They were mean, vile, meddlers and opportunists. Insatiable and hungry cockroaches, a mess of insects. No wonder he was on the lookout for them, no wonder he had them in his sights so he could stay one step ahead of them . . . Didn't I realize the seriousness of the situation? Everything with them came down to a battle of wills, a war of egos to see who was the bigger macho, who had the bigger balls, who had the most testosterone. He had to be on guard. Because if he let them get their way one time—just once—then they'd most likely try to make him believe even more preposterous lies than before, even stinkier, fouler lies. And then there would be more and more of them . . . it would be never ending. And they sure weren't going to get him like that! No way. He had his strategies. As the ancient Romans used to say: *si vis pacem, para bellum.**

In the meantime, I should stop with the crying and drama, get up once and for all before he had to get me up with a good smacking or by dragging me by the hair so I'd go to the den downstairs (there's a clandestine bar on the first floor of Happy Hammer Corners, which is owned by Pancholo Quincatrece, my buddy, where it's possible to buy marijuana; I live upstairs) so I can buy him a liter, oh, and cigarettes (whenever he was really furious, when he was a total beast, the darling liked to smoke two at a time, one in each hand, taking turns inhaling), because there wasn't a more indecent sight in the whole world than a subnormal fat girl splattered on the floor, with her smudged mascara, crying black tears and playing the victim as if she were *La dame aux camélias*. Man, had I ever turned out tragic! I could have been Greta Garbo. He put the money in my hand and shoved me. Get out! I'm not sure but I think Moisés resented me a little over the deal with the transit cop, because

---

* Before he lost his marbles, Moisés had been a brilliant lawyer. When he dropped out completely, at 46, he'd been a judge in the republic's Supreme Court. A very cultured and eloquent man, he liked to spice his pronouncements with bits of Latin. Since I know most people have no reason to know what these mean—they're busy and don't have time to find them in the dictionary—I've made it my job to look them up myself. This one means: If you desire peace, prepare for war.

they'd taken away his driver's license—how unfair!—and now he depended on me (only to a certain point, only to a certain point, he made that quite clear to me) to get from place to place looking for new clashes.

At the beginning of our adventure, when he was still married and completely hysterical because his wife and children didn't understand him (I understand them), I thought that if I just kept my trap shut during his long, fiery rants against the cheaters, counterfeiters, perjurers, charlatans, gamblers, and hustlers, that he would, in fair reciprocity, keep from hitting me. But no. How silly of me. Where did I think I was? Whether I was quiet or not, there was always at least one blow. He *had* to hit me because, in his crazy mind, I was deceiving him too. Of course, it wasn't a matter of sleeping with other men—who was going to notice such a fat stupid girl with a look about her like an eighteenth-century French whore? (Although a bit rococo, I found this description fascinating.) Besides, I don't think he cared much for fidelity: He wasn't the type of guy who dealt in details. The way he saw it, I deceived him when I tried to trick him, cajole him, and make him look like an idiot by pretending to understand him, when I called him boo and baby, when I sang to him, "Oh you're so cute/ so precious you are," or when I undressed him with my teeth, or when I circled him like a satellite of love, purring like a cat in heat, or when I performed a striptease just for him (for years I've dreamed of undressing before a crowd, on a counter or something like it, but I've never had the chance) to a soundtrack of music from the 40s, lit only by a bamboo lamp with a red silk frame; when I touched his anguish, his pain, the terrible desperation he felt living in this cruel and soulless world chock full of enemies.

Boo and baby, him? A serious man like him, nearing fifty, tall and strong and with a certain Hebraic patriarchal air? C'mon, what kind of disrespect was that? What the fuck was I thinking? Did I think he was a faggot or what? Where did I think I was going to get with all that cooing? Didn't I take him seriously? Was there a chance I understood even a smidgen of something as complex and subtle as the theory of authority (the most abominable of all arguments, he said, because it was purely scholastic), Cartesian doubt, Kierkeggardian (what a word) doubt, or Pirron's skepticism, the greatest doubt of all? What did a fat girl with a big butt know about the different stages of doubt, about the precariousness of existence, about the insignificance of being here, about the scandal implied by death itself? Frankly, zilch. I didn't even think that thinking about death was amusing. Because, in the end, there's no escaping it, it's going to get us anyway . . . So why so much morbidity? That's like living in perpetual agony, dying every five minutes.

But, sometimes, these scoldings served to make me question how it had been possible for me to survive surrounded by so much ignorance and so much neglect. How I'd managed to avoid things I never saw coming, how I'd escaped wrapped in such unprecedented, exuberant, and eerie unawareness. I was then hit by a surge of good intentions: the desire to go to the library, to read big fat cryptic philosophical treatises, all swollen with concern over the scandal implied by death, with a lot of quotes in Greek and German (mysterious languages), to ponder them, develop my intellect, and evolve until I became a tormented, somber, and taciturn person . . . But that inspiration never lasted long. It wasn't my fault: generally speaking, things don't last long in the Caribbean. I got lazy, relaxed right away. I was seduced by the sweet satisfaction of doing nothing at all, of vegging out, of languidly fanning myself while resting on the window sill and admiring the shape of the clouds, or the elephantine steps on the ceiling, or the lines drawn in the air by the flight of a botfly. Someone told me that, more or less, that's what Muslim heaven is like.

Frequently, Moisés would forget about me. He'd disappear from the Corners for days, even weeks. Using fuel or a little mechanical work as payment, I'd put the car in the garage of a neighbor who would solemnly swear he wasn't going to steal the tires or the wipers or the rearview mirror or anything else, and I'd dedicate myself to waiting patiently, to thinking about the complications of staying put in order not to think about the hospital, the police station, or the morgue. If Penelope weaved and undid a tapestry, I, in turn, would retire to Muslim heaven and tra-la-la that song about one hundred bottles, the one that goes: "One hundred bottles on the wall . . . / one hundred bottles on the wall . . . / If one should fall . . . / ninety-nine bottles on the wall . . ." Later, another would fall and there would be ninety-eight, then another and another until the end, when there would be zero. It was quite entertaining and the little sing-song also served as a spell to avoid catastrophe. I liked to think that if I reached zero, nothing awful would happen. I never knew where my baby went or why (although I could imagine) and he'd return bruised, scratched, cut, bearing all kinds of injuries. I never knew when he'd come back, or even if he'd come back. Of course, he never explained. According to his own words, he'd gotten a divorce so he could be free, not so that I could control his every step.

He also had the habit of disappearing inside himself, down into the labyrinths of his deep rage. He'd sit in a corner, hating, alone with his liter, in the same pose as Rodin's *The Thinker*. Father Ignacio, a little old man practically heroic in his commitment to dealing with the neighborhood's 83,000 sins (the worst: domestic violence, child abuse), who generally happily, and honestly, accepted any kind of joke about his surname—Loyola, no less—told me once that that statue made him anxious.

"You tell me, child, what kind of position is that to sit in a chair, with his head hanging like that and his spine all twisted up?" Father Ignacio aped the pose with obvious disapproval. "Let's not even talk about the scoliosis that's bound to come from that, but what kinds of ideas can come to a man sitting like that? Nothing that's not dark, atavistic, and destructive. Thinker, my foot. That's no thinker in my book. He's bitter, resentful, envious, frustration personified. An enemy of communal peace. A public nuisance."

In fact, my "Thinker" cursed them all in a low voice. He shit on each and every one of their mothers. He gave them all the stink eye. With gritted teeth, he insulted them all, smacked them with condemnation and contempt, and wished them all dead. A million deaths. If only a cobra would bite them. Or if they could be poisoned with methane gas. Or get AIDS. Or get run over by a truck. Or hit by lightning. Yes, yes! That was it—an avenging ray of lightning! His hands would brutally twist an invisible neck until it emitted its last breath.

"Die already, goddamn it, die, die!" And then he'd laugh. "Heeheehee . . . checkmate . . . heehee." He had that little liquid laugh, Luciferian, which made my hair stand on end.

Later, he'd come to and look at me as if he were lost, as if he was about to ask me where we were and who I was. Then, suddenly—bam!—he'd snap out of his amnesia. Once he recalled that every now and then he shared a bed, a shower, and a cup of coffee with someone else, someone who, no matter how retarded she was, could see him and hear him up close, touch him and know his vulnerabilities and insecurities—then his first and almost always sole response was suspicion. And he'd start in on me, quite naturally, by accusing me of spying on him.

Moisés appreciated darkness not just in the figurative sense. Because of an ophthalmic or cerebral imperfection, I'm not sure which—he didn't like to talk about illness (one time, Dr. Frumento mentioned the word "photophobia" and his favorite patient told him to go to hell)—Moisés's eyes didn't have a good relationship with the sun. They stung, they oozed, they got red and bloody.

On the streets, he used dark glasses that made him look like a Mafioso, drug dealer, or contract killer, like a John Dickson Carr character; the lenses were diabolical mirrors that took images apart and then put them back together with a sinister touch. When he was home, our enormous window (the sill goes down to about my knees, maybe a centimeter off more or less; to lean against it and enjoy the view after our battles, I have to sit on the floor), our only window, had to be closed and black curtains strictly drawn (double, triple, dense, impenetrable, a real horror). He had taken it upon himself to patch all the holes so that the most inoffensive ray of light—even those fringes of sun in which tiny multicolor particles float about—could not gain access. We used electric light even at twelve noon. In case of blackouts, we lit candles. The neighbors assumed we were involved in a satanic cult. I wasn't particularly surprised, since all we really needed to complete our healthy vampire life was to sleep in coffins. It was incredible it hadn't occurred to him yet. When it came to the heat, we pretended it didn't exist, which is a lot of pretending in the Torrid Zone, until it reached 35 degrees Celsius in the shade and the room boiled like the ovens in the crematorium at Auschwitz. Then my baby said, Enough, what a country, what a fucking country where you melt and then evaporate, and he installed an air conditioning unit so that we could freeze our asses off the way God intended. In case of blackouts, we went for a stroll or we simply roasted.

Moisés's love—he hated the word "love," which is in and of itself fraudulent, meaningless except for a stupid red paper heart pierced by an even stupider arrow—consisted of screams, insults, and threats so horrible that, had I followed them to the letter of the law, would have meant I wouldn't be here now to tell the tale. He was a supreme master at the art of humiliation and the poetics of mockery; he didn't miss a single entry in any vocabulary designed to denigrate a human being. In short, I was the most despicable creature he'd ever met in his life. A particle floating in a fringe of sunlight, a microbe not worth taking into account. His love also included hitting, with his fist or the belt buckle, bites and pinches that left bruises, scratches, dry penetration, and other delicate acts. I think he kept waiting for me to suddenly confess my insincerity. He nearly accomplished it that memorable day he grabbed me by the shoulders and started smashing my head against the wall: "Die, just die, goddamn it, die, die . . ."

Oh, that's when I learned how fear can overcome pain, how it eclipses and overrides it in extremely dangerous circumstances, how a person can transmute not just her neurons but, rather, all of her cells into pure fear—really, a beautiful experience. In the end, he let me go so he could smash his own head in the same way (that's when I understood Dr. Frumento's insinuations about getting a room with padded walls), which allowed me to get a bucket of cold water and pour it over him to put out the fire. This incident forever affected the hearing in my left ear.

Of course, my pleasure struck him as fake. Why did I sigh? Why did I moan? Why did I get wet so quickly when all he ever wanted was to torture me? And everything else, why? How could I like a man whom I couldn't understand at all, who was old enough to be my father, and who wiped the floor with me? No, of course I couldn't. He wasn't some idiot standing around on the corner. Go tell somebody else that story! I was just like the others—a liar and a fake, an evil whore. Very evil. The kind who lie with their entire body. Exhausted, he'd look at me skeptically, the way criminals look at their dogs, those strange creatures who adore them no matter what. He'd light a cigarette, just one, and hide behind the smoke.

Now I ask myself if I really did like sleeping with him. Yes or no? He was convinced I didn't, but I did. A lot. In the deepest way, until I got dizzy from it. He was a beautiful man, Moisés, with those big, black, rabble rouser eyes, always hiding from the light, and that aggressively curved Nazarene nose, and his venerable Leonardo da Vinci white beard. His mouth . . . Frankly, there had been many before him, but none like him. I was aroused by his smell, by his deliriously low voice, by the atrocious things he said and forced me to repeat (in truth he didn't have to go to much trouble to get himself an echo, *talking* gives me the shivers), his body temperature that was almost always feverish. His way of walking, so feline, as if he was lying in wait. Even his red aura of fury. Ah, Moisés . . . There are still days I miss him, especially when it rains or it's cold and the city crumbles outside.

It isn't easy to confess this. Some people are disgusted by it. For example, my friend Linda thinks I'm a degenerate with only half a neuron, and that I'm not worth more than an earthworm crawling up a dirty spout. Poor girl, she's ashamed of me. She's a professional writer, a *real* writer, a traveler, ambitious and full of energy, feminist in her way and full of very important thoughts. Her tendency to generalize made her consider that when Moisés the Caveman hit me, he was hurting all the women on the planet. Those here now and those still to come. But beyond the politics, she took it all very personally, and very hard. Oh, if only one day that ogre, that Cro-Magnon, that thug, that troglodyte, that Nazi would get confused, get his wires crossed and try to hit her . . . Ha. Then he'd see, yes sir, he'd see what could come out of a little box of guava sweets. She practically wanted him to. Yes, because those who live by the rod . . . —sometimes my friend also suffers from that same impetus that makes people scream and hit the table with their fists—What the hell was that guy thinking? Who did he think he was? So impotent, such a failure, such an insect . . . Because I was a fool and brainless, I'd given him too much leeway, too much license. Too much. And the sonovabitch took advantage and abused me. But one day, he'd come to his Waterloo, because not every woman was as timid, unhappy, or willing. Absolutely not, goddammit.

Without ever having laid eyes on him, Linda hated Moisés with the same intensity with which he hated "them." Deeply, dizzily. Like Hannibal the Carthaginian hated the ancient Romans. His mere existence offended her, drove her out of her mind. Of course, I never went to her with complaints or tears, not only because my situation (to give this thing a name of some sort) didn't exactly cry out to be made public, but also because I didn't want to add fuel to the fire. I've always believed that everyone should take full responsibility for their decisions and shouldn't go crying on other people's shoulders. But a bruised eye or a broken lip can be very hard to hide, even under three tons of makeup; to make things worse, my friend is very observant. She's very keen, quite astute, and always finds a way to get everything out of me, point by point, and then she gets even angrier. As a matter of principle, machos in general only provoke her disdain, but my lover became a question of honor for her. She'd get even with him and put him in his place or her name wasn't Linda Roth. To this day, I still don't know how I managed, in four and a half years, to avoid that dreadful meeting, especially in the summer months, which is when people get most intransigent and bellicose, and thus avoided my little home becoming a battleground. I think if for no other reason, I deserve the Nobel Peace Prize. Who would have won in that war of titans? Who knows? Me, I wouldn't have bet on either of them. I would have simply hidden under the bed. Because if Moisés, in the red corner, counted on brute force like an orangutan, then Linda, in the blue corner, counted on a certain cryptic evil, like a serpent. They were both magnificent, whole and spectacular.

She would have loved to castrate him. Wasn't I familiar with the delightful story of Pierre Abélard, the French rhetorician? A fabulist in the end, she even made plans to do it. First, two sedatives dissolved in one liter. Or better three, considering the complexity of the beast. It was imperative to take advantage of the enemy's weaknesses, and she was well aware the animal was a major-league alcoholic. Then, to wait for the magic potion to take effect. No hurrying. Patience, great patience. To watch the slow descent of his lids, the tension, the collapse of the tower. Then, the pruning shears, clip clip, and the transition from bull to bullock would be complete, mission accomplished. Deed done . . . oh, and an artistic detail: we'll put it in his mouth, like a cigar, ha ha. Didn't I think that was an excellent idea?

I don't usually argue with Linda (in general, I don't usually argue), because she's wiser, shrewder, and always struggling to bring light into my dark life, even if sometimes it's by force. Nor do I like to inhibit her initiatives, as she says, or clip the wings of her imagination. But on this issue I gave myself permission to underscore a few tiny problems with the plan. What if he woke up at the precise moment and caught us both red-handed? He'd be pretty mad. And what if he bled to death? A heck of a problem. Could we get away with it? Almost certainly not, because it would be incredibly hard to get rid of the evidence, to clean up the blood and hide the body, the murdered body which weighed 91 kilos. Maybe she wouldn't but I'd get really nervous and would confess everything to the first cop who crossed my path; they'd have to slap me to get me to shut up. And, did she know that in our country the death penalty is still in effect, that the majority of the judges are men, and that, quite probably, not a one of them would be amused with our little prank, especially since we would have played it on one of their former colleagues? Yes, he'd been a judge on the Supreme Court and a full professor at the Law School, a real celebrity. Anyway, the whole idea of castration struck me as unfair, a bit excessive, since Moisés had never mutilated me in any way.

"You can write about those things," I told her, "but you can't act on them. If you're so intent on playing with scissors, don't you think it'd be best to do something more symbolic? Maybe you could cut his beard . . ."

Linda was horrified. She raised one brow and then the other. She looked at me as if I were monstrous. What did her sweet little ears hear? The little man's beard? Wow. There was nothing more repulsive to her than facial hair, so a man's face would never be as caressable to her as that of a girl. When had I lost my taste? Of course the beard was unnecessary. Beards were disgusting. But to be happy about cutting off a beard when you could cut off . . . ? Why the hell was I so passive, conservative, and silly? Did I have the soul of a yam? Or was I completely lacking in self-esteem? What century was I living in? My tongue ached to tell her the eighteenth century, my favorite century, but I controlled myself, in case she thought I was mocking her or something. Instead, I tried to change the subject. I asked her about her latest novel—how was it doing? I lauded the previous two, which were absolutely majestic and had had great impact. I told her she was a genius, that no one admired her like I did, and I even compared her to Virginia Woolf, but no go. Her latest novel, *One Hundred Bottles on the Wall*, was the story of a double homicide, but she still didn't know who to kill—she pointed at me, as if she wanted to kill me. The previous two had also been bloody and truculent, but they were out in the world on their own now. In the not-too-distant future, they'd be classics of the thriller genre, noir classics. Her agent was negotiating translations. And there might be a movie version . . . That was a great dream: to write for the movies. That's where the real money was, in the movies, and who was going to deny it, money made the world go 'round. Anyway, she *knew* she was a genius, much more so than that hypocritical English lizard I'd dare to mention in her presence. She didn't need to hear praise or bullshit, so I could spare her all my stupid admiration. Did I really think I could manipulate her with such sweet nothings? How pretentious, how arrogant the little fat girl could be. And she turned on me. As they say, in full force.

She got quite sarcastic, poisonous and cruel, as only she can get. She felt really sorry for me. Really sorry. Practically wanted to cry; she gave me a twisted grin. Yes, my story was a real tearjerker, like melting ice cream, a soap opera for retired ladies. I reminded her of women in Islamic countries. (She'd only told me about the beauty of the Aya Sofia when she went to Istanbul, so what could she be referring to now? I didn't dare ask.) The women in Islamic countries didn't have any choice in how they were. But in my case . . . I was pathological. It must be some sort of trauma to the cerebellum, a virus. In all honesty, and to be precise, I reminded her of certain characters from Patricia Highsmith's *Little Tales of Misogyny*. I couldn't possibly guess which one. Yes, that very one—she didn't actually wait for me to guess—"The Victim." The cheap provocateur. The imbecile, the nothing, the mentally retarded one. The one who got raped a bunch of times. Wouldn't I like that? Divine, right? Surely I entertained those sorts of fantasies before going to sleep. Why didn't I beg the Caveman (because all my communications with him, of course, were pleas, on my knees and kissing the floor) to invite all his buddies over for a private party between them and me? For an instant, I wanted to tell her that Moisés was very much a solitary man, that he didn't have buddies, but I controlled myself once more. It's important not to torment friends.

With a metallic voice that was at once as screechy and sharp as the blade on a dagger or a carving knife, she was off: all about victimhood. That little whore, more dolled up than a clown, her hair dyed, a masochistic cockteaser to the extreme, always playing with fire . . . until she got burned. Didn't I want to know the end of the story? Well, of course, it's as expected, the victim gets lost in an Islamic country. She's a pitiful thing, despicable, pathetic. A trashy woman. Revolting.

Sometimes Linda would overwhelm me with her readings but, by coincidence, I'd read the aforementioned book in this case. Yes, very original. An exhaustive catalogue of diverse female depravations. All the stereotypes. Strangely, the only one missing was "The Bostonian." That is, the dominant homosexual: caustic, totalitarian, and a busybody. Needless to say, I didn't bother to express my astonishment to Linda. It's important not to offend friends. But she didn't give me any credit for that. In spite of my silence (or perhaps because of it—I imagine that for argumentative people the absence of an adversary of the same caliber must be disconcerting), she slammed the door and stayed away for months. She didn't even say goodbye before she left for the Frankfurt Book Fair. I called her house three, four, a bunch of times, but she just hung up on me. I found this all quite terrible, because this charming girl is the person I love the most in the world.

Now that it's winter and I'm alone again (though not for long, since something small has decided to live), I think about Moisés. I don't mean "think" in a direct way, with rigor, following the logic of the word. I don't think I've ever known how to do that. Which is a shame, considering how important it is. Mostly I muse, I let my memory go free and it takes off, like a wild animal which surges, snakes, curls, and ends up leaping onto Moisés's neck. There are many questions and very few answers. Why did I accept his conditions? How did I let things go so, so far? At what moment did I lose control? What control? Did I ever have it? Was it ever really in my hands to stop what finally happened? I don't know. I don't think Moisés hated me. In fact, I don't think I mattered much to him. I wasn't important at all. His only obsession was with "them," the rascals, the rogues, the bandits. The enemies. His entire existence was based on trying to stop them from deceiving him, to catch them red-handed, to rip off their dirty masks, destroy their Machiavellian plans, confuse them, smash them, annihilate them, pulverize them. He was more misanthrope than misogynist. In his battle against humanity, I was his sparring partner. So that when he hit me, he was really hitting them.

In this unfortunate personal intervention, I symbolized the worst of the human condition, the worst side of all earthlings, so repulsive, obnoxious, and sickening. To break one of my fingers meant razing Prague. Strangling me until I couldn't breathe, that was the massacre at Tlatelolco. If someday he'd managed to choke me to death (just a suspicion), well then, Hiroshima and Nagasaki. Now that I think about it with some calm, it's possible poor Moisés was a little sick.

Chapter 2

Happy Hammer Corners

PERHAPS MOISÉS'S PERSONALITY MAY PROVE MORE INTERESTING, but for now I'd like to talk about me, even if it's just a few words, because everybody's important in this story and, for that reason, we all have a right to a wee bit of egocentrism. This business of "everybody's important" is the kind of thing that someone with a devastating inferiority complex comes up with but, what can I say? My name is Z, which leads Linda to all sorts of wisecracks about my place in the alphabet, which she says is identical to my place in the world. In my readings, I've learned that Tchaikovsky used the Z—a kind of Cyrillic Z, I suppose—in his letters and journals as a secret code for homosexuals, e.g., "it was a pretty good party, there were lots of Zs . . ." But I also know that, because the Z is barely used in English, it means that in Scrabble, that game in which letters are used to create a kind of puzzle on a board, and each letter has a different value, mine has the greatest number of points: ten. Apparently, English speakers have a really tough time placing a Z in its proper place. I'm not surprised that they eye it warily and that we are indebted to Shakespeare for this exquisite saying: "Thou whoreson Zed! Thou unnecessary letter!" That's what he said in one of his comedies, that resentful man. But I couldn't care less. I may be lacking in practically all the virtues possessed by Don Diego de la Vega, but my signature (because I do have one, though I never use it) has an air about it like the mark of Zorro, and that's saying something.

It's best if I don't talk about my physical state. I know that I *should* exercise, I know. I don't exercise plain and simple because I don't want to, because I find exercising horrific, because I'm intimidated by pools, tracks, and squash courts; I'm so horrified that I haven't even taken the trouble to come up with a more decent excuse, and my poor conscience carries the weight of that guilt night and day. I have no peace or tranquility, and no matter how I try to avoid my responsibility to deal with the problem, to turn the corner and just live my life, as much as I try to forget the whole matter of kilograms, I can't, because Linda reminds me with particular cruelty every time we run into each other. Thirty-five pounds overweight? What kind of shamelessness is that? How could I neglect my appearance so terribly? Was there a creature in the world with a bigger sweet tooth than me? How many miserable pizzas and croquette sandwiches and pieces of peanut brittle had I dared gobble down in a day? Better yet, why couldn't I focus on vegetables? Had I not seen myself in the mirror? Who the hell did I want to look like? And so on. I don't want to say anything to contradict her, but the truth is that I don't understand why we, humble and inoffensive fatties, are the victims of such fierce intolerance, why we're disdained, stigmatized, marginalized, why we're jeered, why we're called whales, tanks, porpoises, wardrobes, amplifiers, hot air balloons, and other fine things—why we're persecuted and have to surrender to the whims of the skinny. As Oliver Hardy might say, the fatso always loses.

Since I've known her, my friend has always shown a great talent for cornering people, for grabbing them by the neck and throwing them up against the wall. According to her critical eye, the most appropriate thing for me to do would be to take up a combat sport like judo, kung fu, or tae kwon do—in other words, to kill two birds with one stone, since these kinds of disciplines are not only good to burn fat and help a person look like a person—she explains this to me in a condescending, practically maternal tone—but because they also raise self-esteem, subvert the most elemental power dynamics, and offer a new and interesting vision of the world to the practitioner.

"How delightful to be able to knock out some big fat guy," says Linda, "hit him with a coupla good ones, smash his nose, disconnect his jaw, break his teeth, crash, crash, crash . . . I get shivers just thinking about it." And in fact, she shivers. "Because the thing isn't just to do it, no. So what? That would be too crass. The thing is to know that you could, *if you wanted to* . . . Aha!"

As a fan of women's boxing, she deplores the mental deficiency of certain obtuse and meddling officials who insist on banning it because women are delicate flowers, or, in other words, out of pure machismo. Flower, my foot. What an abomination. I consider her quest for justice quite laudable, I applaud it and cheer it on and all that, but, as far as I'm concerned, I'm sure that if I ever found myself with a pair of gloves in a ring . . . I'd just die. Maybe the truth is that I *am* a delicate flower, a timid violet, an opulent rose, a lily of the valley, who knows? A squash blossom. I'm quite the coward, the dope. I'm afraid of anybody determined to pluck my petals.

Still, sedentary, like moss on a stone, I've lived in the same place since I was born, a little palace in Vedado that's an architectural jewel, a monument to extravagance, a marvel of odds and ends and patches and sutures, an eclectic Frankenstein fashionable in 1926 and in ruins according to this year's style. This little palace, across the street from the nearly collapsed and dusty Christian Science Library, right on the corner of a main avenue and an alley-like street of ill repute that's a disaster, has suffered so many brutal transformations in the course of nearly a century that it's really astonishing it's still standing. It could fall down any day now, especially with these tropical hurricanes . . . we'll just have to wait and see. In the meantime, the roof leaks a fine grit and pieces of stucco. I've thought about wearing a construction helmet, just in case I get my skull fractured one of these days. There are also cracks in the walls. Vertical cracks, the dangerous kind. During hurricane season, water comes in everywhere (except the faucets, of course), and my life consists of catching leaks in pots and buckets. At the beginning, though it may seem incredible now, this was home to somebody with a lot of money, some anonymous oligarch who owned sugar mills or tobacco farms or coffee plantations or ranches and, of this I'm sure, he had very broad taste, the kind that inspires happiness just from breathing under a colonial roof with neo-Gothic windows, Roman arches, baroque balustrades, art nouveau gates, and Greek columns from different eras. Anyone with knowledge of architecture just looks at this place and scratches their head: it's a wonder there's no Mudejar minaret, no Byzantine dome, no Egyptian pyramid.

On what I imagine as a blustery night, the oligarch disappeared. He vanished without a trace, as if a genie from a magic lamp had spirited him away. Other than the Cadillac in the garage, all he left behind was a maid, a black woman named Petronila Hamilton, who, of course, didn't know a thing. And even if she had . . . well, that's the first hole in the story of this place: a broken thread, an empty space in which delirious hypotheses and crazy arguments proliferate with an eagerness for fictionalizing. It's possible our big shot, bored with his little palace, had ordered that something even more schizophrenic be built on the shores of the Almendares, just three kilometers from here, charmed by the idea of owning both a mansion and its reflection. Or maybe he traveled to Tibet and the monks convinced him of something that's very difficult to put into words. Or he was ruined because of a lie, because of a stupid fat girl with an air about her like an eighteenth-century French whore, or some damned twist of fate, and so, sick with cancer, he hanged himself from the roof with barbed wire. Or he was assassinated and since then his spirit has roamed the halls hovering between blue smoke and squeaking chains. Perhaps he's behind me right now, reading this very page over my shoulder with oligarchic disapproval, dying to take the pencil from me. Who am I, so audacious, to talk about his private life this way? Who gave me permission? And what kind of bullshit is this, writing with a stub on tattered newsprint? Why don't I try to get a computer? Or at least a typewriter—in any case, something more fitting with his lineage? Oh, if he only knew! I like people who disappear. If I could, I'd disappear too.

We're told what happened next by a bronze plaque (firmly embedded in stone, so it can't be stolen) next to the front door. Between 1954 and 1961, the big house was the headquarters of some kind of organization, an esoteric club affiliated with the now-defunct Pythagorean Party, which was casually referred to as El Xilófono and organized practitioners of black magic and fortune-tellers against Halley's comet, Saturn's rings, flying saucers, cosmic dust, the conjunction of Uranus and Neptune and other space debris which, I suppose, destroyed them in the end. It's not good to fight such powerful enemies. According to them, what was above was isomorphic to what was below—that is, both the cosmos and human life had the same composition and would respond in the same way to stimulus, or something like that. And since human life was just a tad fucked, they launched themselves with great quixotic zeal into the war of the galaxies. They never counted on popular support. Ingrates, the neighbors always saw these people—black magic practitioners and fortune-tellers in revolt—as a bunch of kooks. What can you do? To be honest, I haven't found much sense in their activities either, although I did think it was a good thing they didn't fire Petronila. It's possible I haven't really tried to understand; I hardly ever try very hard to understand what I don't understand. Now and again I think there's nothing to understand, that things are as they are and that's that.

My great-uncle W., the marquis's grandson (well, yes, there's a marquis among my ancestors whose title goes all the way back to the time of El Cid, so it's true that in my ghetto veins there are in fact a few drops of the most authentic blue blood, which I won't deny no matter how often Linda accuses me of being a snob) and the honorary president of whatever that club was, sometimes likes to visit me and have a little chamomile tea and smoke a pipe and yak and predict the future and all that, but he doesn't dare, the poor man, because as it turns out, on the front door, the one downstairs, a huge heck of a door, there's no doorbell or anything remotely like it, and since I live upstairs, the only way to access my charming self is to stand on the sidewalk and scream your lungs out: "Zeeeeeeeee! Zeeeeeeeee! Zeeeeeeeee!" My great-uncle, the marquis's grandson, resists this vociferous method, not just because he considers it vulgar and one of the worst of the local customs, but also because since I live on a busy avenue, and since he is a famous astrologer, a passerby might recognize him and that could provoke adverse comments, rumors, and whispers about his inappropriate conduct.

"Hey, Manolo, my man," the gossip would go, "you're not gonna believe who I saw the other day! None other than W., . . . the fortune-teller, dude, the fortune-teller! The mystic, yeah. And you shoulda seen him! He was plain crazy, screaming like a banshee in front of the house where El Xilófono used to be . . . You've heard of El Xilófono, right? Yeah, I'm pretty sure it's with an X. What a riot! Well, it looks like the old man finally had the lights go out or got hit on the head or lost his marbles and now he's all fixated on that again. A relapse. Of course, that old guy is like a hundred years old . . ."

No, no way. My great uncle, the marquis's grandson, couldn't allow that. It's true that he's about a hundred years old, but he doesn't want people talking about it out in the streets. He's asked me for a copy of my key, and I'd gladly give it to him if I had a clue where the key is. I have to admit that I'm one of those people who never have a clue where anything is. To get to my own apartment, I have no choice but to stand on the street corner and bark at somebody's balcony until a sympathetic neighbor throws me *his* key. Perhaps someday I'll find mine; after all, Woody Allen says that Einstein said that the universe is not infinite. In other words, the damned key has to be somewhere. While I'm looking for it, I've asked the potential visitor to play a xylophone instead of screaming. That way, every time I hear the soothing notes of the xylophone, I'll know it's him and I'll go down to open the door for him. But no way. For reasons that I can't quite fathom, my great-uncle, the marquis's grandson, refuses to accept my suggestion.

The esoteric club was closed after the Pythagorean Party fell into disgrace. The practitioners of black magic and fortune-tellers dispersed, each went his or her own way; most of them are probably dead now. According to what Moisés told me, this isn't uncommon: all Pythagorean parties end up in disgrace. They crash, soar, explode, pop just like soap bubbles. There's no other way to end for them. Occasionally, a raging rabble will even set fire to their headquarters and chase its members with sticks and stones with the express purpose of lynching them, because the public gets tired of their cheekiness and their disrespect and their shamelessness—my baby's voice would start to bellow here—those with self-respect get sick of those who want to swindle, daze, trick, laying out all those Pythagorean lies morning, noon, and night. This has been going on since centuries before the Common Era and it's part of philosophy's dark traditions. As the ancient Romans used to say: *nihil novum sub sole.** That bit of Latin impressed me because of its fatalistic charge, inexorable like the blade of a guillotine or the volts from an electric chair, but I was also secretly glad (I mean, behind my boo's back) that my fortunate great-uncle, the marquis's grandson, had emerged without harm from that dark tradition, never having to personally experience any of the bloody and violent consequences of those acts of vandalism.

Once El Xilófono was shut down, and to take advantage of the little palace's proximity to the newly created Cuban Institute of Cinematographic Arts and Industry, which included an extravagant screening room that showed all, or almost all, of the essential work of Méliès to date, my little palace became property of the state and was turned into a boardinghouse, more or less a charity really, for film folks: directors, screenwriters, actors, cinematographers, big critics, and the rest of the lot, with their respective dogs, cats, and lovers. Like ants drawn by sugar, they came from the four cardinal points, from the most remote corners of the city, from the provinces, from abroad, from under rocks. How tumultuous. How noisy. The most eminent among them came from Cinecità, fascinated by Italian neorealism, the vicissitude of being on the streets with a camera at all times, always ready to capture vivid scenes

---

* There's nothing new under the sun.

in authentic locations, or something like that. Enraged just like the "angry young men," they navigated the French New Wave in the company of Goddard, Truffaut, and Resnais, before they dropped anchor with the Brazilian *cinema novo* and the sweet air of marijuana they smoked with Glauber Rocha, avoiding haggles about tributes to Howard Hawks, also known as Scarface. I heard once that they hated Chaplin because, they said, he couldn't begin to touch the sole of Buster Keaton's shoe. Between Visconti and Kurosawa and a bunch of names for which there's no room here (just like at a flea market, there was much to choose from), almost all were in a cult to the god that was Welles, who would later be overthrown by the god Bergman, although they also bragged about their understanding of Tarkovski and Miklós Jancsó. Generally speaking, they bragged about a lot of things. They were arrogant. They argued at the top of their lungs, they crossed swords over their various and often antagonistic obsessions; they praised or buried their subjects in absolute terms, argued, recriminated, contradicted, made themselves hoarse, and got drunk. They believed they lived intensely. They believed that. I imagine them rebellious, enthusiastic, dynamic, and full of vitality, optimism, and new ideas. It must have been a moment of great hope. The atmosphere, so effervescent, was perfect for creativity. The mantra was: Great Film with Limited Resources. The forecast, reserved. Now very old and without much hope of successfully getting up the stairs, Petronila persevered. Set up in perpetuity on the first floor, she made them coffee cut with lentils, some other squalid snack, washed their laundry now and again, and made sure that none of those depraved perverts messed with her grandson, Pancholo. Those were the hard years, when there was not one bit of anything, rice with hake, dreams, and that's it. (Nobody could imagine then that, twenty years later, the hard years would return, even harder, without rice, without hake, without dreams.) It's from this era, both famished and bohemian, that the Corners' three most famous nicknames come: for those who are precise, The Village of Misery; for the ironic, Beverly Hills; for the people from the neighborhood, The Cave of Whores and Faggots.

My parents took up residence in this splendid place, like partners in crime, a pair of not-too-conventional adventurers (or rather, conventional in their way), more like brother and sister. My dad, a native of Camagüey—born inside a tinajón (those large ceramic jars native to that place), as he liked to say—dedicated himself to Z pursuits with his pals and other good friends and, every now and again, he'd edit films and later put together some funny shorts in the style of Norman McLaren. My mom, a native of Paris, dedicated herself to being a native of Paris. Don't existentialists dedicate themselves to existing? She read *La nausée* and took it seriously, maybe because she read it in French. She was a leftie, a total hippie, and a little disturbed (it's the only way I can imagine that she'd be interested in my dad, because my dad was notorious, flamboyant, a feathery fan with a pink neon Z emblazoned on it); she later made a point of getting pregnant and dying in childbirth (I was born feet first and almost wasn't born at all, and so, for many reasons, I'm living proof of fate), leaving behind a fat little daughter in the care of her bachelor father, more bachelor than father, who still couldn't believe all that had happened to him, so libertine, so unstable, so incapable of taking care of anyone. So that when I finally opened my eyes to the beauty of the world, the first thing I saw was a perplexed and infinitely astonished look back. He was in anguish. In a panic. What is this that the black hand of misfortune has brought me? Why is she looking at me? Where did she come from? Where do I put her? And what if I drop her? Why is she crying, since I haven't dropped her yet? What does she want? What does she want from me? What do I do? Oh, my God! On the verge of a nervous breakdown, my troubled father carried me with extreme care, as if I were an atomic bomb. He'd look heavenward like a Christian martyr about to be sent to the lions and sing in a hurt voice: "You left me in the darkness of the night . . . / And left me aimlessly . . ." It was a truly moving spectacle. When I was very little, he'd put me to sleep by telling me a story about an evil stork who'd brought me from Paris without warning, which is actually more or less true.

"That damned bird," he'd sigh, "always determined to complicate lives . . ."

Although he hated his paternity, he never questioned it. Many years later, when, in his opinion, I was more apt to understand the naked, brutal, and sordid truth about life—he loved to talk in those terms—he attributed my origins to a stupor in which he was the victim, the poor boy, which doesn't mean that it wasn't more or less true, since he had never been with any other woman before or after my mother.

The victim of the stupor, who firmly believed in democracy and free expression and freedom of association and I don't know what else, and whose ignorance about childhood things was stunning (as far as he was concerned, a little girl and a baby vulture were more or less the same thing), gave me complete and total autonomy from the very beginning to do whatever the hell I wanted. He could have given me up for adoption, but he didn't. And

I'm grateful to him for that. I was very happy, growing up like an animal in the leafy forests, wild, savage, like Huckleberry Finn. I have no memory of a single rule, a single prohibition, not one taboo. Smelly, full of fleas, and illiterate, I was delighted with my life, playing ball by throwing strike after strike (a lefty, like my hero back then, the mythic Changa Mederos) at the neighborhood batters, or flying kites or racing carts until all hours of the night. How marvelous! Nobody ever told me those were boys' games (according to Linda, there's no such thing as "boys' games"—and to call them that is one of the insidious ways the patriarchal system has to distribute roles for its convenience and to perpetuate gender discrimination, etcetera, etcetera), but who cares? I probably wouldn't have given much importance to the info anyway, and the truth is that I always found boys more entertaining than girls. In fact, *much more* entertaining. In other words, I'm not one of those girls who refuse, who know how to say, "No, not now, later, later, some other time, maybe tomorrow, move over, hey, don't be an ass . . ." Instead, I'm one of those who opens up like a compass and spreads out like a game of jacks. I'm one of those who doesn't waste any time and immediately begins to dance and enjoy the show provided by the National Symphony. I love a mess. I don't even remember ever having been a virgin, which Father Ignacio tells me isn't such a good thing, but I can't help it, that's who I am. Perhaps in that way, I'm like my dad, and if it's a matter of chromosomes, who knows?

In honest defense of his principles, my dad had broken with the entire tinajón tribe in Camagüey, those retrograde, prudish, sanctimonious, puritanical, Victorian assholes (I don't know them, it's my dad who called them that), so there weren't any aunts or grandmothers to stop the madness and put a bit of order into my crazy coming of age. Only W., the marquis's grandson, tried to make his noble and unselfish contributions to my development: he took me for walks, to eat ice cream at Coppelia, to the rides at Jalisco Park, to look at the monkeys in the zoo. I loved the monkeys, who were so naughty. I would have liked to have one, even a little one, but it wasn't possible. According to my Dad, we had nothing to feed it and, when it came to monkeys, he already had me. Adversity. My great-uncle, the marquis's grandson, also warned me that my horoscope was one of the most depressing and calamitous he'd ever seen. According to his calculations, I was born marked and what awaited me was a series of tragedies and sufferings. If I wanted to survive, I had to be wary of Uranus and never lose sight of it. That bothered me a bit, of course, but not much: I've never worried very much about the future. My very best friend, my soulmate, Pancholo Quincatrece, taught me the most useful thing I've ever learned in my life: to drive the oligarch's ancient, practically ghostly Cadillac, an authentic relic, and, also, rudimentary skills in automotive mechanics; in other words, how to take apart a vehicle and put it back together without leaving a single part behind. Later, I'd figure out the astrologer's Peugeot, Linda's Mercedes, and Moisés's Lada. If I didn't starve to death during the crisis in the '90s—and I almost did—it was thanks to that skill. With a few tricks, of course. That's still how I get along, how I get by.

In order to keep me off the streets as much as possible, Father Ignacio let me spy on the most isolated corners of the neighborhood with his telescope, an incredible privilege which added to my already considerable reputation with the other kids on the block. And, of course, I also took advantage of the situation to keep an eye on Uranus. In other words, to try to watch him, because this Uranus character proved quite elusive. I couldn't really say, but I don't think I've ever actually set eyes on him. Later, I got into catechism and learned that there's no need to be afraid of planets. Except for ours, all the others are harmless. Thank God. Even though their ideological differences were obvious on sight (one of my dad's favorite pastimes was his weekly and detailed confession, in full narrative bloom, of each and every one of his erotic adventures), Father Ignacio liked my dad because he never hit me.

I finally got to go to school—only one year behind—thanks to Petronila, who, in spite of her problems, made sure I bathed and combed my hair and brushed my teeth now and again. I didn't find any of this especially interesting, but I got used to it, and I eventually became a civilized human being, addicted to the social contract to the point that I let Linda drag me to the university, to the Alliance Française, and to other whimsical activities. Petronila also taught me not to steal popsicles (even as her grandson was teaching me how to steal cars, to take them apart lickety-split, and to sell the parts, hee hee), not to throw rocks at the mango tree, not to stick my fingers in my nose, and not to stick my tongue out at old people. My inclination to stick my tongue out, it's true, had certainly become alarming, so that, even now, I can't claim to have bested it completely. Even today, in certain circumstances, it's all I can do to contain myself. The thing about not pulling a cat's tail I learned from, precisely, a cat: empirical science. In the end, my childhood was a paradise, and my dad, a great dad. No matter what anyone says, I have no complaints. I'm not even resentful about the monkey. I think that, given the circumstances, he did the best he could. There are many others who would have liked to have a dad like mine, if only they could. About ten years ago, he immigrated to the United States, and last I heard, he was part of some scat group in San Francisco, the folks who wear brown handkerchiefs and play with shit, and that it was going great for him. I'm really glad for him, from the bottom of my heart.

Eventually, however, disenchantment came to the Corners.

"As can be expected," Moisés would have added, "or did you think you could feed your illusions, or, in other words, stupidities, without paying the price? If you believe that, you're screwed. Well, you're screwed anyway."

And so, yes, after the blinding grit came the chipped tiles, or what is otherwise known as "The Black Decade." Little by little, between proscriptions and persecutions, and pure and simple Stalinism, according to my dad, the party came to an end. The film folks moved on, to other houses and other countries. The Village of Misery fell into the shadows (the misery not so much: it only fell into shadows because, among other things, the lightbulbs kept getting stolen), into oblivion, became an antique, anachronistic, always a little off, something just not talked about anymore. Subtly, without scandal, the little palace fell from view. It became a kind of tenement, like certain renaissance palazzos, which are just shells of their former selves, exactly as they're supposed to be on the outside, while on the inside, they've been consumed. The new residents, many with accents from the eastern provinces and not familiar with urban living, brought with them new fauna, heretofore unseen on the city scene: hens, turkeys, pigeons, turtles, a pig, a goat with a bell around its neck, a hutia, and some kind of megatherium, a cross between a mastiff and a rhinoceros, which barks and bites and believes itself to be the hound of the Baskervilles. All of these creatures piss and shit wherever they want, as if this were a grove or a glade. To say it perhaps in a more romantic way: the tenement smells like the jungle, like the wild, like savages. I get along fine with the hutia. I'd never seen one before, but this one likes to be petted and will eat from your hand and everything, so it's a pretty sweet animal. But not the megatherium. I've grown to hate that damned creature, and I don't feel even a little guilty about it, since I'm convinced he hates me too. He's a real s.o.b., all black, hirsute, with many fangs and scary red eyes. It's his fault I had to get a rabies shot and now have a scar on my ankle. Father Ignacio insists we must forgive our enemies, regardless of species. Perhaps in a thousand years I'll be able to forgive the megatherium.

In terms of the neighbors, you never know. None of them works. It seems they've all got their schemes going, but I don't really know, and I don't want to know. I think the less you know, the better. Although they think differently, that's for sure. You'd think they'd get bored, that soap operas and American movies with sex, violence, and adult language were not enough entertainment. With solidarity as a pretext, and sometimes without a pretext at all, they love to meddle in other people's private lives, to eavesdrop behind closed doors, to peek through keyholes, to open correspondence, rustle through the garbage in search of evidence, keep tabs on who comes and goes, criticize other people's habits and clothes, find out how much they earn, how they earn it, who they sleep with, what's in the bag, and everything else. You almost feel like you don't have a home, like you live on the public sidewalk. Luckily, I don't give a damn about any of that, but I know people who'd go crazy if they had to live here. And I'm not being paranoid, that's just the way it is. My neighbors can be real fuckers. Every now and then, they knock on my door with something to sell, from a can of sweet coconut to a razorblade, an aluminum bucket to a bottle of cod-liver oil, a pair of plastic slippers to a spool of orange thread, anything at all. There's one, a pale, miserable, little fellow—a Jehovah's Witness—who also knocks on my door now and again, but only so he can babble his nonsense about the ways of the Lord and all that. I let him in because I feel sorry for him, because the others are always kicking him around, and because Moisés once slapped him a couple of times and dragged him out by the ear. One of these days, I'll have to say something to him myself, just to see if he'll come to his senses.

As soon as Pancholo's grandmother died, he immediately began getting in trouble. As orphaned as me, or perhaps more so, he got four years in jail for stealing and illegally slaughtering a cow. His crime, committed while he and a friend were completing their compulsory military service, was basically holding the cow's leg, given that his munificent heart made it impossible for him to kill her in cold blood (he says he had to look away), while his accomplice beheaded her without a second thought. The car hustle was actually going well, so I don't really get why he had to go into another business. City boys rob cars; cows are the business of boys from the countryside. My buddy had lost his way and got screwed.

"That's what you get for not minding your own business," Petronila would have said. "I warned him, but he never listens when it comes to consequences."

But it wasn't actually Pancholo's fault.

"Don't be so overprotective, girlee," Petronila would have said. "You're always defending him, and he doesn't deserve it."

But I'm sure of it, because my buddy is allergic to that olive green uniform, and he'd already committed all kinds of mischief and done all sorts of juggling to avoid his compulsory military service. Poor guy. He claimed to be asthmatic, hemophilic, deaf, a flatfoot, a psychopath, a Buddhist, and even a faggot, but nothing worked. The recruitment officers weren't fools and they never believed a word of any of it. How could they, when he had that perverse and impish face of his? Then, like somebody just holding onto a hot poker because he has no choice, my unfortunate little friend decided to try and shave his age in an obsessive, compulsive, and untimely way. Thus his nickname. One time, my dad asked him how old he was (I can imagine why, though in those years homosexuality was outlawed and it was no small thing to mess with a minor), just like that, point-blank, and sly Pancholo, who imagined government officials everywhere, said, Oh, no, not him, my lieutenant, definitely not him, he was just a child, a tender babe, a little baby barely "quin . . . ca . . . trece"—fif . . . thirteen—little years old. And then he gazed at him with shiny eyes.

"Listen, dearie," my dad said with great restraint, trying not to laugh, "let's leave out this business about 'my lieutenant,' okay? Now, fif . . . thirteen? What age is that, dear? What you have is called the Peter Pan complex. The boy who doesn't want to grow up. And it's pretty serious, you know that? Serious, serious indeed. And it won't do you any good. I can just imagine you green, green as a little lettuce leaf . . ."

But when that green baby came out of prison, he was more than ripe, mature, turned into a wise man, a maestro of the mess, of the tumult and the lie, licensed in the art of the occult and surreptitious, master of all knowledge and necessary skills to play the coppers and operate a clandestine bar downstairs where they'd just as soon serve cheap rum as chispa'e tren ("train spark," a hair-raising ethyl-based moonshine, more like old rat poison, which, in order to sell it better, he'd renamed "loco spark," the "loco" short for "locomotive") or whatever herbal cure we might need to keep up with the misfortunes that destiny has brought—at the crack of dawn, Pancholo's conversation took on the rhythm of a bolero—that we might drag our sorry carcasses through the disgusting and remote roads our miserable lives have taken us down.

Not counting the bar's regulars—a bunch of drunks who hang out on the terrace amidst their own urine and vomit and sing that song that says, "Gimme a hand, cuz I'm falling . . . / cuz I'm falling cuz I'm so high . . ."—nor the transients, which include a crew of uncles, cousins, nephews, and in-laws, all with accents from the eastern provinces and peasant habits like having their picture taken in front of the Capitol—there are forty-four residents in our little palace, unless my count is off, and the majority suffer from construction fever. Where they get the materials, I don't know (they say all the benches on Paseo Avenue have been robbed of wood), but what's certain is that from one day to the next, there's a multiplying of partitions, dividers, screens, niches, lofts, little bathrooms, one apartment in the garage, two on the roof, an attic studio, and, I suspect, a secret passage. The citadel grows inside, becomes dense, a beehive, a wasp's nest. Some days it feels like it's going to blow like a firecracker or a Pythagorean party, although sometimes I can't tell if it's the place or my head. They hammer and hammer away, hammer and never cease hammering. You hear the tock tock tock at every hour. It's as if their mantra was, "Raise the roof, carpenters," letting loose a hammering epidemic. Tock tock tock over here, tock tock tock over there. When it's not these guys, it's the others hammering, a stubborn, interminable, everlasting tock tock tock. This tock tock tock is absolute, the permanent fixture responsible for the little palace's latest nickname: Happy Hammer Corners.

When Virginia Woolf talked about the importance of a room of one's own, a refuge from the noisy world, a place to listen to your own internal voice, the vital space necessary for any writer to write, even an amateur like me, she never imagined a place like Happy Hammer Corners. Well, we all know that imagination wasn't exactly that hypocritical little English lizard's greatest strength. (She's never done anything to me, but Linda says that Virginia used feminism as a cover while she raked Katherine Mansfield, condemned Anna de Noailles for having as big an ego, and dismissed Victoria Ocampo as a fool. Father Ignacio says he's not prejudiced but that all Anglicans are like that, soulless heretics.) Back on the subject of a room of one's own, I can honestly say that I'm the happy proprietor of a small room with a huge window and a stupendous bathroom, luxurious with its blue tiles, the house's original bathroom . . . ever more demonically noisy than Vía Láctea. It's no doubt an evil wish, the result of frustration and resentment and even envy, but I would have liked to see Mrs. Woolf writing *Mrs. Dalloway* amidst the screeching chickens; the thunderous barking of the megatherium trying to eat the bill collector from the electric company or that poor and good hutia; domino pieces smacking against a table: "Make way cuz here I come, cuz I got some and I can, the dirty and the squat, I pass you by and pass you by again, cuz you're a macao, my friend, a real macao"; the honking of the horrified pig running when they try to hose him down to see if they can get rid of a little bit of the stink; the war of decibels between Compay Segundo, El Médico de la Salsa, NG La Banda, Orquesta Revé, Paulo F. G. and his Elite, Adalberto and his Son, who knows who and his Trabuco and the Charanga Habanera in an every-man-for-himself battle to see who's the wildest, the loudest, the baddest—and let us not forget Radio Reloj, marking the time, beeeeeeep . . . : "Twelve-thirty in Havana, Cuba; three a.m. the next day in Wellington, New Zealand"; the goat's braying added to the bell's ding dong; the drunken brawls now spiced with a whole arsenal of choice vernacular, folk sayings, and other stridencies; the fights among the sober (same as before), like the sonic one with lightning, thunder, and crashes between the owner of the megatherium and the pig's owner, because that abusive megatherium raped the pig and the pig in turn gave the rapist pestilence and the pig's owner told the owner of the megatherium that she should stop being such a bitch and she responded that he shouldn't be such an asshole and that he shouldn't mess with her, because she had no problem getting into a slapfest with him, and she tried, and then he returned the favor and pulled out a knife used to peel taro to poke her in the stomach and everyone else ducked inside so the blood wouldn't run like a river, and all along, the soundtrack to this was that implacable, inhuman, and everlasting tock tock tock . . .

And all this din is nothing compared to how it was back in the days of Poliéster, may God rest his soul, though it's possible that not even the Lord Himself in His infinite love may want him anywhere near. At least, if I were Him, I wouldn't. No way, not even if they paid me in dollars. The son of a ghetto black woman and a Soviet technician, the boy wasn't actually named Poliéster but rather Dniéster, like that really faraway river, all the way over there where even the devil uses three voices and nobody hears him anyway. But "Dniéster" is an incomprehensible word, and also unpronounceable, and so the neighbors turned it into Poliéster and that's that. Oh Poliéster, how we knew and loved thee! That sublime creature distinguished himself for his infinite capacity to make noise with everything and anything. Just like Nero, he was an artist. An enfant terrible. An absolute lunatic. A genius from a distant shore. What would the world have been like without the divine Poliéster? With square ears, a weak voice—soprano with a tilt toward a wail—when he wasn't dedicating himself to bel canto, his favorite instru-

ment was the coronet, without any less love for the conga, the bongos, the
batá drums, the maracas, the guiro, whether it was twelve noon or three in
the morning of the following day, always with the same enthusiasm. But he
never quite got the beat right, no matter what. And oh, he was so off tune!
Linda called him The S.O.B. with the Lil' Horn. And Moisés wished him the
same finale as all his other enemies, that a cobra should bite him and all that.
Pancholo would just get drunker to more or less deal with this new nuisance
that misfortune had brought us. The drunks sang along with him from the
terrace. The megatherium wanted to eat him, congas and all. Even his long-
suffering mother would stare at him with astonishment. Who'd ever seen a
mulatto with so little rhythm? Could it be because of that Soviet spermazoid?
He wouldn't stop. Since art implied sacrifice, Poliéster never rested. And so
neither did I. And that wasn't fair, because I'm no artist. I think at one point
I came close to losing the hearing in my right ear too.

Following Linda's advice and with the slight hope that the great percus-
sionist, cornet player, and singer would see that his musical vocation was a
far, far off dream, I tried taking him on by playing *Don Giovanni*. That way
I could also give my hearing a cleansing. But that jovial idea lasted about as
long as a piece of cake at a school door. Troy went up in flames. The neighbors
openly rebelled, bitched and cursed, came to complain in a mob, and made
the biggest deal out of it, the biggest in the history of the Corners, because
the noise that came out of my tiny room made them nervous and gave them
terrible headaches. I was driving them crazy. They were all going to wind up
in an asylum because of me. (I thought of recommending Dr. Frumento but
I didn't dare. What if they got angry? Mobs scare me.) Cohabitation has its
rules, the first of which is respecting the rights of others. Wasn't I aware of that?
How could I victimize them like that? What had they done to deserve such
a thing? With my little mouse of a heart, I gave in immediately. I raised the
white flag, acknowledged that majority rules, and, as usual, tried to surrender.
I already said I'm a dope. But Linda was incensed. What did I mean, "surrender"? Why surrender? What the hell for? No way. Turtles could surrender.
She couldn't allow those social climbing eastern provincial immigrants to get
the better of me. If they had a problem with me, then they had a problem
with her. If I was a meek little mouse, fine, but she certainly wasn't. What
balls. She sure as hell didn't bow before anyone. The supreme incarnation of
warrior fury, looking somewhat like the owner of the megatherium and even
like the megatherium himself, my friend was quick to signal that whoever

wanted a fight would get more than their share. So these immigrants didn't take to *Don Giovanni*, eh? Well, we'd see. Of course we would. They had to be educated. Mozart, after all, was smooth, easy, popular. Undoubtedly, they needed something more aggressive, more forceful, something that would put us all into orbit. And so, without asking permission, my guardian angel began playing Arnold Schoenberg full blast. Let us now draw a curtain over the events that followed.

Chapter 3

She wanted to be a writer

PERHAPS IT'S BEST IF WE GO BACK TO THE BEGINNING OF THE STORY. I think everything started at the cafeteria half a block from the high school, at the counter, when Yadelis, my buddy from the Los Muchos tenement, told me that Pancholo was beautiful. That was exactly the word she used, "beautiful," and she said it so naturally that I just started to laugh. To crack up, with my entire body, as if I was coming undone, and like I hadn't laughed in a million years. As if I were being tickled with a little feather on the soles of my feet. I practically peed from so much laughter. It was, without a doubt, a great joke. Very funny. Because Pancholo is my buddy, my soulmate, practically a brother, my "ecobio," or blood brother or whatever it is he means when he says that, but the truth is that, no matter how much we search the entire archipelago (and probably Jamaica and Haiti and all the Dutch Antilles and everywhere else), we would never find an uglier black boy. Not even Petronila, who looked at him with the partiality appropriate to a grandmother, would have ever considered him "beautiful." As black as the bottom of a kettle, with a narrow forehead and eyes like a toad, with the flattest nose and the thickest lips ever, he was fit to scare the kids at night: "Sleep, little child, sleep . . . / cuz Pancholo's coming to eat you up." Maybe the Kaffirs in Rhodesia might consider him the most handsome man in the tribe, or an anthropologist might be amazed to run into him among the masses in a mestizo country and think he's found a real link to Africa, I dunno. Though it has nothing to do with beauty, I won't deny the virtues of his immense, splendid, and steely member, so seductive for certain types of women (older than him, experienced, moneyed, white, whiter than white, European) and so desired in vain by people like my dad. But Yadelis wasn't a Kaffir nor an anthropologist nor older nor expert nor well-heeled nor white nor European nor Z, so her enthusiasm struck me as incongruent and, as a result, funny.

I was laughing about his being beautiful while my friend watched with increasing disapproval, her mouth tight and her brow furrowed, as we waited to be served our orange sodas. My singsong laughter, exuberant, luxurious like a fern (the height of vulgarity, according to my great-uncle W., the marquis's grandson; when would I learn to laugh like a lady?—and what's with the fern?—it was evil Uranus who made me laugh like that), was the result of that great joke but was also kind of silly, and was in some ways similar to happiness. Back then, I was fifteen years old and Yadelis was fourteen. She was certainly pretty, very pretty (she still is), like a model, like those black girls from the United States who star in movies, Whitney Houston and Vanessa Williams, the former Miss America. She could have whomever she wanted. All the high school boys swooned over her, just like years later, guys from a variety of nationalities would also swoon, including that Swedish magnate who would propose marriage and to whom she'd say no, of course not, who do you think you are, don't be so fresh, quit your drinking, look at that gut, an old man, and look at that face, just drop your hundred bucks and get lost. But that Viking must have been one of those who, no matter how badly you treat 'em, just keep coming back, stuck on her like a disease, and the boys from Los Muchos (because they're all family, a clan) would take his side and pressure Yadelis morning, noon, and night, saying who do you think you are, you're the fresh one, you stop drinking, your head's full of smoke, you can't spend your whole life chasing that Quincatrece fellow, he's just an under-evolved monkey anyway and full of shit to boot, a deadbeat, a bad guy, cunning, who ever heard of such a stupid jinetera, you tell this story and nobody's gonna believe it, God sets up millionaires for idiots, your youth will go by in a flash, girlee, in a flash, and you're going to look like a scouring pad in no time, think ahead, use your head, this is your chance, foolish girl, how many women out there wouldn't want to be in your shoes, you've got to take advantage of this, if for no other reason than your daughter—until they managed to get her deported to Sweden, where she was welcomed by a bloody pneumonia that almost killed her. But in the mid-eighties, who knew things would turn out that way? Yadelis was very much in love (love is blind, or at least myopic) and I imagined that Pancholo was also in love with her, after all, who was he not to fall in love with her? And they would be happy, very happy, sort of like Beauty and the Beast and all that, like a very tender telenovela. I was happy for them. And I laughed. Because I'm like that, full of cheer.

They finally served our sodas, in real glasses. At that moment, I didn't care that they were glass. Why should I have cared? I may not have even noticed. At that point, my friend had concluded that I was making fun of her shamelessly, brazenly, right to her beautiful face, and she was indignant. This happens to me now and again. I laugh, for the heck of it, because I'm happy, and people think I'm making fun of them. Or I say something, something utterly insignificant, any ol' thing, and they think I'm being ironic. Why do they believe this? I don't know. But the fact is that they get intimidated. They get very mad. For example, Moisés. One time, he assured me—as he pounded the table in his usual style—that we were sinking into disaster, catastrophe, a massacre, Hell, into pure shit. As the ancient Romans used to say: *O tempora! O mores!* * There was nothing to laugh about. In fact, while I laughed, I looked exactly like what I was: a great imbecile. He said that if I laughed like that one more time, he was going to throw me out the window, head first. (Which would have been entirely possible, given the size of the window. My body, and his too, could easily go through that window. And death was certain whether we fell or jumped, because both this apartment and the one downstairs have extremely high ceilings. I'm suspicious of the architect who designed the window. I think he should have put up a guard rail. The thing is, I don't like guard rails.) In fact, Yadelis did not threaten me. She merely threw her soda in my face, which was pretty daring. I wasn't actually bothered by that little baptism, I really wasn't. I simply did the same thing back. Or, more precisely, I tried to do the same thing back. Yes, because she was fast, but me . . . I'm a snail. A gentle, lazy, languid mollusk. She was always telling me: "You're too slow, pudge, too slow to live in the West." She very elegantly ducked and the little orange shower fell on the person behind her. Oh.

That person was a girl from our class. A skinny girl with curly hair and a prominent nose, like a witch, wearing pince-nez lenses, Italian loafers, and a

---

* What times! What customs!

gold Rolex on her wrist (in our country a gold Rolex is not just a very luxurious watch, it's more, much more: a myth, a legend, a symbol of power. I only recognized it because I'd seen it once in a magazine), a stiff creature, arrogant, who sat in the front row and didn't talk to anybody or look at anybody and got good grades on all her papers and responded to the teachers' questions with great confidence, as if she were saying, "I know it all, you have nothing to teach me, why are you asking something so obvious?" She walked like she was marching, like a soldier in a ceremonial battalion, like the guards surrounding the Queen of England, as if she had a stick up her butt. Yadelis couldn't stomach the girl.

"So imperfect, and such a braggart, a four-eyed . . . she thinks she's the star of the circus," whispered my little friend, "as if her shit didn't stink . . . check out that penguin nose—it looks like it's gonna poke you! She struts like a boy, but she's just a fart. I'd love to get my hands on her!"

I confess, I was afraid. I don't even know why. Maybe because I thought she was too clever, too cool, too adult, distant, mysterious, so like a foreigner. *Different*. When I saw her drenched in soda, I gulped. I stopped laughing instantly. I didn't know how to explain my awful behavior, my insufferable eccentricity, or how to apologize. It was terrible. I would have rather been a thousand kilometers away. Or for the earth to open up and swallow me. It was all I could do not to stick my tongue out, which would have no doubt only made things worse. Then, to really complicate things, Yadelis started laughing in a way that was not at all innocent. Through her wet lenses, the witch with the Rolex looked at me in silence, sizing me up. It wasn't just her nose that was sharp, but also her eyes. She looked at Yadelis, who was all caught up in her own amusement. Then at me again. She took off the pince-nez, folded it, and dropped it in her blouse pocket.

"I . . . hmm . . . hmm . . . look . . . I wasn't trying to . . . you know . . . hmm . . ." Those were the lovely words that I managed to articulate just before my inadvertent victim, following the rule of an eye for an eye, bathed me in soda from head to toe. She did it with a killer's cool, as if drenching someone in soda was the same as drinking the soda. For just a fraction of a second, I imagined her pulling a pistol from her purse and firing at me: bang, bang, bang. How frightening. The imagination can certainly take us to some dark places.

Even though she'd left me all sticky, a real mess, I didn't complain this time either. How could I? In truth, I deserved it; I'd earned it with my own bad behavior. In a way, that direct, immediate, and proportional revenge was a relief for me, because I don't like having outstanding debts of honor nor long-term enmity: this way, we were even. Everything should have ended there; it would have been better if it had ended there. But Yadelis didn't feel the same way. She didn't like how things had turned out. She'd stopped laughing. She couldn't stomach that girl, she had a grudge against her, and, all of a sudden, she went nuts. She screamed something like, "What the fuck is your problem?" and since we'd already drained almost all of our soda and were a bit short of munitions, she grabbed a glass from a guy who was just standing there (she was so quick, he continued drinking, out of inertia, as if he still had the glass) and threw it at the witch in the Italian loafers. I don't mean that she threw soda at her again. I mean that she threw *the glass*. Sometimes Yadelis got a little too aggressive.

Luckily, the curly red-haired witch had very good reflexes. She reacted in a flash. She screamed something like "Up yours!" and put her hand out just in time to deflect the glass from its deadly trajectory. I think what she had wanted was to catch that projectile, pluck it out of the air and declare Yadelis "out," what a baseball commentator would have called a "defensive gem." But that would have been too much to ask for. The glass continued its flight, now perpendicular to us, and headed toward the other side of the counter. The three of us followed it with our eyes, unable to move, in suspense, holding our breaths like the stadium fans who squint their eyes at the thunderous hit that might turn into a home run: " . . . and there it goes . . . going . . . going . . . gone!" Ah! It could have shattered against the wall or the soda tank. But fate is implacable. The damn glass went and broke on the manager's face, a poor guy to whom it had probably never occurred that his job could be so dangerous. We fled like rats.

I couldn't sleep a wink that night. I usually sleep pretty well, with only an occasional nightmare, almost all having to do with the megatherium: I'm walking on a deserted plain lit only by the moon and the monster comes after me, barking and barking until it splits my eardrum, then he shows his fangs and his blackened tongue, drools, foams rabidly at the mouth, takes a few giant steps, coming ever closer, all the while smelling of the pig he raped, then finally he reaches me and goes for my neck . . . essentially, nothing too terrible. But back then, the megatherium didn't exist yet and so I was assaulted by something else: insomnia. It was a miserable night, one of the worst ever in my life. Everything had happened so quickly, so much quicker than it takes to tell (I've told it in slow motion) and so much faster than it took for me to recover from it. If I can remember every detail now, it's because I spent that night alone, very studiously replaying the scene over and over by myself, the whole scene, from the first guffaw until the shattering of the glass, not forgetting a thing in spite of the anguish and obsession with precision, until I got dizzy and wanted to throw up. I kept playing and replaying the vertiginous scene in my room, all alone in the darkness. I kept trying to find the initial mistake, the first screw up, the origins of the tragedy. I wouldn't do this again under any circumstances, even if I could go back in time and had a second chance. I was looking for my own culpability. But I couldn't place it. Everything seemed so casual . . . I prayed for a miracle, so that it could all be a bad dream. I was drowning in cramps, shivers, and I also had a terribly jumpy stomach. I smoked an entire pack of cigarettes. I almost had an asthma attack, even though I'm not asthmatic, or a heart attack without having a heart condition. I think I got some grey hairs out of the deal. In a low voice so as not to wake my dad, I sang, "One hundred bottles on the wall / one hundred bottles on the wall / if one should fall . . . ninety-nine bottles on the wall . . ." until I reached zero, and the floor would have been a clutter of glass shards. (Even though the song doesn't say so, I've always imagined the bottles made of amber-colored glass.) I repeated this two or three times. But I got nowhere. I couldn't get that poor man and his messed up face out of my mind. It had been so unnecessary, so useless, and all because of my stupidity. To be honest, I hadn't actually seen his face, but I could imagine it, which was worse. His messed up face. Because of my cursed stupidity. Goddammit, it was really easy to do some damage! And then . . . to run like that. I felt like a cockroach. I don't think the idea of the shattered glass helped much.

The next morning, I met Yadelis at the corner of the high school. She didn't dare go in; she practically didn't dare get any closer. But she didn't dare go back to Los Muchos either. Basically, she didn't dare make a move of any kind. Where did she leave her audacity, her aggression, her terrible impudence? Grey, opaque, trembling, transformed, she seemed like a different person. Poor girl, I felt sorry for her. She talked with the vaguest thread of a voice. She hadn't slept all night either. She'd spent it praying to Ochún, begging for her help, promising heaven and earth if she'd just get her out of this fix. She had, in fact, ended up threatening the saint in the yellow dress with all sorts of reprisals if she didn't solve the problem. Of course, she felt she was innocent. She *was* innocent. Had she done something wrong? Of course not.

She never did anything wrong. But she was not unaware that others might see things differently. Always so ill-intentioned, so evil, so envious, people always thought the worst—no, no, she wasn't going to say it. Man, it was so easy to get in trouble! She talked only to me about her complicated relationship with the Virgin. Nobody in school could know anything about it because, back then, religion was considered obscurantism, a step backward, and it was practically prohibited. I didn't talk about being Catholic either and the two of us kept each others' secrets.

In a low voice, so no one would think I'd lost my mind, I started singing: "One hundred bottles on the wall / one hundred bottles on the wall / if one should fall—" until Yadelis begged me to please cut that crap out. Hearing a song about bottles made her even more nervous, because her stepfather was an alcoholic and abusive and hated her and her nine siblings and he was going to kill her if he found out she was in any way involved in any kind of trouble that involved throwing glasses. The worst part was that her pig of a stepfather was also a police officer. He was used to smacking around outlaws, big and small, to beating them to a pulp with a solid rubber blackjack. What a nightmare. I don't how I managed to drag her to school. I was scared too, but less of what might happen next than of what I had already done. But I couldn't just leave her there, alone, abandoned, replaying her misadventure. When we went in, the big-nosed witch was already in class. In the front row, like always. She didn't look at us, like always. She seemed very calm, healthy and punctual, that witch, with an air of someone who'd slept like a baby. Incredible. Even if there was some performance in her behavior, it was still incredible. That girl had nerves of steel. I considered that she'd make an excellent poker player, capable of putting up her own mother as a bet on that green felt, totally capable of winning it all with the worst hand. I was so jealous.

Still, I wasn't very sure about how cool this witch in the pince-nez would really be. Nothing seemed to bother her. Nothing scared her. Nothing moved her. She was made of steel. She was queen of the bluff. This I found out later, during math class, when the little old man who was our teacher was killing himself to explain one of the complexities of his subject, what an equilateral triangle was or some such thing. Then a few rumors started leaking into class from the hall. A murmur. A blah blah blah. A horrible story, told in incomplete sentences, in parts, fragments, in little pieces of amber-colored glass which drilled into Yadelis's and my ears. A public scandal. An assault.

Violence. Juvenile delinquents. Facial disfigurement (this about killed me). The Center for the Re-education of Minors (this killed my buddy).

"That's what they call it," she whispered in my ear, "but in reality it's like a prison, and much worse than adult jail. There are some huge black women there, and some shameless white ones . . ."

I wasn't thrilled with the news. My hands were sweating. Her legs were trembling. I got goose bumps; my hair was standing on end. She was biting her nails. We both needed to make doodies. And all along, there was that poker face, immutable, nothing. Like a cactus, who doesn't care if it rains or not. And that's exactly how she was, too, when she was called to that terrible place where the Great Indian Chief Head Scalper furiously barked from behind his desk at terrified students who got into any sort of mischief: the principal's office. Cool as a cucumber, she gathered her book, her notebook, and her fountain pen, put them in her bag, excused herself to the little old man who was our teacher, and left, her head held high, very smug, very sure of herself, very much in charge. The little old man was stunned. That girl? They wanted to see her? The best student in the class? In the principal's office? No. Impossible. There had to be a mistake. The kids in the class were also stunned, although I got the feeling that they were happy to see Miss Perfect in trouble. There were winks, raised eyebrows, giggles, and coughs. Under any other circumstance, Yadelis would have been the happiest of the lot, would have jumped for joy. But she was mute this time. She merely looked at me, like a trapped animal, with all the world's terror reflected in her eyes. I suppose I must have looked at her in the same way, since a frightful chill ran up my spine and froze my brain. I imagined they'd call the two of us in at any moment. And I can't speak for Yadelis, but I'm sure I would have told them everything until someone slapped my mouth shut. I think I was born to confess crimes, which is maybe why my dad used to joke around about my "papal predisposition."

But things didn't happen that way. A half hour later, when we heard that the Know-It-All had been escorted down to the nearest police station in a squad car, well . . . that was really something. The little old man who was our teacher almost had a heart attack and had to be helped and everything. The kids went from sweet joy to morbid curiosity, while Yadelis remained totally immobile, paralyzed, as still as a statue, as if struck by lightning. I felt a pain in my lower abdomen, like a steel blade stabbing me inside. Struck by a presentiment, I got up in a flash. I didn't want to stain my skirt. And yes, in fact, a thread of blood was already running down my leg, eleven days early.

I went back home like a zombie, unable to see anything or anyone, only forms and colors that didn't make much sense. There were cars honking in the distance. I heard a squeal, a brake, somebody's voice calling me a cretin, stupid, a jerk, telling me that if I wanted to kill myself I should just cut my veins and not screw around with other people's lives. Bah. I went up the stairs hoping the steps would never end, would just go on and on, interminably, all the way to heaven. But they ended and I got to our apartment. My dad wasn't home. I washed up, even though in the midst of the ruckus, I'd come to believe the contrast between the red and my skin was just fabulous. It's just that I'm a very light-skinned brunette. I don't know if I'm part black; probably not, although on this island, you never know and it doesn't matter. I'm a lazy little white girl. The sun makes me bronze, but it doesn't burn me or make me look like a boiled lobster. It actually gives me a very touristic tone. I like it. So much so that I thought I might get somebody (who?) to give me a traffic-stopping red dress as a gift. I might have been delirious, but I don't think so. It seems that sometimes, in the vortex of tragedy, just before the actual disaster, there's a tendency to focus on details, on silly things.

I took some diazepam for my cramps, to deal with that piercing jabbing that was coming in waves now, and another to see if I could calm my nerves. It's not necessary to lose your mind; there's no need to fall into the temptation of losing your mind, even if, in certain situations, it may be the easiest thing to do, the path of least resistance. It's important to keep your wits about you, I told myself, I think I even said it aloud, even if the world itself is going nuts. The police had arrested a child, had taken her from school? What the heck was going on? Things are different now. To illustrate my point, just last week, two girls from that same high school armed with a couple of steel bars from a construction site charged a teacher and beat him to a pulp. Why? Very simple: they didn't like him. They sent him off to intensive care and the likelihood is that the guy will never walk again. In my day (I know I talk like an old lady, an old lady of twenty-eight) that would never have happened. The most we ever did was stick a turd or a dead cat in the disliked teacher's desk drawer, that's all. As far I know, there weren't any drugs or guns in schools. Outside, yes, of course. There was everything outside: razorblades, billy clubs, hole punchers, knives, the occasional handgun (alcohol and matches were reserved for suicide or, as a last resort, for crimes of passion); there was all kinds of traffic and all kinds of people acting all sorts of ways. Because of optimism or habit, people get strange ideas about Vedado. It's true that in the '50s, it was a bourgeois neighborhood. Kinda dicey in some areas but always pretty decorous. It's certainly true that there are worse places in the city. Centro Habana, for example, is fucked. But, when I was born (at Sacred Heart, precisely in the sacred heart of the neighborhood), Vedado was already full of tenements and you could find just about everything, from the landowner's daughter who had refused to leave the country to the bandit ex-con who planned to assault the landowner's daughter in order to steal her paintings and lamps. It was already a hodgepodge, a melting pot, a carnival. In spite of the mask of fake respectability so characteristic of an area with so much contradiction, there was a certain hardness on the street. But not in the schools, no. School was progress. You went there to get ahead, to take advantage of the opportunities (at least that's how Petronila saw it), to sign up on the good side in the war between civilization and the barbarians. The thugs hadn't infiltrated the schools yet and it didn't even occur to the cops to go looking for them there. That's why, when they arrested the witch with the fountain pen, I felt like the floor had just fallen out from under me, that I was living a nightmare, that the world had gone crazy. I took a third diazepam to take care of the nightmare and slept like a log. Logs don't dream.

When I woke up, emaciated, with dark rings under my eyes, a disaster, it was dusk. A tenuous light, between a pale pink and old gold, smoothed everything out with a certain calm. Perhaps, even, a kind of sadness. The first thing I heard was Yadelis's laugh. Laugh . . . ? Oh. What was that? Supreme confusion. My dad was telling fag jokes and she was laughing. My dad was a jester, an epic poet, a master specialist in fag jokes; he knew thousands, hundreds of thousands, and he also made up a bunch, and told them with a lot of style, but . . . With one foot already in The Center for the Re-education of Minors, without even counting the threat posed by the stepfather with the blackjack, how could my buddy be laughing like that? But there she was. I'd never seen her happier. They both celebrated my return to wakefulness with great enthusiasm, with cheers and applause, as if it was a resurrection or the arrival of the Messiah. They sang "Las Mañanitas" as a duet (substituting "tardecitas" for "mañanitas," the rascals), as if I'd taken twenty instead of three diazepams.

"Well, my dear, here you have Waking Beauty," exclaimed the Great Jester, "and I surrender her to you; she's all yours. And to you, sleepy usurper of cigarettes"—he pointed at me with an accusing finger as I stuck my tongue out at him—"I'm leaving a thermos full of coffee. Well, almost full, and $1.20 so you can buy a pizza, since you're so skinny and must nourish yourself"—I stuck my tongue out at him again—"Don't make faces and pay attention. The $1.20 is here, look, right here next to the thermos. Don't tell me later you couldn't find it. And now—ho! ho!—we're switching cameras and mics to . . ."

Just for the hell of it, I asked him if he was going to sleep at home that night. He winked and said no, of course not: other parts of the world were competing for his modest efforts. He gave me a little peck and went flying out the door. Yadelis followed him with her gaze, her mouth agape and, I'd say, in awe, until he disappeared into the shadows on the stairs. Although they'd known each other all her life, Dad's style never ceased to amaze her. What a guy. He was so funny. He was such good people. He'd leave like that, so as not to be in our way, and didn't even try to get with her. Why couldn't she have a father like that? Why couldn't we swap? I'd get Los Muchos, the cops; she would get my dad. Ha ha. And, well, I shouldn't look at her like that, with such a frown, so humorless—I had not frowned at her, but was instead rather astonished. She said I had to be very nice to her because she had brought me the latest news, the banner headline. "We have been saved." She paused, got up, poured some coffee into the thermos cap that served as a cup, gave it to me, took it from me, had a sip, gave it back to me, sat on the bed, and lit a cigarette. "Yes, saved." Because something a little strange had happened, something which she couldn't quite wrap her head around, but which, in the end, was a beautiful thing. Life was beautiful, just like Pancholo. She looked at me askance and exhaled a cloud of smoke as if she were facing a movie camera.

After the morning's hullabaloo and my sudden disappearance, she'd stayed behind, just hanging out, to see what had happened. By mid-afternoon, the girl was back in school, escorted by the same squad car, followed by her parents, who were in a Mercedes. A silver Mercedes, check that out—Yadelis offered me a cigarette but I was sick of nicotine by then. And then everything started all over again. The police officers assured Chief Head Scalper and his assistant principal (so boring, like a piece of lead) and the little old man from math class (poor guy, a fossil), and all of humanity, that there had been a mistake, a very lamentable mistake . . . Was I listening to this? A lamentable mistake. The fossil cried out, "I knew it! I knew it!" The girl's father spoke in a very low voice, softly, pronouncing each and every letter. He was a thin man, not very tall, also wearing glasses, and what a nose. But even so, he was frightening. He threatened to sue them all for "defamation" and "slander" and "arbitrary arrest" and police "brutality" because they were all "anti-Semites" who'd just shat on the "constitution" (yeah, he said "shat"—my buddy wasn't so sure about the other words but she had no doubt about that one), and he was going to take the matter as high as he needed to, all the way to the UN, to be precise. What a speech. The guy talked so oddly. Other than "shat," the only other thing that made sense was the stuff about police brutality, and of course he was right about that, no doubt about it. Brutality and a half. The lead officer explained, a little nervously, that it wasn't their fault, that the aggrieved citizen had initially identified the girl, as had two other witnesses—she was the only one from the whole gang who had been identified (Yadelis smiled happily, all perfect white teeth)—and, then, later, they'd reconsidered. The three had been wrong, said the lead officer. That could happen, couldn't it? They'd probably confused her with someone who looked just like her. That's where my buddy had left them, as the officers tried to appease the guy who pronounced every letter. Did I understand any of this? Because she didn't understand squat, but so what? The thing was, no one had seen us, only the other girl, and the girl had kept mum, which was great, and no doubt she wouldn't give us up now, when things had turned out like this. What luck. What incredible luck. Thank you, Ochún.

The news burned through the high school like prairie fire. The witch continued her routine, not saying a word to anyone. She strolled along, quite calm, as if she had nothing to do with the stories, and as if she didn't notice the looks or hear the commentary. But everybody, both students and teachers, were talking about the same thing at recess and between classes. So, in the days that followed, before the anecdote became a legend, I found out, little by little, the rest of the story. I didn't ask too much, of course. Just kept my ears keen, so as not to raise suspicions.

As it turns out, we had, in fact, been seen, since they certainly weren't blind. As they say out there: there's always somebody watching. But not to the extent that they could express it to a sketch artist. The aggrieved citizen and the two witnesses had described us this way: a little black girl, a little fat girl, and a little girl with glasses, all three in high school uniforms. Yadelis was very hurt that the little black girl came in first: always the same crap with the little black girl, of course, because everything is her fault, the racists. Nonetheless, the implicit racism in the saying, "All black people look alike," had been very useful.

Neither the aggrieved citizen nor the two witnesses, all white, were any good at distinguishing one little black girl from the others, and in our school there were a lot of little black girls, some quite beautiful. It may seem strange but it isn't. I know people like that, who see black people as if they came in bulk (they're the same way with Asians), like carbon silhouettes, vague darknesses, so no matter how beautiful she might have been, I don't think they could have recognized her even if she'd been standing in front of them. Little fat girls were fewer, perhaps not so many, but enough that I could pass inadvertently. As a little fat girl (or anything else), I'm very common, nothing out of this world, there are a zillion girls like me out there. In other words, Yadelis and I could blend into the crowd. But not so the witch. Curly hair (the real thing, not a cold wave, curly from the roots on up), an excessive nose, pince-nez, a spectacular watch . . . too many details. This is the problem with looking like a foreigner. The police had shown up in the principal's office with those details and the two witnesses. Chief Head Scalper sent for her and the witnesses immediately identified her. Up to that point in the story, fine. The officers probably thought they'd solved the case. Heh heh. How wrong they were.

They expected a quick, terrified confession and the names of the others. She could have said, "I was minding my own business, perfectly at peace, and the little fat one splashed me with soda, out of nowhere, because she's so stupid, and the little black girl threw the glass at me; that little black girl is something else, you wouldn't believe how she talks. What could I do? I just tried to make sure the glass didn't hit me. In fact, I tried to grab it, but I couldn't, and then I just ran and I didn't go to the police because I was afraid; anybody would be afraid of people like that, so vulgar for so long. That's why I'm so glad you're here today. They're in my class, So and So and So and So." She would have been released easily. Nobody would have held it against her because we weren't friends. In fact, nobody really expected anything else from her. But no. She decided to deny everything. A glass? On his face? Her? No way. Even though it wouldn't have been a good idea to admit it, she was the best student. She was very proper, very well mannered. She spoke three languages other than Spanish. She was into fencing. She'd never been in trouble of any kind, much less a violent incident. The principal, who was sitting there, and the other teachers could attest to that. In other words, her word was to be believed. Also, she had not been in the cafeteria yesterday. She didn't know the aggrieved citizen and, of course, had no reason to aggrieve him. She always hung out alone, studying, without little black girls or little fat girls following her around. They would not find a soul on the entire terrestrial globe who would testify to the contrary. With utmost respect, she suggested the witnesses needed to take another look—she stood where there was the most light, pushed her hair from her face, and showed her features and profile; they should try to remember very carefully, because they were making a grave mistake, a very grave mistake with incalculable consequences. She *always* told the truth—and this she said in the presence of the witnesses, cool, undaunted, convincingly, without a single muscle twitch, without blinking. She would repeat it later, in the same tone, to the aggrieved citizen, without being intimidated by the many cuts on his face, the stitches on his forehead, or the eye patch. She showed compassion but not guilt.

"Oh, I am so sorry, I really am. Believe me, I would like to help you. I hope they catch the bastard who did that to you very soon," she said quite seriously, "because a criminal like that shouldn't be on the loose. No, he shouldn't be. His place is in jail."

The officers had taken her down to the station to pressure her. That troublesome girl with her Pinocchio nose, her worldliness and her three languages besides Spanish, was not going to pull a fast one on them. What did this snot-nosed girl think she was doing? This was no game. She had to say what they wanted her to say, without excuses or pretexts. They didn't let her call anyone. They didn't let her drink water or go to the bathroom. Various officers took part in the interrogation. One was kind, paternal: "I have a daughter your age, so, you see, you can trust me. We know it was an accident, but we have to clear the matter up, for your own good, so just tell me what happened and you can leave and that's that; I'll take you home myself." She smiled at him. Another, like Lt. Columbo, played dumb: "I believe you, of course; now tell me, where were you at the time of the incident?" Naturally, she had no idea when the incident took place. "Where were you at 11:30 a.m. yesterday, Thursday, June 9, 1987?" If she remembered correctly, she was on her way home. Yes, because they'd gotten out of school early. She was on her way home. "Ah, yes, very well. And what kind of proof do you have?" She had no intention of proving anything. With all due respect, they were the ones who had to offer proof. Another officer, who liked to stir things up, said: "You don't have to continue with these lies. Don't be stupid, girlee. We already caught your little friends and they told us everything. They both blamed you. Aren't you going to defend yourself? It's probably best if you do." She congratulated them for having caught the suspects but she didn't have any little friends. To be frank, she found the whole idea of "little friends" pretty ridiculous. Another one was threatening: "Look, if you don't talk, it's your problem. The one who's in trouble is you, because from here you're going straight to Juvenile Detention, and we'll see if they don't straighten you out. And just so we're clear, I'm going to make sure your life is a living hell. Do you know why? Because I'm a very bad man." She sighed sadly. If they locked her up, tough luck. But they'd be committing a great injustice, because she hadn't done anything. Their guilty consciences wouldn't let them sleep at night. Or during the day. And, how weird, since she'd been taught at school that the police were good, and friends to children . . . Another officer, a beast: "Hey you, whassup, wha's goin' on 'ere; don't play crazy or clever wit me cuz I don't buy any of that crazy or clever crap; just tell it once an' for all, godammit; don't make me haf to slap you one." She gave that one a faraway look, with divine disdain. Slap her one? Fine. She couldn't stop him. But it wouldn't be worth it. The Nazis had slapped her grandparents way more than "one." And she certainly wasn't better than her grandparents, and wouldn't pretend to just go along, like a good girl, just to avoid her "one." The beast lost his mind and had to be held back by the others. He screamed to let him go, that he was going to show her how to have respect for authority. She took refuge in a corner, like a timid little mouse, covering her face with her hands and trying to take up as little space as possible. And that was the delightful spectacle that was offered to her parents upon their arrival; they had raced over, not allowing anything or anyone to get in their way from the moment Chief Head Scalper had notified them. By that time, the witnesses and the aggrieved citizen had already begun to have their doubts.

A couple of weeks went by. The school year was nearing its end. It was the ninth inning, the last classes at the high school, and we were taking final exams. Yadelis, pregnant (three months but she'd just recently begun to show), had decided to never crack open a book again. According to her own words, she would never again face the printed word. What for? She could read by sounding out the syllables, she could count on her fingers, and she didn't have the remotest idea what an equilateral triangle could be. It's not that she was dumb, she was simply not interested. Her goal was to move in with Pancholo, attend to him, take care of him, spoil him, produce many babies, and play house. (It didn't seem like a bad idea, but that was the exact moment my buddy chose to hold the cow's leg and get sent to jail.) Her opinion about the witch had gone through considerable modification. She'd changed, she'd done a 360, that's how much she'd changed.

"She took it like a man, pudge, like a man," she kept repeating, astonished, full of admiration; she said "man" as if she were saying "god." "I knew she'd be like that. I told you, pudge, I told you a million times and you kept telling me no. I always liked her, always. You and your prejudices . . . That girl is hard, hard as a rock."

If I had been afraid of that girl before, I was now terrified of her. She struck me as a dangerous freak, some kind of alien, a Martian in disguise or some such thing. It was pretty difficult for me to accept such an invulnerable creature, with so much personal power, able to leap tall bounds over human and divine law. I'm scared of people who don't get scared. But Yadelis took her admiration very seriously and wanted to get up close and everything; she wanted to talk to her. I tried to dissuade her. Get up close, for what? Talk about what? Did my little friend think that dangerous freak was going to pay any attention to us? Wasn't it obvious she didn't give a damn about us? Yadelis shrugged. No, it wasn't obvious. In fact, it was the contrary. That dangerous freak had saved our asses without asking anything in return and we should be grateful, social, and friendly. I insisted. What if the cops were still watching her? What if they saw her talking to a little black girl and a little fat girl? We'd all be in a mess of trouble. Yadelis cracked up and told me I watched too many movies. Basically, she was stuck on the idea of getting to know her.

I kept thinking about the cafeteria manager. What about his face? More than just thinking about it, I tortured myself with it. I know now that if you follow your religion to the letter of the law, you can't live, but at fifteen I was very confused. Smoking, drinking, fucking (sometimes with married, atheist, and communist men), using profanity, lying, skipping school, sticking my tongue out, stealing cars with Pancholo, stealing plantains on my own . . . those were all minor details, nothing that couldn't be taken care of in the confessional. Father Ignacio had a forgiving nature; after all, it's not the same to preach in the barrio as in Rome. But violence, no. Violence was inadmissible. It was wrong to hurt anybody, period. This time, Father Ignacio listened to me calmly, like always. But later he gave me quite a lecture, a real talking to, and like three million Our Fathers and who knows how many Hail Marys. It didn't work. A week later, I felt the same, like a cockroach. Then Father Ignacio explained that it's one thing to be Catholic and quite another, and very different altogether, to be a Nazarín. I asked who that was. "Some nut," he said, "some nut invented by that shameless Luis Buñuel. He drank in the gospels the way the Quixote went through novels on chivalry. He didn't understand that to love your neighbor, you have to love yourself first. Right? Of course, if you feel so bad"—Father Ignacio smiled—"you could probably clean the sacristy, dust a little, get rid of the spiderwebs, wash the pews, and weed the garden . . ." So that's what I did, and I got great results: I was so tired that I didn't have the energy to blame myself for anything. I was also unable to resist when he demanded that I not follow the example set by my buddy, the pagan, and instead stay in school in preparation for college. Even though his vows might have been from another order, I think Father Ignacio was a bit of a Jesuit, just like his illustrious namesake. I never saw the cafeteria manager again; it's possible he may have found a job with fewer risks. His heir continued selling soda for many years after that, but in plastic glasses.

I'm not eloquent. I've never been able to talk anybody out of anything. It's always everybody else talking me into stuff. When Yadelis decided to go tell the dangerous freak about her fervent admiration, I decided to go along, just in case. Although I was afraid, I stayed by her side to make sure there wasn't a new tussle. We waited for her at the park on Paseo, two blocks from school. She always walked by there at exactly the same time, the chronometric witch. She barely looked at us, and half-smiled, sorta sly or mocking. (In time, this smile would lose its playful air to become more and more sarcastic.) She stopped in front of us, as if saying, "Ah, very well, so you finally made up your mind," as if she'd been waiting for that meeting. I relaxed a little. Yadelis said one or two stupidities, which didn't erase the smile from the dangerous freak's face. She even gave her a little kiss. (My friend used to be extroverted and sickly sweet, just like me. But the Malmö mists have really changed her.) I don't think the freak cared much for the little kiss: practically imperceptibly, she pulled back a couple of millimeters. And she spoke. As I suspected, she didn't give a shit about us. It wasn't that she didn't like us, no. It was just that: she didn't give a shit about us. What was astounding to me was not this fact in and of itself, but that she could admit it so freely. I think most people don't give a shit about others but almost no one will admit it, and much less with such sincerity. I thought she was cynical but, also, interesting. She had not lied to protect us; what a strange idea, that. She was training for the future, to best practice her chosen profession.

"An actress?" Yadelis asked.

"Secret agent?" I asked.

No, nothing like that. Actresses and secret agents played out scripts written by others. She wanted to compose her own scripts, make up her own lies and fool the whole world. She wanted to be a consummate con artist, a sublime pretender. She wanted to be a writer. That turned out to be Linda Roth's first big speech.

Chapter 4

Mangos and guavas

"THEY TEACH US TO EAT MANGOS . . ." SAID THE GREAT PRETENDER, nine years later, as she launched into her second big speech. "No, no. Not like that. Maybe 'teach' isn't the right word"—a writer to the end, she's always worried about the right word—"More precisely, they *program us* to eat mangos. It doesn't even matter if we eat them right or not, often or not, if we like them or not: the issue is to eat them. Mangos or nothing. They program us so that there won't be any other option."

We were alone in my room. By that time, my dad had ceased all transmissions from Happy Hammer Corners and had made a definitive move to North America with his cameras and microphones. He lived near Dallas. He had been floating around Miami before that, where he must have made a play on the wrong person, because they chased him out of there amidst gunfire, threatening to blow his brains out if he ever showed his face around those parts again. Later, he'd move to San Francisco, because the proximity to Love Field made him nervous, what with the echoes of the JFK assassination (probably echoes that only he heard, although you never know) reminding him of his recent shoot-out, and he was, after all, a pacifist. He'd sent me a thousand dollars with Linda, who'd just returned from New York, two hundred for Father Ignacio, and (I don't know for whom) a pair of green cowboy boots with red fringe, yellow heels, and innumerable multicolored decorations, not to mention gold sequins, and fake rocks—one of those delicate products that hit the markets every year with a tag that says: "Made in Texas by Texans." There was also an unforgettable letter, terrible, hilarious, with lovely lettering, an epistolary gem in which he told me about his adventures, with a postscript that included three fag jokes and in which he asked me to tell them to Father Ignacio as part of his donation.

The economy wasn't doing so well in those days. To be frank, it wasn't doing anything at all: it was paralyzed. I don't know if we were living on the brink of collapse or in the midst of it. I'd lost my little editing job at an obscure farming magazine (there were no more farms or paper on which to print the magazine), and I wasn't doing a thing on the side with my mechanic skills. Total downer. The day before (and the one before that and the one before that and the one before that) I'd gone to bed on an empty stomach. A glass of sugar water, a piece of bread that seemed to be made of sand or an aluminum scouring pad, and that was pretty much it until I got to school. No rice or hake or illusions. What a shame. Instead of the song about the bottles on the wall, I was singing that other one: "The coconut got no water . . . / it got no meat . . . / it ain't got nothin . . . / nope, it ain't got nothin . . ." I'd lost the energy to count down to zero bottles. I think I was afraid to get to zero. I felt exactly like that coconut, upset by the maracas making music in my belly, because if there's anything that'll depress a fatty like me, it's a lack of provisions.

Like a lot of other people, I'd tried to raise a little pig. An ill-fated initiative. My little one's name was Gruñi, to which I then attached my surnames in a fit of maternal love. That was the first mistake: giving it a name. I hadn't quite realized the rigorous anonymity to which, without exception, my neighbor's hogs were submitted. Because to name something is to individualize it. Name equals spirit, name equals a singular personality. Then it needs to be cared for, because, in some ways, it is unique and unsubstitutable. Following this theme, there's a very clever question which goes like this: "Between the Mona Lisa and a baby, if you could only choose one, which would you save in a fire?" I have my answer, but I won't tell. We'd be better off phrasing the question this way: "Between the Mona Lisa and Juan Carlos, grandson of the woman who lives down the block and sells lollipops, if you had to . . ." And then? Of course, there are always people who hate humanity and all our splendid creations, who would call this question a matter of "shitty humanism," who believe the world would be much better off without the abominable Mona Lisa or that imbecile Juan Carlos and wouldn't lift a finger to save either of them. But let us return to the story of the little pig.

Really cute and sweet, Gruñi Álvarez La Fronde loved it when I stroked him behind the ears. He lived well protected in my room. I never let him out to the hallway where that perverse and anonymous megatherium could commit some outrage against him. He ate the same as me, whatever it was, whatever we could get. He slept with me in my bed. Sometimes just with me and sometimes with an occasional lover, who invariably protested, made a face, declared that he was allergic to such a creature on his pillow, said that it was unacceptably disgusting, and took advantage of my sleep to put Gruñi on the floor. The little angel, how he put up with all those insensitive stepfathers. There was one who tried to throw him out the window, but I caught him just in time. "What are you doing?" I screamed at the ruffian, and saved the little thing, who was terrified. What a nightmare, that window; it's almost like its uncommon size awakens the worst instincts in people. And, for the record, Gruñi did not smell: I bathed and combed him everyday, even if it meant I had to carry the buckets of water myself up the stairs. We were very happy together until one day while he was still very young, he got sick and died. I cried like Mary Magdalene, but it was probably for the best, because I never would have had the nerve to sell or kill my pet. I don't know why, but I suspect I'm not very good at hog farming.

The thing is, I was dying of hunger in the middle of a city with several million inhabitants but with no one I could go to for help. After crashing his Peugeot against a ceiba tree and reducing it to a tin can, my great-uncle W., the marquis's grandson, was recovering from his many fractures in Camagüey with the tinajón family, from where he sent me a telegram to warn me that Uranus was near, lying in wait, ready to launch the cosmos's evil forces into our miserable lives. Uranus (perhaps Neptune or Pluto, I don't quite remember) had made him lose control of the car and was, therefore, the cause of the accident. With my heart aching, I supposed that the astrologer, so blind he couldn't make out a ceiba tree three feet in front of him, and a little nutty to insist on driving at his age, was probably in his last days, about to kick the bucket. But no. Thank god, and perhaps a benevolent planet, my great-uncle, the marquis's grandson, is what we call a survivor. He's still there, without his Peugeot, with a cane, still flatly refusing to touch a xylophone, but alive and kicking and still divining the future.

Father Ignacio could sometimes resolve some groceries through the Church (in a very stealthy way, the verbs "to resolve" and "to get" began to replace the verb "to buy" in the lexicon of the economic crisis), but a collection of homeless and kinda crazy old women, with black veils, rosaries, and crucifixes, depended on him. Between all of them, things were pretty dark, like the veils on those little old ladies, like certain characters invented by that shameless Luis Buñuel. It broke your heart. It's not that I thought it was wrong to live off charity, because what's important is to live (it doesn't matter what for, it makes no difference, the important thing is to live), but it wasn't right or possible to ask my confessor to also take care of somebody who was young and healthy. My dad's donation, to which I would add another $200, would come in very handy, although I refrained from telling him about the pacifist's North American adventures. Who's ever heard of a confession by mail? But maybe, it occurs to me, it's possible that Catholics from the developed world are already confessing via the Internet, who knows.

Pancholo was in the same straits as me, hungry, gaunt, and penniless, in plain decay, except that he didn't give a shit about food. What was the big deal with all that chewing and swallowing? What a waste of time. His thing was liquor, which he would offer me freely because I was his "ecobio" (in truth, ecobios are all male and make up some kinda lodge or fraternal order where there's no room for mistakes or women, so I'm only his "ecobio" by his word, and between us), with the addition of some grass to get us through the misfortune which has been our fate so that we might drag our sorry carcasses through the disgusting and remote roads our miserable lives have taken us down. Of course, I think rum and marijuana are good. They're good until, in fact, they're not; so long as it's a matter of mixing "loco spark" and grass, but in those famished circumstances, they only served to accompany the concert already going on in my stomach. The hangovers were infernal.

In the meantime, Yadelis was agonizing amidst the mists of Malmö. She'd come through with both lungs intact, thank God, the little Virgin of Charity, and perhaps Odin, the chief of the Scandinavian pantheon, according to the encyclopedia. Sometimes Father Ignacio scolds me for what he considers my heterodox tendencies, my excessive tolerance of whatever superstition or idolatry appears on the horizon, and my persistent attachment to syncretism. I understand. He'd already gotten quite upset because I attended a toque de santo, a celebration of an African orisha, at Los Muchos (I don't know if it's because of the music, the sweets, the colors, or the dancing, the fact is that I'm attracted to toques de santo like a moth to a flame; somebody once told me I'm a daughter of Obbatalá, the chief of the Yoruba pantheon, and I confess that I love the idea of being the daughter of such an illustrious being), and later he was upset by my reference to the benevolent planet, and still later because I paid attention to a Jehovah's Witness, and that's not including my flirtations with palmistry, the Ouija board, the I Ching, and the tarot. The thing with the Scandinavian pantheon struck him as the topper.

"But child, that perversity isn't even actually practiced anymore," he protested. "What are we going to do with you, huh? Impish, frivolous, wayward, and, as if it weren't enough, now anachronistic."

It's possible that I'm such a bad Christian that I would have been burned at the stake during the Dark Ages, but at the time I had no choice but to pray to everyone and everything, including Odin, a local divinity with a specialty in Nordic problems, because "dying" was the precise word to describe my friend's condition that the inconsolable Viking used on the other end of the phone line, and I was terrified. It was a matter of life and death, and I love Yadelis very much. Here, without her, I never dared go out with foreigners. Although the truth is that I've never been very good at business, witness the matter with the little pig. I'm a complete failure as a jinetera. In the first place because, though I'm more understanding and patient than Yadelis (there are tourists who, when it comes to sex, don't have a clue where their left hand goes, so it's important to teach them, but without insulting them or laughing at them or any of that; it's important to repress any giggling), if someone wants a beautiful little black girl, it's going to be tough to get them to be satisfied with a mousy little white girl who's got a few too many kilograms on her. Second, I know how to fuck but not how to get paid for it. It's just really hard for me to demand payment for doing what I most love to do. I'm happy if they just take me out to eat. Besides, not all tourists are drooling old men. No way. There are also young men, handsome Italians and Galicians who know what they're doing. How can you charge those guys? I must be an idiot. According to my friend, the problem is that I don't value myself. She does. She feels that all men (except one—the important one, the beautiful one, of course) *have* to pay to sleep with a girl, because it's not a game but a job like any other. I tried to see it her way but I couldn't, so I quit. I couldn't ask Pancholo to charge for me because, poor guy, he already had a rep for pimping because of Yadelis, and the laws on the subject had just been tightened, so they could send him back to the tank without a second thought. I have to admit I was also scared off by the warning I got (me, of all people, who'd stolen so many cars with impunity), because I'm not amused by problems with cops.

And I was still a few months from meeting Moisés. I don't mean to say that my boo was even a little bit interested in the tourist business. To my knowledge, he's not interested in business of any kind. Besides his somewhat gruff manners, he wasn't exactly overflowing with diplomacy. He disliked most people and did very little to hide it. How could someone like that negotiate? The only people with whom he was never aggressive were Father Ignacio, who never tried to convince him of anything, and in fact didn't even look at him (to Father Ignacio, my relationship with Moisés was some kind of affair with the devil); Pancholo, because of his very lucid theory about our sorry carcasses; and Alix Oyster, the most notorious of Linda's girlfriends, as quiet as her nickname implies, who lived with us for a while, until . . . Well, it's not Alix's turn yet; I'll talk about her later. The thing is that the sweet man used to give me money. Pesos or dollars, always money, perhaps with the objective of establishing a certain distance between us, or to compensate for his excesses, or, who knows, maybe Dr. Frumento was right and deep down Moisés really was a noble and generous guy. Where his money came from, I don't know. I have no idea. He'd put it in my hands and that was that. I once dared to ask him about his mysterious finances and he pinched my butt (really hard, that savage) before recommending that I shouldn't be such a gossip, that curiosity killed the cat. But as I said: when Linda came back from New York, Moisés hadn't yet entered my life and I was really down, struggling and just plain wiped out.

For fatties, according to Linda, hunger has certain advantages, a certain dignified compensation that needs to be taken into account: the loss of kilograms. On that memorable night in 1996, after not laying an eye on me for six months, she discovered I have a good figure. Probably too voluptuous for her tastes, but quite acceptable. She's more inclined toward the athletic look; she melts over Olympian beauty: during more recent times, her idol has been that super stellar multi-champion hyper-glorious ultra-divine Marion Jones, the one who won five medals in Sydney, grinning ear to ear. Moisés also liked women like that, perhaps because they're a little tougher and require more of a beating before passing out on the floor. It's also possible that they might throw a strong punch of their own to liven up the party. As the ancient Romans used to say: *altius, citius, fortius.** In any case, I looked quite different from the ter-

---

* Higher, faster, stronger.

rapin Linda had left behind in Havana six months before. It was important to her not to be too demanding with such a longtime pal: with a wee bit less ass, slightly narrower hips, a belly a teeny bit firmer, my tits slightly less perky, and my cheeks a little less chubby, I'd be almost perfect. The "almost" was necessary because, above and beyond everything, I lacked height. Just a little bit of height. Losing kilograms because of a forced diet struck me as pretty cruel and confusing, but it seemed right to her, which was typical. She called me a terrapin, an interesting comparison, because terrapins last a ton of years, they're very long-lived, and I have a great love of life. And the thing with the height, that was just shameless, since Linda and I and millions of other women are the same height: a little less than Yadelis and a lot less than Marion Jones.

But, as usual, I didn't argue with her. Not just because no one in their right mind would ever get into an argument with her (my friend has always been extremely eloquent, quite the sophist, very talky, very capable of demonstrating that green really is red and vice versa; there are some who believe she should get into politics), but also because I'd missed her terribly and here she was, suddenly, to save me, perhaps not so much from my impish, frivolous, and wayward spirit, but from my aching belly. We were now swimming in money and that always provokes a good mood. That's the banknote's spell: all (or almost all) our agonies disappear as if by magic. As the poet says, "Don Dinero is a powerful lover." There's no better psychopharmaceutical. Aside from my dad's thousand dollars, there were several thousand more for each of us. What opulence. Other than in movies in which there's a bank robbery, or in which drug dealers leap from boat to boat, I'd never seen a treasure like this. I felt like a Rockefeller.

Our habanos business was off the charts. A little before she'd left on her trip, I'd hooked up with a guy who worked at a cigar factory. Very playful and creative, with a steaming sensuality, he loved doing crazy things with cigars. The details don't matter; the fact is, I had a very good time with him. We only slept together a couple of times but he liked me and gave me two boxes of Cohíbas so that I could sell them on my own, without giving him anything, and without my even asking for them. Oh, if only all men could be that generous. Each box had a street value of thirty-five dollars. That's a Havana street, because on a New York street they were worth about six hundred apiece. As soon as I found that out, I took one to Linda. As a gift, of course, so she'd have something to spend in New York, where it's said everything is so expensive and there's a subtle little hand, invisible and sly, which keeps pulling cash out of your pocket without your knowing. My friend wanted to know why there was such a difference in price. When I explained how it was illegal to sell Cuban products in the United States because of the embargo and all that, her eyes grew shiny behind her lenses.

"In other words, it's some sort of contraband, right?"

"Well . . . yes. More or less." This business of calling a spade a spade was an awfully bad habit, I thought. "You can take two boxes from Cuba without having to declare them. It's legal. But you can't take a single one into the United States. That's why they're so pricey there. It seems that yanquis just fall to pieces when it comes to smoking a Cohíba."

"That's good. They should fall to pieces." She was thoughtful for a moment. "Hey, Z, and if they catch you with a shipment, here or there, what happens? Do they send you to the gas chamber?"

"Oh, I don't know about that. But I think probably not." I thought "shipment" was so over the top. "And, at least here, there is no gas chamber. Here we have firing squads."

She started laughing. Her fear of the gas chamber was congenital, she explained, part of a biological inheritance that I, so young, lacking in expertise and the last letter of the alphabet, could not understand. Nobody likes to be slapped one and poisoned and suffocated and then turned into soap and their skin into lamp shades and their bones into buttons and other artisanal objects—ha! ha!—she loves talking like this, which in my opinion is both unfortunate and a little pathetic, but the other Jews at the synagogue also think it's hilarious, so I dunno, maybe there's something to it after all. But, well, seriously, I *had* to give her the other box of cigars and put her in touch with the pervert from the cigar factory—my friend doesn't ask, she demands, which makes some people think she should have been in the military, although I can't picture her obeying orders, ever—because she'd decided to invest her capital gains in this business, since it had such excellent prospectives. She wouldn't tell me how much capital she was talking about because . . . well, she just wouldn't—she's a little obsessed with money; I think she's stingy, but like all tightwads, she thinks she's thrifty—but she promised we'd split the profits in half because information also has its value: no business could prosper in ignorance. As always happened with us, she convinced me.

I gave her the other box and put her in touch with the pervert, from whom she bought I don't know how many more boxes, but they filled two suitcases and a backpack, about half the factory's production. At first, the guy, who thinks he's a genius, a wiseguy, when it comes to business, tried to nail her at thirty-five a box, but she warned him not to try to play the shark or smooth or sly. She suggested he take advantage of the opportunity to make a tidy profit instead of wasting time trying to play her: she wasn't born yesterday and she knew perfectly well that "wholesale" implied a discount. What a vocabulary. I think the guy thought she was a foreigner trying to pass for Cuban (he asked her nationality and she said Japanese; he didn't ask anything else). They went back and forth for a good while. He had doubts, resisted, tried to convince her, gave her this ironic look that, according to Linda, is typical of men when they're confronted by a woman who bests them. But she never lost her footing. On the contrary: she seemed to enjoy the duel. She'd speak in a low voice, softly, pronouncing every letter. She was implacable. Prodigious with her resources, she was colder and crueler than the iceberg that pierced the *Titanic*, and she ended up getting the pervert to take the price all the way down to twenty a box. I'd never seen such a performance of negotiating wizardry. I was so impressed that I decided to make her the proposal I hadn't dared present to Pancholo. She looked at me incredulously. Me, a jinetera? Her, a pimp? Where in heaven's name—from what battered brain had such a brilliant idea sprung? Who'd ever head of a fat jinetera and a skinny pimp? She smiled before asking me, please, to quit talking about such lewdness.

So she took off for New York with her two suitcases and a backpack full of cigar boxes. She was invited by Hunter College at CUNY, the state university, for the First Hispanic Caribbean Women Writers Conference or something like that. To be frank, this college had actually been interested in a series of lectures by Carlos Fuentes, but the great Mexican had politely declined the invitation (according to my friend, they paid very little) and so they organized the meeting of Latinas instead. Linda is not Hispanic, doesn't have a drop of Hispanic in her, in fact had somehow managed to get herself an Austrian passport (later, she'd trade it for one from the European Union, which is wine colored, very pretty, and very useful, so they won't mess with you at customs and will allow you to happily continue to traffic), but she writes in Spanish. She was going for two weeks and ended up staying six months. Of course, she lost her job at the publishing house. But that wasn't particularly important: later, no one really knew when, perhaps in a few years, she'd *buy* a small publishing house, or better yet, she'd be a shareholder for a big and powerful one. I don't know if she really meant any of it. It's possible she did, because she'd already begun to have problems with editors, who don't seem to last beyond the first light of dawn with her. The fact is that from such conflicts dreams are born, although she presents them as faits accomplis, as if she had a crystal ball where she could see the future with the kind of detail available in the present. Her faith is so absolute, her conviction so profound, that I'm always frightened by the possibility of failure. But, of course, I don't tell her. I don't like to be a harbinger of bad news.

As might be expected, she got through customs with no trouble at all. Just to warm up her act, she'd gone through at Rancho Boyeros without declaring a thing. If she'd taken into account the possibility that she'd have to bribe somebody, it didn't matter—she didn't need to. Her good girl look (in a lot of ways, she's still the best student in the class) inspired a certain trust. She had a layover in the Bahamas without the slightest hitch. Then she landed in Newark, in New Jersey. She was twenty-two years old. She'd never set foot outside the archipelago, not even outside the big island, but she conducted herself with utmost confidence and ease, as if she were Phileas Fogg, the man who went around the world in eighty days. Well, actually, better than Mr. Fogg, since that conspicuous traveler had a slight tendency to get into all sorts of trouble, contrary to my friend. She chooses her battles. She'd considered the possibility of having to explain herself in English with a German accent, since by that time she spoke four languages other than Spanish (her talent for languages is terrifying) and she loved mixing it up, making up fraudulent arrangements to confuse the non-specialist, so that the non-specialist could never guess the speaker's origins, but none of that proved necessary either. No one attacked her. No one stopped her. No one paid any attention to her whatsoever. I think that Austrian passport helped a whole bunch.

"Of course. Nothing succeeds in this life like passing for European. Pacifist, fresh-faced, financially solvent, and very proper, a first-class citizen," she'd say later, with a poker face and a neutral tone, and without the slightest trace of Third World bitterness.

She dedicated herself to selling the boxes, one by one, with tremendous patience, on the streets of Manhattan, in various bars and discotheques, on the subway, in Little Italy, in Chinatown, on Broadway, in Soho, at the skating rink at Rockefeller Center, at a Thai restaurant, at an Indian place, at a Greek diner in Brooklyn Heights, at Strand Books, in Chelsea, at a vaudeville club in Harlem, under the trees in Central Park, at the zoo, as the opera let out, amidst the work of the great masters at the Met and MOMA, on the ferry, at the Statue of Liberty, even *inside* St. Patrick's Cathedral, in front of

the altar, which reminded me of the bible passage about the money chang-
ers in the temple (I don't know why, since no one threw her out of there for
being sacrilegious). She trolled everywhere, using her four languages other
than Spanish, although Spanish too, but not much—she smiled a lot—and
in spite of the many absurd laws against the healthy habit of smoking (she's
not a smoker), many New Yorkers fell to pieces over the prospect of smoking a Cohíba. They literally drooled. It was as if they'd never seen a cigar and
had spent their entire lives waiting to lay their eyes on one. And to smoke
it. They didn't care about the laws or the environment or the risk of getting
lung cancer or any of that. Their eyes grew wide, their mouths dropped;
they'd check it, sniff it, exclaim "Oh God!" and would drop their green on
the spot, before some other freak got to their treasure. This way, my friend
managed to sell all the boxes for more than seven hundred, and some for
more than eight hundred. I was astounded that her clients carried so much
cash on them, without fear of being mugged . . . On them? Oh no. Not on
them. I couldn't let my underdevelopment betray me like that. To avoid it,
she happily finished the story by explaining that she had to drag quite a few
of them to an automatic teller to get her full price. She felt very good about
her transaction, not only because of the generous bounty, but because of her
recently discovered talents for international hustling.

Upon her return, the very first thing we did was to go eat at a very modest but attractive and cozy little restaurant called El Gringo Viejo. I ignored
her evil insinuations about how I'd go back to my former terrapin silhouette
and concentrated on chewing and savoring and swallowing a colossal steak
that was almost too big for my plate, nicely cooked from end to end on the
outside and practically raw on the inside, with its abundant mushroom sauce
and its accompaniment of huge, crunchy fries. Oh, the glory! How divine!
Yum yum. Delicious. Exhilarating. Fantastic. How . . . oh. It may seem
utterly crude, a barbarity, an atrocity, but the truth is that, after so much
involuntary fasting, all that eating caressed my insides in such a way that it
practically provoked an orgasm. Why deny it? That's the way I am. Voracious,
primitive, gluttonous, one of the hordes. For radical vegetarians, like Linda,
so orthodox that they're practically herbivores, the mere sight of a steak
dripping blood can be something like a spectacle of Dantean proportions.
Entrenched behind her lettuce, brussels sprouts, watercress, celery, chard,
cabbage, spinach, beans, and other weeds, she'd look at me like a fawn peering
at a lion: in horror. But I don't care. I've been hungry all my life, sometimes

acutely and always chronically. I've lived day to day, between hustling and inventing. I've been walking a tightrope (I still am), a trapeze act without a net that might cushion my fall. Maybe it sounds a bit dramatic, but it's not. I suppose the image of the tightrope is familiar to everyone, all of humanity; it's just that hunger makes it more evident, more vivid. I dunno. Among one of my laws of survival is that, if the opportunity to eat presents itself, it must be taken advantage of to the max, because you don't know when it will come again. It's that simple. After the steak, I had myself a delicious slice of cake followed by three scoops of ice cream with whipped cream, syrup, and a pastry. Yum yum. Then a cup of coffee, a cigarette, and that's that. The joy of being alive, paradise on a full belly, nirvana. That's when I asked Linda how it'd gone with the Hispanic women writers. As soon as I saw the look on her face, I knew the answer would be long.

The Hispanic Women Writers? Ha ha. The Conference, capitalized, was more like sci-fi, like an episode of *The X Files*, except it lasted four days. And thank God for that, because it had been incredibly boring, irritating, more social than literary, and a little nutty. In other words, what you'd expect. Was it possible to expect anything else from these kinds of things? She'd make a surreptitious escape early each morning. She'd step out to those dusty streets and run around the Big Apple, take a look at a few museums, and play tourist for a while, which meant, among other things, staring in awe at the World Trade Center and other natural phenomena, taking pictures, and, for one insane moment, considering the idiotic possibility of buying a little sign that said "I love NY," or better yet, "I ♥ NY," or a Lilliputian version of the Empire State Building. Oh, and she was taking care of business. Above and beyond everything else, taking care of business. She'd get back to the conference in the afternoon, just in time for the final applause and to congratulate the Hispanic women writers for the lucidity of their ideas, the keenness of their proposals, and the elegance of their respective rhetorical styles. She was unable to avoid the last session, dedicated to public readings of stories and poems. She had to justify her honorarium in some way, in spite of its squalidness. So she read a brief, hair-raising tale which went on to win the Semana Negra prize for crime fiction: "The Cannibal Who Liked Mayonnaise." The audience applauded, of course. Not because they liked the cannibal, the author explained, but because they applauded everything there. She could have winked, stuck her tongue out, stood on her head, or farted, they would have clapped just the same. That's what's called "feminine solidarity."

Night was another story, though. The New York night has many faces, some beautiful, some horrible. My friend found one that was both beautiful and horrible. Dreamy and nightmarish. Spine-tingling. Unexpected. Turbulent. If she'd ever been innocent, she ceased to be so in New York. In the safety of shadows (and neon signs), some of the Hispanic women writers transformed themselves, forgot they were writers, women of ideas, proposals, and rhetorical styles, and went out to have fun. Yearning but unsure, and perhaps a bit restless, she went with them. And what had to happen happened. It started at an East Village disco, a very peculiar and crazy disco where there were only . . . But we have to go—she stood up—it was late, almost evening, and it didn't seem like good manners to spend the entire night at El Gringo Viejo. What she was going to tell me, the most important part—she smiled enigmatically—she'd tell me at home. Not her house, because there was family there (I remembered her brother Félix, the violinist, a very good lover with a large nose, riotous hair, and his circumcision) and she was not in the mood for family. She showed me the contents of her purse: a beautiful bottle of Clan Campbell. Oh. All right. A secret spiced with whiskey. Now I was dying to know the most important part. There's nobody like Linda when it comes to creating suspense.

"... the thing is to eat them. Mangos or nothing. They program us so there won't be any other option," she was saying later, as she paced in my room in the light of a candle we'd lit because of a blackout. "Supposedly, mangos are the tastiest fruit in the world . . ."

"And they are," I affirmed emphatically from the bed. "I'll say they are. Mangos . . ."

As I've said, I don't usually interrupt Linda, because I know she can't stand to be interrupted and we shouldn't irritate our friends. But her words had reminded me, quite painfully, of the cruel fate met by the mango tree that had for many years been at the door to the Corners, dropping shade and mangos into our lives. It'd get stubborn sometimes, that tree, and in spite of Petronila's intervention, there was no choice but to throw rocks at it to get it to drop its fruit. We didn't do it because we were bad: Pancholo, Yadelis, and I and all the other kids in the 'hood would die to sink our teeth in that sweet scented yellow flesh (sweet and scented in a thick, strong, violent, practically sexual way more than anything else) and let the juice run down our shirts, our chins, our necks, chests, all the way to our feet, making a supreme mess. Ah! Mangos made us feel sticky and happy! But one day the storm of the century arrived on our coasts, that terrifying hurricane that lasted a whole week. It wasn't the worst of them; the thing is, we tend toward an apocalyptic tone and refer to any storm that's a bit much as "the storm of the century." This one was a bit too much. Among its many misdeeds, it tore all the tiles from the roof of the little palace, shattered various neo-gothic panes, dangerously opened up various cracks on the walls, and uprooted the mango tree. That poor tree ended up horizontal but still alive, with its roots intact and protected by moist clumps of dirt. We thought they'd replant it when things calmed down. You don't have to be a botanical expert to know mango trees are perennials, which take a bunch of years to mature, that is, to give fruit, and so they shouldn't be allowed to die just like that. But no. There was no move to replant it. Some guys with a crane came and picked it up as if it were a piece of junk. "Make sure to get that s.o.b.," they groaned, and they took it who knows where. My dad asked them why they were doing that, and they said "that" was their job and he needed to move outta the way and not screw with them anymore. We never saw it again. It may sound absurd, but I think there are people who hate trees. ". . . they're the best, Linda, the best. Get over it. What do you have against mangos? What have they ever done to you? Weren't you a vegetarian until not too long ago?"

"Vegetarian? But Z . . ." She looked at me, confused. "What the fuck are you talking about?"

"Same thing as you. About mangos."

She started to laugh. Just like the guys with the crane, she didn't give anymore explanations, just poured more whiskey for me. She said she was sorry we didn't have more ice. (Whether there's a blackout or not, she always complains about the same thing: the lack of ice. The problem is that there's no fridge. If she needs ice, I think she's going to have to go get it at the North Pole. But I don't say anything, of course. I just shrug.) She plucked a cigarette from the pack in my purse, put it in my mouth, and lit it with the candle flame, because in that infernal darkness, we'd already misplaced the lighter. How weird, all that kindness. It wasn't at all easy, she said cautiously, to tell me the most important part. It meant she had to really concentrate and choose the right words so there wouldn't be any misunderstandings. I needed to just keep my trap shut until she was finished with the story, okay? She was asking nicely, so I took off my shoes before I got in a lotus position and ready to listen in absolute silence. I would have done it anyway, but it's always more pleasant when you're asked nicely.

"As I was saying, supposedly, mangos are the tastiest fruit in the whole world. From the moment you're born, they're telling you that. At my house, for example. My parents eat mangos, same mangos they've eaten for a million years, and they still haven't gotten tired of them, as is plain to see. Within the parameters of that diet, my parents are happy"—they seemed that way to me too—"They are living proof of the benefits of eating mangos. My brother. That's another one. He changes mangos the way he changes shirts. He chews on them and tosses them. The only thing he cares about is the violin and becoming a great soloist like Jascha Heifetz or Isaac Stern or Yehudi Menuhin, and the mangos help ease tension, help him relax, and that's it. If somebody gets hurt, that's not his problem. He certainly has talent, but that doesn't give him the right to . . . You know, sometimes I've come to believe my brother is a real sonovabitch. Well, you already know that."

No, I didn't know. Like in romantic songs, he'd lied to me. He told he loved me and it wasn't true. He never loved me. Or maybe he did, but only for one week. It doesn't matter. Those kinds of things are usually said to caress the ear and not to be believed. I love to hear them, especially if the liar has a low, deep, sly voice that creeps in your ear and shakes you up inside. I've always remembered Félix fondly. If I didn't come to his defense just then, it was because I'd promised his sister I'd keep my trap shut.

"And then there's TV, school, the movies, the telenovelas, even the cartoons. Everywhere you turn, the same message: we must eat mangos." She sighed as I began to understand that "to eat mangos" meant, in this moment, something quite different from what it usually means. Sometimes I'm a little slow. It's just that, you never really know another human being. It's just that, who knew that Linda had also had a childhood, that she'd watched cartoons? "The problem is that I've never felt attracted to mangos. Do you understand? I don't like them at all. Not even a little, nada. Mangos make me sick. Down with mangos. What I like are . . ." She thought about it for a moment. ". . . Guavas. Yes, that's it. Guavas." As if it weren't enough to find the precise word, she underscored it. I must have looked at her with a certain confusion. Because I also liked to eat guavas and I didn't understand why she had to admit this with such grandiloquence. Unless "to eat guavas" also meant something different than it usually means.

"Wipe that idiotic look off your face and listen to me, Z. I've felt like a weirdo for so long because of that. I thought it was so strange, the only person in this blissful world who didn't want mangos but guavas; how silly. I wasted all my adolescence and who knows how many opportunities. I was so stupid."

It was incredible that Linda was saying such a thing about herself; I almost interrupted her to disagree. "You know what I did once? I ate a mango." I had to make a huge effort not to say, Oh, big deal. "I don't know what crap I was trying to prove to myself, but I swear it was the worst experience of my life. I was seventeen. We were in high school. And don't ask me who it was"—she pointed at me with her finger and smiled mysteriously—"because I'm not going to tell you. It's nothing. It was horrible. Hor-ri-ble. Aside from the pain, the only thing I felt was disgust; I almost vomited. And, lord, the imbecile decided to court me, to insist he was in love with me and all sorts of silly stuff like that." But wait, "to eat a mango" couldn't possibly mean "to fuck a dude" because neither Félix nor her father ate those mangos; what a mess. "But now it's different. In New York, I ate a guava . . ." Again with the grandiloquence. "Well, to be frank, I ate more than one. All these months, I've been staying in the apartment of a Puerto Rican guava. And it went well. But then it got bad, because the Puerto Rican guava paid all the bills but demanded exclusivity, fidelity, and eternal love in exchange. A non-stop talker, that romantic. Coke drives her a little crazy, she throws tremendous tantrums, and it got to the point that she threatened me with a handgun. It was exactly as I'm telling you, exactly. The gun was empty, but I didn't know that. I was immobile. Then she loaded it with one bullet. And there I was, stuck, as if my feet had been screwed to the floor. She spun the cylinder and, you know, Russian roulette. She fired at my head. Do you realize what that means? *She shot to kill me.* Later she dropped the gun and sobbed and said that I was an ingrate and a traitor and all that. What fun, right? That scared me a little, as you can imagine"—I'll say: my hair was on end; could it be true?—"but it doesn't change the bottom line. From here on, I'm going to eat all the guavas I can. Even if they shoot me, I'm going to eat guavas. If I fall in love with somebody, great. If not, that's great too. It isn't necessary to fall in love to eat guavas. There's no justification necessary. Because eating guavas is a natural act, you know? It's as normal as eating mangos. It's not an illness nor an extravagance nor a crime. Just like there are left-handed and right-handed people, there are people who devour mangos and people who devour guavas . . ."

By this time, the situation was clear to me. "To eat" meant "to fuck." From a glutton's point of view, a "guava" was a person of the same sex and a "mango" was a person of the opposite sex, so that . . . Oh lord God in heaven! I couldn't believe she'd gone through all that gibberish just to tell me something so simple! I was going to tell her I already knew, that my dear father (whom she knew perfectly well) had told me that story very early on, in fact before he even mentioned Little Red Riding Hood and the wolf, quickly and quite explicitly, without mangos or guavas or subterfuge, long before any prejudices had set in. But my friend was off, going on and on about the left- and right-handed. She didn't hold liquor very well; she didn't drink very much and so she got really talky when she did. I didn't dare cut into her inspiration. In the candle's faint light, she paced my room immersed in her argument that I should understand her since I was a poor left-handed person obliged to function in a right-handed world. Just as I had not chosen to be left-handed, she hadn't chosen to desire guavas. Nobody could deny their own nature without risk to their psyche. And we shouldn't hide it from anybody, since that made us vulnerable to blackmail. Nobody . . . And then, in the midst of the blackout, like the bell that rings at the beginning and end of every boxing round, Poliéster's cornet sounded. It was a savage blare. Then there was another. There was a brief pause and then the first notes of a very innovative, exciting, and very off-key version of "The Peanut Vendor." Oh! I'd been wondering about the quiet.

"Shit!" cried Linda as she jumped up and down. "He's still alive? Isn't that sonovabitch ever going to die? I don't even know what I was saying . . . Fuck him! Where was I?"

"You were saying . . . Look, Linda, calm down. If you want, we can just leave it there. You're . . ." I paused to find the right word, which, of course, wasn't "dyke" or "dagger" or anything of the sort. " . . . You're a lesbian, so what? As far as I'm concerned, you could be a cannibal who likes mayonnaise. You don't have to explain anything to me. I love you no matter what."

"Lesbian? Where did you find that fancy word?" She looked at me with pity. "I know you love me and all that, but don't get sentimental. And I also know I don't owe you any explanations. But I have to give them to other people. Unfortunately. I do have to explain myself to *them*, because I'm not just going to hide in my house. This was a kind of rehearsal, you understand? A draft which I'll copy anew tomorrow."

And that's exactly what she did. I don't know exactly what happened, because Linda has never told me and I haven't dared to ask. All I know is that a few months later, her parents and her brother immigrated to Israel. It's possible that she too will go one day. But, for now, she's here.

Chapter 5

Searching for new anxieties

CLOISTERED IN THE STUDIO OF THIS MAGNIFICENT PENTHOUSE, SHE continues to write her novel, *One Hundred Bottles on the Wall*, the one about the two homicides. She has told me not to bother her. For any reason. Am I listening? For any reason! Even if a dinosaur comes through the door—her finger points and her eyes shine. Even if a hydrogen bomb explodes or we're attacked by Martians or the government collapses, I cannot interrupt her work! Is that clear? There's cauliflower in the pantry. I can eat it. (Cauliflower? Eeewh. Green brains.) Or I can have orange juice, which is in the fridge. Or read a book, and see if I can get a little culture. Or listen to music (with headphones, of course). Or watch a video. Or smoke, although I shouldn't. Or work on a crossword puzzle. Or stare at the ceiling. Anything except bug her. Poor me if I interrupt her. She'll kill me. My friend is not a great hostess; she's not interested in wasting time with idle chat. She hates anything that hints at a workshop, a salon, or boho. Time, *her* time, is sacred. I would understand this if my life—this is what she says—had meaning beyond simply being, simply flitting about.

There are books everywhere. On floor-to-ceiling bookshelves, covering entire walls. On top of or under furniture. On the bench of the upright piano, mingled with scores. In the kitchen, between groceries and vegetables.

Even in the bathroom. I once found her favorite, *The Maltese Falcon*, in the fridge. She swore she'd never put it there, that it was no doubt some mischief on Félix's part. In any case, I've never seen anything quite like it. Hundreds and hundreds, thousands of books in five languages other than Spanish (a polyglot beast, Linda can now read Russian, but she says she can't quite give up the dictionary as a crutch). She has friends on every continent, including Australia, and they always give her books, they put them in her suitcase when she's traveling or they mail them to her. In any case, books. And magazines too. Has this terrible bookworm read all this? Maybe. Certainly the crime fiction, which, between the classics, the contemporary, and the rare, make up legions; she's gobbled those down from beginning to end. I'm sure of it. Her knowledge of sensationalist lit, as well as Sherlock Holmes, is very wide and quite exacting, deep and erudite.

It doesn't matter if she leaves me alone, abandoned like a dog on the streets. I come over because it's quiet. Up here on the twentieth floor, close to heaven, nobody sneaks in to sell anything, or yaks on and on about Jehovah, or asks to borrow a little bit of sugar. I'm over the nausea and dizziness. But I still don't dare to go out on the terrace. I used to, before. I'd hang out there and look at the city, so white and so beautiful from afar, from heights that hide the devastation, tending a modest veil over the misery and horror; an iridescent Havana in a pinkish twilight, with cars like beetles, pedestrians the size of ants, the Malecón interrupted by the Focsa Building and, further on, the bay. Pure air, a sense of plenitude. Vertigo. It was Félix, not Linda, who took me out there. That is, she invited me to the penthouse (she also invited Yadelis, who never came because she was always too busy dealing with Pancholo's mess and other messes), but we only moved between the living room and her large, well-lit bedroom, with an antique gramophone with a horn and everything, a fern hanging from macramé, a photo of Djuna Barnes and Thelma Wood (definitive and emblematic from before the trip to New York, just like the one of Gertrude Stein and Alice B. Toklas, although she quickly got rid of that one because, what was the point of having to look at such ugly faces when she was barely awake?), various bookshelves jammed with books, and more books under the bed. That was Linda's most private space, a room of her own. My friend is a homebody, a snake-woman, a little crouched animal who'll only step out to do battle when she's assured of victory. It had to be the violinist who'd show me the world from the terrace, that singular perspective of the urban landscape, with the majestic and somewhat ironic gesture of someone who's offering up a kingdom for conquest. I'd never been up that high. I sat on the rail with my legs hanging off the side, balancing myself on nothing at all, without using my hands. He held on to me. If he'd let go, I would surely have died. To do something like that, you have to have a great deal of trust in the other person. I trusted Félix Roth, I don't know why.

The last time I was on the terrace alone, a few months ago, I wanted to fly. It was a sensation all over my body, an incredible desire to sit on the rail again, to face the streets again, to walk on air, slowly, very slowly, in slow motion, to breathe deep and then . . . to fly. I heard the voice of the edge, as seductive as Félix's or Moisés's, an almost irresistible temptation. The worst part is that I wasn't even afraid. Or maybe I was, but I was enjoying it. The pleasure of being afraid. Like a little devil with a coiled tail. I told Linda, who raised an eyebrow and determined I needed professional help. Immediately. A psychiatrist and an exorcist (for the little devil, to exterminate him). In spite of her incredulity, my friend doesn't take any "preventive measures" when the circumstances call for them. She doesn't consider herself an atheist, but rather agnostic, which means that, in her opinion, God doesn't exist, except maybe He does. According to Father Ignacio, this is shameless, opportunistic, and plain intellectual dodging. We didn't find an exorcist, only a babalao. For his part, Dr. Frumento went on and on about a personality type—mine—with a depressive core, with maniacal episodes and I don't know what else, something latent and dark that could well be traced back to the frightening experience of living at Happy Hammer Corners. In other words, I'm loony tunes. He gave me a script for pills that aren't available in a single drugstore here (Linda's agent sends them to her from Spain) and recommended I avoid dangerous situations. But what is a "dangerous situation"? I dunno. I think about people, about men and women, with that erroneous sentiment we call gratitude. About Alix Oyster's disturbing tattoo. About the window in my room, that cathedral-like window . . . But I haven't been back on the terrace, just in case.

So I stay in the living room. I'm not really interested in reading a book to see if I can get a little culture. Nor helmeting up with the headphones or facing a crossword puzzle. I'd like to smoke, but I shouldn't. Because of the baby. Oh. It's not easy, everybody knows, to give up cigarettes. You get all anxious, restless, a disaster, your nerves on edge. Maybe I'll go eat one of those green brains . . . No. There's no way. Never. A movie then. I shuffle through the cassettes. Oh, it's the same stuff. A bunch of cassettes but it's always the same: film noir classics, adaptations of crime novels, cheap thrillers, shootings, hangings, kidnappings, persecutions, stabbings, blood, viscera, horror and more horror . . . What an obsession. Sometimes I wonder how my friend can sleep at night. And they say I'm the crazy one! Actually, I confess I used to like watching those films. But not anymore. When it comes to gruesomeness, I've had my fill with real life.

I end up deciding on the same film I watched last week: *Romeo and Juliet*, the one from 1968, Zeffirelli's version. I've seen it a million times; I practically know it by heart. It's so out of place with all the others, if Linda hasn't recorded over it to capture more atrocities and throat slitting, it's because of me, because she knows how much I adore love stories, and also, probably, Nino Rota's music. Ah, the lovers of Verona. Here's a wonderful tale in which the only thing I don't like is the ending, which is so sad. Why do Romeo and Juliet, those angels, have to die, huh? And why in such a random and terrible way? It's just the director being cruel. I know the original story is terrible too, but so what? Even if Shakespeare was a bastard, there's no reason Zeffirelli had to be one too. What would it have hurt to improve the ending a little, huh? After all, a version is just that: a version. I do think it's different to *read* a tragedy in some ancient book, where these are words, only words on yellowed pages, than to *see* the catastrophe with our own eyes. There's nothing like the impact of moving images. And then there's the music. But don't pay attention to me. Linda thinks I'm a silly sentimentalist. She's way more intelligent and it bothers her that after so much conniving, the Jackal doesn't get to bash DeGaulle's brains. "What a piece of shit!" she bitches. But she doesn't give a damn about Romeo and Juliet's wasted love.

I have an unusual problem with Romeo: I'm not attracted to him. What I mean is that if I saw him hanging out on the streets of Vedado, I wouldn't be interested in getting close to him, to smile or wink at him, to flirt, to party, to share a bottle of rum with him and drag him to my room, etc. It's strange, because he's a hero and, generally speaking, I'm attracted to heroes. To men that do crazy stuff. Vagabonds, explorers, adventurers, caudillos, national heroes. But Zeffirelli's Romeo, with all his glamour and his cute and precious face, definitely doesn't attract me. Maybe he's just too young. Or maybe it's that he's untouchable, exclusive, obsessive, stubborn, madly in love, and a little slimy. I prefer that crazy boy Mercutio, or better yet, the troublemaker, Tybalt Capulet. The first time I saw the movie, I was deeply hurt that they killed Tybalt, who no doubt deserved it. Tybalt reminds me of Moisés. Romeo reminds me of José Javier, alias El Titi.

Suddenly, I remember JJ, his singular story, and I wonder if it might shed any light on the present cloudiness. I don't know why we called him El Titi, though I suppose it had something to do with all his glamour and his cute and precious face. Although this business of his physical attributes may be deceiving. On one of those turbulent days back in August 1994, when the riots happened, when everybody was trying to leave, when the streets were in revolt (I shut myself up in my room because I'm too much of a coward, but somebody told me about a parade of tanks down a certain avenue), JJ and two of his buddies hijacked at gunpoint one of the ferries that goes back and forth between Havana and Regla; there were still passengers aboard when they aimed its prow northward. That is, where they thought north was. Without a compass, without food or drinking water, the spontaneous mariners took several days to reach the coast of Florida or Key West, I'm not sure which. It was pure luck they didn't run out of fuel, and a miracle they survived such an anguished journey. One of the hostages, an old woman, died from some sort of stroke. Poor woman. It must have been horrible to see yourself subject to a half-crazy boy as your fragile embarkation continues toward the open sea, tossed by the currents of the Gulf (just thinking about it brings back my nausea) and surrounded by hungry sharks under a scorching sun. When I told Moisés, he thought it was great. If he were twenty years younger, he would have done the same thing. "Man needs to try his powers," explained my baby, "to test the limits of his territory, to conquer new spaces, to conquer the ocean. As the ancient Romans used to say, *Mare Nostrum.** One less old woman, who cares?"

El Titi, who is the only human being who's ever proposed to me (a church wedding, with a white dress, which would have just been utterly shameless on my part, but which really had Father Ignacio going), had also invited me to go with him across the Caribbean on that little ramshackle ferry, side by side with accomplices and hostages and everything else. Oh, yes. Fantastic honeymoon. He didn't put it quite this way, of course. A hopeless romantic, he would talk about the trip, a cruise ship, a nice change of pace. After all, didn't birds migrate in search of better climate, in search of food? Of course they did. Two days before taking action, he'd detailed his buccaneering plans to me, point by point. In spite of his vast knowledge and survival training in the Special Forces, I never thought he was serious. Especially because his imagination didn't stop

---

* Our sea. They were referring to the Mediterranean.

in Miami, in some hut near the beach where we'd sell cold Coke, hamburgers, and pork rinds, a tropical paradise in the shadow of wild palms. No, sir. That would have been too simple. Anybody could come up with that. El Titi aspired to more. Our first child, born on American soil on the Fourth of July, would be a great success: the first Latino president of the United States. It all sounded a bit fantastic to me, but . . . In any case, I would have never gone with the future father of the future president. To steal a ferry *without passengers* didn't strike me as a bad idea; I even considered that my experience with cars might be useful. But guns, no. Goodbye to guns. Pancholo says whoever picks up a piece, even if it's just to impress the Coast Guard, always ends up using it, and it's not right to go around killing people.

When I met him, JJ was the prettiest boy at Vedado High School. Tall and thin, dark-haired and blue-eyed, with long and curly lashes, he had dimples when he smiled. He was not at all sexy, just a doll that made you want to wrap him up in cellophane, put a gold bow on him, a Christmas bell or something like that, and stick him on the mantle. With his air of helplessness, like a figure made of porcelain or any other easy-to-break material, he gave the impression that he'd shatter on contact.

"Baccarat crystal," my dad determined the one and only time he saw him. "Women are going to mess with him, get him to do their bidding. All in good time. Just you wait."

Back then, women weren't approaching JJ with the malicious intentions my dad, due to the trauma he had suffered with my mom, was so willing to attribute to us. I suspect the other girls in school felt the same way I did about El Titi, which is what you usually feel when faced with a very beautiful being from some other species, perhaps extinct or mythological. A Uranian butterfly, a quetzal, a unicorn. A weirdo. It never dawned on anybody to even flirt with him. Plus, to try to get something out of him would have required a will of steel because JJ adored his girlfriend and didn't have blue eyes for anyone else, not even by chance. His love of Martica was rock solid, or so it seemed. It was a love that would survive fire, hurricanes, earthquakes, volcanic eruptions, and acid rain. A Great Shared Love. They were always together, hanging out all the time, very attentive to one another, kissing, touching, saying sweet things to each other. They were like a pair of octopi, the most cloying and celebrated couple in our high school. Romeo and Juliet. Who could have ever thought of coming between them?

I didn't know Martica very well. But if JJ's head was in the clouds, hers was in another galaxy. She was a luxurious blonde, well dressed, very attractive, exuberant, and probably too adult for El Titi. Just like in Zeffirelli's film, in which Juliet is a woman, at least from the physical point of view, and Romeo is still a boy, skinny and disheveled, strutting along. She was good people, Martica. Affable, quiet (rather than talk, she more or less purred), with a dreamy look. Satisfied. Very boring. When everything ended, when JJ left her at the end of our twelfth year, Martica did the same thing I would have done in her place: nothing. She went through the sequence of emotions typical of docile women: first, fright; then weeping; desperation; melancholy; exhaustion; oblivion; rebirth; new partner. Zero scandal and, of course, zero resentment. She didn't go after him. She didn't pretend to be pregnant. She didn't take it upon herself to cry out about all his many cruelties and infamies. She didn't sleep around with his friends. She didn't contract some thug to beat his ass and break four or five bones. She didn't put any spells on him. She didn't even try to find out who it was that had come between them. She didn't believe her Titi, with his cerulean eyes, had left her *for another*. It just happened, like an abrupt bolt of lighting in an otherwise serene sky: Romeo fell for some unknown outlaw girl and kicked Juliet to the curb.

Ultimately, JJ was lucky with poor Martica. He was able to break up with her without incident. Others have it much worse. For example, Pancholo had a miserable time trying to separate from Yadelis. In fact, he never quite managed it. If the Viking hadn't shown up, they'd still be together. My buddy wasn't interested in other women; his occasional European girls only represented extra income to supplement illicit liquor and grass sales. His problem was that my buddy had had enough. More than enough, goddamn it, enough! Why couldn't I, his favorite ecobio, understand that that babe was beyond demanding, controlling, domineering, jealous? A real dictator. Of course, I did understand, it's just that I don't like to get in the middle of other people's private lives, especially husband and wife.

"Oh, balls . . ." my buddy sighed. It was impossible to live that way. That black slut had him up to here. She was driving him way too hard. She was pretty, sure, but insufferable. She earned a lot of money, yes, but she wouldn't let him breathe. She was on him all the time, telling him what to do in front of his crew: do this, do that, do that other thing, shut up and buy me an avocado. He was the laughing stock of the neighborhood. She'd completely dissed him. People were beginning to think he was a fag. Not even the drunks on the terrace said hi to him anymore. When they saw him, they'd sing in unison: "María Cristina wants to tell me what to do . . . / and I go along, go along with her . . . / because I don't want people talking . . ." What disrespect. He decided to tell her to go to hell. But he couldn't. Yadelis didn't allow it. She blackmailed him by saying he wouldn't get to see his daughter anymore, even if Los Muchos was only a block away from the Corners. Leidi Hamilton (yes, it's written exactly as it's pronounced in Spanish, and the surname is my buddy's: Francisco Hamilton is Pancholo Quincatrece's real name) would take refuge in my room every time her parents got into it. She's an ugly little girl, exactly like her father. Brainy, imaginative. Smart, she could fool anybody. She managed to conquer even Linda, who detests children. The three of us would play "I Spy," in which you have to guess an object in the room by its mere description, and Leidi always came up with grey and subtle things: the spider webs on the ceiling, the smoke from my cigarette . . .

"Ah, yes. Of course. Very clever," the writer would say, having fun.

Yadelis put sixty thousand spells on my buddy, even some ingested through the mouth, which are the most powerful. But she didn't have the patience to see if the spells would work. No way. Her mantra was: Prayers to Ochún, club in hand. She threatened to burn herself alive, to turn him in to the cops for all his wheeling and dealing, to cut his dick off when he was sleeping (Linda was fascinated by this), to beat his sorry carcass to a pulp. Given that Pancholo insisted on the utter depravity of separation, my friend had no choice but to carry out at least one of her threats. So she beat his sorry carcass to a pulp. With a baseball bat (the club). She caught him unawares, a total betrayal, and hit him until the bat broke. She almost killed him. Later, of course, she took care of him in the hospital day and night. First in intensive care and then in the recovery room. She'd take him dulce de leche, candy, bon bons, marijuana, and other sweets. She'd caress him all over, call him "papito riquito," and nearly died trying to please him. In fact, she behaved like the most obliging of lovers, the kind who defends what's hers and never lets it get away. In the midst of all that love, "papito riquito" surrendered any ideas of independence.

Nothing even remotely like that happened to JJ. He had come out fine, so that his behavior in the last few weeks of school, immediately after the breakup with Martica, seemed incomprehensible and even alarming to those of us who knew him or thought we knew him. He was always seen alone. His head in the clouds still, but alone. As if going through storm clouds and lightning, a tormented prisoner. Maybe he was terrified, who knows. The thing is, he looked like hell. Those blue eyes were out of orbit. He didn't shave his three little measly chin hairs. His shirt was faded and buttoned the wrong way because of some weird inability to line up the buttons and the corresponding buttonholes. He started smoking, so much that he lit a new one with the stub of the old one. I think if he didn't smoke two at a time, the way my baby did years later, it was only because it didn't occur to him. If somebody had suggested it, he might have. He moved along, disheveled, his hair on end, as if he'd grabbed a high voltage wire with his bare hands. Nowadays, it's very fashionable to have hair like that, even dyed green, orange, or cinnabar, but in those days, that kind of preciousness was considered extravagant: even without realizing it, El Titi was an avatar of punk fashion. His hands shook like a professional drunk in need of a bottle at breakfast. Sometimes, he'd bust out laughing hysterically or bend down to pick up non-existent objects. He chased after flies. Basically, he was nuts. As if the blonde had kicked him to the curb and not the other way around.

"Forget that cretin," said Linda, so understanding. "He's probably doing all that to get attention. Really, what do you care?"

El Titi had never been particularly talkative, but his silence those last few weeks very nearly reached absolute. He was completely quiet, except for the hysterical laughter and the occasional indecipherable nonsense. No confidences with anyone. No clue that would allow us gossips to find out the identity of his new and apparently devastating partner. Why didn't he show her off? Why so much mystery? There was great speculation; some said he was hysterical. There was a story going around that it was the wife of a high-ranking Air Force officer, a gorilla with blue stitches and gold stars on his epaulets, who'd caught him under the bed, grabbed him by the neck, and told him between beatings that he'd given the order to have him immediately executed by firing squad. Later, the spotlight fell on the daughter of a foreign diplomat who was forced to return to his country because he'd been declared persona non grata after having been caught spying for the enemy and aiding and abetting dissident groups, among other crimes. There were some who were betting it was a disabled girl, paralyzed from the waist down, forever in a wheelchair. Or some woman imprisoned somewhere for having dismembered her husband, her mother-in-law, and all four kids. Or sick with AIDS, with sores all over her body and breathing through a tube. Or a very elegant drag queen, the kind who confuses even the most savvy, the kind who only give away they're really men because of the size of their feet. And so on. But none of this could be verified. Martica's successor kept her anonymity until the very end. All the talk died down and ended up getting lost, like salt in water, amidst the hassles with the upcoming and terrifying university entrance exams.

About three years passed before I heard from JJ again. My high school graduation coincided with my dad's exile. He couldn't take me with him, so we said goodbye like good friends who swear they'll meet again, why not, but who don't depend on each other for survival. It may sound a little cold, but the truth of the matter is that separation really didn't cause any suffering on either part. Nature, ever wise, provides examples. As soon as the baby bird can barely fly, the mother bird pushes it out of the nest and it's every bird for itself. It may seem cruel, but it's not. It's the best thing that could happen to that baby bird. If it were up to that baby bird, it would stay forever in the nest, lazy and shameless under the mother bird's protective wing. It would never have its own life. So no. The baby bird should learn for itself. And certainly, the knowledge the baby bird needs, like the wherewithal to find crumbs and all sorts of schemes to avoid cats, are not the kinds of things one learns in college. I was never interested in that. Should I have spent my whole life amongst books? To what end? I prefer having a trade and hustling to books. I like to read, but not because I have to. Although what I prefer is to do nothing at all. Muslim heaven. But Father Ignacio, indignant with this new heresy ("the first quarter moon's secular evils," he muttered), took it upon himself to get on my case at all hours with a sermon about the sin implied in wasting one's gifts, gifts given by the Lord, Our Lord, the one and only true Lord who under no circumstances is ever to be called Allah. According to him, I wasn't nearly as dumb as I pretended to be. I could very easily find crumbs, avoid cats, and get a college degree. What an optimist, that Father Ignacio.

In September 1990, Linda and I enrolled in the School of Arts and Letters at the University of Havana. If I'd been given a choice, I would have signed up for a technical career. Some kind of engineering, say, mechanical. Not only because I already had a certain amount of experience with motors, but because in those careers there's as much a scarcity of women as there is an abundance of men. Excellent for husband-hunting: many candidates, little competition. It's not that I wanted to get married to "comply with societal norms," like the women in my parents' generation, who had to go through a quickie married stage before they could enter a quickie divorce stage before they could devote themselves to simple promiscuity (although there have always been those who skipped both stages, e.g., my mom). Even though there are days when I feel frighteningly alone, I wasn't trying to build a relationship that was more or less stable in and of itself, to have a partner in good times and in bad, no. Even then, at eighteen, I wanted to have a child. I wasn't interested in deceiving or obliging anyone, but I wanted to have a child with someone who, in spite of the economic crisis that was beginning to show its hairy and mangy head, would want to be a father because of his own desire for it. It was an inexplicable longing on my part, a little crazy, I know. But very intense. For me, being a mother meant the same thing as being a writer meant to Linda: it was a sensation that went deeper than just being present, than just being in the chaos. But my friend stubbornly decided that I had a sensibility for art and a talent for letters. So much for engineering. Who'd ever heard of an engineer named Z? She convinced me, of course. Thanks to her I learned a ton about film criticism and maybe about being a writer. Because of her, I wound up in that very artsy and lettered school that was, yes, chock full of women. I was scared stiff. There were about twenty women for each man. And to make this worse, the man was usually a flaming fag. There was nothing I could do. Nobody could have caught a husband there, not even the mightiest of hunters.

One night, just before the nightly firing of the cannon at nine o'clock, I was musing about my misadventures while sitting at the Malecón in the company of a trash can and a couple of aromatic joints, grass from Baracoa. I had a serious problem. I had to prepare an oral presentation for the next day about a very extensive and boring epic poem, a horrible thing called *La araucana*. It was by instinct that I knew it was boring and horrible because I hadn't, in fact, read it, and I suspected I never would. But I hadn't been able to come up with a single scheme by which to avoid the task without coming off as a total loser. These things always happened to me, because I was always such a procrastinator. I was in constant avoidance and left everything until the last possible minute. Later, I'd pass by the skin of my teeth or I'd simply flunk. I think I must have been a terrible student, nearly expelled at various points, and with my career hanging by a thread. It's not like I'm trying to make excuses, but the business with getting crumbs was getting tougher by the day and it was getting harder for the baby bird to do everything. There, in front of the sea, smoking a joint (at risk that the cat might get me), I gazed at the luminous line of light from the Morro lighthouse that shone on the bay in regular intervals. I focused on the sound, also rhythmic, made by the dark water as it hit the reefs. Northern winds, the refreshing kind (not like southern winds, like at Lent, which drive people mad). The smell of salt, of oil, of rotting mollusks. What peace. Oh, if only time would stop . . . Little by little, I got my sweet high, time finally stopped, and I lost track of those awful araucana thoughts.

There was a "shooter" sitting on the seawall just a few meters from me. In other words, one of those guys who happily masturbates in crowded public places, whether it's on somebody else's porch or the bus stop, in a tree, sorta hidden behind trash cans with worms crawling around their feet and fruit flies buzzing around their heads, or hidden in the shadows in a movie theater, very focused on the screen even if it's an Asterix movie (I saw that particular show once at the Yara Theater). Some exhibit their dicks for women who pass by, perhaps convinced it's quite spectacular. This one was now getting off on me, all dressed up, kinda high, my back to the city. How imaginative. I watched him out of the corner of my eye and he continued, working at his task with great enthusiasm. It occurred to me to help him out just a little bit. Not very obviously, of course, because I didn't want him to run off; some of these shooters are pretty shy and they have to be treated very carefully. So, as innocently as possible, as if it were utterly casual, I began to raise my skirt a little at a time. Heh heh. It was then that . . .

"Hey you! What are you doing? Jag-off! Shameless! Get outta here!"

Completely freaked out, my jag-off ran off. Startled, and with the noble (and useless) purpose of trying to come off like a decent woman, I fixed my skirt and threw the roach I still had in my hand into the reefs. Another hand rested on my shoulder.

"Oh, sweetie, you really don't change. As crazy as ever."

"Meeeeeeeeeeeeeee?" Automatic response.

"Yeah, you. Turn around, c'mon. Tell me to my face."

Scared to death, I turned around. What did this dude want me to say to him? I hadn't recognized his voice. But I recognized him, yes. Immediately. How could I not? Dark-haired with blue eyes. Dimples when he smiled. Hair really short, almost a buzz cut. He'd gained some weight. Not much, but some. He looked older, less pretty and more manly. The Special Forces uniform looked good on him. Really good. He was incredibly handsome.

"El Titi?"

"Ha ha! That's me. Aren't you going to give me a kiss?"

Of course I was, I could do no less! He presented his cheek, very proper on his part, but I kissed him on the mouth. And it wasn't a peck, a Russian kiss, no. It was a helluva kiss, with tongue and everything. I can be quite uninhibited. Although I sometimes use being high as an excuse for many of my various misdeeds, this time it was not the reason for my flirtation with the ranger. No way. I've drunk and smoked hash practically since I came into this world (I also like to sniff coke, though I've never gotten hooked because it costs too much money), but I would have never dared to come on to JJ in that way when we were in high school. As I've said, back then, I wasn't attracted to him. But even if I had been, I still wouldn't have done anything. First, because of his long and very public romance with Martica, and later because of his insanity with the terrible unknown girl; they made him remote, unapproachable, a brutally sincere Romeo. Now, I didn't know what, but something profound, mental, had changed in him. Something inside which was obvious in his new look. He looked more common, more settled, available, *resigned*. "More manly," Yadelis would have said. And, in fact, JJ didn't reject me. He let me kiss him and then he laughed.

With great agility, he jumped over the seawall precisely as the cannons fired at nine o'clock. We ended up emptying the trash can and finishing up a roach. At some point, he got up and went to get a bottle of rum, which wasn't easy without an empty bottle already in hand (it was as if all the bottles, all one hundred, had fallen from the wall and our city was suffering from a tremendous bottle shortage), but he managed. And pretty quickly, which I suppose had something to do with his uniform. We talked a lot about old times. About all the minutia from three years back, our prehistory. I was now twenty and he was twenty-one, but we loved talking about before, when we were young and immature and didn't know a thing about life. What had happened to our classmates? Oh, so many stories, some quite mind-boggling. Yeyo was a secret hunter, terrorizing crocodiles and other creatures in the Zapata Swamp. El Johnny, the long-haired one, had a rock group, or more precisely, a hardcore group, Metallic Crab (whatta name), and gave concerts at Patio de María and dreamt of recording an album. Luisi Drácula was studying medicine and had decided to specialize in forensics; he'd discovered he loved cadavers and was quite talented with a scalpel during autopsies. And Boliche—whatta surprise—was now a seminarian with the LaSalle brotherhood. Martica was a flight attendant on international flights with Cubana de Aviación, and very happily married to a pilot. El Titi was glad for her, of course. She deserved it; she was a very noble person.

That sounded like an epitaph. The kind of comment in which what matters aren't the words, but the tone. And the tone was cold, Frigidaire cold, supinely indifferent. El Titi had never regretted that separation, had never tried to get back with Martica. She may have been very noble but nothing special. Rather bland, insipid, common. A girl like a million others. I begged him—between caresses and sweet nothings in his ear—to please not be so unfair to her. Martica struck me as fine. You didn't need to look any further than her job. You had to be pretty to get on with an airline, didn't you? The way I saw it, any guy would like Martica. His skin all goosebumps from the tickling caused by my whispers in his ear, JJ shrugged. Aha. *Almost* any guy would like his low-life ex. Did I know why? Because most guys didn't know squat about women. They thought they did, but no—he took his blue eyes off me to stare into the darkness of the sea. They had no idea what an exceptional woman could be. To find out, of course, you had to be prepared to get fucked over . . . I don't know how much truth was contained in such absolute affirmations but I was impressed. Maybe it was just a matter of resonance. I would have liked to ask JJ what *his* idea of an "exceptional woman" was. I didn't out of discretion, because I didn't want to force a confidence. Instead, I hugged him and kissed him anew. I'm sometimes blown away by the colossal distance between my nerve when it comes to bodies and my respect for the soul.

But why were we still talking about Martica? Maybe it'd be better if I told him what I'd been doing with my life. Because the stuff of his—martial arts, parachuting, survival training, submarine maneuvers, wall climbing (like a cockroach) and other outrageous things—he didn't want to talk about them. Other than flirting with jag-offs at the Malecón, what was I up to? I skimmed over things, leaving out the business with *La araucana*. We were feeling good, happy, a little drunk, and there was no need to ruin the night, our night, with lamentations and pouting. I'd lean on Father Ignacio's shoulder later, since that's the function of a confessor anyway. My ninja boy was much amused by my sexual frustration at the School of Arts and Letters. What was funny, he said, wasn't the fact that there was such a dearth of available spermazoid but the carnivalesque way in which I'd told the story. I was one of the most delightful weirdos in Havana, capable of lifting anyone's spirits.

"Spirits and what's not so spiritual, too," I whispered in his ear again, as he took me like a belladonna in his arms.

My amazing revelation didn't seem to bother him. Not even a little bit. In fact, it might have had the opposite effect. His blue eyes sparkled. So, as innocently as I could, as offhandedly as possible, I began to curl up with him.

Heh heh. He was all smiles, dimples. At first, he was expectant, curious. Let's see what was up with me, how far would I go with such a casual encounter, right there, on the seawall at the Malecón. Later, I found out that others had talked to him about me, at length, with that mixture of admiration and disdain that good lovers who don't ask for anything seem to provoke. I'd had a reputation as a slut in high school, as crazy, French, shameless, a libertine, a flirt. There were girls who wouldn't even speak to me, as if I had a contagious disease. But it doesn't matter. I don't think I ever did anybody any harm. And so I continued with my excitement over this parachutist who'd fallen out of the sky, with his supple body, flexible, easy to maneuver. Plus, he was getting excited too. He started getting loose, hungry, possessive, like an octopus. I thought there were eight hands all over me. It was all good. His kind, amiable smile transformed into something else when he discovered, after certain exploration in heretofore unknown territory, that I didn't wear panties: it was the kind of smile I love to provoke in guys. Ah. And then, opportunistically, he asked about my friend, the skinny girl. Whatever happened to her?

For an instant, I was confused. My friend. Who? Perhaps by that time I should have figured things out. But I hadn't. Without letting go of the ranger, I told him, fast and furiously, that my skinny friend sat next to me in my college classes, that she was still the best student, that she let me copy off her on tests now and then, and that she still loved traumatizing professors with her cunning questions, which inevitably revealed them as majestically ignorant, illiterate, barely worthy of their university degrees and the departments they taught in. For the sake of brevity, I left out any stories that involved a young Arab boy in the same class whose father had died in Gaza or the West Bank or one of those places, the kind who appear now and then on the news, massacred—that's what they said—by the Zionist army, or the Polish girl (Polish from Warsaw, not from Havana), a very fervent Catholic, very strict, both of whom looked very intensely at my friend the skinny girl, as if looks could kill. Of course, she was not intimidated by these insects—that's what she called them—who weren't even able to speak halfway decent Spanish. Without a care in the world, she'd stroll by her enemies wearing a white pullover with a huge sky-blue six-pointed Star of David on her chest, singing, "Party . . . / party hearty / cha cha . . . / sweet little cha cha cha." The Cubans—that is, the Cuban girls and the one Cuban flaming fag—we didn't really understand that odd warfare, how whatever that cha cha cha (the one by Jorrín, an old pal of my great-uncle W., the marquis's grandson) was about could be an insult to anybody, but both the Arab boy and the Polish girl from Warsaw would get furious whenever they heard it. Mostly, we didn't understand because in the School of Arts and Letters at the University of Havana, in spite of its many problems, there was a certain air of tolerance at the beginning of those troublesome '90s, especially when it came to political, religious, and racial matters. Moreover, I asked myself, why did any of this matter to JJ? But instead of talking about it, why not use my mouth toward a more useful, more substantive end—that submarine maneuver for which I was accused of being "French"? So I did.

We wound up making love on the seawall. In the most discreet of ways: I straddled the ninja, who was sitting down, and so peace on earth and glory in the heavens. Nonetheless, passing cars screamed all sorts of things at us. Well, the truth is that those drive-bys directed themselves at him, not me: "Shameless soldier!" "Soldier sonovabitch!" "Let her go!" There were a lot of honking horns as well. More focused than a yogi, JJ didn't even hear them. Nor did he notice the return of my jag-off friend, now accompanied by a pal who was as enthusiastic as he was; the two of them took up strategic positions just a few meters from our debauchery. In spite of so many people around to distract me, and against all probability, there came a vertiginous moment in which I too stopped hearing and seeing; a few seconds later, the shameless soldier came inside me and called me linda, or pretty. We were both so pleased. So much so that if he hadn't looked at me with such embarrassed blue eyes, as if offering apologies, I would have never realized that he had, in fact, called me "Linda" rather than just "linda." I hardly ever notice the evidence right away. A truck can run me over and I won't see it. I'm just like my great-uncle W., the marquis's grandson, and there are days when I can't make out a ceiba tree three feet in front of me.

Once I was hit hard by the realization, what was my reaction? I don't remember very well, but I know exactly what I *didn't* feel. Neither shame (mine or anyone else's), nor resentment or anger, disgust, or a desire to beat the shit out of the guy. What I had in front of me was a portrait of human misery: a man in pain and there wasn't a thing I could do to help him. In order to do so, I would have had to become someone else, someone very different from me, an "exceptional woman." Because the differences between my friend the skinny girl and me, physically as well as character-wise, were easy to distinguish on sight. What to do? The most immediate thing was not to hurt this repentant Romeo anymore as he separated from me with the bleak air about him of someone who's expecting to get hit with a torrent of (deserved?) insults. If I remember correctly, I brought him back toward me and said something about how frequently we have sex with somebody (in fact) and, inadvertently, someone else comes up (mentally, the unknown girl). It's not something that can be controlled. For example, as he was caressing my breasts, I'd been thinking about Bruce Willis. When he was holding my hips, I was with Mel Gibson. It was Andy García who penetrated me. And Antonio Banderas who came. That was all bull, of course. A story, a tale, pure b.s. But it worked: JJ looked at me in disbelief, with certain relief, and then he began to laugh, to laugh heartily. It's always good to find somebody a little crazier than you are.

As dawn was fading, with the sun practically risen, he walked me to the Corners. Very chivalrous. I didn't think I'd see him again. But, in fact, he came back. Like the killer returns to the scene of the crime. Once in my room, we had the best of times. And not just once, but many times. I let him call me Linda because it didn't matter; she was who he thought about twenty-four hours a day and a good part of the night. I called him Bruce, Mel, Andy, or Antonio, indistinguishably, and we had a lot of fun. Every now and again, he'd ask me about my friend, the skinny girl, with curiosity but calmly, without freaking out. I would tell him about the "exceptional woman's" college adventures and outrages and he'd be left in awe, ecstatic. Wasn't she just splendid, fabulous, extraordinary, he'd ask, that little witch with the big nose and the electric personality? I was surprised he didn't try to approach her, not even to see her from a distance. One time they almost coincided in my room, but he sensed the danger and ran off, terrified. I never knew the details of their high school encounter, though I suspect the kick to the curb must have been very violent. I never said a word to her about the matter. Never. Not even in '94, when JJ set to sea. Nor in '96, when, during her second great speech, she made that allusion to the only "mango" she'd ever eaten. Regardless of how close we were as friends, who was I to break her confidence like that? I suppose she'll find out when she reads this book, if I ever finish it, if she ever reads it, and I pray to God she doesn't hate me then.

El Titi never fell in love with me. He wanted it to happen, in fact he made a tremendous effort, but it wasn't up to him. He loved Linda in a kind of magical way, his idolatry almost the result of witchcraft. His passion was so persistent that it lived even far away from the object of his desire. A Great Unrequited Love. I could not be the new Juliet, the virtual one, hidden, phantasmagoric, the one who refused to play Juliet. Not me or anyone. As the bolero goes: "I've kissed other mouths searching for new anxieties . . . / other unknown arms encircle me, full of passion . . . / but all they do is remind me of yours . . . / which are unforgettable . . ." If he proposed marriage it was because I was the only woman he'd ever met who would accept his condition, who understood him without being offended, feeling undervalued, or anything like that. He was comfortable with me, relaxed, and he didn't need to pretend. And who knew if maybe, with time . . . As far as I'm concerned, if JJ hadn't been struck by that buccaneering dementia, I would have married him. A child of his, even if he never reached the White House, would have been beautiful (I hope the same of the one on the way, Moisés's). A little after he arrived in the United States, he wrote me from Ft. Lauderdale to tell me all about the adventure that had been his trip. Later, he wrote again. He'd gotten a job, very well paid, as a bodyguard for somebody who seemed like he was quite the devil, since everybody wanted to kill him. Later, nothing. I lost track of him. Wherever he is now, I wish him luck. I hope he runs into another woman like me. Of course, the ideal woman would be another Linda. But that's not very likely to happen.

Chapter 6

The Thursday girl

WHAT A COINCIDENCE. WHAT AN INCREDIBLE, DISTURBING, AND macabre coincidence. Just now, as I try to re-create the story so I can get some order in my poor head, I realize that both incidents occurred on the same day nearly five years ago. I met him during the day and her at night. Back then, I didn't notice anything in particular. Who could have ever imagined what would happen later? For clairvoyance, there's God. And my great-uncle W., the marquis's grandson.

But let's not kid ourselves. To know somebody, really know somebody, in the sense that they reveal *all* their secrets, their schemes and their hidden resources, their complexes and frustrations, their most secret longings; to have somebody undress before us, not just take off their clothes but also their skin, their muscles, their organs, until they're just a skeleton, until they're entirely foreseeable—no, I didn't get to know either of them that way. To be honest, I've never gotten to know anybody that way. Not even those who are closest to me: my dad, Father Ignacio, W., Petronila, Pancholo, Yadelis, Linda . . . Not even myself. These portraits are just approximations. More or less. Just fragments. Maybe the coincidence isn't so particular after all: it comes down to the fact that I ran into each of them for the first time on the same day, that's all. They strike me, now that they're both gone, as totally inscrutable, profound unknowns.

One timid tropical winter morning in January 1997, I went out really early. I was on my way to the vegetable stand to see if by chance I might run into some potatoes. I was very happy because Yadelis, far away in the mists of Malmö, had lived through the pneumonia, the panic, and the nostalgia that had been strangling her since her arrival in that inhospitable, icy, and twilight land that seemed populated by specters, where no one looked at anyone on the streets (at least not in the eye), noise was prohibited, and everyone talked gibberish. To celebrate the news, I'd invited Pancholo and Leidi Hamilton to eat up a big pot of french fries, just the three of us. My little soulmate has never been interested in fries, cooked or raw. Fries? What do you mean fries? What kind of childish crap is that, to celebrate with fries? he protested, the vague silhouette of a bottle of rum reflected in his eyes, like always. Couldn't we get a party together, like normal people, the kind of get-together that actually really helps with the dragging of our sorry carcasses . . . etc.? Of course we could, yes, except that I wanted to please his daughter first and foremost. Poor girl. Perhaps I'm wrong, perhaps I'm just being a gossip, perhaps I'm making up something monstrous and being unjust, but every now and again I get the distinct impression that her parents don't pay much attention to her.

As I walked to the vegetable stand, I was thinking about faraway countries, developed and reasonable. I was making a list of pros and cons for moving to another country, I was trying to figure things out. The abusive cold, snow, and wind, sorta like a freezer, didn't do much for me. I've never been any-where, but I've seen movies with landscapes filled with snow and I've heard a few stories about the world below zero, hair-raising stories about people who were frozen stiff in Alaska, who turned blue on the Baltic coasts, or who wanted desperately to kill themselves during white nights in St. Petersburg. How scary. Also, I don't know any other language: a little English, with a heck of an accent, four or five words in French, and that's that. When a foreigner talks to me in gibberish, I just smile at him, beatific, so the poor man doesn't feel misunderstood. He could be telling me to go fuck myself and I'd never know. This business with the smile, however, isn't always the best way to go. There was this one guy once, during my time running around with Yadelis: very dumb, Dutch or South African Boer, I dunno, but he thought I was making fun of him (me, who never makes fun of anybody) and he slapped me one so hard I can still feel it. The bottom line is that I'm not especially into skin that's whiter than mine, those super white epidermises, translucent, the color of fish bellies, with freckles and little red or blondish white hairs; no. But there are also good things. Other than food and progress, of course. For instance, I like the idea that noise can be prohibited. I'd like to see, even if just through a peephole, how my neighbors from Happy Hammer Corners would live in Malmö. Up there, in the northern quiet, in the stealth aurora, how could the divine Poliéster have written his opus?

That's where my mind was at when I saw him. All of a sudden, under the flamboyan trees in John Lennon Park, which wasn't called that then. The guy that's turned me on most in my life, my best lover, the philosopher, the savage, the mysterious one, the devil, the craziest among the crazies, was pacing back and forth, talking to himself. He'd take five or six steps, super big steps, then he'd stop, turn halfway, walk five or six steps more in the opposite direction, then another halfway turn, and so on. It was impossible to understand what he was saying, he was barely audible, pure muttering. His gestures suggested rage, absolute rage, especially his arms, moving like windmills, or when he posed like a boxer and threw a hook. After a while, he took a pose, like a butterfly on a squash, a choleric butterfly on an igneous flower, on the same bench that, years later and with much fanfare, there would be a seated and carefree effigy of the ex-Beatle whose glasses would be stolen shortly thereafter by some jokester (or some fetishist into retro stuff). He went on from there, this great man, hitting ghosts. None of this surprised me much, since Havana is full of indignant people who talk to themselves.

I stopped. He'd caught my attention from the start. Not because of his furious soliloquy, nor because of his beautiful or ugly spirit, which I didn't yet know about, but because of his amazing anatomy: about one meter 90 centimeters and close to 200 pounds, all very well distributed. Oh. Where had this come from? (Yes, if I remember correctly, I thought "this," not "this guy.") A work of art. A live colossus. A Greek god. He had nothing to do with Apollo, more like Zeus, exactly as he is on the altar at Pergamum: the head of the pantheon, the leader, the patriarch, the still-good-looking older man who seduces all the women and strikes dead all the rascals with his lightning bolt. A miracle of Creation. One of those Men who, when I see them, make me understand my dad's inclination 100 percent and force me to question what in the hell Linda sees in girls. Of course, I would never dare say such a thing *to her*.

I got a little closer, I couldn't help myself, and then my admiration turned into astonishment. From what hole in the ground, trash can, or whatever had my colossus with the fierce monologue come from? How long had he been bingeing or fleeing or fighting? Because his silver beard, still close-cropped, was the only clean thing on that majestic figure. His physical beauty contrasted with his grey curls, a little greasy and scattered every which way. Wearing dark dusty glasses with streaks and fingerprints all over the wet lenses . . . from dew? He was wearing an Armani suit, shiny from so much grime, with hair and confetti and bits of leaves and other things on the dark blue jacket and a shirt that had once been white. He was covered from head to toe, down to his fine leather shoes, with something that could have been blood, mud, or tomato sauce. What a splendid disaster. I wouldn't have been surprised if cockroaches had started coming out of his pockets.

You see beggars on the streets all the time, tons of them, people pleading at the door of the church, in cafeterias, in line for the bus, everywhere. They're disabled, lepers, abnormal, bums, street artists, and even Prophets of the Apocalypse. But not like this. Not with a beautiful silver beard, not with a body whose strength you could imagine, not in an Armani suit and fine leather shoes. This man came from some other world. I imagined something very bad had happened to him, something horrible. Of course, something horrible has happened to all beggars. Because to be on the margins means there's been a fall, a final letting go that means you've wound up in that frightening hole that is also an attraction. I know this well. And I also know that we don't all fall from the same height. Some get more mashed up than others. In fact, there are some who don't survive the impact. That very beautiful man came from very high up. What had brought him so far down? I still don't know. I never managed to find out the hidden reason (actually, what hidden reason?—I never even got a superfluous reason) behind his horrible state, just something that probably had to do with the end of the world and the fall of the gods. After admiration came astonishment, and after astonishment came pity. I sat beside him. It was possible the problem still had a solution. Maybe he needed help. I could go with him to the hospital, or to his house, if he had a home. Or I could call his family, if he had a family, if we could find a public phone that actually worked. Or I could invite him to eat french fries at the Corners. Or whatever. At that historic moment, I wasn't thinking I would become involved in a tragedy. That's how idiots like me get in trouble.

My mistake with the pity was in telling him, years later, in my room. How could I know it would offend him so much? He slapped me one so hard I fell on the floor where he kicked and kicked me until everything got dark and I couldn't see anymore. I was incredibly stupid, he screamed, a cretin, a degenerate, a yokel, a pig. I didn't understand a fucking thing. Who the fuck did I think I was to feel sorry for him? Did I for a second think myself superior to him? What the fuck did I, a fat imbecile, know about his life? When—in what moment of our relationship—had he ever had any confidences with me? Pity! Fucking pity! Me and my fat ass! What he wanted was to kill me. To cut me up in little pieces, pack me up in a bed sheet, and throw me into the Almendares. Because he *knew* he was a Man, in the way that Nietzsche meant that word. And pity, fucking repugnant Christian pity, was, according to Nietzsche and according to him, a sentiment for whores . . .

That's why, because of my smart mouth, because of Man and Nietzsche's susceptibility (another angry man, that one), I ended up floating, not in the Almendares, but in the emergency room at Fajardo Hospital, with two fractured ribs, a splitting headache, aching arms and legs, stomach, kidneys, bleeding like a faucet from my nose—basically, a wreck, a broken aura. The doctor, who was very young, perhaps a student, wanted to write up a complaint for the police and told me that the station was right there, across the street. I couldn't convince him that I'd fallen down the stairs when I'd stepped on a banana peel. A banana peel? C'mon. Who was going to buy such an absurd story? He insisted I shouldn't be afraid of the angry man who'd brought me (how polite of him) and still waited outside for me in the car, even though his place was clearly in jail. Or in the psychiatrist's office. Or the cemetery. I didn't know it then but I found out later that the angry man had told them all to go to hell: they could think whatever they wanted, tough shit, the bunch of faggots, or did they also need to have the crap beat out of them? Whatta show. When it came time to make a spectacle, he never cared how close the cops were. I lacked the strength (and the temperament) to argue with the young doctor, the courage to tell the truth no matter how obvious it was, or the imagination to make up another story. Thank God another doctor showed up, older, with a bored look on his face, and told my protector to leave me alone. They'd had enough, or so I thought I heard, with the Thursday girl, yeah, the week before, when the young doc wasn't around and no, how awful, imagine that, the girl . . . My ears were ringing and so the only other word I understood was "acid."

In spite of that majestic philosophy lesson, I've never understood what's so bad about feeling pity for another's misfortunes. Even if we know nothing about them, even if we shouldn't care, even if they deserve their predicament.

Especially if that pity only lasts a few seconds, if it suddenly transforms into desire, as happened that morning under the flamboyan trees in John Lennon Park, when I sat down next to my colossal disgraced aristocratic vagabond and smelled him. Ah! I know it's not right to go around sniffing to see what cologne people use or how many days it's been since they last bathed. But there are some aromas that impose themselves with their intensity. They sneak into our nostrils with such force, they take up inside us without any chance of stopping them, and then, once there, they arouse all that's been dormant, they rattle us, excite us, hook us. That's what happened with that mixture of sweat and a very virile perfume—expensive, dry, French, sorta sweet, emanating alcohol and something else, something indecipherable. Shit stink, according to Linda, and sulphur, according to Father Ignacio. But no. What fools. Neither shit stink nor sulphur is indecipherable and neither of them ever smelled that man.

In the meantime, my Greek god was going on and on, muttering. It didn't seem as if he'd noticed I was there. Fascinated by his scent, by the absurdity of the situation, I listened in a bit on his words. Death. With a low voice, he was talking about death. About writing a book about the putrefaction of corpses, how a guy would turn greenish black and malodorous while he was being consumed by bugs, short and fat voracious little worms, rats too, and the guy would just be there, unable to get rid of them, how the belly would burst on the functionary from the ministry, the sonovabitch bureaucrat, poof! And then more and more bugs would come to the funereal banquet, huge white cockroaches, swarms of creepy-crawlers would cover him from head to toe, and the guy would just have to be there, horizontal, defenseless, fucked . . . hee hee . . . checkmate . . . hee hee—I heard his little liquid laugh for the first time, Luciferian, his only laugh, and for the first time it made my hair stand on end. "Yes, it would have been good to write the book," he said with a sigh, "and to include a few color photographs and then dedicate it to one of them, to someone still alive, adding an R.I.P. to the name of the future deceased, or better yet, 'in memoriam,' like a warning . . . hee hee . . ." Because we know death is coming, he said in a grave tone, but not when. It could overtake us anytime. As the ancient Romans used to say: *mors certa, hora incerta.** Although liars will insist otherwise. Goddamn it, of course, this was such old shit! Ah, but not to them. No way. They weren't ever going to die. Them, those cursed hypocrites, reveled in their specious immortality. And

---

* Death is certain, but not the time of death.

not because they believed in reincarnation or transcendence or anything like that. They didn't even believe in the whore who had birthed them. They didn't believe in fuck. They simply closed their cynical little eyes so they couldn't see the disaster that was coming their way. So they wouldn't have to see the worms or the rats or the big white cockroaches. They couldn't do otherwise, the fucks, because fear was eating them alive. And they pretended that he— yeah, him—precisely him—should act in the same disgusting way. Oh, those frauds. But they'd see. Yes, those ruffians, those rascals, those miserable jerks, those pigs, those fucking bastards would see.

"Because death . . ." He lit a scrunched up cigarette that dropped bits of tobacco from both ends and turned to me. "And you? What are you looking at? Do you know anything about death?"

"Me? No."

I wanted to add, "Not as much as you," but I didn't dare.

"Oh, no? Then get lost."

"What?"

"Are you deaf or idiotic? I said, get lost."

"But . . . why? Am I bothering you or something?"

"Why? Because. Because I said so. And, yes, you are bothering me. I don't like to be looked at," he grunted. "If you want to look at something, go to the zoo and look at the monkeys. So go, go, get outta here."

I got up. I'd never been told to get lost quite like that, so much like being thrown out. If he didn't want to be looked at, he could stick his head in a paper bag. Or, I thought, in a polyethylene bag. But I didn't want to leave. I didn't want to leave him there, all alone, talking about death and all that other crap, with his silver beard, his Armani now in tatters, his low voice, and his scent. I didn't want to stop smelling him. Sometimes I behave like a dog who doesn't care if he gets kicked and always comes back, wagging his tail (not the megatherium, he's a fucking bastard). So I sat back down beside him.

"Listen, look, don't get that way. I'm not going to bother you or anything. The only thing I . . ."

"Oh, no. Not this. What do you want, mamita? C'mon, tell me. Do you want me to . . . ?" And then he made a terrible and barbaric gesture about sex, very explicit and strident, dirty, crude, vulgar. Unforgettable.

I was rendered speechless. I must have blushed. And it wasn't because I'm embarrassed by such things because the people in my neighborhood say that stuff when they're kissing the same as when they're punching each other's lights out. No way that's going to embarrass me. I've heard that crap a million times. In fact, I've spent my whole life hearing such things since they are in the air all the time at Happy Hammer Corners. I'm so used to them, they go in one ear and out the other, meaninglessly. If what he said stayed with me, imprinted full of meaning in my brain, it was because *he* said it, in a helluva voice, looking straight at me through his disgusting lenses. Because he was just fine. From the bottom of my romantic heart, I would have loved if his words could become reality, that he would actually do to me what he was proposing. Could he have said it seriously? Or did he just want to frighten me so that I'd get outta there once and for all? I decided to see.

"Well, yes." I was talking to him informally, forsaking "usted" because it didn't make any sense to address him otherwise if he was going to talk to me like that, even if he was twenty years older and knew a lot about the putrefaction of corpses and the ancient Romans and all that.

"Yes what?"

"Nothing, just that I like the idea." I picked something off his jacket.

For an instant, he didn't move, indecisive. He threw his cigarette butt away. He looked me up and down various times. Not with the look of someone who's checking out merchandise before buying it. More like how a manufacturer of coffins discreetly takes measure of a future client. It made sense: wasn't death his theme? Finally, he smiled. Sardonically, but with incredible teeth, whiter and cleaner than his beard; not at all a beggar's teeth.

"Tell me something, little girl, are you making fun of me?"

Oh, why does everyone always think the same thing? Do I look like a clown? I wanted to stick my tongue out at him. But I controlled myself and got very serious instead; I did my best to come off like a very serious person. And I said no. Why would I make fun of him? He looked me up and down again, then looked me in the eyes. And he drew his own conclusions.

"You're a little crazy, aren't you?"

"No. Not at all."

I started to laugh. After all, it was pretty funny that a guy who looked like he'd crawled out of a trash can, the sewer, or deep in Cruz Key, a guy who talked to himself in the middle of the park and argued with invisible beings under the flamboyan trees, was worried about my mental health. But he didn't like that I laughed. To the contrary. He got mad. My laughter only served to confirm his initial hypothesis: I was making fun of him. He grabbed me by the arm, his fingers squeezing tight. I didn't laugh anymore.

"Hey, hey, let go, that hurts. Let go!"

But he didn't let go. He squeezed even tighter. He was hurting me. I struggled to get that vise off me but it was in vain. It was like steel. With his other claw, he slapped me around on the cheeks and started to unbutton my blouse. Right there, in the light of day. I tried to stop him, I swear I did, but I couldn't. He unbuttoned them all; in fact, he popped one. What an animal. And to think he was asking if I was crazy! An old man with a shopping bag and a newspaper walked by and gaped at us. Then he took a quick look around. Thank God there wasn't a cop in sight. The old man picked up his step. The animal was looking at my tits, which jiggled because of the struggle. I was embarrassed by this, I don't know why. His glasses fell from so much staring; he stepped on them and broke them by accident. The glass made a crunching sound and the colossus muttered, "Bah." His eyes were big and black. Without the grimy glasses, his face was very attractive. But he was still squeezing my arm. It hurt a lot but he didn't care. I knew he'd leave a mark (and that Linda would see it right away and get infuriated, of course, because there are times she acts like my mother or something like that). With his other claw, he felt up my tits, pinched my nipples very hard. He was whispering things that had nothing to do with death. He planted a kiss on my mouth, a kind of bite, and left me with the taste of blood, rust, and something else, something indecipherable. I thought I would choke to death. I couldn't breathe. Not his marvelous scent or the city's polluted air or anything at all. It was too much.

"Let go of me, please, let go of me, seriously . . ." I must have cried. "Let go!"

He stopped. He didn't let go, of course. What madness. There are people in this life who get desperately attached to objects but never in my life had anyone become attached *to me* in that way. In a weird way, I was flattered. I breathed again. He looked at me, again sardonically. He was blinking a lot, as if the light hurt his eyes.

"Well, what do you say, yes or no?"

"Yes, but not here. C'mon, let go of me, don't be a jerk. Goddammit, it hurts!"

"But why not here?" He squeezed even harder, as if he were a thug or inquisitor trying to make a prisoner talk.

"Ow! What do I know! Because there's a bunch of people going by and it's daytime and they're going to pick us up in a squad car and nail us with a fine for creating a public scandal and . . . owwwww!"

"For creating a public scandal? That's all?"

"Yeah, a public nuisance. What more do you want? For immorality and indecency and the whole works . . . owwwww!" My eyes were stinging too, maybe because I wanted so badly to weep.

"Look at that, the little whore knows about laws." All of a sudden, he seemed to realize something. "And for rape? Would they take me to jail for rape? Would you report me?"

In spite of my misfortune, I couldn't help but smile. The word "rape" reminded me of the adventures of the megatherium and the pig, including the owners' fight, all of which was very recent then. That bellicose beast, so much like this man, had grabbed the docile fatso by the ass and . . . Well, better to leave it at that. Why make comparisons?

"Hey, not that I'm trying to offend you, but I think you're a little off. What fucking rape? Just so we're clear, I've *never* reported anyone."

He seemed disappointed. Who knew what his fantasies were, what he'd imagined about rape and police reports and all that mess. He let me go. Finally. I rubbed my arm. And my nipples, which hurt a lot, too. Although he couldn't stop blinking, he watched all these moves with interest.

"I like seeing you do that. You know you're a little shameless, don't you?"

Yes, I knew. But I got embarrassed all over again, I don't know why. I've always been a heck of an exhibitionist, but he intimidated me. I didn't have a clue then the price I'd pay for adjusting to him, for letting him lead me, for becoming completely free of inhibitions with him. My Greek god, the most difficult guy I've ever known. I quickly buttoned up the few buttons left. I looked on the ground for the one he'd popped but nothing, gone forever. Suddenly, I remembered something.

"Listen, I'm attracted to you, I really am," I said, "but, first, I have to see about resolving the matter of some potatoes. If it was up to me, I wouldn't go . . ." I pulled another loose thread from his jacket. "But I promised the girl, you understand? French fries. You can come with me if you want. Later, we can go to my house, which is near here, and you can have some french fries, too. What do you say?"

Amidst all that blinking, he looked surprised.

"The girl? You have a daughter?"

"Oh, no. I wish. She's my little niece, my brother's daughter . . ."

"You live with your brother?"

"More or less. In fact, I live alone." I said this with emphasis. "Pancholo lives downstairs, in a kind of . . . well, downstairs. I live upstairs. In a small room, but don't start thinking it's any big deal . . . So what do you say, eh? Are you up for it? C'mon, say yes."

Incredibly, he said yes. The only thing he added was that I shouldn't get used to it, since his general tendency was always to say no. From the time he was very little—he stood up—he'd learned to say "no." First the *N* and then the *O*. It was a delicacy. He loved the sound of the word, so voluptuous. He started walking, very sure of himself, taking huge steps in the direction opposite the vegetable stand. I went after him to explain, but he stopped next to a maroon Lada parked by the side of the park. I imagined he'd open it with a slim jim or a hook, but no. He opened it with a key he took from his pocket. I should have known. My colossus wasn't an ordinary bum. He came from another world, one in which people owned cars and opened them with keys they took from their pockets. To top it off, the Lada looked like its owner: dirty, with the paint peeling off, the antennae all twisted, the windshield covered with dust and bird shit. It smelled like vomit inside. Perhaps out of consideration for his large black eyes, which were apparently hurt by the light, I offered to drive. He took advantage of the situation to say "no." He snorted. His eyes, he said, were not my problem. Nothing of his was my problem. Perhaps for that same enchanting reason, he refused to give me his name at first.

"Well, my name is Z, the letter Z. Understand?"

He looked at me out of the corner of his eye. We were on our way to the vegetable stand with me giving directions. We arrived; I got out alone and hunted down the potatoes. Ha! There was no question, it was my lucky day, a great day. Because in Havana, the time for potatoes is even more uncertain than the time of death. I was so happy I gave my Greek god a bunch of little kisses. He looked at me askance but didn't reject me. He took me to the Corners. But he didn't accept my invitation. He didn't want to come up to my room. He would not eat french fries. No, under no circumstances would he eat them. Because, he said, he was too old for such silliness. Plus, he didn't like children, no matter how intelligent and niece-like they were. Why did people have children, huh? He couldn't think of anything worse. All kids were useless, starting with his own, he affirmed, that pair of imbeciles, those dimwits, the little monsters who were just like their mother. I noticed the ring on the colossus's finger just as Leidi came out of the clandestine bar, saw me in the car, and came running. There she was, that skinny little black girl, with her naps gone crazy, shouting, "French fries! French fries!" That must have affected him at least a little (he'd never admit it) because a slight smile lit on his lips.

"Look at that," he muttered. "It's better if she's not kept waiting. I should go."

I got out of the car. Neither shy nor lazy, Leidi immediately pulled on my skirt. "C'mon, auntie, c'mon—you're so slow!" I peeked in the car. Would I ever see him again? Hopefully, he wouldn't feel compelled to say no. "C'mon, auntie! Let's go!" Yes, I'd see him again. Maybe tomorrow, or the day after, or next week. "Auntie, please! I've been waiting forever for you!" He'd come back.

"My name is Moisés. It's written with two S's." And then he left.

"I'm huuuuungry!" wailed Leidi, as if she were the Tasmanian Devil.

"I'm coming, girl, I'm coming."

I thought that if Petronila was still alive, that girl wouldn't be looking like that, with her naps all out of whack. But that's how they were. I really don't know how to comb hair like that. I tried once, but I bet that girl's screams could be heard in Hong Kong. I got scared. I thought it atrocious that she should suffer like that because of me. I thought it better to let her live her boho way. I liked that Moisés, with his two S's, wasn't frightened off by my black family. A lot of people would deny it, but there's a great deal of racism in this country. Years ago, when I was a kid, people tried to hide it a little better. Not anymore. Everyone has the right to their own prejudices, that's for sure. But it never ceases to be discomforting when another white person shows theirs in front of you, with tremendous ease, assuming you share the same thought: that black people are the worst trash on the face of the earth. Moisés had a broader mind. I'd learn later that, according to him, the worst trash on the face of the earth—the lowest and most abject, the most repulsive and nauseating—were human beings. Each and every one, without racial distinction.

A little after the french fries, about mid-afternoon, Linda came for a quick visit. She was clear that she only needed five minutes of my precious time. She was in a *big* hurry. She had a commitment that night, an unavoidable commitment, and she was still trying to figure out a small detail. Perhaps I could help her. By chance, did I still have the cowboy boots my Dad had sent with her six months ago? Yes, girlee, the one with the label that said, "Made in Texas by Texans." Those green artifacts with red fringe, yellow heels, and innumerable decorations in various colors, not to mention the gold sequins and embedded fake gems—I find her capacity for visual memory disturbing.

Some time had passed, yes, unfortunately. Enough time to have sold them, or exchanged them for rice or black beans, brutally ripped off the sequins and inlays and fringe, or eaten them boiled like Chaplin in *The Gold Rush*, perhaps hurled them through that uncommon window of mine which makes us so want to throw things through it so that they'll fall—splat!—on the empty head of the Sonovabitch with the Cornet. Had I done any of that? It would be too bad because she *needed* them and had come to buy them from me at whatever price I wanted. Within reason, of course.

I was more astounded than the old man with his mouth agape from that morning, the one who was strolling by the park with his shopping bag and newspaper. The boots were intact, brand new and still in their box, never worn. It was possible they hadn't even lost their American smell yet. I hadn't saved them for any particular reason, I didn't have plans for them. At the moment, thank God, I didn't need them. I could just give them to Linda. But I couldn't imagine her wearing them. If it had been Yadelis, yeah. The Viking's flamboyant wife loved lots of color, bright things, ostentatious things, like a parakeet. She would look good in them. But Linda? Unless she was going to a costume party . . .

"Well?" She was getting impatient.

"No, nothing. I mean, yes. I'll get them for you."

She took them out of the box and looked them over, admiringly, satisfied, as if she'd found exactly what she was looking for. She put them back in the box after first stroking the fringe. How much did I want for them? I didn't want anything. What was this business of asking? I would just give them to her, a gift from the heart. If I'd known she liked them so much, I would have given them to her sooner. Wasn't she going to try them on? Well, no, that wasn't necessary. They weren't her size, she indicated. Almost, but not quite, they were about a half size too big; it was obvious just looking at them. She had a good eye for shoes. But they'd look good on La Gofia. I looked at her questioningly. La whaaaaaat? La Gofia. For her birthday. La Gofia was celebrating her thirty-first birthday in the gay company of her friends and enemies that night, all together in that celebrated little apartment in Centro Habana, and the least she could do was . . . But, what was I thinking? That she, Linda Roth, translator and novelist, future Nobel Prize winner, would wear those folkloric and grotesque things on her delicate little feet? Who did I think she was? Janis Joplin or some Almodóvar character? Gifts, according to her, shouldn't please who gives them but who receives them.

In a good mood, she wanted to pay for those silly things. It was La Gofia's birthday, not hers. I was too loose with things, too unselfish, wasteful, too much of a giveaway; in other words, a calamity. She wasn't going to take advantage of my shortcomings. If I didn't want money, which she found deeply incomprehensible, she could give me something else. Within reason, of course. I thought about it. I wanted the fern in her room, the one hanging from the macramé. Or her fine-point pen. Or the collected Mafalda stories. I thought a little more and proposed instead that she let me go with her to the party that night. I didn't know La Gofia, that was true. Although I loved her name, assuming that was her name (it wasn't; later I found out it was Ana Cecilia); she'd never mentioned her before. Not her or her friends or enemies or the celebrated little apartment. I could take a bottle of rum. I love birthdays, weddings, baptisms, little jam sessions, etc. Basically, to have a good time. Dancing, drinking, joking, laughing at others' jokes . . . Did La Gofia like rum?

My friend hesitated. Of course La Gofia liked rum. And marijuana. And cocaine. And fun in all its forms. She was quite jovial, loved to dance and party, La Gofia. In a certain way, she was a lot like me. Hmm. But only in a certain way. I . . . well, let's say that I might not be entirely comfortable at that party. I might feel like an intruder, or dislocated, out of place. Something like that. Not because the hostess would treat me badly. Not that. La Gofia treated everyone very well; in fact, she was excessively kind . . . But—tsk! Linda clicked her teeth, as if her own words bored her beyond even what she could stand. What the heck. It's not as if they were going to eat me alive. I was an adult, right? It was decided. We'd go together to La Gofia's birthday party. She'd come by at eight to get me in a cab. Yes, a cab, because she wasn't going to drive the Mercedes down those black tunnels, full of potholes and without a secure place to park. I didn't need to worry about a bottle, she'd already bought some Havana Club. So, at eight then. Was that clear? At eight. Not eight-oh-five, even less so eight-ten. Yes, she said while giving me a stern look, I was just too casual, too much of a slacker, and the taxi meters were unforgiving . . .

I came down at eight-twenty. The horn had been blasting intermittently and Linda was waiting for me on the sidewalk with an unfriendly look. Even so, in spite of being furious with me and my lateness, incapable of letting it go even once we were in the cab, she looked beautiful. She was wearing a very short satin dress, salmon colored, with long sleeves. Very dark shoes, very elegant. Light makeup, so that her lashes wouldn't touch the lenses on the pince-nez. Her hair—like the lions at the Metropolitan Museum—was thoroughly domesticated. I was thinking there are days (and nights) when this skinny girl really honors her name. Not because she's generally ugly, no. It's just that sometimes it's really hard to appreciate that she's not. The total opposite of Yadelis, who dazzles from the first moment you meet her, who shines like an August sun, who can't go anywhere without attracting everyone's attention, who'd be the perfect candidate for a Miss Cuba pageant if that contest actually existed; Linda has to be looked at more than once. She needs to be *discovered*. In that sense, she's very similar to Félix. And there's also what JJ calls "the beauty of intelligence." According to him, intelligence is the main virtue, the only one which can overtake all others, like an ace in cards. When intelligence is real, not just a pose derived from having read too many books, it shines a kind of light on the person, illuminates them, makes us see them differently.

"What are you looking at?" she grunted. "If you're going to tell me how good I look, just shut up. At this precise moment, I don't like you very much. You're quite the clown!"

She didn't say another word to me for the duration of the ride. Not even to criticize my neckline, which was pretty low in spite of the chill in the air, or that I'd painted my lips a fiery red. When I offered to pay for the cab, she gave a look like she was going to kill me. With my blatant and evil anti-Semitic prejudices, I thought she only thought about money, she babbled. And that wasn't it. What nonsense. It wasn't about money, but about the order of things. Seriousness. Punctuality. Of course, I didn't have a fucking clue about any of that. She paid the cab and we got out at the little shadowy street perpendicular to Infanta. The music was thunderous, I think it was Adalberto y su Son, that one about "dancing the touch-touch-me-here . . . / I touch you and you touch me . . . / let's dance the touch-touch-me-here . . ." It led the way to the blast at La Gofia's. We went up some dark stairs, steep and smelly, which reminded me of the Corners. On the first landing, under a trembling light provided by a low-wattage bulb, we ran into a boy in jeans and a plaid shirt. He was dancing, repeating Adalberto's refrain, with a little glass in his hand. He said hi to Linda very excitedly.

"Hey, baby, so glad you're here!" The voice, though raspy, was that of a girl. "La Gofia was starting to worry."

"Worry? The Super Flying Gofia? Yeah, right. Like I believe that."

The ambiguous person started to laugh and looked at me sideways.

"Listen, babe, angelface, seriously . . . They've been waiting for you upstairs. That girl . . ." I got another weird look my way. "You go on and see for yourself. I've got to go. I'm going to the corner for a minute."

The figure tried to scamper down the stairs, but Linda held on to a sleeve.

"Wait a sec, Danai, stop right there. What kind of manners are those? This is Z." She pointed at me. "Don't be afraid of her." What madness, I thought, no one had ever introduced me like that before. "Who's waiting for me?"

Danai smiled at me a little, unafraid. Then she turned to my friend.

"The Thursday girl. I think her name is Alix, but I'm not sure."

Chapter 7

Happy birthday, girlee!

WHAT ACTUALLY HAPPENED IN THAT CELEBRATED LITTLE CENTRO Habana apartment is pretty confusing to me now. It was confusing at the time, too, but I wasn't thinking about telling the story back then. So I didn't give a shit if it made sense or not. Perhaps it's true that stories should be intelligible, but life certainly isn't always so. Especially when you go to the party without any major expectations and immediately become part of the festivities in the darkened room, where streaks of light from the tiny hallway to the bathroom and the other room barely allow you to make out the furniture against the wall or a multitude of silhouettes dancing in the middle, clustered in corners or taking a break out on the balcony. Especially if you get drunk on such beauty, if you sniff various lines of coke, if you're feeling good, laughing, having fun, having a blast, and you dance with La Gofia and maybe her friends and enemies to that chorus: "I'm normal, natural . . . / I'm normal, natural . . . / but a little excitable . . ." In those conditions, right in the epicenter of the merrymaking, how could you possibly know what's really going on?

We'd barely stepped inside, Linda and I, when somebody yelled out, "Oh, there's the angel!" And then several silhouettes advanced on her to greet her, I think, to touch her and squeeze her and eat her up with kisses, like a bacchanal; they were so ardent that they practically tore the presents from her hands and her clothes and all. My friend backed away a few steps. Then she tried to escape by going further into the apartment, maybe to the bathroom or to hide under a bed, but she couldn't. Quickly, she handed me the little bag with the Havana Club, trying to make sure it wasn't shattered by some impetuous fan. Luckily, nobody even looked at me. In the midst of the tumult, I heard a contralto voice, a voice I remember as authoritarian.

"Where's my Agatha Christie? She's mine! Let go of her! Let go of her right now!"

Somebody took her by the arm and dragged her inside to the light. She turned her face my way and signaled me to follow. I slipped into the mob, without ever losing sight of her and still holding on to the little bag with both hands. Somehow, I made it to the other room where Linda was straightening her dress and grumbling while fixing her disheveled hair in front of the mirror on the dresser. What absurdly silly women, how ostentatious; damn, it wasn't as if she was a movie star or anything. There was a girl at her side: a willowy mulatto, wearing very ripped denim cutoffs, very tight and short, a blue silk blouse with a collar, long sleeves, shoulder pads, and a Chinese dragon hurling golden flames on her chest; her hair was up in three pigtails—the left one parakeet green; the right one red like mamey; and the middle one yellow like a baby chick. She bit her black-lipsticked lips. I got the feeling she was trying to keep from laughing. On the bed, sitting in a lotus position and decked out in a terry cloth kimono, a freckle-faced girl with a buzz cut insisted on staring up at the ceiling.

"The angel's here . . . the angel's here," she repeated. "The angel's here . . ."

"Fuck the angel," my friend complained. "These things only happen to the angel of Sodom."

Sure I wouldn't be making a mistake, I pulled the bottle from the little bag and handed it to the girl with the Chinese dragon.

"Happy birthday . . . Gofia."

"Oh!" She immediately turned around, smiling from ear to ear, black lipstick smeared on a tooth. "Thank you very much."

She grabbed the bottle by the neck and opened it, all very sure of herself, and without even asking who I was or anything like that. She let a little dribble on the floor, for the orishas, and then served up two glasses. She handed one to me. So what were we going to toast to? It was just her and me, of course. Because Marilú, drunk since she was born and crazy like a fox, didn't need any. And Agatha Christie became a public danger with alcohol in her veins—ha!—she even looked shady with her glasses on. She winked at me and Linda growled "Brrrr" as Marilú insisted on the business with the angel. So it would be just her and me, the last two respectable people left in that damn . . . she stopped all of a sudden. She looked over my shoulder with her brow furrowed and all three pigtails standing on end, as if she'd seen the Phantom of the Opera.

I turned around, expecting a joke of some sort, because I thought the multi-colored Gofia was probably very fond of jokes, but no. There, at the door, on a noisy dark background, hung a truly spectral figure. "Strange" is the first word that comes to mind to describe her. Very pale. Very tall, very young. Almost like a little girl who'd abruptly shot up to one meter eighty, or almost one me-ter eighty, and didn't know what to do with herself, or with such uncommon stature. She seemed fragile. Ethereal. With dark rings under her eyes. Dressed in black. Blue-black hair like a crow's wing fell like waves down to her waist. She had a disturbing air about her. Like a somnambulist, a medieval witch, or a taciturn gypsy. I felt pressure on my chest, a shiver. I was afraid. I don't know why, because in that moment I had no idea about the dreadful connection that would be established (that was perhaps already established) between that girl and me. I gulped down the rum in a single shot.

"Somebody's looking for you, baby," La Gofia muttered.

Linda stepped back from the mirror, still a little shaken up by the previous assault. But as soon as she saw the gypsy, her face softened. She went from bitter to sweet. She wore a huge smile, a real rarity for her. She was tender, kind, without a hint of sarcasm. It was a singular moment. A transformation. Before this, I'd never seen anyone affect her except Leidi Hamilton. But with Leidi, it was more maternal, probably because Leidi also has "the beauty of intelligence" and very few opportunities to show it off. There was, and still is, a great affinity between my friend and my little niece: they're both restless, skinny, they both cheat, and they both get impatient with me; the big one tells the little one that black women shouldn't ever feel lesser than anyone else, or allow anyone to make them feel inferior, and she lends her books by Alice Walker and Toni Morrison, which are pretty tough reading for a twelve-year-old, but which, in the end, help get the ball rolling. Leidi loves all that. She feels adult, respected, like she's being taken seriously. The only thing wrong with Aunt Linda is that she doesn't make french fries. But that's all right. Aunt Z has to be good for something, right?

The thing with the gypsy was different. It wasn't reasonable. If I didn't know for a fact that Aunt Linda was just fine, lucid, sensible, and even pragmatic, I would've thought it was delirium. I would have thought my friend had started losing her mind long before that night at La Gofia's. Many years later, during her third great speech, she'd explain it to me.

"Yes, I fell in love with a ghost, with someone who didn't exist and will never exist. It happens. We writers invent all sorts of things because we're a bunch of neurotics. We know that two and two equals four because we're not totally crazy, but we don't like it. We'd like it to be five. Or nine, or eighteen, or the square root of negative one, or whatever. Anything except four. And so we cause drama, hassles, and create spaces in which this can happen. And it's okay. Sometimes we even get paid for making stuff up. The problem, the real problem—which has nothing to do with rogue editors or the blindness of the critics, or the boorish social climbing souls of those bureaucrats who propose censorship but not against mediocrity, intolerance, envy, hypocrisy, and those other terrible bugs that populate this lettered city—the true problem begins, I believe, when we try to transfer our fantasies to the real world, to that arid and opaque land where two and two is four, only four, always four, and nothing else. In other words, when we get caught in our own web, when we believe our own lies. Or some other writer's lies, which is more or less the same thing. There are writers who are just terrible, who hook you right away and turn your life upside down, squeeze you until your last breath, mash you down to the ground, twist you up like that sapphic Aphrodite, the goddess of love, does with lovers' bodies. In my opinion, the best one of all was that poor peasant, ignorant, sullen, ugly woman who died young without the slightest success.* Don't think I'm trying to impress you with cheap arguments. Generally speaking, none of this matters to me, it's all random. If it's your turn to go, it's your turn. It's just that she managed to translate her many impossibilities into a truly powerful fiction, strong, solid, *believable*. I probably wouldn't want to trade my life for hers, but I probably would with one of her characters. Do you understand what I mean, Z? To live in a novel! Now it sounds absurd to me, even idiotic, but I didn't think that back then. Nothing, I just swallowed the story whole, that's all. Then I met that girl with the black hair and it was chaos. I thought I'd finally found my Heathcliff, the taciturn gypsy. But the truth . . ."

---

* Linda loves really obscure references, riddles, and brainteasers. Since she's a genius, she doesn't give a royal damn if anybody else gets them. When she said this about the best writer, I didn't know who she was talking about. Others might find themselves in the same situation, so I'll clarify that she means Emily Brontë, the author of *Wuthering Heights*.

The truth is that, one night in 1997 in La Gofia's room, Linda was hypnotized, enchanted, made silly, transformed into something very different from herself (at least from her usual self), her eyes so focused on that creature who made me nervous and left our hostess with her hair standing on end.

"The angel's here . . ." said Marilú.

"Oh for God's fucking sake!" my friend snapped. "I just got here, dear. Can you just wait a hot minute?"

"Yes, of course, have a seat, make yourself comfortable, make yourself at home," mumbled La Gofia. "Do you want me to fan you for a bit, give you a little breeze?"

"Listen, Gofia, don't be a bitch . . ." said Linda.

"A bitch, me? Well, yes, of course I'm being a bitch. I was born in a kennel. Bow wow."

The two of them started laughing while the girl at the door remained silent, imperturbable, as still as a statue, and the girl on the bed declared the arrival of the angel for the umpteenth time, and me . . . well, I poured myself another shot of Havana Club, sat myself down in the only chair in the room, and lit a cigarette. A head would occasionally pop in the door, make a face, howl, or laugh and then disappear into the darkness and the salsa music. Linda hugged La Gofia, who'd been barking, and they kissed on the lips: "Happy birthday, girlee!" When they separated, my friend went looking for the present she'd left on the dresser. En route, she checked herself in the mirror. The big kiss (in fact, it was a pretty normal kiss, it's just that I'd never seen two women kiss on the lips) had left black lipstick smeared on her lips and face.

"Check this out," she said, amused. "You come all cleaned up, all dressed and decent, and they just ruin you the minute you walk in . . ."

La Gofia opened the present. She screamed to the heavens when she saw the boots. Oh! She leapt up and down. Oh! They were divine. Oh! That—that very thing—that very thing and nothing else is what she'd been wanting from the day she was born, from the first bow wow she ever emitted at the kennel. Bow wow! Nobody was as good to her, as loving, as special as her baby, her Agatha Christie, her little Polish girl with glasses, her Exterminating Angel, her woman. As she spoke, she shot a sardonic look at the girl at the door, who hadn't moved and remained as mute as an oyster. She kissed Linda again, this silly Gofia, on the lips, on her chin, on the neck. She squeezed her, ruffled her hair, and smeared black on her again. When she stuck her hand under her dress—the whole time looking at the girl at the door—I . . . well,

I poured myself another shot. My friend, who was now a mess, stopped her in her tracks (stopped her cold, I thought), slapped her butt really hard and asked, please, mamita, sweet thing, little bitch, please, girlee, listen, please, don't be such an idiot, Ana Cecilia, goddammit, and let me go talk to Alix.

"The angel's here . . ." Marilú continued as I tried to put my cigarette out on the floor because I couldn't find an ashtray.

I don't know if she was furious or sad or happy, or everything at once, but La Gofia began to stomp. She grabbed the bottle with one hand and with the other she grabbed me, very violently, by the same arm that Moisés had grabbed me earlier in the day. Quite strong, she lifted me up off the chair with one tug. I almost dropped my glass. Oh! Dear God, what was happening to everybody? Why was this happening to me?

"I really love it," she said, "when I'm thrown out of my own room. But it doesn't matter—do you sluts get it? I don't give a damn! Do whatever the fuck you wanna do, whatever you're itching to do, because I'm outta here with this gordita I just got me . . ." She yanked me outta there just as Linda was making a gesture my way, maybe to reassure me, and somebody—guess who?—announced the angel's arrival.

To be frank, I was scared to death. That's why I emptied my glass in one gulp, as if it were vodka, which is a lot less intense on the throat than rum, but gets you just as drunk. And it was as if I'd swallowed a live sea urchin or a ball of fire. Arrrrgggghhh! In other words, I got plastered as Adalberto sang from the speakers, "Who turned out the lights, eh? . . . / who turned out the lights," and La Gofia pulled me to the middle of the living room, where the silhouettes were dancing. When she put her arm around my waist, I realized I needed to pee. What could she have meant by referring to me as the gordita she'd just gotten herself? What was she expecting from me? Perhaps I needed to explain to her that the answer was no, a very kind no, of course, but no, that there was no way, that she'd gotten it wrong with me, that . . . Ow! I felt a sudden pain in my bladder, as if I was being stuck with needles. I needed to pee badly. Peremptorily. In the midst of the darkness, the tumult, and the suffocation, I asked her to let me go to the bathroom for a moment. She looked at me with sly eyes. The bathroom, eh? Sure. We could go to the bathroom.

Stumbling, I entered the tiniest bathroom, very clean, with a shower but no tub. She happily slipped in after me and locked the door. Oh, mother of God. In other circumstances I would have told her I prefer to pee alone. Or at least not in front of a willowy mulatto with a Chinese dragon on her chest, a bottle of rum in her hand, and three pigtails on her head. But I was in a hurry. If I tried to explain my preferences just then, I'd pee myself for sure. So I ignored her. I sat on the toilet with my eyes focused on those boots that had once been mine. They looked good on her, as if they'd been made just for her. She had sinewy legs, like an athlete, just like Linda. I was finally peeing. Uff. Whatta relief.

"So you don't wear panties either . . . Ha ha! How funny!"

I might have looked at her with a certain astonishment, I dunno.

"Funny? Look, Gofia, I . . ."

"Yeah, baby, yeah. It's no big deal. It's just that I don't wear them either . . ." She sat on the edge of the bidet. "They're incredibly uncomfortable, aren't they? I only use them when I have my period."

"Yes, yes, of course; me too."

Sometimes you find unexpected affinities, even in the bathroom. I liked that girl. She scared me a little, but she was okay. I've always liked people who are uninhibited, spontaneous, who talk naturally about bodies, without complexes. I'm not talking about people who do it in a hostile way, to shock, to seem like they're more than they really are or to hurt their unsuspecting neighbor. Not that, no. People who are really honest are the ones I like; they remind me of my dad. Because Petronila died while I was still very young, he was stuck—poor guy—explaining menstruation and other things that come up in adolescence. Now I realize he probably had to do a bit of research at the library, because he really didn't know much at all about feminine ways. But he spoke directly, that's for sure, straightforward, without metaphor or evasion. Black was black, white was white. Just like La Gofia, who was looking at me now with her brown eyes, very clear brown eyes, practically transparent, like cane juice.

Suddenly, I felt better, more relaxed, without the slightest urge to leave the toilet and flee. She took a chug from the bottle and passed it to me. I drank less hurriedly than before. The traces of my red lipstick blended with the residue of her black lipstick.

"Hey, gordita, I like you," she said. "So let's just get to it. C'mon, before those crazy girls start pounding on the door and everything goes to hell."

"Get to it?" I was alarmed. "Oh, Gofia, no. You're mistaken. I don't like 'getting to it.'"

"Oh really? With that little face of yours? Ha ha! Don't play innocent with me, gordita, I wasn't born yesterday. I'm La Gofia from Havana, and I've got what you need. Try it and see."

Oh, God in heaven. How to explain, without offending her, that she didn't have what I needed?

"Look, Gofia, I'm very grateful, but the problem is that . . ."

"What problem? You try it and then you tell me."

She stood up. Terrified, I took another drink. I was practically drinking fumes now. If things continued like this, I was going to leave that party an alcoholic. And anonymous too, because I wasn't even going to remember my own name. She kept looking at me, all smiles, kinda seductive, as if saying, "Come to daddy." I thought she was going to undress or try to undress me or something like that. But no. Sometimes an active imagination can be a bad thing. La Gofia from Havana took a folded piece of paper out of the pocket of her cutoffs. She opened it up and showed it to me. White powder. I stuck my pinky in it and tasted. Yes, she had what I needed. I felt stupider than ever. But she was totally cool about it. Linda would have read my mind, but she didn't. Or maybe she did, but she didn't say anything. There are generous people in this world who forgive and don't make a big deal of things. She sat on the floor and drew the lines out on the edge of the shower. Someone knocked on the door but we didn't care. I sat down next to her and we got to it.

This is the point where my memories get fuzzy. They get superimposed, distorted, confused. They scatter like the colored glass in a kaleidoscope or the hundred bottles shattered on the floor. Maybe it's because I'm not an addict, because I only run into it between Christmas and the Feast of St. John, I dunno, but coke gets me high pretty fast, much faster than liquor or marijuana. It takes me up to the stratosphere, to heaven, and beyond. It makes me feel marvelous. I've only ever tried one other thing that makes me feel better.

"C'mon, tell me," said La Gofia, still on the floor and indifferent to the pounding on the door.

It happened by chance, during my romance with JJ and my first pregnancy. I didn't know I was pregnant and I wasn't careful. I must have made a strange movement, or carried something too heavy, who knows. The thing is that I had a miscarriage the first month. Just like that. It hurt so much, and there was blood everywhere, so much blood. I was alone in my little room and scared and I dragged myself the best I could to Sacred Heart Hospital. There I confirmed, like so many other times in my life, that misfortune is never simple: The miscarriage hadn't been complete. No one asked me anything. There was nothing to ask. I was given an abortion right there in the emergency room, which, as everybody knows, means no anesthesia. I don't know why. Supposedly, at least according to the doctors, it's bearable pain. Since I'm not a doctor, I'm going to keep my opinion to myself. If you don't struggle or get hysterical, the whole thing is over in five minutes. But they're a nightmarish five minutes. Between the bearable pain, the fear, the weakness, the guilt, and the hum of the machine, I thought I was in hell. But I was a good girl, a real woman. That may be why somebody felt sorry for me and, after they turned off the damned machine, brought me that tiny little white pill and a glass of water.

"What's that?" somebody asked.

"Nothing, an analgesic," came the answer.

In an instant, the analgesic erased my pain. Of course, that's what analgesics do. But not only did it erase the pain in my lower abdomen, it erased *all* my pain. All the little things with which we live day to day without even noticing and are only aware of when they're gone. Fear. Weakness. Even guilt, which is no small thing. Most often, because we can't even figure out where it comes from, probably because we don't want to know, it's really hard to get rid of guilt. Confession helps, of course, but even so, it's really hard. And here was a simple little pill that did away with it in the blink of an eye! And without a fuss. There was no euphoria or ecstasy or pink elephants or journeys to Iztlán or any of the things people call "interesting experiences." I don't really know how to explain it. It was like a change in perspective. A view of my problems, my baggage, and my fuckups from another angle. An adjustment in my stimulus review: what I'd previously judged as horrible now seemed normal, natural, quite acceptable. It was a feeling of harmony with myself and the universe. Peace. Cozy, sweet, exquisite peace. Happiness. If I could, I'd take one of those little pills every morning.

"Morphine," La Gofia determined; she was sitting against the blue-tiled wall. "Whoever gave it to you is an imbecile, or crazy, or really, really liked you."

There was more pounding on the door. I don't think it had ever stopped.

"Why do you say that? I can't even remember his face. If I saw him on the street, I wouldn't even recognize him. But I think he must have been a good person."

"A good person? Ha ha! That's beautiful. Of course he was a good person! Morphine is incredibly expensive. It's pricey as fuck. That is, if you can find it. Because sometimes you can't find it even at Mass."

"Oh yeah? What do you know?"

"Meeeee? I don't know anything." La Gofia looked up at the ceiling. "Tell me, something, gordita, where do you come from, so misinformed? Don't you watch movies? If you take one of those little pills every day, you'll get addicted right away. There's no going back. You start needing two and then three and four and then you need a needle—you know that—and then you can't think about anything else until you're completely fucked up." She seemed to be looking inside herself. "Maybe it's worth it, who knows. I mean, in the end . . . Oh, enough! What morbidity! Do you want to depress me or what?"

I'm not sure, but it seemed the pounding on the door was getting increasingly more violent, as if somebody had lost all patience and now simply wanted to kick the door down. There was a great clamor. Was the city falling apart out there? How scary if there had been a cataclysm, an earthquake or nuclear war, and here we were, in the bathroom, like zombies, enjoying our morbidity, speculating about the pros and cons of morphine. I started to laugh. At some point, La Gofia stood up, very calmly, like nothing, and opened the door. There was a bunch of people, so many girls, shaking their heads (I'd dare to say one of them stuck her tongue out at me, and I responded in kind, of course—what did she expect? I'm the master at that!), ha ha, little happy heads, one with a silver mask, another with a cardboard hat, curious little heads, howling, braying, laughing, ha ha, a trumpet playing salsa—"Let Roberto touch you . . . / let Roberto lay his hands on you . . ." First off, there was Danai with her jeans and plaid shirt, who yelled and accused La Gofia of being selfish, criminal, shameless, outrageous, always locking herself in that disgusting bathroom with the first slut who showed up and got her all to herself and never shared anything with anyone, because she was a bitch, a big butch bitch, a jerk, an ingrate, and to top it off, a cuckold—she was waving her hands around La Gofia's face, almost touching her—yeah, a cuckold, because that Polish dyke and corrupter of minors was practically eating that little girl alive right there in front of Marilú, poor bald Marilú, who suffered so much, who was so sad, and who now had to watch that indecent spectacle—fucking A!—they were pigs, that's what they were: degenerates, cynics, disgusting, shitty dykes . . .

La Gofia slapped Danai a couple of times. I thought all hell was going to break loose, that there was going to be a riot, so I hid in the shower, swiftly and stealthily, just in case they were going to hit me too. But blood was averted. The slapping had a sedative effect and Danai, so bellicose, calmed down immediately. There was a lot more bark than bite there. She came down so hard she started sobbing on La Gofia's shoulder, who should have been more understanding, yes, more understanding—she wept like Pancho Villa, if in fact he ever wept, as the pig-tailed girl patted her on the back and murmured, "It's okay, it's okay, there's no problem, girlee, it's over, it's over, it's okay . . ." She, Danai, felt bad, very bad, so very bad, the worst ever, and just wanted to die, to kill that slut, to break her face, to twist her neck, to do who knows what, goddammit, because people always fall in love with people who don't deserve it . . . And so on. I stopped listening. I got lost inside myself, lost in the refrain about the hundred bottles mixed with the refrain about Roberto and other refrains, with the refrain from a not-very-optimistic bolero, the one that says, "I'm not going to cry . . . / because life is the school of pain . . . / where you learn very well how to handle . . . / the hurt from great disappointments . . ." I remember being there, with my head full of noise, hiding in the corner of the shower. Safe for the moment. Far from the future. From the malevolence of Uranus. From Moisés and his invisible enemies. From my second pregnancy. From Alix and her tattoo and her perpetual silence. From the window in my apartment, back then without the black curtain, so big and thick, which, years later, wouldn't let us see, in the shadows of dawn one 19th of December, if it was open or shut.

"Hey, gordita, what are you doing there?"

"Me? . . . Um . . . um . . . me? Nothing."

"Well, c'mon." La Gofia stretched out her hand. "C'mon, let's dance."

I think I was thinking about, well, nothing at all. And not only that, which is quite entertaining, but about how very complicated, how very complex, it must be if it's just women, and passionate women at that, in this business of who loves whom or who was jealous of whom or who would bring on the drama with whom. Who was going to break whose face. The possibilities multiplied; any combination was possible. And, of course, any misunderstanding. I didn't dare leave my refuge. Not without some guarantees.

"Tell me, Gofia, is Danai mad at me?"

"At you?" She was surprised. "No, my dear, no. How could you think that? Not at you. That crazy girl is furious with Agatha Christie because . . . well, because Agatha Christie isn't much interested in her, that's why. I think they slept together once, I'm not sure. Danai is very tragic, very decadent, and she loves to suffer."

"Well, poor girl, no?" I sighed, relieved.

"Poor girl? Fuck that poor girl crap. She's just stupid. It's true that the Polish girl can drive anybody crazy—she's a great girl, an exceptional woman . . ." Right then I thought: hmm! "There's a reason they call her The Exterminating Angel. But it's for that reason you can't get worked up about her, you just can't. No outbursts or drama or anything like that. If you try to control her, zap! She leaves you. That's how she is. If you can take it, fine, if not . . . Oh, but I'm probably talking too much." She winked at me and stretched her hand out again. "C'mon, gordita. Come out and dance with me. And don't worry. You be cool. If anybody picks on you, I'll take care of them. I can be one very mean bitch. Ha ha!"

None of that sounded very encouraging to my pacifist soul, enemy of all fights, but what the hell. We went out to dance in the middle of the living room, in almost total darkness, a thick black fog that only cleared up a little after my eyes got used to it. Out there, in the very vortex of the bash, with La Gofia leading and the speakers blasting my ears, I had the best time. She dances well, very well, as one should, which isn't exactly how people think. There are people in the world who think that every Cuban, just because we're Cuban, is an expert dancer and adores salsa music. But that's not true. Not by a mile. Some are stiff as brooms (JJ), some have their ears screwed up and they go one way and the music another (Poliéster), some just abuse their pelvic dexterity and look like they're fucking standing up (Yadelis), others are very technical but don't have a drop of swing because salsa doesn't come to them naturally (Linda), some actually think dancing is dumb (Moisés) and a waste of time (Pancholo). Modesty aside, I'm a total star. Once, a long time ago, I danced with Pedrito Van Van, who's a superstar, at La Tropical and everybody circled around us to watch and applaud. That was my shining moment. So, you see, La Gofia dances just like Pedrito. She never misses the beat, ever, and is in complete control of her body: smooth, sinewy but not vulgar, balanced, elegant, hooked in to the music, perfect. Later I found out she's a professional, a cabaret dancer, and that she makes a living by giving lessons to foreigners.

"They never get it," she told me, "because they're like vegetables, and dumber than rocks, but I don't care as long as they pay me . . ."

Besides dancing, we also drank all sorts of liquor. From the most ghastly moonshine to Johnny Walker Black, which my cautious and esteemed dancing partner had hidden in a hole in the kitchen, somewhere no one would stick their hand for fear of cockroaches. We also strolled back to the bathroom a few times, to sniff and recharge our batteries, with Danai along now so she wouldn't have another fit. I was super high. I felt like Super Flying Z. It was delicious.

All through this, I kept going past Gofia's bedroom door, which was ajar. I couldn't resist the temptation to peek in. What could be going on in there? Nothing. No indecent spectacle. At least, not to me. That far gone, with so much alcohol in my veins and so much coke in my soul, I'm not sure what, exactly, I would have considered indecent. Every time I glanced inside the room, I saw a different scene. Linda and the gypsy kissing. Linda sitting on the edge of the bed, the gypsy on her knees in front of her, looking into each others' eyes. The gypsy trying to disrobe and Linda, her glasses off, trying to stop her. The gypsy, still on her knees, with her black shirt off, with her breasts covered by a cascade of black hair and Linda shaking her by the shoulders. The gypsy, the shirt back on, sobbing, and Linda with her arms crossed. The only thing that remained the same was freckle-faced Marilú in her terry cloth kimono, as bald as a billiard ball, her eyes fixed on the ceiling, announcing the angel's arrival. I didn't understand a thing. And perhaps there was nothing to understand.

At some point, La Gofia caught me spying on them and joined me. Just to keep me company, just to keep me company, she said chuckling, because the scene was actually sleep-inducing. Ha ha! How boring those girls were. How silly. What a lack of imagination. She and I were infinitely crazier, especially with our spying. Ha ha! Whatta bore . . . she yawned. What she really wanted to do was jump in there, with all of them on the bed—well, actually, Marilú didn't count—and start a big ol' orgy. Just to get things rolling. Just to get them past this romantic b.s., this wide-eyed sentimentality and bleeding heart shit with the I-love-yous and you-love-mes, love of my loves. Ha ha! As if she'd heard us, Linda turned her gaze our way. She put her glasses on so she could see. I thought she might get mad, so I tried to pretend we weren't watching, but La Gofia didn't let me. Of course, she grabbed me by the same arm as before. Now I'd get to see, she said in a wicked tone, what utter immaturity really was. Ha ha! But Linda, having fun, waved at us. The gypsy saw us too. She quickly got to her feet. All fired up, she rushed toward the door. And practically bent from laughter, La Gofia let her through. I didn't have time to do the same. As Yadelis liked to say, I'm too slow to live in the West. Neither fragile nor ethereal, the gypsy shoved me aside. How strong. What silent strength. I didn't get mad or anything; I think I was getting used to the fact that everybody pushes me around. Linda got up and went after her.

"Alix, Alix, don't go getting a complex . . . c'mon, girlee . . . Alix!"

But La Gofia blocked the door.

"Let her go, baby, let her go."

"What did you say?" My friend looked at La Gofia with incredulity. "Get out of the way."

"Don't overdo it, okay? Don't overdo it. What's done is done, but don't overdo it. You don't have to run after her in front of everybody. Look, if you want, tomorrow I'll go to the dorm and catch her, tie her up, and bring her to you. You know I'd do anything for you. I'll eat a slab of ice between two pieces of bread or throw myself off the fifth floor. But don't go after her. Don't do that to me, please. Not today."

Linda, scrutinizing the situation, looked into La Gofia's clear eyes.

"Fine," she said, throwing her arms in the air as if in surrender. "Is there any rum left? I'm dying of thirst."

"The angel's here . . ."

And so the tension was lessened a little bit. As soon as Alix left, I felt, strangely enough, as if a weight had been lifted from me. I can't be sure, but it seemed La Gofia felt it too. We danced again, and drank, and had our fun. For the rest of the night, and well into dawn, Linda acted as if what had happened was not at all important. She confessed she'd loved the bit about the slab of ice between two pieces of bread. How romantic. We sang "Happy Birthday to You" to La Gofia. Kinda drunk and very enthusiastically, my friend also sang it in German. The girl with the mask then wanted to know how to say all sorts of obscenities in German. In a very sensual tone, from a corner of the balcony where the music wasn't very loud, Linda delivered a whole string of gibberish. Danai and I applauded. The girl with the mask tried to repeat the gibberish, but couldn't.

La Gofia was thoughtful for a moment and then said that, though all of that sounded just fine, she preferred to *talk* in Cuban. (As an aside, my friend told me that it was something about a poem by Heine.) I don't remember the details, but I know we had a fine time. At about three thirty in the morning, the upstairs neighbor came down to complain to La Gofia about the noise. He was up to here—he barked just like the megatherium—with that scandalous racket. He didn't give a damn about how other people lived their lives, no sir, but what a fucked existence living above a den of iniquity. He hadn't slept in years. Conciliatory, La Gofia put an end to the party. "There's no problem, maestro, don't worry about it." And so everybody went home.

She didn't say more than she had to. To the contrary. She's one of the most discreet people I've ever met. She can yak about a thousand silly things and give the impression that she's got a loose tongue, but that's not the way it is. In fact, she has a rare talent for figuring out what's most important and keeping it to herself, no matter how drunk or high she is. That night, for example, she didn't tell me that she knew who I was. It took her several months to tell me that, the afternoon before the birthday party, Linda had called to tell her she was bringing her best friend. A sorta foolish girl. Slower than a slug. As jumpy as a rabbit. Cute, but with a few too many kilos. Extroverted. A little too forthcoming. A party girl. A really, really good person. Happy for no reason, mocking sometimes, but not someone who'd ever deliberately hurt anybody. One hundred percent heterosexual. In other words, a disaster. But all in all, her best friend.

Not only did La Gofia spare me that glowing description, she also didn't mention how she'd met Linda at the fencing club, right after she got back from New York. My friend might have been a great sniper if she'd not wasted so much time practicing the saber, a weapon only for men, very heavy. But Linda preferred the saber because, once she lost the duel—that is, if she managed to confuse her opponent for a personal enemy—she could take the blade by the tip and bash the sonovabitch with the bell and guard, something which wouldn't have been possible with a sword or a foil. The whole business with the saber had struck La Gofia as very erotic. She said Linda was great in bed, crazy, very creative, talkative, but a witch without feelings. She said she'd sleep with anyone for pure entertainment, for fun, to relax, because the only thing she really cared about were her detective novels. She was very destructive and left a trail of tears and suffering behind her, with many victims who would then come to her, La Gofia, for a little therapy. The stormy relationship between them had lasted a few months but was just about over because the thing with Alix was serious, you had to be blind not to see it. And she, La Gofia, wasn't angry at Linda. Though it might sound ridiculous, Linda was the love of her life and she could count on her for whatever, now and forever.

I found out about all this bit by bit over the course of several years. Because La Gofia and I became very good friends. We still are, although we don't see each other very much. About a year ago, when things got really tense, really intense, I brought Alix to live in my room and Linda was furious. Oh, what a Malaysian tiger . . . I had no right. She didn't scream, but her words had bite. It was a betrayal, a sordid stab in the back. Wasn't the bearded lunatic enough trouble already? I was going to regret it for the rest of my life. She was not going to set foot ever again in Happy Hammer Corners as long as that imbecile was living there. By that point, Alix was no longer "the girl with the black hair" but "that imbecile." But La Gofia understood. She made fun of my sympathetic bent. Of my damned and repugnant Christian charity, as Moisés would say. Of my inclination to consider others as those "poor, miserable" people when they were, in fact, sonzabitches. My real name was Mother Teresa of Calcutta. She insisted I be careful day and night. Since I'd already screwed up, she insisted I keep one eye open when I slept (I tried, I really tried, but I couldn't do it; both would close up); I needed to be alert. Because Alix wasn't an s.o.b, but she was demented, out of her mind, a dangerous crazy who could ruin my life on the count of three. But I know she understood. I know La Gofia understood. Because she also lived with tragedy, a tragedy that continued every single day. It was the tragedy of Marilú, which was also her tragedy and that of many others. It was horrible. And it was something she never said a word to me about. It was something I only found out about thanks to Linda, who didn't know that much either.

Chapter 8

Next Year in Jerusalem

LT. LEVÍ'S PROBLEMS ARE NEVERENDING. ARIEL LEVÍ, THE PROTAGO-
nist in Linda's stories and novels, is about fifty years old. But he seems more
like five hundred. Life has given him such a bad rap, as they say, that it's hard
to imagine that he was once young, just a boy. He's a skinny guy, not very
tall, with glasses and a nose that makes him look like a ferret. He talks in a
low voice, softly, pronouncing all the letters. Even so, he can be very scary. He
intimidates delinquents without touching a hair on their heads. He's street
smart. Astute, persevering, with a good memory, a great capacity for work,
and an exquisite nose like a bloodhound; he seems destined for greatness. But
there won't be any of that. He's unlucky. And when a detective, whether he's
private or state-sponsored, is unlucky, he's screwed. And so Lt. Leví can never
solve a crime. He can finger the killer but never capture him. There's always
something that gets in the way.

At first, things weren't so bad for him. He did manage to catch the cannibal
who liked mayonnaise. But that story, according to Linda, is too immature,
juvenile and naïve. An attempt, she says, from when she was trying to imitate
Raymond Chandler. When she'd read *The Simple Art of Murder* as if it were the
bible and was convinced that words were good for more than just deception,
how idealistic—she says this aloud as if she were talking to herself, which is why

I don't quite get it. Later, the skies got cloudy for Lt. Leví. He got screwed. He was disgraced. Adversity began to encircle him until he found himself drowning, finally, in a swamp of misfortune. The guy suffers like mad. And for good reason. He's stuck dealing with horrendous crimes, appalling, the kind that kill your appetite (I remember this phrase: "He hadn't seen injuries like this since the train accident"), and he just stands there, like a rag doll, paralyzed, impotent, as if he were blindfolded and his hands were tied. Whatta drag.

Depressed and lonelier than an oyster, Lt. Leví can't sleep in spite of his fatigue. When he's not chasing fugitives, his nights vacillate between insomnia and nightmares. He shaves when he thinks of it, doesn't talk to anybody, smokes whatever, drinks too much sometimes, and then has to deal with the hangover, a migraine, and the desire to hang himself. In essence, he's the very portrait of failure. Every now and again, he asks himself what he's still doing in Havana, why he insists on this battle with what seems like a monster with a thousand heads which grows two new ones for each you cut off and drips a green and fetid blood; disgusting. He has no answer. But he never leaves. It might be too late now. He probably doesn't have the energy for a long journey anymore, who knows. All his stories end with him muttering on the terrace of his penthouse, slowly smoking a cigarette (I see him between clouds of smoke, somber, hardened, bitter; I imagine him as if it were a movie).

"No way. I can't take this shit anymore. Next year in Jerusalem."

Linda's first novel, whose title is precisely *Next Year in Jerusalem*, was first published in 1997 by a modest publishing house in Barcelona. According to her, it was an onerous contract. She knew it when she signed, so there was no deception on either part. She was a young writer, probably too young, practically unknown, who came from a peripheral country—yes, peripheral—underdeveloped, primitive, wild, and because she was Cuban, regardless of what her passport said, and a piece of paper could say anything—this is what she explained to me—she couldn't aspire to more with her first contract. That's how it was with business, she concluded, and sometimes, when faced with something more powerful, you only have two options: conformity or surrender. You take it or leave it. And, of course, you can't get emotionally involved. My friend is usually at home in cool, dry, nonsensical situations; they strike her as very honest, and so based on that criteria, she came to an agreement with the owner of the small press. How could she criticize him, she acknowledged, if she would have done the same thing in his place? Besides, the guy made it easy for her. In other words, he paid for a trip to Spain, put her up in expensive hotels, took her out on his yacht, to see a bullfight, to a concert by the Three Tenors, gave her an enormous bouquet of Bulgarian roses (she doesn't care at all for flowers, but she appreciated the gesture), introduced her to his friends, and acted, ultimately, like a gentleman. And none of that was in the damned contract.

It was a different story with the editor, who was a leftist. Like Father Ignacio, my friend claims she's not prejudiced toward these people. It's just that she loathes the term "leftist." It sounds to her like a dusty piece of junk and makes her want to sneeze. It was fine to defend the rights of ethnic and religious minorities, women, gays, the disabled, children, animals and . . . plants—a vegetarian, she smiled, and then reminded me of the mango tree's sorry fate. It was fine that there were workers' strikes and that peasants from underdeveloped countries should struggle for agrarian reform. It was good to be against nuclear proliferation. Yes, all that was fine. But a leftist politician could still act, according to her, like a "savage capitalist"—she relished those two words—when it came to business, like a street thug, willing to fight dirty, the only difference being that you had to put up with their bouts of conscience, whether they were real or not. Their constant rationalizations. Their paranoia. Their intellectual masturbation. Their need to believe that they're good, objective, noble and generous, philanthropic, angels come down from heaven, even if the meaning of the words had to be inverted in order to make any of it true. When that editor demanded gratitude from my friend, even though he'd done her a great favor by publishing her novel, she started to laugh. The whole time they were at a café with a magnificent view of the Sagrada Familia, and she held her fists under the table so as not to slap him one. Grateful for what? For an implacable contract? For a cheap edition full of errata, with an ugly cover and a foreword that would make anyone sick? Oh, yes, if the man's personal contradictions hadn't been so obvious, she sighed, she would have thought he was just being cynical.

As it turned out, the foreword had been written by an enemy of my friend, a secret enemy, a serious hypocrite, the author of a really stinky little novel— she made a face of disgust, as if she'd eaten a raw toad, without sugar—who, by sheer accident, had reached a certain level of success. A rotten, envious, miserable, vile, quarrelsome, egomaniacal sonovabitch—so she said, among other things—who took advantage of any and all opportunities, even the most inappropriate, to talk about himself. He had told my friend in a condescending tone that he considered her *his equal*—she smiled again—an affirmation which, from a certain point of view, was pretty amusing. Kindly, she responded that no, there was no way they were equals. And he—ha ha—was flattered. What an imbecile. The gentleman and the leftist were both Catalonian. The big hypocrite, Cuban. Of course. Although she didn't have any prejudices with respect to nationalities either—she cleared this up so as not to confuse me—there was no worse treatment than from your own people. She didn't take it personally. How could she be upset with such stupidity? No, sir. She just slammed the table three times (at home, not at the café). Then she declared the whole thing over with. She got herself a literary agent (in fact, it was the leftist who had introduced her to the agent, against the gentleman's wishes, because life was just that complex and multicolored and very rarely in black and white), and so she began another novel, a very sardonic novel even more pessimistic than the first. I listened, perplexed, to all of this, from which she'd left out all the hassles that came later. Life for a *real* writer must be very complicated.

She needed money, a steady income before her balance reached zero. The penthouse needed maintenance so it wouldn't end up like Lt. Leví's: dilapidated, frail, leaky, transformed into ruins of absolutely no archaeological interest. The Mercedes also needed maintenance. In good faith, I volunteered to take care of it, at no charge, but she refused. She didn't want to take advantage of me because we were friends, she said, and, where the hell did I get new parts anyway? Her housekeeper, an old woman who was half deaf, came by twice a week to help her with domestic chores. She had a salary, as would be expected. And there was the electricity, fuel, the phone, vegetables, which were so expensive . . . whatta drag. To top it off, she'd barely gotten back from Europe (a quickie tour of Madrid, Barcelona, Paris, and Brussels from which she brought me an album of reproductions by Velázquez and Leidi a fountain pen in the shape of the Eiffel Tower), and Alix had moved in with her and didn't contribute a cent, not even a brown penny split in two. It wasn't her fault. She was only seventeen years old, newly arrived from the countryside, from the rainforest, from some lost hut deep among Cuba's palms and thicket; she'd come to study journalism at the University of Havana and my friend wasn't going to let her starve at the dorm on G Street and Malecón. Not that little girl with black hair, so lacking in malice, so without resources, so without the necessary cunning to survive in the capital of disaster, said my friend, where it was so hard to dig and come up with a yam or cassava. Let me say that I was surprised by Linda's generosity. She didn't want to have to get rid of her place or the Mercedes or the half-deaf old woman or Alix, or even her gold Rolex, and so she had to get a little side job giving private language lessons. Spanish for the children of diplomats, which a staffer at the Austrian Embassy helped her set up. English, French, and Italian for a whole troop of hustlers, which La Gofia helped her with. All under the table, of course, so she wouldn't have to pay taxes.

I admit, from a very selfish perspective, I was glad she was so busy back then. That way, so tied up with her own stuff, she didn't have time to visit me and meet Moisés, who had moved in with all his insanity to Happy Hammer Corners. Well, "moved in" in a manner of speaking. Alix attached herself to Linda like a limpet, a magnet, a decal, like the Viking had done with Yadelis, but my lover didn't do the same with me. A week after the skirmish in John Lennon Park, when he came to stay (it was that simple: "I've come to stay, crazy girl, so here are twenty dollars, but do me the goddamn favor of closing that fucking window—why all that light anyway?"), I assumed he'd act possessive in some way, jealous, controlling. A lot of men act that way even when they don't give a damn about the woman. I have no idea why. Maybe they think it's entertaining. In Moisés's case, my conjecture was perhaps influenced by the brutal fashion in which he had attached himself to me *physically*. As an example, the first time we slept together, he almost strangled me. While he was penetrating me, he had the brilliant idea of squeezing my neck with one of his giant hands. Although I don't think it was actually an idea but more like an instinct. Nothing was more exciting to him than to feel something (because that's what I was to Moisés: "something") agonizing in his hands. A body contracting, sucking, pleasing him—basically, struggling to survive. A defenseless being, dependent totally on him, on his goodwill, even if it was just temporary, to continue being. It's possible Dr. Frumento might have been right and there's something wrong with me, because I loved his barbaric ways, that whole sadomasochistic trip. I was so crazy for it that I became totally addicted and needed it like a drug. I felt fear, of course, but also the pleasure of fear. A little devil with a coiled tail.

Out of bed, though, Moisés wasn't interested in controlling anything. At least nothing that had to do with me. In his corner of hate, huddled with his liter and his two cigarettes, he seemed far away, remote, on other coordinates and transmitting on other frequencies. A Thinker deep in his bellicose plans, his strategies, his career in firearms, his crusade against "them." He couldn't stand it when I asked him questions about his life (the answers came in screams, insults, and assaults, so I ceased being curious), and he certainly didn't ask them of me. He considered that not getting involved in my affairs was the best way to maintain a healthy distance, of preserving his own independence. If I told him stories about the Pythagorean Party, about the filmmakers who used to live in the Corners, about JJ's hijacking of the ferry with his accomplices, etc., it was because I wanted to, because his comments and annotations on the side struck me as interesting, but not because he asked for them. And if I was rigorously faithful, something unique in my romantic life, it was only because I didn't like anyone as much as I liked him. Not by a mile. To sleep with anybody else after sleeping with Moisés would have been the equivalent of being satisfied with a carrot or a cauliflower, a miserable green brain, after having tasted a filet (and I am very carnivorous—not as much as the cannibal who liked mayonnaise, but almost). I still haven't tried it. I don't dare. I'm afraid I'll get frustrated and that I'll frustrate some poor guy who's probably just average, normal, and trying to be kind, sane, civilized. There's no hurry. We'll see what happens later, after the baby's born.

During one of Moisés's habitual disappearances, instead of getting lost in Muslim heaven or sing-songing about the hundred bottles, I decided to read *Next Year in Jerusalem*. I leapt past the foreword like a bullfighter. Not because of the intrigue, wickedness, infamy, and dirty tricks which Linda had attributed to its author, whom I didn't know, but because, generally speaking, I'm not into forewords. I think I'd had plenty of those, in fact too many, in college. It's not that it bothers me that people write forewords, of course not; everybody should write whatever they want. The problem is that they bore me, they make me sleepy. It was the opposite with the novel: I got hooked right away. From the moment the old woman, very elegant and matronly, very much old Vedado, couldn't open the second drawer on her Louis XV dresser, which was emitting a very penetrating and mysterious rotten smell. What could it be? An amputated human member, a fetus, a codfish, a . . . ? Oh, how creepy. All that had the terrified old woman with her hair on end, and me as well. I devoured chapter after chapter in one night, until the very end, until dawn, until the sad scene of Lt. Leví on the terrace with his cigarette and his depression. It really left an impression on me. Not so much with its literary excellence—which I don't doubt—as for the terrible story it told. Or, more precisely, because of the implications of that story. Was it possible, *in real life*—in other words, in end-of-the-century Havana—for such a horrible murder to occur with impunity? Whatta book. I didn't think the cover was so ugly after all and I barely noticed the errata which irritated Linda so much.

When Moisés came back, I told him about the case. I know that telling someone about a detective novel or a thriller almost always messes with their expectations, curiosity, and suspense. It's depriving them of future pleasure. It's just fucked. You don't do that, even to your worst enemy, or to Poliéster, or to the megatherium if it was human. The eleventh commandment should be: "You will not tell your neighbor who the killer is." Even Father Ignacio, who usually disapproves of my modest contributions to Christian dogma, agrees with me on this point. He also read my friend's novel and the few hairs on his head also stood on end, although his favorite detective continues to be his colleague, a certain Father Brown, created by a writer named Gilbert Keith Chesterton, who is much more famous than Linda ("for now," she says). In terms of Moisés, however, my indiscretion wasn't so harmful since my lover didn't read novels. Not noirs or pink ones or novels of any color. What kind of stupidity was that? The novel in and of itself, in his opinion, was a genre for fools, the homeless, for pigs, the retarded, for people who sucked their big toes, who were always on idiotic swings, swinging away with the hope of being deceived someday or, if possible, every day.

I told him about it, not as if I were recounting a novel, not as a string of lies, but as if it had happened in real life. A rumor. Neighborhood gossip. A little tidbit from Radio Bemba, the people's network which keeps us Cubans informed about everything, or almost everything, that's behind what's censored in the sensationalist press. He listened to me attentively, immobile, without blinking, his black eyes wide open. Just like me and Father Ignacio and my great-uncle W., who'd also read the novel and considered that only Uranus could inspire a crime like that, the story hooked him, too. Every now and again, he'd ask: "And the old woman? How'd the old woman take it? And what about the guy who was hiding behind the tree? And the other cop—not the Polish guy, the other one, the younger one? And then? What happened then, when they realized there was a poisonous snake under the bed, eh?" It scared me to death that he might realize I was deceiving him, that he would catch me trying to pull one on him. He'd accused me so many times of being deceitful when I never had! Oh, no one could have saved me from that beating. And that's just for starters. Later, he'd strangle me with barbed wire or something like that. I think I took a big risk. I did it, like I've done so many things, without thinking twice, or even once. Perhaps this kind of audacity is what Dr. Frumento is referring to when he says "dangerous situations."

Moreover, to my surprise and the astonishment of the universe, Moisés believed me when I told him Linda's fictions. Putting aside a few folkloric touches, like the thing with the snake and the part where the psychopathic killer ties the victim to a chair, gags her, and entertains himself dancing around and singing, "The Martians are here . . . / and they're dancing ricachá . . ." (this victim was a poor little old man, a knickknack vendor, whose life was spared, but who was left with a stammer as a result of the trauma), exaggerations and urban legends that sprung from neighborhood fantasies, Moisés thought the case was perfectly plausible. If you take into account how many guys I've known, and that none has been more skeptical, less trusting, and more suspicious than my boo, and let's keep in mind that I'm not the best liar, then it's easy to see the force of my friend's fiction, the enormity of her talent for making things seem real. She had managed to achieve the goal she'd announced for herself ten years before: to become a consummate fraud, a sublime liar.

According to Moisés, stories like that happened with frequency in Havana. Much more than newspapers and news shows ever reported, since they didn't report crap, he said—and for the first time I was glad I didn't have a television set, glad to have gone with Yadelis to a neighbor's house to watch cartoons—especially during the crisis of the '90s, those ten years that really made the city shudder. Things happened because too many guys were just too hungry, needed drugs or guns or moonshine or things for Santería rituals; they betrayed each other, cheated each other; their women cheated on them in front of the entire neighborhood; or they hated people from Oriente province, who were really hateful, he assured me, just like those from Havana, from Pinar del Río, all Cubans, foreigners, basically all of humanity, which was abominable and false; or there was no water in the building, or present or future either, and it was hot as fuck; shit, the building was about to fall apart like all the others that had already crumpled and now there was debris and dirt and stink and blackouts and bugs galore and . . . He'd get all worked up, as if all this really amused him. Well, I knew. Or I should know. He made a twisted gesture. Given how streetsy and slutty I was. Or had going to college made me a dimwit? Yes, because on our "glorious hill," and he underscored the phrase with sarcasm, he'd come to understand how things were after so many years of lecturing on the law faculty: how they filled people's heads with shit, how they made them believe they were what they were not, how they were taught to obscure the sun with just one finger, he mumbled. How grotesque my look of astonishment, what an idiot. Was I going to change that look or did he have to do it by slapping me one? There was nothing stupider than an educated whore, a little sexual object with intellectual pretensions. Oh, women! As the ancient Romans used to say: *Oculos habent et non vident.** Then he threatened me with his fist. And I ran, just in case.

I have to admit I liked the part about the little sexual object. It sounded better, more affectionate, than being called a dumb fatso, or a retarded fat-ass, or an insect brain. What I still can't figure out is how that man managed to blame me so often. It's true that I live at Happy Hammer Corners, with neighbors that are pure shit. It's true that I haven't worked since I lost my job with that obscure agricultural magazine. It's true that my University of Havana degree, in spite of the effort to get it, is absolutely worthless to me. It's true that I make a living however I can, breaking the law now and again, like so many others, I suppose. But none of that means that there are murders going on every day in front of my very "oculos." At that time, I hadn't witnessed any, and God knows how much I would have liked to go on like that. If he knew so much about terrible crimes, in spite of the utter lack of transparency (I got this very elegant phrase from Linda), it was surely because of his former profession. While practicing it, he must have run into real charming characters, since death sentences can only be dictated by the Supreme Court. When it came to life in prison, which was instituted as part of the last Penal Code reform, probably the same thing happens, although, I dunno, he didn't like to talk about those matters very much. Before, I was interested. Now, I'm not.

By that time, my boo had already fully demonstrated all his bellicose splendor in public. First, he hit the peasant at the pharmacy over the head with a bottle. He left him unconscious, beaten to a pulp behind the counter, drenched in blood. The jag-off, my lover bitched, had refused to give him a psychopharmaceutical Dr. Frumento had prescribed to see if he could calm his nerves a bit and which he, giving in for once, had agreed to take. The disrespectful hick, the peasant cowboy, the shitty-smelling mujik had even pulled a machete on him. On him! From the pharmacy he went directly to his therapist's office and slapped him a couple so he wouldn't prescribe such troublesome pills in the future. Then there was the hassle with the transit cop, because he, the insolent man, had given him, of all people, a ticket for speeding and driving while inebriated. He punched the cop and managed to remain free, but they suspended his driver's license. He was only in jail for a week (isolated, to avoid fights with the other inmates), thanks to Dr.

---

* They have eyes but do not see.

Frumento's statement, because he wasn't resentful and took the assault from his patient in a very professional manner.

But the patient couldn't keep still. No way. He didn't care about the psychiatrist's insinuations about the relative effectiveness of electroshock. He threw a bench against a mirror in a bar and made smithereens out of it; he knocked out the barman, caused massive chaos, then snuck out the bathroom window. Later, he kicked the shit out of the megatherium, who'd tried to bite him, because that hairy beast was out of line. Even the lowest species, he complained, had turned into assholes. That beautiful morning, my boo showed up in my apartment with his mouth full of black hair. I suspect he bit the megatherium, which strikes me as very fair and just, what we could say was giving the thing a taste of its own medicine. Later that afternoon, he got into a major row with those three guys from Los Muchos. They were acting like hot stuff, like big men, according to him, and though he had nothing against black people (nothing against blacks, everything against people), he recognized that between the age of slavery and our times, barely a century had passed and, he said, that was barely enough to erase the damage. And he went at them with incredible fury. He fractured the jaw on one of them. After he grabbed a blackjack from another, he crushed his finger (I called Yadelis to tell her this part of the story and my friend felt very happy, very pleased—oh, if only, she sighed, she could have a man like mine!). The third guy managed to get away more or less untouched, making all kinds of threats, although it was just to save his honor because he never acted on any of them.

After this fight, the folks in the neighborhood began to avoid Moisés. I think they took him for some kind of madman, an orangutan escaped, not from the zoo, but straight from the jungle itself. Where else could he have gotten so strong? And what nerve, because when he fought, he didn't care if he got hit, if they knocked out a tooth or bashed an eye. He didn't care about anything. He went straight to his task: to bash the crap out of his opponent, leave him unable to engage in combat, reduce him to dust. The drunks on the terrace would open a path for him like lackeys before a king. When the king had gone some distance and couldn't hear them anymore, they sang a little ditty after him: "Don't you mess with me . . . / cuz I'm a fire eater . . ." There was one who actually took his hat off. He did it until one day when Moisés caught him in the act, grabbed the hat, and shoved it down on the wiseguy's head in one swift move.

The big deal that my neighbors made out of the duel between Mozart and

Poliéster occurred, of course, in his absence. It's not that I'm underestimating them, nothing could be further from my intention, but I'm sure it never would have happened if he'd been present. It was when Linda decided to cram Schoenberg down their throats that things got really ugly. For me, I mean. They didn't put up with it for even two days. Sure that the Caveman wasn't around, this time the jerks from the Corners weren't happy simply yelling insults, barbarities, and various other interjections. They also weren't satisfied with just waving their hands around, snorting, and making faces. Their intention, I think, was to lynch me, to get rid of me and my fucking eccentricities once and for all. They couldn't take me anymore. Basically, they'd had it up to here. It was one of the worst moments of my life, one I'd like to forget but which I can't.

I didn't even get a chance to scream for help or to call Pancholo, who's an expert when it comes to calming people down. Oh. They surrounded me. They pushed me around as if I were a sack, a sack of potatoes. They screamed. They screeched. They barked. All I could see was a sea of faces distorted by rage; everything was going in circles. I couldn't seem to articulate anything, though I don't think it would have helped much. The wiseguys from the Corners were beyond words. The megatherium's owner threatened me with her famous taro-peeling knife. Ow! That's all I needed to immediately surrender. But that wasn't enough for her. She grabbed me by the hair and put the blade to my throat. Ow! She pinched me. Very lightly, but she pinched me. Owwwww! I was so scared I couldn't speak, I was sweating up a storm and I needed to pee. She was a motherfucker and women had to respect her, because she did in fact have papers proving she was crazy, really crazy, howled the frenetic owner of the megatherium, alluding, I suppose, to her psychiatric history, I dunno. She would kill me for free. The mob encircled us as if we were at a cockfight. Well, maybe a fight between a cock and a little mouse. I didn't hear them making bets but I wouldn't have been surprised if they had. Thirty pesos that the crazy old broad would kill me, forty that she would only slice my face or some such thing. I could hear them bellowing.

"Kill her! Kill her! Cut off her ear! Break her neck!"

Others took the opposite view.

"Leave her alone, Usnavy, leave her alone! Leave her alone already cuz you're just going to get yourself in trouble."

Still others, in honest abstention, had never ceased hammering. Tock tock tock. Poliéster provided a soundtrack with his cornet. Horrified, his mother tried to take it from him, but it was all in vain. The artist held tight to his instrument. Something hot was running down my neck. The Jehovah's Witness cried out about the path of the Lord; I think he was crying. Somebody kicked his ass and the Witness, poor guy, continued his crying, now more enthusiastically. I didn't feel any pain, just fear, a lot of fear. Panic. The goat with the little bell was braying. The chickens were clucking. And Schoenberg was going full blast. It looked like the ancient Roman circus.

And then the comandante showed up, meaning Linda, and she ordered everyone to stop. I'm a lucky girl after all. Somebody—probably God—had left the big door open downstairs, which allowed my friend to quietly come up, like a lynx, and rescue me, sorta like Robin Hood. With just one look, she understood the gravity of the situation and quickly pulled a pistol out of her handbag, disengaged the safety, and aimed it at the owner of the megatherium. The party was over. Everybody shut up. Even the goat and the chickens. The damned cornet was no longer heard. The only sound was Schoenberg. And the Jehovah's Witness's hiccups. And maybe a distant hammering, maybe from up on the attic. My friend came closer and closer to the crazy woman, who hadn't dropped the knife or my hair, and put the gun's barrel to her temple.

"Let her go or I'll blow your brains out."

She let me go. In the end, she wasn't that crazy, thank God. I fell to the floor, confused, in a sitting position and with the firm resolve to never stand up again. The hutia, trying to be nice and in solidarity with me, climbed up on me, on my lap, as if trying to tell me that it loved me, that I was important, that it didn't support this mistreatment or injustice. Sometimes animals can be very expressive. I raised a hand to caress it and I think that's when I peed, right there on the floor. What decadence. I'd never before felt so miserable, like lice, so insignificant.

Without moving the gun, my friend took the knife from Usnavy. "Gimme that." She put it away in her bag, like a trophy, like a war souvenir. I'm not sure, because these ghetto characters, no matter how streetsy, boastful, and loud, turn grey and shit their pants when they're in front of a firearm, but I think that crazy woman meant to whistle for the megatherium, which was who knows where. That monster, which bit people on the leg of its own initiative, could bite your neck if he was ordered to do so. He was, and still is in spite of his age, capable of killing.

"Linda! Linda! The dog! The bastard! Don't let her call him!"

For an instant, my friend stared at Usnavy in disbelief, like someone looking at tiny things through a microscope and being surprised by their mere existence. Then she grabbed her by her yellow Oriente naps (because she's from Guantánamo, near the American naval base, back there where the peasants have spent a hundred years looking up at the sign that says U.S. NAVY) and stuck the gun barrel in her mouth.

"What the fuck is wrong with you?" she asked her in a low voice, softly, pronouncing every letter. "Do you want me to fill your head with lead? I don't give a royal fuck about you, your dog, or your mother. Suck this!" And she moved the barrel in and out of her mouth. "Go on, suck. Like a dick, yeah. Oh no? Well, you'll see. I'm going to count to three. One . . . two . . . Ah, good. You see? That's good."

That woman hasn't bothered me again. No one has. Since then they act like nothing happened. They don't even avoid eye contact. Some greet me, and those who don't, never did, because they're unaware that civilized people say "Good morning." They throw me the key, insist on trying to sell me things, and ask me for sugar because they prepare their coffee as if it were syrup. Every time they offer me a sip of their sticky brew, I want to die, but I swallow anyway so they won't be offended. Although they continued, and continue to this day, to make all kinds of noise (I'm listening to them now, between the music, the hammering, and Radio Reloj), I haven't bothered anyone anymore with Schoenberg or Mozart or anybody. I'd rather avoid violent situations, the type whose beginnings we know well but not so much how they'll end; Father Ignacio agrees with me on this. Besides, I don't think anyone should be put up against the wall, without alternatives, without a way out. The saying is right: For the enemy who flees, a silver bridge. With some folks, and you never know whom, it's the same as with rats. You chase a rat to beat it with the broom because it's infectious, because it's disgusting, a filthy rat, and it flees. It doesn't defend itself, just runs. But only if it has someplace to go. If you corner it, if you don't give it a way out, the rat turns around and bites you. It fights for its life. I don't want to be bitten by a rat. So, I voluntarily surrendered on the matter of the noise. I surrendered on a lot of other things too, which aren't relevant now. I put up with the divine Poliéster's acoustic excesses until the end, until the night of the catastrophe.

When it came to the pistol, which appeared as if by magic in the writer's bag—even though she's a smart girl, cultured, civil, very skilled at making herself understood with mere words—Linda assured me there was no strange mystery. It had belonged to her father, just like the Mercedes. Of course, she didn't have any kind of license to carry it. But she *had* to carry it. She didn't have any other choice. Maybe it was just her imagination, she confided, but Alix was getting the same look as the Puerto Rican guava just before her breakdown. A sinister, obsessive look. Death threats. Russian roulette. Bang! She, Linda Roth, was not going to go through that again. No way. She wasn't going to throw Alix out of the penthouse, not right now, because she was too attracted to her. So quiet, so inscrutable, so elemental with her gypsy air, Linda sighed, she was attracted to that little girl with the black hair like she'd never been to anyone else. She felt like Alix was part of her, as if she was her own dark side. A wild side, atavistic, intuitive, unable to reason and quite irrational. A violent side which, if unleashed, would be very difficult to control. Of course, no one forced the lion tamer into the cage. But once the risk was assumed, because the deal with beautiful beasts *always* involves risks, it wasn't a bad idea to carry a gun on your belt. Just a precaution. And it wasn't just because of Alix. She'd also been—why deny it?—quite moved by Marilú's tragedy. It was horrible. Did I remember that freckle-faced girl with the buzz cut, the one wearing the terry cloth kimono who kept announcing the angel's arrival at La Gofia's birthday party? She seemed a little off, right? Well, she wasn't like that just for fun.

I didn't pay much attention to the matter with Alix. Now I think I should have. Maybe then things wouldn't have turned out the way they did, although I dunno, I can't imagine another ending to the story. The fact is, I didn't think about her for a good long time. At first, I'd found her aura disturbing, but Father Ignacio quickly convinced me that there are no such things as auras. The only real auras are auras tiñosas, or vultures, he said in a severe tone. Everything else was superstition. Who was teaching me these things, eh? Who was I hanging out with? Again with the heresies? How far was I going to go? The truth is, I wasn't hanging out with anybody. Back then, I *saw* people's auras, it was just that simple. But my confessor attributed this to rum and marijuana. He took advantage of the situation to also lecture me against esoteric practices such as white magic, pyramid energy, biorhythms, psychoanalysis, kabbalah, and other things. Conclusion: Alix was a common, average girl. Stubborn as a mule, that's for sure. Capricious, intense, really dumb. Very difficult to deal with. But not an alcoholic, a drug addict, or the least bit aggressive. At least not then. To say otherwise sounded more like one of Linda's novels, like just wanting to add a little spice to the romance. The thing about Marilú's tragedy, however, did make me curious. What had happened?

I bathed, I put a little bit of alcohol on the scratch on my neck, and we went to the penthouse so we could talk in peace, without anybody interrupting us. Once there, while the girl with the black hair looked on in silence (if I didn't think I'd sound paranoid, I'd say she was watching us with her owl eyes), my friend told me a terrifying story. Very similar to the story of the Corners' first resident in its incompleteness, its holes and ellipses, its atrocious doubts, and the blank spaces left to fill with speculation. La Gofia had told her something, but not everything. In fact, Linda thought that not even La Gofia knew the whole story. After I heard the tale (which I'll recount later), I became convinced that, yes, a crime like the one depicted in *Next Year in Jerusalem*, and perhaps even worse than that, could in fact occur in end-of-millennium Havana and, yes, with impunity. Although, to be frank, the impunity part doesn't matter much to me. I think that once the crime has been committed, nothing will ever be the same, without regard to whatever happens to the perpetrator. I think the ideal situation would be to anticipate the act, eliminate the causes, and avoid it. Linda thinks the opposite: she thinks crime itself is part of human nature, that it's occasionally unavoidable, and that I have a cerebellum (she said "cerebellum") full of utopias.

"And the police didn't do anything?" Alix asked with a certain anxiety, as if it were personal.

"No, my love, nothing at all."

"But, Linda, isn't that supposed to be their job?" The instant I asked, I realized it was a pretty dumb question.

"Well, the truth is they did what they could. You know, Z, there's a routine. In some cases, like this one—and it's obvious why—they even put in a little extra effort. A little more concentration. To be honest, I think . . ." She paused. "I think the officer in charge did know who did it, but something kept him from doing anything about it. Something very powerful. Something which he couldn't fight against. His attitude towards Marilú seems to suggest that and nothing else."

"Pure Lt. Leví, right?" I tried to smile, in spite of how somber all that seemed to me. Maybe I just wanted it to be lies Linda was telling.

"Well, yes. There you have it. If you were to tell these things, write them up in a newspaper, a lot of people wouldn't believe them. They'd say these are exaggerations, that Havana's a boring city in which nothing happens. It's possible some sonovabitch could even accuse you of spreading the enemy's political propaganda and you know the hassle, the stupid messes that can bring . . ." She sighed. "So novels. You use them to tell a real thing as if it were false. You rearrange the facts, you invent a little bit." She winked at me. "And there. Everybody buys it. Even the sonovabitch. Who won't shut up, of course. He'll say you're being overly dramatic, morbid, truculent, commercial, that you write literature for tourists and all that shit . . ."

"Who's Lt. Leví?" asked Alix.

"That guy? Some poor cretin, my love. Don't worry about him."

In spite of the explanations and the stories, the fact of the pistol in Linda's bag didn't cease to worry me. I don't like guns, as I've said before; I think they're bad luck. From carrying to using doesn't seem that big a leap to me. And in this case, the carrier thinks crime is part of human nature and all that. For example, what would have happened if Linda had responded to her own nature and blown Usnavy's brains out? A heck of a problem. When I asked her, in front of Alix, she looked at me with such fury, I thought she wanted to blow my brains out. She *never* got out of control, she assured me, she had complete control over herself. Later, alone, she confided that the pistol wasn't loaded, that her entire performance at the Corners had been a magnificent bluff. Like in poker, when you fake like you have something when you don't. Ha ha! Wasn't that amazing? But I was to be careful about telling Alix her secret. If I let it out, she whispered in my ear, she would cut my throat herself with the knife she took from the crazy woman with the yellow naps. Was that clear?

"I'm like a tomb when it comes to secrets," I said, making like I was zipping my lip.

But she didn't show me the pistol and I didn't ask her to. I didn't know whether to believe her or not. I was overwhelmed with a terrible feeling of doubt.

Chapter 9

Love forgives everything

THE YOUNG MAN'S NAME WASN'T SEBASTIÁN, BUT IT FIT HIM, SO that's what the writer called him in her second novel, *Nocturne Sebastián*, for which she won the Dashiell Hammett Prize for best thriller of the year. This prize must be very important and much desired. Like winning the lottery. At least for my friend, it meant a huge pile of dollars. There were presentations in various countries, a bunch of interviews and raving reviews, one of them in the *New York Times*. There were now new friends and enemies with illustrious surnames, the very cream of the crop of crime writers. And, of course, there was still a problem here and there with some obtuse and good-for-nothing bureaucrat whose teeny brain didn't quite understand that the time of Stalinist censorship, retractions with mea culpas and forced exile, was definitely behind us. But let us return to Sebastián, to real life.

The story is that he was very good looking, although Linda never saw him in real life and doesn't really know. Unfortunately, La Gofia didn't keep any of his photographs. She burned them all to keep Marilú, who'd suffered enough, poor girl, from being tormented anymore. I think that, yes, he must have been a very beautiful man. A master seducer, a collector of victims of passion, an authentic heartbreaker who was also called the Exterminating Angel. This kind of person, everybody knows, doesn't really have to be handsome when it comes to entrapping women. It's enough to be interesting looking, to perhaps have a nice voice, and the rest is mental, very mental. The ability to catch and the talent to leave. I think, for example, that's a pretty good description of Félix Roth. But Sebastián was gay.

From what I remember from my dad and some of his good, as well as fair-weather, friends, whispered conversations, and secret meetings heard from the shadows, I got the impression that gays are frequently much more demanding than women when it comes to physical beauty. I couldn't be sure, of course, and perhaps it's just a bias of mine. But in Sebastián's case, there's no doubt that's how things were. Other than an Apollonian body and a face like a movie star, what could be the attraction to that timid, slippery creature with only one neuron in his head? In high school, he got into the habit of hiding behind La Gofia, who defended him and fought the other boys so they wouldn't mistreat him and call him a "little fag." The blond boy, son of a brigadier general, and the little mulatto girl from Centro Habana who was always in flip-flops, had coincided at a sports magnet school where he played water polo and she fenced. From that point on, they were friends for life. Those schools, Linda assured me, were full of kids from the neighborhoods with an aptitude for sports who aspired to get out of the neighborhood, and kids from "good families" with no aptitude for anything whatsoever whose parents aspired to get rid of them.

La Gofia loved him very much, but the brigadier was not very happy that his son, his only son, blood of his blood, educated with so much care and sacrifice in this new and just and luminous society and all that, was a shitty little faggot. That's what he called him, among other fine things. For years, he'd made his life a living hell. He was on him constantly, called him names, humiliated him, persecuted him, and even hit him. Don't walk like that, don't cross your legs, take off that shirt, don't look at yourself in the mirror like that, put your hands in your pockets, don't watch the soap opera, watch baseball instead, get yourself a girlfriend, go hunt lizards, go fight with that little black boy or I'll slap you one, and so on. His stepmother, a big zero, and barely ten years older than the boy, didn't dare take his side. She may have been afraid that he'd slap her one too, for spoiling him and being his accomplice. I understand her. If Moisés had done the same to his kids (not shitty little fags but, yes, useless, good-for-nothings, lazy asses, idiots, dummies, and plain retarded, in their father's opinion), if he'd massacred them in my presence, I'm not sure I would have intervened. No way. Not in my craziest moment. Nobody can be expected to be that brave. Well, except . . . But Linda just shrugged when I asked about Sebastián's mother.

It's not that the brigadier was depraved exactly, no. Contrary to La Gofia's opinion—she considered him a psychopath, a cruel monster, perverse, inhuman, criminal, and sadistic—it sounded to me like he was a pretty common guy. Yeah, you kick a rock and ten thousand just like him come crawling out. A lot of people in the new and just and luminous society don't like fags, just like in any other society. For centuries, they've been assaulted and harassed. Because most people, according to Moisés, can't tolerate difference. Any kind of difference. As the ancient Romans used to say: *homo homini lupus.** (He, on the contrary, couldn't tolerate anything at all. Not difference or similarity. He abhorred fags with the same intensity with which he abhorred everyone else. Why distinguish between one or the other, he grunted, when every one of them, homos and heteros, were *all* a bunch of degenerate sonzabitches?) Of course, I'm not saying it's good to discriminate against anyone. Only that the brigadier didn't invent homophobia. My dad taught me that word, "homophobia," when I was a little girl. According to him, it means "fear of fags" and it's an illness. I'd dare to say that the brigadier, sick and suffering from a fear of fags, wanted the best for his son. It's just that the "best" is a rather relative term and such subtlety doesn't always get through to a military mind. He must have suffered, too, through the whole ordeal. As strange as it may sound, Linda agrees with me about this. Although not without a certain bitterness.

"Things don't always get through to other minds, either," she says, "which are supposed to be more intelligent."

In any case, as a last resort, as a last-ditch effort to straighten out that wayward branch on the tree, the brigadier sent the kid into the army. Head first, at seventeen years of age, straight into an artillery squad. To see if they could reform him, to see if they could make a proper man out of him. Of course, he gave orders that he be treated with maximum rigor, without mercy, without pity. La Gofia wasn't on top of the details because her mother, God rest her soul, had died around that time after a long and terrible agony. She became totally depressed, gave up fencing, dropped out of school and everything.

---

* Man is like a wolf to mankind. Taking off on that famous Latinity, Linda proposes this version: woman is like a wolf to womankind. Let us not forget that, to her, "woman" means "human being."

Even so, she felt terrible about her friend's disgrace and she was furious with the psychopath for his malevolence. It must have been a very dark time for poor Sebastián, a kind of Middle Ages full of wicked omens.

Linda thinks differently: she feels that the wicked omens never came to pass, and that, in fact, there really wasn't any disgrace. We shall see. Supposedly, Sebastián was to spend his days doing many interesting things, including hammering mud off the tanks, mud which was already dry, petrified, and had adhered itself in chunks during nightly manéuvers or something like that. Perhaps the brigadier thought that kind of therapy could provoke a change in his sexual orientation. There are people who'll believe anything. But it turned out that the company chief needed a secretary in the office, a boy who could type. Back then, computers weren't in vogue yet. Our pretty little soldier didn't know how to type, but he did know how to write, a skill with which none of the others had any proficiency. With the hope of being saved, the great scribbler exaggerated his abilities and applied for the secretarial post. He was hired immediately, without tests or anything. So they wouldn't discover his lie and send him back to hammering off chunks of mud, the impostor practiced until the wee hours every night with tremendous zeal on an ancient Underwood that was missing a Z. "But, well, what importance can a simple Z have," Linda said. She smiled slyly when she told this part; she's so cruel. I suspect the ancient Underwood, in fact, did have a Z, why wouldn't it? Anyway, he went on like that until he learned, which took him about two weeks. Maybe he wasn't such a dummy after all. His fear of tanks didn't make him a tropical macho, but it did make him an expert typist, a very speedy one.

The company chief justified his decision to the brigadier—this is pure speculation on my friend's part—with the solid, absolute, irrefutable argument that the homeland, in its hour of need, again facing even more brutal aggression from the imperialist enemy, not only needed artillery soldiers but also company secretaries. And where would he find another, since the other recruits were a bunch of yams with a fear of typewriters? The brigadier was furious. It made him especially furious that he couldn't explain to that short-sighted officer that the miserable secretary, his son, his cursed son, was a shitty little fag who not only deserved to be out there hammering mud off tanks but to be run over by them, to be squashed like a cockroach. He wanted to ship him to Africa, with its malaria and ferocious animals and the heat of war, where Savimbi's hordes would eat him raw. But he had to keep his trap shut because there are things that are not spoken outside the home. A real man doesn't air his family's dirty laundry. He'd rather die first.

At first, this hypothesis of Linda's didn't strike me as very convincing. Why had the company chief dared to so blatantly challenge his superior? Weren't military people supposed to obey orders? Did he *really* need a secretary that badly? Or had he just gone nuts all of a sudden? Why had he done that? Why? "Precisely because he wasn't short-sighted, ha ha!" she responded, very happy to continue using her imagination. "Because he knew exactly what Sebastián was, perhaps even better than Sebastián himself. Because he had the upper hand in the matter. Because the boy was so beautiful and so naïve that it was worth it to piss off the old beast. He probably paid for it later because the brigadier wasn't the type to easily forget an affront. In a certain way, the company chief was the first victim of the Exterminating Angel's charms. So, thanks to all this and not so much to his typing, the little patriot was able to stay in the office during his three years of military service, quiet, protected, and to keep his nose clean."

When he left the army, Sebastián knew what he wanted his vocation to be: He wanted to be a hair stylist, the kind who creates works of art with women's hair. When he heard that, the brigadier lost whatever shred of patience he had left and threw him out of the house. Fuck hair styling and works of art and all that shit; that sonovabitch couldn't be his son. Although, according to La Gofia, the two of them, father and son, were physically very similar, the now-angry and traumatized brigadier, having a very serious attack of fear of fags, had begun to embrace the possibility that his first wife had cheated on him nineteen years ago with the butcher from the corner shop. He would have given anything for that to be true.

The sonovabitch took refuge in the not-yet-celebrated apartment in Centro Habana. Back then, La Gofia's grandmother was still alive and she welcomed him with open arms, all sorts of pampering, caresses, and dulce de leches. According to her granddaughter, this woman was the very personification of innocence. She didn't know squat about fags and butches and thought a blond boyfriend with light eyes had fallen out of the sky for the adventurous Ana Cecilia, a yuma† just like in the movies (the movies of her day, so a yuma like Robert Taylor, who worked with Greta Garbo in *La dame aux camélias*), presenting an unbeatable opportunity to advance the race. She even let them

---

† Cuban word for foreigner, it mostly refers to white Americans.

have her bedroom, the only one in the apartment, and went to sleep in the living room. "If it had been a black boy . . . ha ha!" laughs La Gofia. "She woulda kicked his butt back outta there." It turned out that grandma, may God rest her soul as well, was worse than the Ku Klux Klan. The adventurous Ana Cecilia and her blond boyfriend went along with her because, well, poor woman, why disappoint her? So they shared a bed for a little while. Grandma died in peace, happily convinced that she'd done her duty, while La Gofia talked about an alleged pregnancy, about a future great-grandchild who'd be white and blond, a little yuma. The day after her death, Robert Taylor went to sleep in the living room.

It's not that La Gofia didn't love him anymore. No way. It's just that sleeping with him was horrible. Sebastián's nights were filled with nightmares, probably full of terrifying monsters, vampires, ghosts and all that. Who knows. The thing is, he moaned. Howled. Moved around. Twisted the sheets into knots. Begged not to be killed. To please not be killed, Lord God in heaven, please don't kill him, that he'd be good. But he wasn't good. At least not in bed. He shoved poor Gofia, kicked her, elbowed her, kneed her. There were more than a few times she ended up on the floor from a swift kick. Later, sleeping beauty wouldn't remember a thing about his violent nighttime adventures. When she described these nocturnal incidents, he'd look at her in shock. No way. Nobody could take that. Crazy people had to sleep in the living room.

The rest of the time, living with Sebastián wasn't that bad. La Gofia got herself a girlfriend (in love and all other hellish activities, La Gofia always talks in terms of "getting"), Maribel O'Hallorans, or Mari "Jalorán," or, as they called her in the 'hood, simply Mari La Roja, Mary the Red, a dancer who in turn got La Gofia her job at the cabaret. Although she'd never set foot in a dance school and it had never occurred to her that dancing could be a job, La Gofia carried dancing inside her. I should have seen her at the fencing club, Linda told me. So light on her feet. So graceful. She seemed to be in so many places at once. She used the foil as if it were an orchestra conductor's baton. She smiled as she did it. She fenced, in fact, like a knight from the court of Versailles. If there had been a prize for elegance in fencing, as there is in horsemanship, nobody in the world would have been more deserving than La Gofia.

I was going to say that our planet might be too big for that. Not to bring down La Gofia, whom I respect and admire, but to help Linda out a bit, because Alix (we can't forget Alix, quiet but present) had made quite a face when she heard the praise that Linda had so lavishly heaped on the *other one*.

But it wasn't necessary. Linda cleaned up after herself. She said that when it came to fencing, she preferred a more medieval style, which was simpler, more brutal, wilder, and consisted of holding a sword with two hands and swinging it left and right, sorta like Joan of Arc. Still concerned, Alix asked who that Joan was. Laughing her head off, my friend explained that that Joan was the national hero of France—that's how she said it, "hero"—a real gutsy girl who, though it was true that she, Linda, would have loved to meet her in person, it wasn't possible because that Joan had been burned at the stake a bunch of years ago.

Alix sighed with relief and my friend went back to telling the story from the point when La Gofia had begun to work in the cabaret and was earning money, not much, but enough to support herself and Sebastián. Not that he was a good for nothing, she said to clarify, because he took care of the household chores with commendable meticulousness. He cooked, he ran errands, he did the laundry for La Gofia, and kept everything neat and clean. He was a sweetheart of a boy. He still dreamt of being a hairstylist, but he wasn't ready to actually make an effort to achieve it, perhaps because deep down he didn't believe in his own talents. In the hope that God himself would make him a hairstylist, he had put his entire destiny in His hands. In the meantime, La Gofia, a little alarmed, allowed him to experiment with her. How brave. She told herself—to convince herself and not flee—that, at the end of the day, a bad cut doesn't look so terrible on curly hair. The cut with the three pigtails, green like a parakeet on the left, red like mamey on the right, and yellow like a baby chick in the middle, was Sebastián's idea. Very elegant. Exquisite. Super cool. There was no question that the amateur hairstylist had very good taste. And also a lot of lovers. A whole troop of guys who, for some strange reason La Gofia could never understand, always ended up in fits of jealousy, incensed, behaving like animals, and wanting to kill the Exterminating Angel. Every now and again, they'd beat the crap out of him. Or tried to strangle him. Anyone would have thought that Sebastián's real destiny was not to be a hairstylist but to be beaten up. That unhappy man didn't even complain. Since La Gofia couldn't fight the whole battery of lunatics, she forbade him from having them over to the little apartment.

To reinforce the ban, Mary the Red put up a sign on the door that said, "No Men or Other Smelly Animals Allowed." Of course, this caused a scandal in the neighborhood. What audacity. What boldness. What depravity. What a bunch of shameless dykes. Someone had better call the cops to have them arrested. For exhibitionism. For being degenerates. For being disgusting. Because there were normal, decent families with kids and everything in that building and all around. Oh, things got hot. And how. The decent families tore apart the audacious little sign. And if they didn't rip the girls apart too, Linda explained, it was because they were both tough as nails, gators, fighters, the kind who dare you to come at them bare-fisted. The kind who do as they please, give orders, and are always on top. They're the type who eat soup with a fork. In spite of the gossip, the suspicions of the old snoop who was head of the CDR and the other busybodies who congregated on the corner and in line for the newspaper, La Gofia was fascinated by Mary the Red's initiative. And so, with that explicit declaration, the era of the women-only parties began. Of course, not excluding Sebastián. It was a time of piercing jam sessions, scandalous dykes, commotion, chaos, and all-night noise once a week. The upstairs neighbor, the one who complained the night of the birthday party, was screwed. He wasn't able to sleep a wink ever again.

To get into La Gofia's events it wasn't imperative to know anyone or to show a passport or any kind of credential. It was enough to just be of the female sex. Or at least to be trying to be, since drag queens were allowed. Although, to be honest, there were never many of those. The cover charge was ten pesos. In other words, a pittance, a sign of good faith, something to help cover costs since the host and her partner couldn't provide everything for free. In-kind contributions were also accepted: a bottle of rum, a pack or two of cigarettes, marijuana, even a chocolate cake. Of course, none of this was legal. Even with homosexuality decriminalized and the idea that no one could prove a fee wasn't a gift, there were still troubles with the police, in fact with the district chief. There were already a hell of a lot of problems in that area, he must have thought, to have to deal with a bunch of crazy dykes who were always causing a ruckus. So La Gofia and Mary the Red had to put up with insults, threats, warnings, a couple of fines; in fact they were arrested once and accused of . . . Linda paused strategically in her storytelling. They were accused of disturbing the peace. Whaaat? What had my little antenna ears just heard? The peace of Centro Habana? I started to laugh, though Linda didn't think there was anything funny about the situation. I think it might not have been a bad idea to invite that district chief, who so loved peace and quiet, to come over for a little visit to Happy Hammer Corners sometime. He would have to bring a van or two to carry away everyone who was disturbing the peace, starting with the megatherium.

They persevered. They were careful never to talk about politics, no matter how much they were baited. Not only because they weren't the least bit interested in politics but because they thought it was a topic more appropriate to men and other smelly animals, and because a party that's open to everyone is also open to *anyone*. There's always somebody watching and the walls hear everything. It's not that talking about politics was prohibited in the general sense. Not at all and not everywhere. From what I recall, even in the most difficult of times, just before the collapse of the Soviet Union, my dad and Father Ignacio would spend hours on end talking shit about the government. Sometimes my great-uncle W., the marquis's son, would join them and include Uranus, and sometimes Saturn too, in the diatribes. And nothing ever happened. Of course, they were three completely insignificant insects who aspired to nothing at all. Who cared what they said? But in the case of La Gofia, Mary the Red, and the other girls who had started to join the party gang, it was different because the district chief, who probably didn't care about politics either, was looking for an excuse to catch them at something and put an end to the revelry. To be able to accuse them of being conspirators, subversives, enemy agents, to be able to finger them in any way, would have been a nice little treat. Whatta party pooper.

"But he didn't get far in his quest," Linda said, smiling with satisfaction. "He couldn't take them. The news ran all over town and soon the little apartment became quite celebrated. Downtown girls came, as well as girls from the most remote neighborhoods. Sometimes they didn't all fit and the merrymaking would spill out to the hallways, then the stairs, even the streets. And it wasn't because Havana was the lesbian capital of the world," explained my friend. "Ha, ha! It was because there, in La Gofia's apartment, a place of tolerance had been allowed to evolve. It was a place where you could freely express feelings and desires which were usually hidden or repressed. It was a place to get to know one another and maybe even find a lover. An island within the island."

Things came to a head with a visit from a famous German actress whose name Linda told me but which I'd rather keep to myself, because she really is very famous and I don't know if she lets on in public about her adventures on the deepest, darkest side of Havana. The fact is that this woman's attendance, in the company of her Cuban lover, and the generosity with which she paid for two whole parties out of her own pocket, made the little apartment famous on the entire archipelago; it's what made it so celebrated. The decent families in the neighborhood had no choice but to get used to it.

One evening, a little before the festivities got started, Mary the Red showed up with her adolescent sister, who wasn't a lesbian and never would be, but who was very bored and had a right to some fun too, the poor girl. La Gofia welcomed her the same way she welcomed me years later, very warmly and with sufficient tact to avoid misunderstandings. The younger "Jalorán," Mari la Rojita, Little Mary the Red, or Marilú, when you got right down to it, looked a lot like her older sister. Not only did she have crimson hair, shiny, super red, fiery as is typical of the daughters of Changó, the red orisha (or Mars, the scarlet planet, as my great-uncle W., the marquis's son, would say), she was also just as vivacious, enthusiastic, and passionate about everything. She was one of those girls who are very clear about their objectives and very optimistic, who always achieve what they propose, who will climb Mt. Everest if the object of their desire is up there, and who very naturally assume they'll go through life without ever experiencing failure. "Today's Marilú, the one we saw in the terry cloth kimono announcing the arrival—or actually, *the return*—of the angel," Linda said, "is in ruins, detritus, an empty shell. She isn't even a shadow of her former self." That other one—the clear and optimistic one—found herself instantly entertained at her sister-in-law's: she fell in love with Sebastián. It was that simple. A sudden piercing of Cupid's arrow. Love at first sight. A ray of light.

At this point in the story, Alix gave Linda a crazy look, perhaps to show her that she felt the same for her as Marilú had felt for Sebastián.

Our little friend, gentle and peaceful, incapable of killing a fly, had always gotten along well with women. He awakened their maternal instincts or something. He was so helpless, so affable, so docile that everybody spoiled him. He was a mascot to all those scandalous dykes. But fall in love with him? That had never happened. La Gofia thought it was a great joke, the year's best. That little redheaded girl was kidding, right? But no. Marilú wasn't kidding. Oh, no? Couldn't she see that he was gay, absolutely and completely gay? Yes, of course, but that didn't matter one bit. It was probably because of his lack of experience. She would see to it that he saw other horizons. In other words, she got it in her head to hunt down Sebastián, domesticate him, and keep him for herself. Because. Because that's what she wanted, period. Because she liked challenges. The more challenging, the better. Nobody and nothing could get her to see the difference between challenging and impossible.

From that point on, Marilú never missed a party at La Gofia's. Not satisfied with that, she visited the little apartment everyday. She'd show up in the morning, in the afternoon, in the evening, in the wee hours, at any and every hour, always looking for her much-adored source of torment. If for some inconceivable reason (say, school) she couldn't come by, she'd call on the phone and go on and on about how love forgives everything, believes in everything, waits for everything, and understands everything. "Oh my God, could she talk—ha ha!" said Linda, who was mightily entertained by it all, although she did ask with some concern if it wasn't a little sacrilegious to use St. Paul's epistles for these kinds of things. "Although, if truth be told, all that really does sound rather romantic," she added. Mary the Red came to the conclusion that her little sister was a few tiles short of a roof, poor girl. It was adolescent dementia. The lunacy that hits at sixteen. Nothing too serious. The madness would pass. La Gofia also subscribed to this theory.

And Sebastián? At first, the adored source of torment was perplexed and a little frightened when he found himself being pursued with so many sighs, insinuations, beautiful words, plunging necklines, and mini-skirts. Whatta novelty. Men and other smelly animals usually went after him with a convulsive mix of pleadings and threats; sometimes they offered him money (which he'd take to buy things for La Gofia, such as a dress or a pair of earrings), all very out in the open, pure and hard, direct and to the point. But he didn't try to run away from Mari or ever treat her badly. Mischievously, he took advantage of the situation to try his eccentric hairstyling on that beautiful red hair that was handed to him without the slightest hesitation. Lucky him. He'd been yearning for the older sister's hair for a good long while but she—so selfish, such a tease, such a hustler—had refused to let him touch it. Now he had an opportunity to barter. In exchange for a few rather mediocre, lackluster, and insipid kisses, Sebastián gave Marilú dozens of 'dos, each one more schizoid than the one before it.

In the meantime, the brigadier didn't want to know anything about that good-for-nothing. As far as he was concerned, the boy could rot in the fifth circle of hell. What he couldn't avoid were the rumors about his mad life catching up to him. Somebody told him that Sebastián was a pimp living in Centro Habana, in a terrible neighborhood, practically marginal, supported by a mulatta who worked at a cabaret, who treated him as if he were the Prince of Wales. That he always had the house, or more precisely, the den of inequity, filled with women. White, black, mulatto, Asian, most young, some very beautiful, and all just for him. That he organized amazing orgies once a week. Totally out in the open, utterly without shame. That they called him the Exterminating Angel, no doubt because he had such a strong hand with the whores, because he kept them in line, because, by all accounts, he had them very tightly controlled. That even that girl, the German actress, had fallen into his trap and was giving him money left and right. That his favorite, the brothel's star, was a redhead with a rather extravagant hairdo who looked something like an urchin with blue locks, and who appeared to be underage. That this life of his, like a maharaja, didn't portend good things, and that he could end up in jail for vagrancy, pimping, or corrupting minors.

I can just imagine the brigadier's face. Were they making fun of him, of the family's black sheep? Or had they confused his shameless son for an s.o.b. of a different sort? How long was he going to have to suffer on account of his first wife's infidelities with the butcher from the corner shop? What a nightmare with that damned kid. He decided to go see him for himself, so he could know for sure what was going on and not have to put up with one more story. So one beautiful spring day, without warning, he took a little drive to Centro Habana. He left his driver on the dirty and potholed street to make sure the antenna or the rearview mirror or the car itself didn't get stolen. When she told this part, Linda gave me a suspicious look, but I pretended I didn't notice. Anyway, he went right over to the den of inequity. At that time of day, around eleven, the mulatta cabaret dancer was painting her toenails black with sparkles, the Prince of Wales was daydreaming, and the star of the brothel, sitting on the Prince's knees, was eating a banana. They were all in the living room, getting a little air from the open door. The brigadier watched them from the threshold. They looked so happy!

When he saw his father, Sebastián exclaimed "Oh my God!" turned pale, and began to tremble. His heart wanted to beat out of his chest and he almost had a stroke. Frightened, not so much by the incredible presence of a military man at the door but rather by the effect it was having on Sebastián, Marilú threw the banana peel out the window—my friend likes to imagine that the peel fell on the driver's head and the black kids on the block laughed because they thought it was so funny—then turned to her adored source of torment and hugged him tight. La Gofia didn't know whether to greet the intruder or not, because she knew who he was by sight but he didn't know her. The brigadier didn't give her time to decide. Looking disgusted, he took in the spectacle of his son—or more precisely, the butcher's son—hiding and trembling behind a girl, and he ordered him to come down. Yes, to come down to the car immediately. Because they were going to have a very serious conversation, man to man. Well, more like man to pansy. He half turned and walked away. Like an automaton come to life, Sebastián pushed Marilú aside and followed the brigadier. La Gofia had to hold the girl so that she, in turn, wouldn't follow the automaton. "It's his father, girlee, it's his father. Don't go getting mixed up in that." In the tussle, her black and sparkle toe polish got smeared; a real tragedy.

A couple of hours later, a very happy Sebastián returned: his charming father hadn't beaten the crap out of him this time. Whatta miracle. He could barely believe it. But it was true. More than serious, the man-to-pansy chat had been transcendental. Definitive. A great success. The brigadier didn't give a damn about Sebastián's private life. He didn't want to know anything. It didn't matter to him if he was a fag, a pimp, or a cosmonaut. But no way his son was going to live in that neighborhood, surrounded by so many bad elements. It was imperative to keep up appearances, to protect his public image—the brigadier sighed at this point—whatever was left of it. Since Sebastián didn't have a problem living with women, he might as well get married, right? Like normal people. Or was that too much to ask? If he'd marry the redhead, he'd get them an apartment in Miramar. With everything, of course. And a honeymoon in Varadero. And the moon itself, if it were necessary. Why the redhead? Well, yes, the mulatto was the better woman, much, much better, but even from a distance you could see she had a slutty face. (The brigadier's comment offended both Marilú and La Gofia. The poor guy must not have been very charismatic, even though I imagine him as attractive, especially in the uniform. But I wouldn't confess this to Linda. No way.) And so? Yes or no? Sebastián didn't even need three seconds to decide. There, in the blink of an eye, without consulting anyone, not his pillow or his future wife, he promised he'd get married. When she heard the news, Marilú jumped up and down with joy and covered him with kisses while La Gofia, stunned, let out a whistle.

"Wow," she said, "the termites have really done a job on the piano now."

The bride's mother didn't object. This Sebastián character didn't strike her as the best of all possible sons-in-law, but whatever. She took things calmly, very philosophically, so that she wouldn't get a spike in her blood pressure. Since the death of Old Man O'Hallorans, she'd lost all hope of controlling her redheads. Both were stubborn, capricious, rebellious, just like their old man and their Irish ancestors. If the older one was a lesbian, what was so strange about the younger one marrying a fag? And, anyway, what could possibly happen to her? Nothing. Luckily, there was always divorce.

The wedding wasn't very spectacular. Only about three hundred guests at the brigadier's home, not taking into account those wandering around the pool and the garden, but enough so that everyone would know about the return of the prodigal son and his marriage to that girl who was so in love with him. So everyone could see there was no trick, no pretending. So that the old rumors could die. Because if there was something of which there was no doubt whatsoever, it was Marilú's feelings; she was happy and silly in her white dress and never took her eyes off Sebastián—this came to us through Mary the Red, because La Gofia didn't go to the wedding. Like a bunny after a carrot, she followed him everywhere. She behaved so naïvely, so childlike, that even the most skeptical realized she wasn't faking it. She didn't care about the apartment in Miramar or the honeymoon in Varadero. Not even about the moon itself. She was marrying for love, convinced that her flamboyant husband would eventually fall in love with her. And of course he would. Because love forgives everything, believes in everything, waits for everything, and puts up with everything.

The irony of the situation was that Sebastián was also marrying for love, the writer told us. Not toward Marilú, who, at this point, must have been boring him with her clinginess, but toward the brigadier. He'd let him down so terribly, he'd been such a bad son, that guilt was eating him up. Thus the nightmares, the tremors day and night, his inability to complete any task. Now, for the first time in his life, he'd been given an opportunity to please him, to get his approval, to do right by that implacable being who was such an all-powerful judge. How could he not take advantage of it? He wasn't interested either, not in the least, in the apartment or the honeymoon. The moon, maybe a little. Because the moon, so far, so out of reach, seemed so much like the love the brigadier had for him. He would have married anybody, even a monkey, and would have lived anywhere, even in the sewer, so long as the brigadier accepted him. He married convinced that his dad would finally love him. Because love . . . well, we all know.

This whole guilt thing sounded familiar to me, but I didn't quite understand. Guilty of what, dear Lord? The only thing the poor boy had done, for better or worse, was simply exist. I asked Linda if, in Sebastián's place, she would have gotten married. She said no, under no circumstances. Or at least . . . —she thought about it a bit—not with someone like Marilú. That marriage was doomed to failure from the very beginning. But she understood Sebastián. Yes, because it was a fucked place to be to have all of society against you, and worse, to be in the orbit of an influential person who was also stubborn, lacking in scruples, and something of a blackmailer. And to top it off, his father. To be able to face up to that, you also had to be strong, very strong, and even so . . . what a tough spot to be in. All of us, or most of us, would like to be loved by our parents, to count on their support—Linda's voice cracked just a little bit when she said this—what we needed to know was the price we had to pay, and then what we were willing to pay. Sebastián had made a mistake in his calculations. His marriage lasted a year. And it was a year from hell.

It was also bad for La Gofia. Around that time, her girlfriend's health was quickly getting worse. Although Mary the Red hardly ever went out during the day, and when she did, always wearing a sun hat, long sleeves, and dark glasses, the sun's rays had already done their secret and insidious work on her frail skin. It's possible she may have had a genetic predisposition toward that disaster, since Old Man O'Hallorans had been devoured by the sun's rays. It may seem like an exaggeration but it isn't. The tropical sun, the "Indian," is a sonovabitch, a ruffian, a ball of fire, a killer sun that splits rocks, melts asphalt (whoever's a non-believer should come and look at the tire tracks, which look beautiful), and demands a certain number of redheads every year. La Gofia was terrified. Was she gonna have to sit through another long and terrible agony? Was her life gonna be this shithole in which every time she loved somebody the crab—she didn't even dare pronounce the word "cancer"—would show up and destroy everything? What a farce, this life. Mary the Red went through several procedures in a few months' time. They didn't find anything, but the prognosis was still cautious. What was benign could turn malignant in an instant. The only possibility of salvation was to escape from the "Indian," to leave it behind definitively. La Gofia got in touch with the German actress, who moved heaven and earth to finally get the Red Cross to get Mary the Red and her mother out of Cuba and send them to a place called Vancouver. They're still there, the both of them, thank God.

Sebastián and Marilú's problem, because living together had quickly become very tricky for them, went unnoticed by the rest of the family during this hustle and bustle. While they helped Mary the Red in whatever they could, because when it came to this the spouses were on their best behavior, they didn't seem to be discordant and much less embroiled in a kind of civil war. So imagine La Gofia's surprise when, one week after her girlfriend and mother-in-law's departure, Marilú showed up in the celebrated little apartment, wracked with sobs, and wanting to *kill* that miserable, disgusting, idiotic, ungrateful flaming fag. Unable to respond to a single concrete question, the young wife just kept saying the same thing over and over again, so La Gofia wasn't able to get anything out of her. At least nothing that she didn't already know: that Sebastian slept with four hundred thousand million guys and that many of them became fixated on him. That very afternoon, one of them had called on the phone and when he heard a female voice, asked who it was. Marilú had responded: "I'm Sebastián's *wife*. And you? Who are you?" And the guy had said: "His wife, huh? Ha ha! How cute. Nice to meet you, girlee. I'm Sebastián's husband." With that kind of thing day after day, Marilú had begun to lose her self-control. La Gofia took her side on everything, made her some chamomile tea, and put her to bed. What else could she do? At this point in the story, just one step from catastrophe, is where *Nocturne Sebastián* begins.

That magnificent novel has been read by many people all over the world. Of course, my friend writes much better than me. It doesn't make any sense for me to repeat point by point what she already wrote. For those who haven't read *Nocturne Sebastián*, and I recommend it from the bottom of my heart (although I respect their right not to read it if they don't feel like it), here's a brief summary of the fundamental facts.

When she woke up from her chamomile sleep the next morning, Marilú (Sandra in the novel) was much more clear-headed. She hated her husband because her love, so intense and without release, had rotted inside her. But she wasn't going to give him up just like that. No way. She left determined to battle, if it was necessary, all the butch fags in Havana. A little later, La Gofia (Zoe in the novel) got a call from her. There was crying, panic, and hysteria all over again. Except now something serious had really happened. When she got to the apartment in Miramar, Marilú had found the door completely open and then, in the living room, Sebastián's body. He was naked, with his hands cuffed behind his back, a clear plastic bag over his head and his light eyes open wide in horror. That was the summer of 1995.

La Gofia was speechless. Marilú's screams thundered in her head, everything around her seemed to teeter and collide as if they were in an earthquake. She would have preferred to have never answered the phone, to convince herself she'd never heard those words, that it was a joke, a very sick joke. But she couldn't abandon Marilú in a crisis. Something wouldn't let her, and in her place I'd have done the same thing. Somehow, she managed to get her voice back and told her not to touch anything. To get out of there immediately. To find a neighbor and, together, call the cops. For once, Marilú obeyed.

The preliminary investigation revealed the following facts: no window or door had been forced, which would have been difficult anyway since they all had bars; nothing of value was missing, neither the art nouveau lamps, the Sèvres porcelain china, nor the Japanese appliances. In fact, nothing at all had been taken: approximately five hundred dollars were found in the first drawer of a little night table; a Swiss watch was still on the deceased's left wrist, and around his neck there was also a thick chain, gold as well, with a medallion of the Virgin of Charity. Not counting the deceased and his wife, there were a bunch of fingerprints all over the place. Not surprisingly, the autopsy revealed asphyxiation as the cause of death. And also that the deceased had had sex (anal coitus) shortly before, or perhaps *during*, his murder. There was another man's semen inside him. This last detail comes entirely from Linda's tender imagination and later disappeared, all by itself, ever so mysteriously, from the report.

It didn't take a genius, like Lt. Leví, to discard robbery as a motive. Or to assume that Sebastián Loredo (because Lt. Leví didn't like that business of "the deceased," he thought the murder victims he investigated weren't things or numbers on a statistical chart but persons with first and last names) was acquainted with, even if just by sight, the mysterious visitor who'd entered the apartment without breaking a single lock. Or to consider the possibility of a crime of passion or, maybe, an accident resulting from a sadomasochistic practice gone awry—I shuddered at this thought, because my mind went to Moisés. Sebastián's address book had dozens of men's phone numbers which, along with the fingerprints and the autopsy report—the semen would help with determining blood type or something like that—was enough to start the investigation. But everything was left there. After a few false starts, especially because many of the guys were important men, both civil and military, and some had wives and children and public images to keep up, the case was filed away. And that was it. So why was a miserable little big-nosed lieutenant, a Zionist rat, going around poking into the private lives of his colleagues?

Not even the brigadier wanted to help with the investigation. He treated Lt. Leví as if he wasn't a detective but a gossip, a meddler, a piece of shit. He pretty much scraped him off his shoe. At the wake and then later at the burial, which were attended by far fewer people than the wedding, he seemed impatient with the little widow's cries. "Be quiet, my dear, be quiet already. Why don't you go lay down, eh? Go on, go on, I'll take care of this." He seemed indignant. Not with the unknown killer but with the deceased. The bastard.

The loathsome bastard. That shameless son of his, for whom it wasn't enough to ruin his reputation in life, now said his farewell with this repugnant dirty trick. A plastic bag on his head! What a barbarity! The brigadier was enraged with the fag.

Even though she was on the edge of a nervous breakdown, the little widow cooperated in every way she could with the investigation. In the midst of her madness, Marilú had confused her hate and desire to kill with the actual fact of committing the crime. In a convoluted and dark way, she felt guilty about Sebastián's death. A few years ago, this really amazed me; not anymore. In the last few years, I've discovered that the agonizing substance that is guilt is almost infinite, and that there are many ways of accessing it, some quite outlandish. For Marilú, it was very important that the real killer be found. Only that could have saved her from total darkness.

In the novel, Lt. Leví manages to identify the killer after some complicated maneuvers, but not to catch him. It ends the same as always, with him out on the penthouse terrace, depressed, smoking and thinking about the utopia inherent next year in Jerusalem. Sandra, the little widow, turns out all right, if a little worse for wear; the detective makes sure that she knows the truth. In real life, Marilú gave the apartment back to the brigadier. She couldn't live there anymore, just *couldn't*, and she moved in with La Gofia. She spent about a year in anguish, chasing after the official in charge of the case. Did they have new information? Why was it taking so long? When would they have something to tell her? La Gofia tried to dissuade her. "Let it go, girlee, let it go or you'll go nuts. What happened, happened. If they catch the sonovabitch who did it, it's not going to give Sebastián back his life . . ." But to no avail. Marilú persisted. And persisted. And persisted. Until the detective, feeling cornered and very tense, lost it and told her point blank that she was their only suspect. He didn't actually mean it, of course; he only said it to get her off his back, and so she'd leave him alone. But for the girl, this was the final drop, what made the cup spill over. She went completely crazy. She shaved her head and her eyebrows. She cut her eyelashes with a manicure scissors. She tried to kill herself three times, and that she didn't accomplish it is entirely because of La Gofia, who took care of her and kept her in the little celebrated apartment while she went through the process of getting the necessary papers to send her to Vancouver to be with her sister and mother. Not long ago, poor Marilú, daffy as a duck, finally left Cuba. It's possible that filming will begin very soon on a movie based on *Nocturne Sebastián*.

Chapter 10

Shots on the twentieth floor

THAT ALIX WAS JEALOUS OF LA GOFIA MADE CERTAIN SENSE, SINCE Linda and her ex continued to be very good friends. They still are. *Nocturne Sebastián* is dedicated to "Ana Cecilia Ramos, the most generous of all women," which strikes me as completely fair, since when you come right down to it, it was she who told the writer the story. But Alix didn't understand. Well, not this or anything else. She was also jealous of me. Although Linda explained seventy thousand times that I didn't play that game, that I wasn't queer even by accident, the girl with the black hair couldn't stand me. She couldn't even look at me. I'd barely pop on the horizon and she'd curl up and make faces. She was especially bothered that *Next Year in Jerusalem* was dedicated to "Z Álvarez, my best friend." She thought—it's possible that "thought" might not be the best word when it comes to Alix—that the fact that I didn't sleep with women (supposing it was true, because she wasn't sure) wasn't especially important. In her mind, I could reconsider the matter at any moment. And then, of course, try to take Linda away from her.

La Gofia made fun of her. She entertained herself getting Alix pissed off. She called her Alix Oyster. Because if oysters *never* talked, it wasn't out of discretion or timidity, no. According to La Gofia, these silences were due to the fact that they had nothing to say. It was due to the oyster's own crass imbecility. Who'd ever seen such a dumb hick—she'd make this "serious hick" look when she was saying things to her face—or a more yam-like peasant from the middle of nowhere studying at the university? Ha ha! How pretentious. Because if that stupid Russian collective farmer were to fall on all fours, it's very likely she'd take to the grass just like a mule. Or to the dirt itself. Ha ha! So simple, so very worthy of her hometown in Pinar del Río, it was probable she didn't even know how to read. Let's see, girlee, what's two plus two? Ha ha! This attitude didn't strike me as particularly generous, especially coming from the most generous of all women, but whatever, nobody's perfect. I didn't play along because I felt sorry for Alix. It wasn't her fault, poor girl, that she'd been born in the hills. I never gave her a hard time. I think I only stuck my tongue out at her two or three times. But that girl with the black hair looked at us both with hatred, and then took her complaints to Linda. So that she'd scold us, I suppose. As if my friend were the teacher and La Gofia and I a pair of naughty girls.

Linda didn't scold us. She even liked La Gofia's theory of oysters. "Hey, that's what I call anthropomorphic, that's what." She didn't take it seriously. She told Alix not to be such a dud, not to let herself be so easily provoked. Didn't she realize we were jealous of her? Yes, *jea-lous*. In fact, though Alix wasn't precisely pretty, she was very attractive, like a basketball player, a tall woman of about one meter eighty in height who left guys breathless out in the streets. This was true. But not the part about the jealousy. The part about the guys on the streets, yes. They couldn't take their eyes off her, they screamed, honked the horns on their cars, motorcycles, and bikes. Alix stopped traffic and Linda felt glorious, because she likes it when guys find her girlfriends attractive, when they drool over her. Especially because they can't have her. There was a smartass once who propositioned Alix, pinched her butt, I think, and . . . the girl with the black hair nailed him so hard, she swept the floor with him like Muhammad Ali. Bam! A right to the chin and a knockout. I can't even describe my friend's glee. That was her girl!

But Alix didn't see any advantages to her physique. In fact, I think at first she was a little insecure. When it came right down to it, she complained, what good did her size do her? It only drew unwanted attention, caused all sorts of problems . . . Linda wasn't too clear about what was important to Alix. She told her that Agatha Christie, the real writer, was over six feet tall (about one meter eighty, but the English don't use the metric system and so they have be measured in feet and inches), was a huge helluva woman, but that didn't keep her from being the most read author in the world, the most famous of all time, and, to top it off, happy. Alix contemplated the matter for several weeks. Then she went back to her gloom. She didn't want to be famous or a writer or anything. She wanted Linda. And she wanted La Gofia and me to leave her in peace. If at all possible, to never see us again. Only that would make her a happy person.

Oh, so that's what was important. How sweet. Very well then. My friend then talked to her about a well-known feminine archetype which, according to her, is known as The Writer's Lover. The favorite. The companion. The muse. For example, Thelma Wood. She couldn't sing or eat fruit, was utterly useless, a total disaster, but she was Djuna Barnes's great love. She inspired one of the most splendid novels of the twentieth century, *Nightwood*, and she was a very tall woman, really tall, even taller than Agatha Christie. And, of course, very beautiful. There was a photo in the bedroom. But those names meant nothing to the girl with the black hair. Neither did the photo. And so she was furious. She had a helluva fit (something which, I suppose, an oyster would never do). Fuck her height. Please, she needed Linda to stop talking to her about such weird people. She needed her to put her feet on the ground. Because that slippery slut and the sardonic fat girl both looked at her, at Alix, as if she were some strange creature. We called her Oyster and illiterate and a yam and a Russian collective farmer and a mess of other horrible things. We stuck our tongues out at her—and then she stuck out her own tongue so Linda could see the extremes we'd go to in our depravities. She needed to get rid of us once and for all because we were completely unnecessary.

"Them or me," was the ultimatum.

Explanations were fruitless. Alix stood her ground. Her or us. Like that, stubborn. For the first time in her life, Linda felt that she might be losing control, that the situation was slipping out of her hands. She was nuts about Alix, yes, absolutely, crazy in love like she'd never been before and, according to her, like she'd never be again. But she can't stand blackmail, or threats, or terrorism. She can't stand it when somebody, anybody, tries to exercise power over her to make her go against her own wishes. Since I know her so well, I'm certain my friend is one of those people who, when confronted by the mafia, any mafia, with one of those propositions you can't refuse, they refuse. Even if it intrigues them, even if they find it interesting, useful, or advantageous, they still refuse. And if they get killed, which is frequently the mafia's response, it doesn't matter. Life isn't worth living once you've bowed your head. According to Mario Puzo's definition, my friend is Sicilian. Or, as Yadelis used to say, a real prick. Some people find that behavior kinda stupid. But I think it's admirable.

I found out about the ultimatum just recently. Back then, Linda didn't say a word. At the time, our friendship was in crisis. It was a passing thing, but a crisis nonetheless. And not because of Alix, but because of Moisés. As I've already mentioned, she was furious when she found out he beat me. And she didn't even know the half of it, really. To this day, she doesn't realize I'm half deaf in my left ear. Her dismay grew and grew as she came to understand, little by little, and almost purely intuitively, that I would *never* leave Moisés. And I never did. I couldn't say for sure what tied me to that man. But I know it was something powerful, very powerful. Something which I couldn't (and perhaps didn't want to) fight. It was circumstances, horrible circumstances, which finally separated us.

When she returned from Germany, from the Frankfurt Fair, and after a few weeks in Havana in which she'd barely talked to me, she came to see me at Happy Hammer Corners. During her last tempestuous visit, she'd swept the floor with me. She'd said that I was an imbecile, that the victim . . . that women in Islamic countries . . . She'd treated me very badly, almost with the same disrespect as Moisés, as if I were a cockroach or something like that. The worst part is that I love her very much, more than anyone else. And I take her opinions to heart, so I *felt* like a cockroach. Not angry, just sad. A sad cockroach. How pathetic. I didn't know what to do to win her back, to make everything go back to how it used to be. And then she showed up again. Just like that, as if nothing had ever happened. She'd bought me a huge box of chocolates, very extravagant (which I shared with Leidi Hamilton, but not with Pancholo, my little soul mate, because he thinks chocolates are childish and a waste of time), and a bottle of Domecq. Oh, and a surprise. A black dress, a long dress down to my ankles, super elegant, a gift from "a certain someone."

If she hadn't told me who, I would have never guessed. That certain someone and Linda had seen each other in Berlin. That certain someone was still very much a rogue. Single and uncommitted, he had a bunch of women friends of many nationalities, all very democratic. He studied eight hours a day. He'd left the Tel Aviv Symphony to embark on a solo career. He liked to take risks. He'd refused to do military service in Israel. Conscientious objector or some such thing. And also, things were messed up. Same as always, ups and downs, but messed up nonetheless. He liked to take risks but not big risks. He couldn't imagine himself shooting at anybody. Things had been going well for him so far and they'd certainly get even better soon. He was earning a lot of money and making plans to move to New York. He'd started acting a little crazy, like an unbalanced genius; he was popping a string on his violin at each concert, same as that ugly man, Isaac Stern, used to do way back when. "That was sheer bullshit," a certain someone said, "but the public loved it, especially the Americans, who got up and started screaming right away. Heh heh!" He remembered me, of course. Not everybody would let him hold them twenty stories off the ground. Oh, little Z. A very easygoing girl, a lot of fun, with a very peculiar sense of humor and a helluva . . . ah, no, never mind. And speaking of me, he'd always wondered how I put up with his charming little sister.

I was happy to hear all this, I really was. And even happier that Félix's charming little sister should come to apologize, even if it was indirectly. That's how she is, very proud, and there's no need to push the issue. "There are things beyond understanding," she said. Or maybe not. Maybe she *didn't want* to understand. Because, seriously, if you actually think about it long and hard, human behavior, no matter how outlandish or criminal it might seem, always ends up getting rationalized in some way. Of course. Human beings, for better or for worse, encompass all that's both good and evil. Even the biggest sonzabitches, she insisted, have their reasons. That's why it's unnecessary to listen to them. So be it. As far as she was concerned, any man who regularly hit a woman deserves to be castrated. End of story. There are no mitigating factors and nothing to understand. It's a matter of principle. That was her thinking—she banged the table with her fist—and she didn't want to think any other way.

I didn't share her opinion. Maybe it was because of Father Ignacio's influence, or because of my own nature as a relatively easygoing girl, I dunno, but I thought it was atrocious and uncivilized to respond to savagery with more savagery. And, in any case, even supposing there was justice in an eye for an eye and a tooth for a tooth, a man who beat up women only deserved to be beat up. It's a matter of proportion, I suppose. What I found curious in all this was that Moisés shared my friend's intransigence, her falcon-like attitude. But in other areas of interest, of course. His theme was "them." The lying, fraudulent, mendacious, cheating, hypocritical, meddling, gambling, fucking bastards. Same as always. According to him, they all deserved to die. And that was that. He didn't abide mitigating factors and didn't need to understand anything either. To the gallows with all of them. To the firing squad, guillotine, rope, electric chair, lethal injection . . . so they'd learn to be honest. As the ancient Romans used to say: *dura lex, sed lex.**

I didn't tell Linda any of this because I didn't want to upset her. I don't think she would have been at all amused by having something in common with the Caveman. I also stayed quiet, and even smiled, because I was glad to hear her promise not to interfere in my life anymore. I was free, she asserted to my great surprise, to do with myself whatever the hell I wanted. Even put up with punching, insults, and humiliations. I could take all the shit in the world I was up for. I could throw away my literary talent. Drown in obscurity. It was my choice. Yes, it was my choice, as hard as it was for her to admit. Although she wouldn't wash her hands like Pontius Pilate, she warned me, no sir, no way. If someday I changed my mind, or if things got really horrible, all I had to do was call her. A little ring and, bam, she'd come running to my rescue—she smiled—just like Superman. And, of course, I could always take refuge in her house. Friends were good for something, weren't they? I was very happy, quite moved, when I heard her. How wonderful to have a friend like that. Yet, when things got really bad, Linda had stopped speaking to me again and I didn't dare call her. But I'll talk about that later.

From that day on—I don't remember if it was the end of '98 or the beginning of '99—until a few months ago, Linda never came up to my room again so as to avoid an unfortunate meeting. Because if she'd ever actually run into the gorilla . . . ha! It would have been the San Quentin riots right there and then, for sure. He may have been big and strong but she had her ways, plus a gun (unloaded?) in her bag. She didn't stop coming to Happy Hammer Corners, but she stayed downstairs, at Pancholo's place. She didn't much like it, or the singing drunks who greeted her with "don't cry . . . / don't cry for her . . . / because she was quite the outlaw . . . / gravedigger, don't cry for her," or my buddy's quiet style, nor the whole theory about our sorry carcasses. But she didn't want to stop seeing Leidi. "Oh, that little girl, so smart," she'd sigh, "and surrounded by so many bad examples. What can the future bring her?" Not interested in the future and delighted that Aunt Linda had come to visit *her*, Leidi didn't come up either. Aunt Z was a really good person, yes, a real good egg, but Uncle Moisés was something else. So imperfect, and always with

---

* The law is tough, but it's the law.

a sour face. He didn't even wanna be called "Uncle"! Things being that way, I'd go down to hang out with them. Pancholo would let me know when they were there by screaming: "Heeeeey! Ecobiooooo! You got cooooompany!" And I'd go. Whether I was alone or had company, I'd go. Uncle Moisés never tried to keep me from going. If anything, he'd take advantage of the situation and ask me to pick up some rum or cigarettes, no hurry. He didn't give a damn about my visits.

The first crisis that Linda and I had coincided with Alix's ultimatum. In the meantime, La Gofia had met a painter who was very interested in taking her on as a model. This woman painted abstracts. All very lyrical, relaxed, smooth, like Kandinsky and *The Blue Rider*. Very pretty sketches, really excellent, according to Linda. I dunno, but I have the impression you don't really need a model for that. Yet it seems you do. She's a very sensitive, emotional, and temperamental artist, the two of them tell me. Seeing La Gofia naked served, and still serves, as inspiration. It helps her create more and better pictures. And the most generous woman of all couldn't refuse to contribute to her art. No way. She'd have felt guilty for the rest of her days. In the end, this whole business with the sensitive painter struck La Gofia as much more entertaining than bothering Alix. So La Gofia started spending time away from the penthouse. Without breaking it off with Linda, naturally.

That's how both of us, La Gofia and I, disappeared from the girl with the black hair's visual field at exactly the moment she demanded it. She must have felt very satisfied: the slippery slut and the sardonic fat girl were out of the picture, simply out, multiplied by zero, two birds with one stone. Actually, it had just happened. An incredible coincidence that allowed Linda to leap out of the fire and avoid having to make a drastic decision. But Alix believed the ultimatum had worked and, the worst part, that she had a certain power over my friend, that she could get her to do things according to her whims. Crass mistake. How could I not feel sorry for her? Why Linda didn't just tell her the truth at the time, why she didn't just put her cards on the table, which would have helped her avoid all sorts of trouble later, is something I'm still intrigued about. She was well aware of Alix's mistake but didn't move a finger to fix it. As they say, she went along with it. In her place, I would have done the same thing, of course. If the conflict had resolved itself, why run the risk of stirring it up again? But, it turns out, Linda and I are very different people. While I live day to day, attached only to the present, which so often seems to me the only way to continue living, she looks at everything long term, she projects, calculates, edifies, makes plans for the future. What had failed her this time?

No one knows, not even she knows. In her third great speech, the one about the dangerous confusion between life and literature, between the peasant girl Alix and the gypsy Heathcliff, Linda attributed her strange behavior to a madness typical of writers. It was just that—a crazy fit, a schizophrenic episode, a mental breakdown, a blackout. A delirious desire to live in the highlands of Wuthering Heights. The more insufferable Alix's behavior got toward her, the better. The more Alix seemed like Heathcliff, the more it fed her fantasies. Until Alix went too far. Until, as they say, she crossed the line. And then the dream was over. My friend loves this version. I suspect she's trying to get me to see it all in a good light for her future biography, a book which, she tells me, no one could write better than me, in about twenty years' time or something like that, when they give her the Nobel prize.

I'm convinced that, unless something unexpected happens, Linda will run away with the Nobel and force me to write her biography and say everything she wants me to say. There are some tasks that are inescapable: if you're born to make tamales, corn husks will fall from the sky. But, honestly, I can't swallow this silliness about madness. Linda Roth, crazy? No way. Even if I couldn't exactly explain why, the truth is that it just sounds false to me. A little too literary. It's true that some people have done strange things, things no one would have expected of them, and later said they were in the process of writing a book. But I don't trust those people. How can a book be so important, so determining, if at the end, all it is is just a book? Maybe the bible. I dunno. Honestly, I dunno. Right now, I have another version of the story in mind. With all due respect, I'd like to set aside *Wuthering Heights*. Linda didn't have a reason for falling in love with Alix. It just happened. Because people fall in love and there's no reason needed, no justification. Used to breaking hearts (JJ, the Puerto Rican guava, Danai, La Gofia, and who knows how many more), Linda had never been in love before. It hit her really hard. For her, Alix became someone really important. Linda didn't go through the trouble of hiding it, of protecting herself, the way people who've already been hurt tend to do. On the contrary, she was quite vulnerable. And Alix, poor girl, tried to use that to her advantage, to satisfy a caprice. Not because she was a bad person but because she was immature. Linda felt betrayed. Something inside her went "crack" and out came her dark side, her cruel and vengeful side. She let Alix get confused on purpose. Let her feel powerful. The higher the girl with the black hair flew, the harder her fall . . . Of course, this is all hypothesis. The fact is that, from the moment the ultimatum was issued, that relationship was a powder keg. The breakup was just a matter of time.

At this point in the story, as can be expected, I disappeared. Linda has told me a few of the details. Alix, nothing at all. How can I tell the rest of the tale without risking my credibility? After all, what really happened between the two of them, alone up there in the penthouse, only they really know. And God. But, in any case, God speaks even less than Alix and never gossips about other people's lives with me. What I'm about to tell is an approximation of reality. It's possible it's pretty close. But I don't dare assert that it *is* what happened.

It seems the girl with the black hair didn't take too long to make my friend the center of her world. She couldn't imagine her own existence without Linda. She needed her, or thought she needed her, like oxygen. Anywhere that Linda wasn't was an absurd place, dark and definitively uninhabitable. She tried to imitate her. Just like Leidi. It's just that Leidi's a little girl, but, also, she really does resemble Linda in certain aspects. So what was cute in my little niece (Yadelis came to visit a few months back and I think she *noticed* her daughter for the first time ever; she was so pleased—"No man is gonna step on that little black girl—she knows so many things! You can tell she takes after me!"— that I think she's planning on taking her to the mists of Malmö) seemed like a caricature in Alix. I can imagine her going on and on about the intrinsic fraud in Virginia Woolf, that hypocritical English lizard who threw herself in a river, according to Linda, because she couldn't stand herself any longer. Or about Simone de Beauvoir's political mistakes and those of the first wave of European feminism. Or how Frida Kahlo managed to capture the actual experience of physical pain in her paintings. Or . . . No. Honestly, I can't see it. I think that as soon as she opened her mouth, little Alix would have made three or four political mistakes, would have been in terrible physical pain, and wouldn't have been able to stand herself until she threw herself in a river. The Almendares. Poor girl.

But there were other, easier, ways of imitating Linda. Eating only vegetables. Listening to classical music. Exercising. Not smoking. Smiling sideways, with her mouth a little twisted. Looking over her glasses with an air of superiority . . . Well, not that, because Alix didn't wear glasses. Basically, imitating the details. But there was more to it, too. When *Nocturne Sebastián* became successful, and with that success came money, my friend stopped working as a language teacher. She was sick of the diplomats' kids and the troupe of hustlers. I wasn't surprised. She'd never had the patience to teach anybody anything, unless we're talking about a *very* intelligent disciple, like Leidi. When we were studying together at the School of Arts and Letters, she preferred to just let me cheat off her on tests than to actually explain anything to me. And the same with the Alliance Française. Obviously, I didn't graduate from there. It was too hard. I should know French, according to Linda, the same way she knows German: by osmosis, just because, because it was my mother's native tongue and that whole story. Her own ancestors are very curious. In Cuba we call them Poles, but they have nothing to do with Poland. They lived in Prague but they weren't Czech. They spoke German but they weren't German. Prague was part of the Austro-Hungarian Empire but they weren't Austrian or Hungarian. After World War I, they moved to Vienna, where they prospered until Hitler had it in for them. Some managed to escape and come here. Their descendants fled from here and went to Israel. A certain someone fled from Israel, lives in Berlin, and plans to move to New York. But back to Alix's imitations: as soon as Linda dumped her little teaching gigs, Alix dropped out of the University of Havana. Bad decision.

The girl with the black hair had never been interested in studying journalism. Or any other career. Her father had a little farm and some animals in the deepest groves of Pinar del Río. Very peaceful, very bucolic, nobody hammering or anything like that. If it had been up to her, she would have never set foot off that little farm. Since she was little, she'd cut school so she could run in the flowerbeds, pick tender flowers, catch butterflies, eat dirt, etc. But her father, a dummy from the Canary Islands, would grab her by the ear and drag her back to school. That's where progress was, the way forward, civilization. I think this dumb Canarian and Petronila would have understood each other very well. Even though he himself had never gone beyond second grade, if that, he'd forced poor Alix to study like a mule to finish high school in the countryside and then exported her here, to Havana, where yams are magically transformed into doctors or engineers. He deposited all his hopes in her and wouldn't accept failure after so much effort and sacrifice. The girl landed in journalism school like a flying saucer, by total accident. She could have studied anything at all. She didn't want to be a journalist. She didn't want to be anything. Later she realized she wanted Linda and that seemed enough. Dropping out of the University of Havana meant a complete break with her father and, of course, with her entire family. They'd never let her go back to the little farm. This is called "burning your bridges." There's no going back. You either conquer the capital, really aggressively, or you die.

If it'd been me, I'm sure Linda would have screamed to high heaven. But she didn't do anything when it came to Alix. She didn't try to convince her otherwise or make a scene or anything. She just folded her arms. Literally. Since the girl with the black hair had no manual skills and lacked the wits to hustle, and since she had no intention of working out on the street or engaging in any kind of business, my friend laid off the old half-deaf woman who helped her around the house and assigned the domestic chores to Alix. Washing, ironing, doing the dishes, cleaning the floors . . . everything. Without help. Without a single penny for her efforts. "Yup, just like that," complained the writer, "because it was time—enough of this shameless lying about." What was that lazy ass thinking? That she was gonna just lie there for all time? Was she thinking that she, Linda, was gonna pay her for . . . ? Fuck that. There was only a seven-year difference between them, so fuck that. Yes, she, Linda, supported her, bought her clothes, shoes, perfumes, basically everything, treated her like a queen, so the least that lazy ass could do was take care of the house. No work, no eats. No cauliflower, not one pickle, not one green onion, nothing. Nobody was going to live in the penthouse just hanging around. Nobody! Those were the rules of the game. And whoever didn't like it also knew where the door was. When my friend said this, in a low voice, softly, pronouncing all the letters, I already knew Alix had nowhere to go. Because when she dropped out of school, she'd also dropped out of the dorm at G Street and Malecón, where everybody went hungry and there were blackouts now and again, but where there were at least four walls and a roof. She didn't have friends who could help out in a difficult moment or the money to rent, and the rents were sky high anyway. Her options had been reduced to obeying Linda or making her bed under a bridge somewhere.

When I think about it, it seems to me the girl with the black hair didn't mind playing housewife too much. When it came right down to it, there was never a lack of water in the penthouse (to those who really know Havana, the real Havana, the deep Havana, the dry one, this seems impossible—water on the twentieth floor? What? Lies! But it's true, they always had water, lots of it, H_2O, fresh water, which my friend had spent a fortune to ensure and which required hydraulic engineering, a motor, and a cistern and everything); there was also a washer, a vacuum, a dishwasher, good detergent, deodorizers, all kinds of cleaning products—in other words, all kinds of exquisite things that you see in American films and must make the lives of homemakers so much easier. Alix got up off her easy chair and dedicated herself to keeping everything bright and shiny. But she must not have liked Linda's *tone* very much. Why was she treating her so badly? Why so much hostility? Didn't she love her anymore? I think that's about when she began to suspect that her power over my friend, if it had ever existed, had now vanished. Or was at least weakening, losing its strength. Oh. How frightening. Just thinking about it gave her the shivers. It was better to not think about it all.

But, in fact, she became obsessed. Her lover was distancing herself, slowly, surreptitiously; she was inexorably losing her and there was nothing she could do. As a result, Alix became more annoying, more insistent, more possessive. Especially because there were other people around Linda now. Editors, critics, journalists, other writers, both Cuban and foreign. Girls she'd seen before at La Gofia's parties. Folks from the fencing club. A little old man who cultivated broccoli. Jews from the synagogue. Hustlers who sold copies of movies with a lot of violence. A blind man who tuned the piano. Functionaries from the Austrian Embassy. Booksellers from Old Havana. Musicians, poets, and painters. A dentist. Crazy people who'd read her novels and wanted to ask her out for a drink, to fuck her, kill her, or tell her new and terrible stories she could write. So many others. These people appeared and disappeared spontaneously, without a schedule or appointment, and there was no way to control them. Alix, who had so stubbornly gotten rid of the slippery slut and the sardonic fat girl, couldn't quite exterminate these new pests who encroached more and more every day on her time with Linda. She was jealous of all of them. Even the little old man who cultivated broccoli. She wanted to erase them all from the map, destroy them, disintegrate them without mercy. She made faces at them, rolled her eyes, hung up on them, insisted on pressuring my friend to expel them from her life. But she didn't get anywhere. Usually so solitary and allergic to groups, now Linda even hosted those who wanted to kill her. Utterly deaf to Alix's demands, blind to any pleading or angry look, she'd demand she go boil water for tea. And there she'd go, the girl with the black hair, probably wondering what had happened to her old powers.

Some of the people hanging around didn't hide their astonishment at The Writer's Lover. What an eccentric couple. Because it was clear that, intellectually, there was an abyss between them. What did they talk about when they were alone? What the hell did Linda Roth, such an admirer of the intellect, and so wonderful, ever see in that big and obstinate imbecile, in that hick who couldn't even read her novels? (Alix not only didn't read them, she was against my friend writing them because they took up too much time and attracted all those pests.) I'm not sure exactly how these pests expressed their concerns, or to what extreme. I only know that my friend, strangely enough, wasn't offended by their comments about her private life. She didn't reproach them for their lack of decorum or manners. But she didn't defend her relationship with Alix either. She merely put on as bored a face as possible.

She assures me she was never untrue to Alix. Not because of a lack of opportunity or conviction. Of course not. She wasn't the type to repress her emotions. But she told me she'd never found anybody—here or abroad—anybody at all, who she liked as much as the girl with the black hair. This might be a lie. La Gofia, for example, doesn't believe her. "Fidelity? The Exterminating Angel? Ha ha! Man, you're gullible, girlee." According to her, my friend loves sex—La Gofia calls her "viciosa," practically addicted—a Polish outlaw, a maroon, slippery; she says nobody changes like that from one day to the next. But it could still be true. Why not? Contrary to all expectations, that's what happened to me with Moisés. Absolute fidelity. With the only difference being that Moisés didn't give a damn what I did behind his back, while Alix lived in fear that Linda would cheat on her. In fact, she was convinced my friend was sleeping with all the women she was seeing. At first, before the cursed ultimatum, Linda would say no, that it wasn't like that, that love truly transformed people. But, later, she wouldn't say anything. Why bother? If that fool wanted to worry her little head off, reasoned the writer, it was her problem. If she was so determined to suffer, why try and stop her? And so an enigmatic silence fell between them. Alix interpreted the silence as another sign of their growing alienation. Didn't Linda care what she thought anymore? How horrible. Then, in the distance, a terrible ghost appeared. The most dangerous kind, the destructive type. The one who would, just by existing, give the coup de grace to this moribund romance: N. Cohen.

Before I talk about N. Cohen, I should mention that Linda was one of the very first residents of our archipelago to connect a computer to the Internet. I'm not sure but I believe this is not entirely legal. In Cuba, I mean. Only state institutions and certain persons are "authorized" to do so. My friend tells me there are users who connect clandestinely. Sometimes they get caught. Somebody interrupts the connection, no one ever knows exactly *who*, makes a few threats, and then disconnects them. But these users never give up. No way. They just reconnect right away. They happily cruise down the virtual highway until they're caught again. And so on. My friend has never been caught in any of those little skirmishes. Technically a foreigner, the prohibition doesn't apply to her. And, oh, pity whoever might try to disconnect her! She loves to go browsing around in cyberspace, or whatever they call it. She's a great navigator. Christopher Columbus. Me, I'm the cabin boy. I confess that, at first, I was a little scared of that thing; I thought it was weird. I didn't understand it. I still don't understand it. But my friend has explained that there's nothing to understand. You use it and that's that. It doesn't bite. To use it you only need half a neuron, she tells me, thus its popularity. Even Alix, who was also afraid of it, eventually learned. The Internet brought e-mail, with which Linda communicates with her friends on other continents, even Australia; it's much cheaper than calling on the phone. It's possible this may sound naïve, since millions of people are familiar with e-mail. But there are also millions who aren't. At Happy Hammer Corners, for example, the only two people who've ever seen it are Leidi and me.

The thing is that Alix learned to use it. She and Linda would send each other messages practically every day whenever Linda was traveling, which happened more and more frequently now. From Rome, the writer told her all about her first impression of the Sistine Chapel: "Oooooh!" From here, Alix pleaded with her not to hook up with any Italian girls and demanded that she come home immediately. From Istanbul, the writer commented on how dazzling the Aya Sophia was in daylight. From here, Alix pleaded with her not to hook up with any Turkish girls and demanded she come home immediately. From Paris, the writer wrote up a review about the scandal provoked—at the end of the twentieth century!—at the d'Orsay by the Courbet oil which until recently had been hidden away in some alcove because of the sheer indecency of its subject matter: a vag. It was very realistic. And hairy. Splendid. A genuine Western vag which stirred up great enthusiasm in the hordes of Japanese tourists. From here, Alix pleaded with her not to hook up with any French girls, especially with that Courbet, so shameless that painter of vags, and demanded that she come home immediately. Linda was having a lot of fun.

But the girl with the black hair used e-mail not just to make demands and issue edicts from afar. Very interested in knowing who Linda was in contact with, why and what for, she soon got in the habit of checking the other correspondence my friend received. I dunno if this is right. Father Ignacio says no, that all correspondence that isn't yours should always be inviolable. But he doesn't know squat about e-mail and perhaps the very idea that it's electronic introduces relativity to its privacy. Could that be true? I dunno. As far as Linda was concerned, she didn't care about Alix's fierce spying. Or maybe she did, but she didn't say so. When Alix, not making eye contact, or pretending to be casual (or sly, as Moisés would say), asked about the identity of someone she considered to be sending too many messages, my friend would respond with complete honesty.

A question phrased something like "Who's So-N-So?" is never easy to answer, no matter how simple it seems. It has its complexity, its philosophical entanglements, its air of Big Question. How to know who So-N-So is if the So-N-So herself probably doesn't know? At least in my case, it'd be extremely difficult to explain who I am to someone who doesn't know me at all. To complicate things, Linda tended to answer with professions. So-N-So was a translator, a journalist, her agent's secretary, etc. And she'd shrug, as if none of it mattered. But when Alix asked who N. Cohen was, she got a different kind of response.

"Cohen is . . . Oh! You can't even imagine Cohen. A marvelous person. Yes, yes. A marvelous person."

It was a hair-raising experience for poor Alix. She'd never heard Linda talk that way about anybody (to be frank, neither had I). She freaked, like a forest animal when it knows a fire's coming. She could smell the danger. It was an obscure sensation suggesting wrecks, earthquakes, imminent disaster. She hated N. Cohen instantly. Hated and feared. She'd never liked marvelous people. Those wicked, meddling, invasive, shitty sluts could put a happy glow on their lovers' faces. They'd provoke that faraway smile, a little mysterious (yes, I've also seen Linda's inner smile, provoked by Leidi, N. Cohen, and Alix herself). They'd try to steal her from her. Take her away forever. Yes, because marvelous people were never satisfied with just one night of infidelity. Not even with a weekend. No, they wanted *everything*. Marvelous people wanted everything. And that couldn't happen. No way. Because Linda belonged to her. She was hers and no one else's. Private property.

After that first initial shock, my friend's owner tried to find out a little more about N. Cohen. Where had she come from? What did she do? Was she pretty? Why did she send Linda so many messages, about one a week? What was the color of her hair? How were her legs? What perfume did she use? How did she dress? Why did she write such long letters? Why did she write them in English? Just to seem deep, wise? Or was it so that she, Alix, wouldn't understand them and have to remain in the dark? So talkative sometimes, Linda said that N. Cohen wrote to her. It was in English because that's how it was, period. That Alix and her tantrums and her caprices and her hysterical fits didn't exist for N. Cohen. The absolute worst about Alix, Linda added, was that on top of snooping where she shouldn't, without anybody's permission, she had the incredible gall of then demanding explanations. What right did she have to do that? None, none at all. She was tired of giving explanations. End of story. Stupefied, very hurt, Alix attempted the ultimatum strategy again: either N. Cohen or her. But this time the trick got turned on her. Linda told her to go to hell.

"If you want to leave, leave. I'm not going to stop you."

As often happens to poker players who, sure of their triumph, bet the house on a single card just to have fate squash them, the girl with the black hair must have felt as if the rug had been pulled out from under her. What vertigo. She couldn't cover that bet. She couldn't leave. She couldn't leave under any circumstance. And not only because she didn't have a place to go, which was the least of it, as far as she was concerned. Yes, it may have been a little nutty because it's so romantic, so romance-novel actually, but at twenty years of age, Alix wasn't in the least bit interested in the material comforts that came with living with Linda. She considered herself perfectly capable of living without any of them. Including a roof over her head. Well, not any of them. There was one thing she couldn't do without: Linda. That's why she couldn't leave. Because Linda was her life. How could she live without her life? And so she didn't go. Determined to get my friend back, in whatever way and at whatever cost, she stayed in the penthouse. To defend her territory. To fight for it like a cat on its back. That slut who wrote only in English wasn't going to get her way. Not if she could help it. If N. Cohen wanted war, she got it.

What happened later is quite confusing. Between that last bit of blackmail on Alix's part and the final confrontation between the two of them—a horrible scene that seems straight out of one of Linda's novels—various weeks passed in which the tension grew and grew in the penthouse. So thick, so unbreathable, you could cut it with a knife. They barely spoke to each other. They avoided each other, secluded themselves, looked at each other askance. Until the storm hit. It seems that Alix took it upon herself to erase a couple of N. Cohen's letters from the computer before my friend had a chance to read them. Maybe she thought if the letters disappeared, so would her rival, that notoriously marvelous person who, faceless and voiceless, only existed in her wicked and indecipherable epistolary. As could be expected, Linda was immediately aware of what she later called "that compulsive, stupid, and dirty move." What bothered her most wasn't the loss of the messages (N. Cohen sent them again), but that such an imbecile—that's what she said to me—would try to fool her. How could she even dare? She'd had it up to here with Alix. It was time to kick her out.

"Get your things and get out."

But, as it turned out, Alix proved to be a difficult lover to get rid of. Really difficult. For starters, she out and out denied her mischief on the computer. Her? Erase her messages? How could Linda accuse her of such a thing? How awful! How unfair! "Fine. You didn't do anything wrong. It's awful and unfair of me. But just the same, leave. I'm bored. Go." Alix cried, screamed, threw fits, howled, got angry, and threatened to throw herself off the terrace. My friend went along with it. "Go ahead, jump, go ahead, we'll see if you don't hit bottom faster than the elevator." So Alix changed tactics. She threatened to throw *her*. Linda cracked up laughing. "Sure, go ahead." That's when it got good. Perhaps Alix gave her a sinister look, or maybe it was just a sign she saw, who knows. What's certain is that, all of a sudden, Linda stopped laughing. Something must have frightened her. Since she couldn't possibly take on such a big girl with just her hands, she pulled out the gun. "Get back, sucker. Don't come any closer. Don't come any closer!" But Alix had never seen a firearm. Maybe she didn't understand what they were for. Or she didn't care. Or . . . finally, she tried to grab it. There was a struggle. And then there were shots on the twentieth floor.

A bullet grazed Linda. On the side of her left temple. She still has the scar and I suppose she'll have it the rest of her life (according to La Gofia, it looks good on her). But Alix was terrified when she saw the blood. Oh! She was paralyzed. What the fuck had she done, by God, what had she done? Linda—who didn't feel pain but panic—took advantage of this temporary immobility to smash a jar on her great love's head. Crash! Alix fell flat on the floor. My friend didn't waste any time asking herself what she'd done. She went bananas. She'd been accumulating resentments and began kicking and kicking the girl with the black hair, kicking her stomach, kicking her chest, her face, until she was exhausted (this scene strikes me as very familiar, but I won't share that with Linda, no way). Then she dragged her like a sack of potatoes to the elevator, went down to the garage with her, put her in the Mercedes, and threw her out on the street, half unconscious and covered in blood, just a few kilometers from the penthouse. I don't understand why no one called the police. It seems very strange to me. Because you could *hear* the shots. The pistol didn't have a silencer or anything like that. There's no question they were heard. I dunno. Maybe there wasn't a single neighbor in the building at that moment. Or maybe there was, but nobody wanted to get involved. Or better yet, even though Linda's pretty experienced with fooling the police, maybe things would have gotten complicated because of the firearm.

In terms of N. Cohen, there's not much to say. I don't know what N. looks like. N.'s forty something. N.'s traveled the world over and read thousands of books. N. knows various languages and, between the two of them, they speak Hebrew. N. teaches philosophy at Harvard or something like that. N. understands what no one understands. According to my friend, N.'s is simply a fierce intelligence. And that's not even counting N.'s sensibility, grace, talent, wit, or sense of humor. A torrent of virtues. A gem. A star. But nothing's perfect in this life. From Linda's point of view, this marvelous person has a small defect: The N. stands for Nathaniel.

Chapter 11

My lover, my friend

THE WAY THOSE GUYS WERE LOOKING AT HIM WAS RIDICULOUS, grotesque, laughable, definitely pathetic. They were watching him—Moisés, now sitting on the edge of the tub with a bottle of rum in his hand—as if they had X-ray vision. As if they could *see* through opaque material, discover what was obscured, decipher forms in the dark, when in fact they couldn't see beyond their stupid noses. How absurd. They fixed their gaze on him as if they could diagram his brain, ideas, and thoughts right through his skull. Or his heart right through his chest. Emotions, feelings, and all the idiocies those cretins attributed to that miserable cardiac muscle . . . Oh, how infuriating! It was offensive. Insolent. Shameless. Disrespectful.

But there was more. Of course there was more. Given their lack of limits . . . —he took a swig straight from the bottle—given their infinite petulance, there was always more with them. Because those homeless sonzabitches didn't just dedicate themselves to the idiotic X-ray thing. No, no way. They were also clairvoyant. Oh, yes. Clairvoyant. They were great seers—he lit a cigarette—diviners, sorcerers, prophets. The tribe's shamans. They weren't like the crazy old man, that relative of mine—he pointed at me as if I was responsible—the one with the horoscope and the xylophone and the marquis and all that puffery. No, these guys were much worse. We could probably forgive the old man, give him a pat on the head. (When my great-uncle W. warned Moisés about Saturn, my boo didn't slap him one because he didn't want to break him. Instead, he patted him on his bald spot, as if saying, "You're being spared cuz you're a mummy, cuz otherwise . . ." The mummy was quite upset by this.) Yes, because he was *too* old, archaic, and already had one foot in the grave. But *they* didn't. No, they didn't. He took another swig and passed me the bottle. Such fakes, such charlatans, they wanted nothing more and nothing less than to read his mind. Even though they couldn't read their own because they didn't have one—he took off his shirt, looked at it with disdain, and threw it in the corner. Whatta bunch of swindlers. Pretending to be mind readers. What nerve.

And what faces they made. Wiseguys. Visionaries. Guys who knew what was up. You had to see those faces—he lit a second cigarette—those masks, those concrete faces. Especially if you wanted to vomit. Christ! Although they probably weren't lacking in experience. Certainly not when it came to hustling, cheating, shamelessness. Not when it came to the stench of their disgusting lies. And they dared to give him advice like doctors, to predict his future, to meddle in his decisions, to tell him what was right and what was wrong, to spit out opinions about a bunch of things they didn't have a clue about. Cursed degenerates. That's why he had to beat them to a pulp. To twist their necks. Kick their asses. Drown them in a pool of sulphuric acid. Hee hee! That's why they had to be squashed, bagged, and annihilated! (This sweet phrase, according to what I've been told, comes to us from the Nazi army: When they felt an irresistible impulse to destroy a city, they "squashed" with their tanks, "bagged" with their infantry, and "annihilated" with their planes. This method isn't at all clear to me, but I get the idea. I think I wouldn't have wanted to be there.) Yes, that was it! Annihilate them. Exterminate them. Suppress them. Bam! Bam! He slapped the air around, as if he were swatting flies. Not even the dust from their bones would be left. Nothing. A wasteland. Salt in the dirt. So they couldn't reproduce, sprout again like worms, like the weeds that they were. As the ancient Romans used to say: *delenda est Carthago.**

And the two of us—he looked at us bewildered, probably asking what we were doing there, standing right in front of him—why were we still awake? Wouldn't it be better if we went back to bed? That way we'd leave him alone.

---

* Carthage must be destroyed. The ancient Romans mixed salt into the fields of Carthage. They salted it, cursed it.

He'd let us know when he wanted the bathroom full of sleepy women. For the moment, he just wanted to be alone. Because. Because human beings, so heinous, were born alone and died alone. It was close to three in the morning, a time for solitude. That bastard with the cornet and the conga drums and the maracas should be asleep too. Whatta guy. He was going to kill him someday. Yes, someday he was going to squash him like a creepy crawler, like a dung beetle—he squashed the two cigarette butts on the floor. Not now. Now he just wanted to be alone—and he pointed toward the door with a weary gesture.

The two of us very obediently went back to bed. When Alix, somewhat upset, whispered that she didn't understand a damn thing my lover said, I passed her the bottle and told her not to worry about it, not to give it too much importance, because I didn't understand him either. She shrugged and yawned. As far as I know, she wasn't the type to strain her brain trying to figure anybody out. And as far as she was concerned, Havana was full of lunatics, monsters, and perverts, which was enough to explain any extreme behavior, psychology aside. She took a drink and put the bottle on the table. Exhausted, she'd spent the afternoon hauling buckets of water up the stairs and a good part of the evening drinking with me and Pancholo while the drunks in the bar sang us that song: "I could have been happy . . . / and now I'm the living dead . . . / living between tears . . . / through the worst part . . . / of this endless drama . . ." She fell back asleep the minute she got in bed. Lucky her. I wish I'd been able to do the same. But no. I was caught up in something akin to anguish. Maybe it was because of the silence; there was an unsettling calm in which the only thing that could be heard was the purring of the air conditioner and the echoes of Moisés talking to himself in the bathroom. An unusual quiet at Happy Hammer Corners. When you've lived for years and years with noise, the much longed for quiet can be disturbing. I dunno, it was as if something was amiss.

Stretched out next to Alix and more wide-eyed than an owl in the middle of the night, I thought about Moisés. He'd disappeared a couple of weeks back, which in and of itself wasn't that strange. Not for him, since he disappeared from the Corners whenever he felt like it. He was a disappearing act. Then he'd show up, as irate as when he left, sometimes with traces from fighting, some scuffle in a faraway neighborhood; he'd come back, always with money and always wanting to fuck. That was the best part. Although, to be honest, I would have preferred if things were different. For instance, I wanted him to stay with me for longer periods of time. Or for him to tell me where he'd been. Maybe deep down in my heart, in my miserable cardiac muscle, I wanted to live like normal people. But I never dared suggest any such thing. No way. Not only was I afraid he'd hurt me for being so fresh and intrusive, but I also feared he'd leave me for being a nag, that he'd get tired of me and tell me to get lost. Instead of chasing him, I tried to adapt. And I managed it. Of course. At this point in our lives, four years from that first clinch in John Lennon Park, I'd gotten used to his routines. Heart and soul, hormones and neurons. So every time he came back from his secret battles, he'd find me available, attentive, desirous, excited just to see him. This may sound a tad excessive, kinda nymphomaniacal, but it's true. As soon as Moisés came back, especially if it had been a long absence, I'd get wet, I'd shiver, I'd shudder, even my knees trembled. Just like Pavlov's dog, the one that drooled at the mere sound of the bell.

Moisés could come home at any hour of the day or night. But he favored the middle of the night. Time for solitude? No. Time for stealth, to tiptoe, to avoid running into the table and everything else. Time to move feline-like in the dark until leaping upon the unsuspecting prey, who perhaps at that very moment is dreaming about a very tall, very strong guy with a white beard and black eyes who bites her mouth (because ferocious creatures are excited by the taste of blood, so similar to rusted steel) and penetrates her with all the savagery in the world. Fast, very fast, so she won't get a chance to warm up, so he can nail her while she's dry, so it'll hurt. And it did hurt, yes, it hurt a lot. Because this tall, strong guy, to put it mildly, was rigorously proportioned. How could it not hurt? And that's not counting the squeezing and pinching, the hitting. Oh! I'd always dreamed of these beautiful things but had never confessed them to anyone. Except Father Ignacio, of course, who took it all very well, without getting freaked out or anything, since, obviously, he'd heard even worse blasphemies and, anyway, he grunted, the apple doesn't fall too far from the tree.

My erotic dreams were magnificent. Very crude, very realistic, and in vivid color. They only lacked a soundtrack. But it didn't matter. Under Moisés in the middle of night, I frequently crossed that tenuous border of wakefulness. That's when I'd get the soundtrack. His radio broadcaster's voice would whisper delicious barbarities. Sometimes I'd have enough time to turn on the bamboo lamp with the red silk shade. That was ideal, that was perfect, because I love to *see* and, more than anything, to be *seen*. And not because I have the most spectacular body in Vedado or anything like that. I just like it, that's all. Because I like myself, I suppose, in spite of the excess kilograms. I think men notice this and, generally speaking, find it attractive. Even Moisés, who called me fat all the time and told me I had a black woman's ass, seemed quite pleased. Now that I find myself a little depressed in spite of the pills that Dr. Frumento has prescribed, I remember those scenes in detail, which always lift my spirits. Memory can have its drawbacks but also its advantages. There were some splendid dawns, and no one can take them away from me.

When he came back this time, at about two thirty, my lover made a mistake. Instead of putting his hands on me, in the darkness he'd grabbed Alix. A monstrous mistake, however understandable. (Not too long ago, I shared this story with Linda and La Gofia. My friend doesn't think it was a mistake at all, but just more of the Caveman's lack of shame, because Alix and I are very different, even in the dark, and as a mistake it's the kind of thing that only happens in the stories in *The Decameron*. La Gofia didn't say a thing: she practically died laughing.) Alix slept in the fetal position, hugging herself, as if she were protecting herself from the cruelties of the universe, poor girl; when it happened, she let out a horrifying scream. A cry that seemed to come from the depths of hell and splintered the silence of the night. Unfortunately, it exploded right in my ear. Oh! I woke up with a start, absolutely convinced it was the end of the world or something like that. Moisés stepped back immediately and turned on the lights.

I'd been wearing a ripped t-shirt in bed so as not to get cold. Alix slept in the nude because she loved to freeze in the air conditioning like a penguin. I hadn't objected. In the first place, because she'd suffered a lot already and it didn't seem fair to keep her from this simple pleasure which caused no one any harm. And, in the second, because I believe everyone has the right to sleep however they want, a simple matter of democracy, according to my dad. But Moisés, for once, was stupefied. Sitting on the bed, Alix wasn't doing a thing to cover up. She looked at him in fear, almost in terror, as if he was the devil, Satan personified. The expression on his face, even after a few seconds just staring at her, reminded me of what I imagine the three bears must have looked like when they found Goldilocks in *their* house and in *their* bed. And if I remember correctly, Goldilocks wasn't naked.

In spite of the scare, I thought it was funny. So as not to laugh, and so my boo wouldn't get pissed and start in on me, I introduced them. My lover, my friend. This changed things. Nothing like the absurd to relieve the absurd.

They didn't shake hands or wink but it was as if they both came to, as if each realized that the other wasn't a demon or an extraterrestrial or anything like that. A man and a woman, that's all. He looked at her curiously, even admiringly. She covered herself with a sheet, pulled it to her chin, and mumbled an apology. It was a very kind gesture on her part, although completely unnecessary. Moisés looked at her skeptically for an instant, doubting her sincerity, but only for an instant.

"It's cool, girl, it's totally cool," he said, pulling a fifty-dollar bill out of his pocket and handing it to me (I was very happy, because Ulysses S. Grant has one of my fave faces). He grabbed a bottle he'd left on the table and then locked himself in the bathroom while cursing "them."

It had been nine days since Alix had come to live with me and this was the first time they'd seen each other. It's not that I was expecting him to have a specific reaction. To the contrary, during those nine days, I'd worked to avoid any kind of speculation about what it might be. Why torture myself for nothing? With Moisés, you never knew what was going to happen, you never knew what was up or down. But I was surprised by his manners; that is, that he didn't try to strangle Alix. I hadn't consulted him before bringing her over. Not because it was my room. No, that would have struck me as too stingy, too narrow, too rancorous and low. I hadn't consulted him simply because he wasn't around. Because he was a phantom. Now I thought that, at the very least, I owed him an explanation. I got up, I gave Alix a shirt, and went to the bathroom. She followed me while buttoning up, not asking a thing. She'd been following me everywhere since I brought her home, always silent, like a cub after mama bear. This made me a little nervous sometimes, I started getting a persecution complex of sorts but, in the end, it's not like I was going to push her away and say, "Hey, you, get away from me," or anything rude like that. Then it turned out I didn't dare interrupt Moisés's tantrum about his friends with the X-ray vision. So we went back to bed, Alix and me. Her to her sweet dreams, now with a shirt on. Me to my insomnia.

The bathroom light was still on. The door, half open. What was my boo up to? Other than raging against the bastards and devising ways to squash the divine Poliéster, was he cooking up something terrible for poor Alix? Suddenly, I imagined him masturbating. Oh God, the things I come up with! Who's ever heard of a guy jerking off while he hurls insults and plans crimes? Although I suppose it could happen, why not? Human sexuality is very complex. The most disturbing part of that interesting image of Moisés is that it excited me.

I mean, excited me again, because I was still hot from before, when I saw him in front of me, stunned by Alix's presence. How could I sleep like that? I did what I could to cool off. I thought of the refrigerator. Of an ice floe. An igloo. Frost, hail, handfuls of snow. But nothing worked. I was drenched, my lower abdomen shuddered in waves, and my nipples were stiff. What anguish. What desperation. If there was something fun going on in the bathroom, I *couldn't* miss out on it. No way. I got up, very quietly so as not to wake Alix, and I went off looking for new adventures.

I found him on the edge of the tub, in the same position in which we'd left him. He hadn't moved, not even a millimeter. I think he was talking about a bunch of sly ruffians who thought they were so smart and so important when, in fact, what they had in their cranial cavities—that's how he said it—was pure shit, a giant turd from one parietal lobe to the other. This seemed to offend him greatly. But when he saw me, he forgot all about those sly ruffians. He gave me an outrageous look, a look of contained rage. It was the look of someone who's been waiting much too long for what's theirs, absolutely theirs, and definitively theirs. It was the look of someone whose patience has reached its limits and is now a bomb about to explode. There were no words. There was no need for them. Not even the ancient Romans would have had anything to say. We fell to the floor and . . . well, it's understood.

At first, I tried not to make any noise. Not because of me but because of Alix. Like all the others at Happy Hammer Corners, I don't give a damn if I'm *heard*. That's par here. As Moisés used to say, when you live in "overcrowded conditions," qualms and scruples don't matter. I remember that we could hear Pancholo and Yadelis even up on the roof, in spite of the hammering. And there are no words to describe the coupling of the pig and the megatherium. They really had fun! But I was embarrassed in front of Alix. If we made too much noise, she could take it as a very vulgar insinuation that she wasn't welcome in the little apartment. And that's no way to treat a guest. Oh, but it wasn't entirely up to me. And there's nothing like the silence of the night to amplify sighs, friction, panting, Moisés's bass tones whispering that I'm a dirty whore with the biggest ass ever and that he was gonna impregnate me, etc. If only there'd been a little band playing (precisely now, when I don't need it, I have this song stuck in my head: "Why do you love me so much . . . / when I'm so bad . . . / I'm so bad bad bad . . . / I'm so bad"), or the Concert for Cornet and Bongo Opus Number 2001 by Poliéster, or some fight, or the slugs slapping dominos, or Radio Reloj announcing the time in New Zealand, or even Schoenberg . . . but no. The silence was overwhelming. And what had to happen, happened. When I came out of the bathroom a couple of hours later, the apartment was empty. I remember I even looked under the bed. Nothing. No trace of Alix.

I put on a pair of shorts and went out looking for her before she could get into trouble. I was beat to a pulp, exhausted, drained, and desperate for sleep (but now with no worries) and I almost killed myself on the stairs. How fucked up, I thought, of all those delinquents to steal the bulbs. I wasn't going to have a choice but to get a flashlight. I finally got to the porch downstairs in one piece, thank God. And there was the fugitive, wearing just the shirt, barefoot, huddled among the sleeping drunks and the smell of piss. She looked like a scared little animal pursued by a pack of bloodhounds, a hellish legion, a horde of evil spirits. I gestured to her to stop with the craziness and come up with me, but it was useless. No way. She flatly refused. Anybody could have thought that what awaited her up in my room with fork in hand was the cannibal who liked mayonnaise.

I sat with her on the dirty floor. Why was she so panicky, huh? Of course, she didn't utter a single syllable. Thus Alix Oyster. I'm not sure but I think that, due to her bad habit of following me everywhere, she may have *seen* Moisés and me rather than merely hearing us. Perhaps an exuberant spectacle, extreme and dizzying, but in the end, nothing all that extraordinary. And although, according to Linda, the girl with the black hair had never slept with a man, she was still an adult. And she was a peasant, so she had to have seen bulls and cows, horses and mares, very violent, savage, and natural couplings, pure bestiality. What could possibly have frightened her so much? She never explained it to me. She looked at me with her eyes popping out of her head and bit her lips like she was trying desperately to keep the slightest revealing sound from escaping. I started to feel guilty, ashamed for having given in to temptation and having traumatized that poor girl that way, because only God really knew the depths of her pain. What to do?

I stroked her hair, I gave her a little kiss on the cheek, I told her I was happy to have her in my home, I promised the next day we'd go buy a chocolate cake. She calmed down but she still didn't want to go up. I'm not usually very convincing, and much less so when I'm exhausted, my entire body aching, and my lids at half mast, so I didn't insist. But I felt bad about leaving her alone with the drunks on that inhospitable and stinky porch, so I got comfortable and fell asleep beside her. My only hope was that the mice and cockroaches would have some pity and not crawl all over us with their usual boldness. A little later, just before dawn, Alix shook me awake to tell me, stoically, that she'd changed her mind. We went up. I took a quick peek at Moisés, who was sleeping peacefully in the tub, and I let myself drop in bed with the simple purpose of never getting up ever again.

It's not hard to imagine that, since her exile from the penthouse, Alix had been through hell. I imagine her battered awakening on some strange street, her head wounded, a tooth chipped, sticky from the dried blood, penniless, without her I.D., without a single thing to her name, without a place to go, and surrounded by a curious circle who wouldn't leave her alone but who also didn't dare stop a car and take her to the hospital; nobody wanted to get involved. Out in the world, people say Cubans are very generous, good people, that we give a hand to anyone in trouble, but that's not entirely true. Maybe it was once, but not anymore. After the crisis of the '90s, Havana, at least, has really hardened. Everybody's into their own thing, their own schemes, their own individual needs. Favors are scarce. Poor Alix. She was homeless. And what an abrupt abandonment. Whatta way to hit bottom. So sudden, so from one minute to the next . . . It would have been an extreme situation for anybody, but it must have been so much worse for a young girl who'd always been sheltered, secure, without the need to struggle for anything. She survived, of course. But that doesn't prove her strength or her fiber or her great luck or any such thing. It only proves that dying is sometimes harder than it seems.

There's not much I was able to find out about Alix's three or four months on the streets. She never said a word to me about it. But through La Gofia, who has friends everywhere, from the highest spheres to under rocks, there's a network of informants (Linda calls it "the butch underworld," though it also includes some drag queens), I found out the girl with the black hair lived on the sly for a couple of weeks at the dorm at G Street and Malecón. Back then, there were a lot of illegals, pals, lovers, and classmates of the residents who just hung around. They were young people whose legal residence was outside the city, or on the other side of the bay, in East Havana, and needed to get to class in one piece, and this way they spared themselves the incredible odyssey that public transportation on a daily basis could be back then, the randomness of the bus schedule or hitchhiking, the madness of the camello,† or the martyrdom of pedaling kilometer after kilometer on an empty stomach

---

† Large trucks, with a hump in the middle, that pulled trailers filled with commuters.

under a scorching sun. The school administration wasn't unaware of this, but it was a real case of "don't ask, don't tell."

I remember the dorm at G Street and Malecón from my own student days. I went a few times because I'd made a few friends at the School of Arts and Letters who lived there. They'd say, "Let's go study," with tremendous optimism and conviction, but we never studied a thing. Instead of breaking our brains over Umberto Eco's semiotics or Lábov's dialectics or Chomsky's abstruse grammar, we dedicated ourselves to gossip, rum, and the boys in other departments. It wasn't a big deal to switch partners; we toasted to our good health, we told lurid stories, we sang along to singer-songwriters like Joaquín Sabina (we knew the words to all the songs on his album, *Física y química*), and we celebrated the mere fact of existence. New to our freedom, open to new experiences, those girls from the provinces came to Havana, the capital, with its perpetual disorder, to leave their inhibitions behind, to live in the very center of the world of vice. I remember a very relaxed atmosphere, where we were hungry but still had fun, where it was filthy but still jovial, and to a certain extent, naïve, like a hippie commune. Later, we graduated, as incredible as that might seem, and everyone went their own way. But the party at G Street and Malecón went on. It got even more intense. There were kids with tattoos, rings in their noses and other places, psychedelic colors, hair that looked more like feathers, a fashion trend in which they all looked like *The Last of the Mohicans*. And then there was pot, not just the consumption, the clouds of sweet smoke that helped find the spark in bad jokes, but also dealing. Still later, there was shameless hustling and, according to rumors, hard drugs. Finally, there was violence. This is what I call total chaos. Linda, who prefers scientific names, calls it "postmodernism."

That's when Alix snuck back in. I have no idea how she managed to survive. La Gofia saw her once, at the "wedding" of a couple of friends of hers, one of the loudest and most celebrated parties ever in the scandalous history of G Street and Malecón, and she couldn't help but be surprised. The Exterminating Angel had certainly had other victims, La Gofia said, but there had never been a more rotund, complete, and devastating example of her destructiveness. The girl with the black hair, former queen of the penthouse, looked like hell. Very skinny, ragged, dirty, more somber than ever, with her pupils dilated and dead drunk. A distressing spectacle for anyone who'd known her before.

"That girl's crazy," her friends warned La Gofia. "But she's not too bad. Right? Even like that, all fucked up, you can tell she's not too bad a catch.

They call her Little John, because of Robin Hood's buddy, the big guy. But she's crazy, man. The other day, she fucked Chicha the Skunk. The one on the sixth floor, the one . . ." They made faces of repulsion. "Yeah, she fucked her, which is already crazy enough. Can you imagine that? Whatta stomach she must have. But that's not the best part. No way. Chicha said that at the peak of the moment, you know, Little John said, that's it, this is as far as I go, and asked her for five pesos to buy a pizza. Fuck!" They giggled. "And that's nothing. Poor Chicha went and bought the pizza. Of course, she wasn't going to just give up her chance. She told her, 'You stay right here. I'll be right back.' And she did come right back, victorious, with the pizza. Little John hadn't left but she didn't remember a thing. Just like that, dears, exactly like that. Outta the blue. A galloping amnesia. When she saw the other girl, she huddled in a corner and started to cry. Such a big girl! She was crying as if she was being gutted. Chicha didn't understand. What the fuck was she going to understand? And just then Little John leapt up, grabbed the pizza, smashed it into Chicha's face, and ran outta there. So, c'mon, dude, tell me, huh: is she crazy or what?"

Concerned, La Gofia talked to Linda. That couldn't go on. No matter how stupid Alix was, no matter how many human errors she'd committed, she didn't deserve such total destruction. What kind of person was my friend who could dump the woman who'd been her companion for four years like that and just leave her to the grace of God? Linda shrugged. She didn't give a damn what La Gofia thought of her—she put on a very sad, serious, hurt face as she said this, as if deep down, it really did hurt her very much. Did La Gofia think she was evil because she lacked Christian virtues? Well, then, fine. She was evil—there was a gesture of resignation. She was a shameless dog, a scorpion. Her, the worst of all. But, why was pious Ana Cecilia so worried? For hundreds and hundreds of years, Christian hordes had accused her race of evil and treated them accordingly, she said, pushing her curls out of her face so La Gofia could see the scar on her left temple, still pretty new, and as if it had been caused by Christian hordes. La Gofia was dumbfounded and my friend talked on and on for a long time, in a low voice, softly, pronouncing all the letters. She talked about diaspora, about pogroms, about Auschwitz. She didn't have any trouble adding a few Shakespearean verses (translated), the famous ones from Shylock's speech at the end of Act III in *The Merchant of Venice*, as if they were her own passionate words flowing from her heart. "You've shown contempt for me . . . you've insulted me . . . you've mocked me

. . . you've gotten in my way." And thus she confused the pious Ana Cecilia. So much that, moved, she decided it was her, Linda, and not that imbecile, Alix, who was the victim. They ended up making love.

In the meantime, violence exploded at G Street and Malecón. Anybody could have seen it coming. The neighbors from the building next door had already made various complaints to the police about the rowdy gangs from the dorm who were always making noise, mixing salsa with Brazilian samba, Argentine tangos, Mexican corridos, boleros, guarachas, jazz, Latin rock, heavy metal, rap, songs from the OTI festivals, the most abominable disco, and even Beethoven's Ninth, all at the same time and well into the wee hours, seven days a week. The din was so outrageous, the volume so extreme, that the unhappy neighbors had begun looking forward to the blackouts so the scoundrels couldn't turn on their sound equipment, or, more precisely, their instruments of torture. The scoundrels, however, refused to give in to the blackouts. No way. They began to play rumbas and sing, full-throated and with great enthusiasm: "I want I want I want . . . / to dance in the light of an oil lamp . . . / talk to me of love . . . / love in the lamplight . . . / I want you to sing me a blues song . . . / before the lights come back on." Basically, they were right up there with Happy Hammer Corners.

Not satisfied with all that, in the last few months, they'd also begun to throw all sorts of things out the windows. They didn't do it with bad intentions. Since the elevators didn't work, even on holidays, they'd found a splendid solution to the problem of taking out the garbage without having to go down eight, nine, ten stories on the narrow, smelly, dark stairs crawling with cockroaches and who knows what other bugs. Shitty toilet paper, used condoms, sanitary napkins, plantain and banana peels, eggshells, empty cans, coffee grounds, and other beautiful things would rain down around G Street and Malecón, and the trade winds, so naughty, would fling them at the windows of the smaller and defenseless building next door. Umbrellas became indispensable to cross the sidewalk that had now become a garbage heap.

Furious, the neighbors kept complaining. But nothing came of it. According to Radio Bemba, it seemed the police were genuinely busy pursuing real outlaws, like the ones who had robbed the Banco Financiero, or burned down the Manzana de Gómez, or planted bombs in various hotels, and they couldn't waste time with some meaningless college tadpoles. So, since no one was stopping them, the tadpoles discovered the ineffable and implicit pleasure of throwing things out the windows. It was a tingle, a deep savoring, delicious, voluptuous, an almost orgiastic feeling of power. How fantastic. Old shoes, boxes, books, old bulbs, hangers, broken chairs, buckets, tables all rained down . . . until one day when a plastic bag full of dirt came down. That little meteorite came from a great height to land on the ground, yes, but only a few centimeters from a little three-year-old boy who had just come home with his father, the president of the residents' council for the neighboring building.

This good man didn't think twice. He didn't think, period. He took the boy inside the building and emerged a minute later with a bat in hand, the kind they used to use years ago, aluminum, and headed toward the notorious dorm. I'm told that, from the look on his face, it was clear he was planning to crush the skull of whoever crossed him as if it were a clove of garlic. He was sick of so much indulgence! What the fuck were these bastards thinking? He swung the bat as if he were hunting mammoths . . . Oh! The bastards who'd been hanging out in the hallways fled to their respective rooms and took refuge. Nobody wanted to confront the anonymous avenger. No way. Somebody—perhaps the old security guard—thought to close the door before anybody could get out. The anonymous avenger, angrier because of the enemy's cowardice, demanded that they open up, that they open up immediately, fucking assholes, so he could beat the fuck out of them. But they didn't open up. Enraged, he bashed the glass with the bat. Crash! Crash! In this way, he reduced it to dust.

The racket alerted the other neighbors, who ran to support their president with sticks and stones. They were ready to triumph or die, because zero hour had arrived, the moment to shred the squalid, stinking bastard sonzabitches with their nose rings and their din and their trash throwing and their wanting to dance in the lamplight. All of a sudden, the dorm was under siege. People outside couldn't get in, in spite of the broken glass, and those inside didn't dare try to leave. Fueled by the hideous afternoon heat, both sides hurled insults and projectiles at each other. A mob gathered. A tourist filmed it all with a video camera. Somebody took advantage of the situation to rail against the government. Others joined in. And then the police finally arrived in various squad cars with their sirens blasting. Whatta show. When I told Moisés, and I mentioned it as if it were gossip, as if it was totally second hand, he spent about three hours lamenting that he'd missed it. What fucked luck he had.

After the battle of G Street and Malecón, Alix was forced to abandon the dorm. In spite of the interrogations and the threats, they were never able to identify the criminal who'd deliberately thrown the plastic bag with the express purpose of killing the little boy. I think it's a good case for Lt. Leví. But maybe not, since the big-nosed little man only deals with murders already committed and in that battle, thank God, there were no deaths. The little bag, as it turned out, was in and of itself suspicious. What was such a thing doing in a student residence building? Had it been used to grow *cannabis indica*, Indian hemp, or, in other words, marijuana? The police sometimes think the worst of people. For better or worse, a rigorous search was conducted in which a bunch of irregularities and negligences were found. Nobody ever went to court over anything, but "competent authorities"—Linda's phrase to delineate nameless and inaccessible power, the power that falls from the sky like acid rain and eats through our skin—decided to restore order and put an end to the chaos, or rather, the postmodernity. As an initial measure, it was proposed that all the illegal residents be kicked out. La Gofia told me that Chicha the Skunk didn't hold a grudge and proposed hiding Little John under the bunk bed, but the girl with the black hair, measuring one meter eighty, didn't fit in such a small space, and no longer being a student at the university and not having family in Havana meant that if the cops got ahold of her they could very well send her back to her native province and, no, that could not happen. She decided to hit the streets.

She left without a trace. I only found out about her months later, when I saw her among a squad of beggars on the porch at La Pelota, a miserable eatery at the corner of 23rd and 12th, just a few blocks from the Corners. I go by there every once in a while. I go to buy bread, or to stretch my legs in the afternoon, or to take Leidi to see cartoons of the Lion King and his friends eating creepy crawlies and Pocahontas and her raccoon and Aladdin (my little niece assures me, and she's surely right, that who I need to hook up with is the lamp's genie, a fun guy who knows how to get things done, because that's the guy she needs as an uncle) during the kids' Saturday matinee at the theater at 23rd and 12th, or to drink a little beer at the bar in front of Colón Cemetery and watch the human parade, the pedestrians, the cars, the movements, and see what happens. The squad of beggars has been a pretty common sight around here for years now. Some sit on the ground with their image of Saint Lazarus and their box for change, others extend their hand and tell you they need a particular medicine, some sell trinkets, others talk to themselves, others dumpster dive; there's one with a leprous lip, two dwarves, one is hydrocephalic, and another imitates Freddy Mercury, I think, though he doesn't look much like him. Basically, these are people just like us, except their lives are more fucked up. When I can, I give them something. I don't think that because of this I'm the great benefactor of humankind, Saint Z of Vedado, as Linda says sarcastically. I don't fool myself like that. I know very well that I do it for myself, because I like to do things that make me feel good.

That's the reason—because I was following my Catholic, apostolic, and Havana-born conscience (sheer stupidity, according to my friend)—that I approached Alix on the porch at La Pelota and offered help. This was a shadow of the taciturn gypsy who'd pushed me at La Gofia's thirtieth birthday party, the jerk who'd called me a sardonic fat girl, the savage who'd almost killed Linda, and the crazy girl who'd smashed a pizza into Chicha the Skunk's face. What I saw was a disabled, tattered, dirty, skinny girl with bruises on her face and arms, with feverish eyes, almost unrecognizable in her devastation. Although it would be preferable sometimes, the truth is I don't have a heart of stone. I was greatly surprised she hadn't gone back to Pinar del Río, that she was still embarked on her conquest of the capital as if she were Hernán Cortés on the Sad Night. There are some people who are very stubborn. Some make it, i.e., Linda, or Cortés himself, but I think this is because they have a sixth sense about when they're being falsely led, when they need to make a strategic retreat. Unless you want to kill yourself, there's no need to go straight ahead all the time.

I had hoped to convince Alix to go back to the little farm. However dumb her Canarian father, I thought, he was still her father. He wasn't going to condemn her to who knows what kind of sordid death out on the streets. In any case, why not give it a try? Why not give the man a chance? I know that convincing isn't exactly my specialty but I thought such a good and commonsense idea would have its own weight in Alix's foggy mind. I thought patience was the only thing I needed. The plan was that she could live with me until she realized she *should* go back to Pinar del Río, at least to get a breather, a rest, and that there would be many wonderful opportunities that would present themselves later to return to Havana and get in trouble. Father Ignacio agreed with my plan. The only thing he asked was that I respect Alix's decision, whatever it might be, and not lose sight of the fact that she was a human being, an adult; in other words, that she was free and responsible for herself. She wasn't a puppy or a kitten, he insisted. Because it was one thing to be Catholic and another, very different thing, to be Viridiana. And, without my asking, he proceeded to explain that this Viridiana was some fool made up by that shameless Luis Buñuel, that she picked bums off the street to keep as pets, and for that little stunt she'd been suffocated.

I actually talked with Father Ignacio later. There, standing on the eatery's porch, I had to make decisions myself. Sitting on the floor—more like crumbled—Alix looked at me in fear, as if she didn't recognize me. I could have turned my back and called it a day, like any sane person. But no. I gave her my hand. She retreated, terrified. I said, "I'm Z, don't you remember? Z, Linda's friend." Her eyes glittered. "You do remember, dontcha?" She didn't say a word. "Well, it doesn't matter, it's not imperative that you remember. The thing is, I live around here and you can come with me, if you want, right this minute, and take a shower and eat at a table and sleep on a bed and all that stuff." She was stunned, still frightened. "Look, don't be scared. You don't have to shower if you don't want to, but eating, you know, yum yum, I don't think that's such a bad idea. Whaddaya think?" She thought about it for an instant, then smiled. It was very sad, but it was a smile. All right. I helped her up and brought her to Happy Hammer Corners. It's that simple. Was it a compulsive act? I dunno. I only know that now, after all that has happened, I still think it was the right decision.

My tenant had not exactly gotten used to her life as a vagabond. In spite of her troubles, she was still a typical Cuban girl in that she *had* to take a shower every day, whether it rained, thundered, or stormed. She loved water. Luckily, I'd gotten some from the little faucet downstairs that morning. Just to wash her hair, she used three buckets. She felt weak, a little dizzy, and I had to help her. The water would wash off black, as if her long dark hair, almost blue, was washing out while she laughed with joy and splashed me and made a great big mess. All that made me happy. In spite of the bruises (and they can't have been from when Linda beat her, because too much time had passed; *something* had happened out there), and although a few kilograms would have done her some good, she had a lovely figure, much lovelier than I might have guessed from her ungainly walk, so brusque, like Big Foot. But the most impressive thing of all, at least for me, was her tattoo. It was a snake with green scales, very well drawn with a fine tip, with a white rose in its mouth. A real work of art, it covered the whole right side of her back, from her shoulder to her hip. Next to the rose, a sign in black: LINDA, MY LOVE. I don't know why, maybe because of its irreversible quality, but that sign scared me. Maybe I'm getting old, settled in my ways, retrograde, and I'm intimidated by young people's extravagances.

Her clothes, rags that were falling apart, had to be tossed. Nothing of mine fit her, of course. That night I gave her one of Moisés's shirts and the next day I got the nerve from somewhere to go to the penthouse to get her things, if my friend still had them. As I had imagined, the writer had a fit. More sibylline than the snake with green scales, she spit all the insults, allegations, offenses, condemnations, and contempt on me she could remember. She insulted my chubby cheeks, my weak mind, my traitorous soul. She offended my religion. All Catholics, starting with Karol Wojtyla, are all a bunch of hypocrites, intolerants, perverts, criminals . . . I'm not going to repeat everything she said, because it may seem as if Linda is a bad person, and she's not. If she were, she wouldn't have handed me one of her suitcases with Alix's clothes, shoes, perfumes, makeup bag, toothbrush, and I.D. It's true she pulled my hair, the abuser, but she did so as to not strangle me. Anybody can have a bad day. Then she stuck two one-hundred-dollar bills in the pocket of my blouse, which, given that it's her, were worth about two gold ingots. She told me that she never wanted to hear from me or "that imbecile" or anyone else ever again.

This is how Alix came to Happy Hammer Corners for an indefinite stay. After the incident at dawn, Moisés accepted her as if she were part of the landscape and, other than sleeping in the bathtub, he didn't change his habits in the least. He remained his usual vampire self at night, with the bottomless bottle and two cigarettes, abusing me in word and deed, devising his exterminations of "them"—in other words, same ol' thing. One time he asked if the new girl *also* liked guys. I said that, as far as I knew, no. Then, very excitedly, he asked if she hated them. And I said that, as far as I knew, no. That she was indifferent to guys. This seemed to disappoint him, and from that moment he lost interest. He was never especially courteous to her but neither was he rude. Unless Alix were to interpret a couple of times that he beat me in front of her, as if she weren't even there, as rude. On those occasions, she huddled in the corner, poor girl, and bit her fists without daring to intervene. Maybe she was generally indifferent to guys, but she grew to hate Moisés as much as or more than Linda did. Except that she, in contrast to the writer, didn't have the words to express her hatred. That's about when the nausea began.

Chapter 12

To escape the vertigo of time

NOBODY BELIEVES ME. I NEED TO SAY IT RIGHT UP FRONT: NOBODY believes me. Not even Father Ignacio, who tells me that because of all the liquor and marijuana I imbibe, I go around seeing things that aren't there. Not Dr. Frumento, who attributed what he considers to be hallucinations and delirium to my manic personality, which is in essence depressive. Nor Linda, who insists that I have an exuberant imagination, a capacity for fantasy that I should take advantage of to *write* stories instead of going around propagating rumors that don't do me any good in any way and that, in the end, could even get me tossed in jail.

And in terms of the police . . . well, from the very beginning they were quite satisfied with the idea of *two* accidental deaths, because it would probably have been very difficult to prove otherwise and they didn't want to get stuck in a quagmire. They went to the hospital, yes, and looked at me curiously and asked me probing questions. But I couldn't talk then. I could hear and understand, at least I think I could, but I couldn't speak. I was speechless from fright, and the presence of the two plainclothes officers flitting around me wasn't helping my state of mind. For whatever reason, plainclothes police scare me the most. If it's impossible to avoid them, if they're going to be there anyway, I'd rather they be in their little blue uniforms.

Later, I got back my ability to speak. It came back pretty quickly. Living through what I did, or similar episodes, affirms Dr. Frumento, has left some people paralyzed, unable to open their mouths again. What threw me out of shock was finding out I hadn't lost the baby. But the police never came back. Kindly Dr. Frumento had taken the liberty to speak to them for me. To say that I didn't know or understand a thing. Good. A little more and he'd have declared me incompetent, outta my mind, which, in certain circumstances, can be all right. The best part, though, was when he added that it wasn't in my nature to hurt anybody and that no one had loved Moisés more than me. Dr. Frumento is a very prestigious psychiatrist who has worked for years in the courts talking to crazy people who've been accused of crimes, to witnesses and judges. So it wouldn't have made sense for me to insist on talking to the police. And, also, if they'd finally left me alone, thank God, why stir things up again? Who would that help? As Father Ignacio says, there's no need to exaggerate.

But back to the incredulous circle that surrounds me: perhaps my friend is right and I should dedicate myself to writing down what no one will listen to with any kind of faith. The outlandish. The novelesque. The incredible. But I'm not too sure. If this book were a novel, it's probable no one would believe me either. Let's see if we understand each other: I know that fiction is beyond what's true or false. It's fiction, period. But it must be convincing in some way, at least while you're reading it, otherwise what's the point? I think they call that "verisimilitude." To tell what didn't happen but could have. When there's no "verisimilitude," it's said the novelist is dumb, inept, a fake, shameless. It'd be better if he or she were a stevedore hauling sacks at the port or selling peanuts at the bus station. No wonder I doubt my ability to convince others, who are so skeptical sometimes, so distrustful, so suspicious, even when it comes to fiction.

Linda, on the other hand, can be quite convincing. That sublime faker can make things up with the sly mastery of a Hollywood scriptwriter. Many readers are enchanted (enchanted in the sense of the snake charmer and the snake) with her lies, even the most improbable ones. She would have told this story—my story—very differently. Taking into account the inevitable variations in style, it would have begun more or less like this:

"At 7:32 a.m. on Tuesday, December 19,* 2000, on a splendid and lovely day,

---

* Talk about coincidences! The outcome of this story takes place, in fact, on December 19, a

the best day all that Havana winter, the citizen Poliéster, alias the Sonovabitch with the Cornet, left his room in the tenement known as Happy Hammer Corners. He was quite jovial, cornet in hand, hopping on one foot out of pure joy. But he didn't get very far. To his misfortune, his mother's stupor, the consternation of Lt. Leví, and the delight of the rest of humanity—it will be clear why later—he decided to stop right under my friend Z's enormous window. Perhaps he was considering serenading her, or catching one of those mosquitoes that carry yellow fever, or scratching his ear, or whatever. We'll never know. Because at 7:33 a.m., barreling out of my friend Z's enormous window like a missile, came the citizen Moisés, alias the Caveman, who fell on him from nine meters up, all ninety-one kilograms of him, and squashed Poliéster. How's that? It hardly seems possible. Still, I think that because of the gruesomeness, there's an immediate desire to know what happened, even though we might worry that we're being fooled."

But that's not what my confessor, my therapist, and my friend refuse to believe me about. There are eyewitnesses to Moisés's fall and the squashing of Poliéster; that is, people who saw it with their own eyes. The little drunks from the porch (those guys may have seen it through a blur and maybe one or another thought it was time to stop drinking); the old folks from the neighborhood who stand in line every morning to buy the paper at the stand and gossip a little while they're at it; Usnavy in her morning hustling; the Chinese guy who sells Chinese fritters across the street, next to the Christian Science Library; a few black kids from Los Muchos; the Jehovah's Witness in his morning sermon; the scissor sharpener who comes by every Tuesday with his particular little philharmonic music; various commuters; and, to my great dismay, Leidi Hamilton, who is always on her way to school at that hour. Although some of them may not be very interested in testifying, they can all confirm that I'm not lying, at least not up to this point.

I woke up in the middle of a riot of voices. Alix wasn't there. In that moment, I could have gone to the window, which *seemed* closed, to open it and look out and find out what had happened, the reason for all the shouting. The black double, triple, impenetrable, and strictly closed curtain, sealed from left to right, was exactly the same as the first day Moisés had installed it to relieve his photophobia, or whatever it was, and wasn't allowing a single

---

Great Day for Cuban Literature, according to Linda. It's her birthday and also the birthday of the great poet José Lezama Lima.

sliver of light, or the most minimal ray of sunshine. But the noon light, the radiant, blinding killer, the one that makes the colors explode, the one that dazzles tourists and makes the natives drowsy, the "Indian," would have come through the curtain in the same way it does our eyelids when we close them to avoid looking at it. In other words, the noon sun would have given away if the window was open. But the indecisive light of a winter dawn can be confusing. Mirages, errors in perspective, failed calculations. This is what led to citizen Moisés's misfortune, and consequently, Poliéster's. My lover may have tried to lean on the black curtain, convinced there was a solid surface behind it . . . and then fell into the abyss. Pure inertia (Linda, who has never been interested in science, made a few rather cynical comments about the implacable laws of Newton). The window was, and is, sufficiently wide that his body could go through it. The ledge, so low, didn't, and doesn't, serve as any kind of guardrail.

I don't know why Moisés was wandering around the darkness of the apartment in the wee hours and leaning on the wall; I suppose it may have been to find his way and not bump into anything. It occurs to me that, in the bathtub, where he'd been sleeping since Alix's arrival, he might have noticed that the temperature was rising in a very suspicious way, as if the air conditioner had broken. The rise in temperature was probably due to the fact that the room wasn't sealed, that the cold air was escaping through a leak somewhere—in other words, the open window. But he was unaware of that detail and perhaps got up meaning to kick the machine a few times. To see if it would work like it was supposed to, goddamn it. That's the way my boo dealt with things, including the car: by kicking. His idea of mechanics was very similar to his idea of love. This is nothing more than a theory because while he walked around like a phantom in the shadows, I was fast asleep, gloriously and irresponsibly unaware of the change in temperature.

What I was saying about the traitorous window is that I could have gone to it when I woke up and fallen just like Moisés. But I didn't. Something stopped me. In that instant, I couldn't quite pinpoint the source of the information, the nugget hidden in the haze of the previous night's drunkenness, but deep down, in the deepest part of my consciousness, I *knew* the window was open. I knew there was some trick, a ruse, some sleight of hand and, behind the curtain, only air. In the few seconds before there was arduous knocking on the door, I had a sudden vision of what had happened. It was a kind of illumination. Bam! A bolt of lightning. And I was glad. It's possible that this may be the most ruinous of my confessions, the most perverse, the most horrible: I was glad. There was a tumult in the hallway, a grave rumor of steps, agitated, increasing, like waves in hurricane season. Above them, screams: "Hey! My ecobio! Little sister! What's goin' on? Open up!" And I was frightened about having been glad. Between the knocks on the door, the voices, the megatherium barking, the chickens squawking, and the braying of the goat with the little bell, I got scared of myself. Of the beast inside me. Of my pagan spirit. Of my recently discovered dark side.

Whatta violent commotion. And so difficult to explain. It was one of those nontransferable experiences that can only be imagined, if that, by those who've gone through something similar. I suspect it's close to what happens when, after an accident, you face the mirror for the first time and are loathe to recognize the disfigured features, asymmetric, vaguely familiar, which look back at you with fear. Who knows. What's certain is that I felt a sudden cramp in my lower abdomen, followed immediately by a sharp intermittent jab, so intense, as if an awl had entered my vagina to poke my uterus over and over. Ow. It was the same shuddering, perhaps sharper now, that I felt when I lost my first pregnancy. The panic and the abortion with no anesthetic and the guilt and the morphine. How horrible. I thought—although "thought" might not be the best word (as usual)—no, not this time, I couldn't take it again. Nooooo!

In the midst of my rage, I dragged myself to the window, not to jump, but to look out at the panorama and confirm what I already knew and, at the same time, what madness, to see if there had been a miracle and nothing had happened. Oh, how wonderful if it could have all been a nightmare! I whispered my magic mantra: "One hundred bottles on the wall . . . / one hundred bottles on the wall . . . / if one should . . ." With my breathing chock-full of longing (the awl had become a drill, my mouth tasted like blood, oh), I opened the curtain a little bit and, with the utmost care, like someone who's getting ready to take a peek at Medusa's head, the one that turned busybodies into stone, I looked down. How dizzying. Midway on the concrete walkway from the building to the garage, there, under street level, lay two lifeless bodies. Two bodies in anomalous positions (from that angle, they looked twisted, deformed, a pair of marionettes with broken strings, a heap of junk), one on top of the other in a cross. I had been imagining one, or none if I got my miracle, and this surprise served as the dagger in my gut. I didn't try to focus my eyes, which were suddenly blurry, to identify the second body, the unexpected one underneath. I couldn't distinguish the profiles in the curious crowd who gathered like vultures around death; I saw only shapes. I may have heard a police siren, or an ambulance, I dunno, because I didn't see any vehicles. I didn't even notice that the mob at my door had ended up breaking it down. I sat on the floor, my back to the wicked window, and buried myself in the darkness. The last thing I remember is the worried face of my little buddy Pancholo.

Later, I found out the second body, the one that left a brownish stain on the concrete, was Poliéster. I wasn't glad this time. I didn't jump for joy or high-five with delight or scream with glee; I didn't sing that ditty, the one that says, "No, you don't have to cry . . . / because life is a carnival . . ."—although God knows I had plenty of reason to. I was undaunted. Maybe the beast inside me had gone back to where it came from. I also found out the artist's death was instant, that his skull was fractured. That Moisés, on the other hand, was taken unconscious in the ambulance. The musician's body had cushioned his fall, not a lot, but enough to extend his life a little more. He was in a coma for a coupla hours and he would have lived, the doctors said, if his heart hadn't given out. It was a massive stroke. I didn't go to either of the two wakes.

This is what we could call, like the Argentine film, "The Official Story." The only acceptable one, the least horrifying, the apparent one. But there are still outstanding issues. At the hospital, the district police posed certain questions that weren't too far off base. Why was the window open if we had the air conditioner on? Who had left it like that, knowing full well that the curtain, which was pretty intense, could confuse people and cause a deadly accident? Who benefited from Moisés's death? Who was the other person who, according to reports, was living with us, and where was she? I can't answer this last question. Other than the daughter of a dumb Canarian with a little farm in Pinar del Río and the great love of Linda's life, I can't say who Alix was. Nor where she could be. She simply disappeared. But I have the other answers. They make up "the other story," the underground version, the one below the official one. The one they won't believe. If I tell it now, it's not because I want to hurt anyone, but because I'm trying to get some order in my own head. It's a mental health issue. Because it's not at all easy to live among people who don't believe me and think I'm an alcoholic, a druggie, delirious, manic, and a liar. I'm very gullible. Between Father Ignacio, Dr. Frumento, and Linda, it's possible that one of these days they'll convince me and I won't even believe myself, I won't trust my own instincts, the evidence of my own eyes and ears—all of which seems like madness, and which scares me a lot.

The whole thing began with morning sickness. To make sure, I went to the clinic at Sagrado Corazón, and, in fact, I was five weeks along. My first reaction was happiness. Crazy happiness, the most ever in my life. I even gave the gynecologist a little kiss. There was so much relief in all that happiness. Like a light at the end of the tunnel. I'd been with Moisés for four years, four years of relative stability, a steady relationship, intense, persistent, without ever using a contraceptive, and nothing. The mere idea of being infertile (how?), or that he would have had that surgery they call a "vasectomy" behind my back—one of the worst things ever invented, according to Father Ignacio—horrified me to such an extent that I'd decided not to think about it. I'd decided to leave the entire matter, like so many others, in the hands of God. And suddenly, this. Five weeks. A little person. Oh! If I might be permitted a little blasphemy, I felt like the Virgin Mary might have when she found out about the Miracle. Later, I hesitated. Moisés and I had never talked about the possibility. Especially because I knew he didn't want any more children, so I thought it was an excellent idea on his part to avoid any explicit discussion of the matter even if it was Jesuit-like, and while he didn't do a thing to prevent pregnancy, the silence also kept his conscience satisfied. Everything was clear, he'd tell me.

But at the moment of truth, I got panicky. My boo didn't want more kids, like so many men, because of a lack of resources with which to raise them, or because of fear of a defective trait that would get passed along, or because he didn't want to take on the responsibility. No. Because he hated humanity, his nay to reproduction was an absolute moral principle, immobile, almost religious, a neon no. The world had enough riffraff—that was more or less his argument—for one of them, namely him, to be making more. It was true that he'd once been young and dumb and married an imbecile—that's what he said one time—blonde, skinny, very pretty, whom he didn't even find attractive, and had had two kids with her, two perfect cretins whom he didn't like at all—in other words, a disaster. All of that had been a grave mistake. It was something he'd left behind forever and couldn't repeat under any circumstances. When he was on top of me, or under, or next to me, or wherever, he'd whisper that he was going to impregnate me, but no way. The idea excited him (me too), but it wasn't meant to be taken literally. As they say in my neighborhood, there's no need to confuse the gymnasium with magnesium.

Given all this, how would my boo take the news? I dunno. I never told him. I tried several times but it was useless. I'd start to talk, but panic would soon take over and I couldn't finish. I'd get tongue-tied. I'd get lost in my babbling, interjections, loose syllables. Whatta calamity. I stammered. He'd look at me with rage and grunt and say some very stimulating things.

"If you're going to say one of your stupidities, just say it. If not, shut up. Or do you want me to untie your tongue by slapping you one?"

No, I didn't want to be hit. I preferred to stay tongue-tied. Or to stay quiet, which is what ended up happening. It might be easy to think that, at this point, after so many beatings, one more punch didn't really make much of a difference. But it did. By that time, Moisés's style had begun to worry me. Not because he'd gotten more savage than he already was (that was hard to imagine), but because of the new situation. Before, there was nothing to lose. Now there was something. The little five-week-old person, conceived in the midst of violence, needed to be protected from the very violence which could inadvertently, or deliberately, destroy it just like that. Oh. Just imagining it made my hair stand on end; my heart raced, I choked, I shivered all over and got cold sweats. The little person could only count on me. Me, though I felt more fragile, more vulnerable, more defenseless than I'd ever felt in my life. It's not like I was expecting violins or feeling sorry for myself like those crybabies in Dostoyevsky's stories, honest. I didn't have the time for that kind of caprice. Morning, noon, and night, my thoughts twisted around the conflict as if I were trying to put together an especially difficult jigsaw puzzle. I kept asking myself what to do.

Father Ignacio counseled me, for the umpteenth time and now even more severely, intransigently, and definitively, to tell that wicked atheist to go to hell, since, he mumbled, we weren't even properly married. Normally, he would have thought twice before telling a parishioner to kick out the father of her future child, no matter how shameless, lazy, alcoholic, or adulterous this person might be. But there was nothing to think about in this case. My lover was the devil. And that wasn't a metaphor. Seriously, the devil—he crossed himself—the diabolical devil, the Antichrist. I had to expel him from my life before he brought on more misfortune. And don't even think about telling him about the baby. Careful, I had to be very careful with that, okay? Not a word. Get him outta there and that was that, the best thing for the child. Didn't I know that famous phrase by José Martí, the one in the letter to his Mexican friend, the one that said that sometimes silence is necessary, that there are some things, in order to make them true, which have to be kept in the dark? That's right, so the child had to be kept in the dark. May God forgive him for such advice—he crossed himself again—but he was speaking to me with his heart in his hand. Was I going to listen to him, for once in my life?

I made a promise to him. In fact, I promised myself. But I didn't keep it. Not because I didn't think it was reasonable. To the contrary. Quitting Moisés meant the same thing to me as kicking heroin meant to others. The same good sense. The same benefits in terms of health. The same challenge. The same impossibility. For a while, I tried to fool myself, the way addicts do, with the silliness that, responsible for myself, in full control of my mental faculties, I could leave him whenever I wanted. So why do it that way, so abruptly? No, not like that. Better to wait for the right moment. That's right, the right moment. Every time I slept with him (then, contrary to what happens with other women, my nausea disappeared completely as if by magic), I would tell myself that was the last time. That it wouldn't happen again even if I was offered a million dollars. That that was the last time. And, since it was the last, it had to be *really* good. Something memorable. Something to remember later, after I'd left him and I was alone. And so everything was marvelous in the best of all possible ways.

The right moment, which had been longed for so often, finally presented itself one afternoon. After a long feverish embrace, we were exhausted, drained, practically bored with each other on the bathroom floor; he was on his back, I was on my side looking at his profile, which seemed lifted from an ancient coin. Far from me, from the goings on at the Corners, with his plans against "them," poor Alix (who was probably wandering around the porch like a lost cub so as not to hear us) was smoking a single cigarette and entertaining herself by contemplating the wisps of smoke. She made smoke rings, one inside the other, which made me jealous because I've never been able to do it. Now, I thought, right now when I don't want him, when I don't need him to touch me, now that he's lying there all crumbled up, trying to seem interesting, the tough guy, the lord of the rings, now that he's drained of the strength and energy necessary to start a fight, yes, now or never. I sat up and told him, looking him in the eye. I didn't want to go on with him. I didn't want to see him again. He needed to go.

He looked at me with astonishment, with a question mark written on his brow. What had I just said? I inched away and repeated it, word for word, as if it was the most natural thing in the world. I didn't want to go on with him.

I didn't want to see him again. He needed to go. His astonishment turned into incredulity. But . . . what was up? What had gotten into me? Was I serious? He had a look about him as if he was searching and searching for a punch line and not finding it. Then came the great question.

"Why?"

And the great answer.

"Why? Well, because . . . hmm . . . hmm . . . because I'm a Christian and you . . . you . . . hmm . . . you're the Antichrist."

Now that I think about it, it was a strange way to say goodbye to somebody. Generally speaking, there are other reasons. Because you're too bossy, like Pancholo told Yadelis. Because I love another, like JJ told Martica. Because you bore me, like Linda told the girl with the black hair. Because you're a lout who tried to kill Gruñi, I told a guy once. Because you're too good and I don't deserve you, Félix Roth told me. Human reasons. But the Antichrist . . . Moisés thought that was really erotic. The rascal took it as a compliment, a wink, a come on, and smiled like he'd finally understood the joke. Whatta slut I was. With this new, surprising, and unexpected shot of adrenaline, he embraced me and pulled me to him to start again. And me . . . since I'm not made of ice . . . It became quite clear to me that I could never leave him.

So then, what could I do? If neither the truth nor lies work, what other option is there? Alix, who was aware of my misadventures because she'd gone with me to Sagrado Corazón, very willingly offered to donate blood so that I could get an abortion behind the monster's back. A discreet option, legal and free. Bingo! This bright idea didn't strike me as either criminal or repugnant (Father Ignacio would have screamed to high heaven, into the very ear of God), but it did seem off-base. Sorta like recommending suicide to someone who's afraid of death. C'mon, sir, just hang yourself and you'll see how the fear passes. What I was most afraid of was that Moisés, in one of his furiously destructive attacks, would cause me to have a miscarriage, and here was this smiling girl, suggesting that I beat him to the punch. She wanted me to sacrifice what I couldn't protect and was only going to bring more anguish and heartache. It was that simple. As if the little five-week-old person was guilty of something. As far as Alix was concerned, of course, there was no little person, just a disposable entity, without a soul, without rights, a miserable little embryo that wasn't even a fetus yet. It goes without saying that I rejected her offer. With the greatest care, so as not to hurt her feelings. I was very grateful, I said in an emotional voice, with one of her hands between both of mine, I really was, but no. No way. I would *never* get an abortion. Why not? What do you mean why not? Because . . . well, because my faith doesn't allow it. This was true, although not entirely true: I spend my whole life doing things my faith prohibits. But it seemed like a good answer to dodge the question so that Alix wouldn't insist. And she didn't. From that moment on, she looked at me with pity.

And so, for one reason or another, all the alternatives, or at least the ones I could think of, began to cancel themselves out. I couldn't tell Moisés about the pregnancy, because it would most certainly drive him insane and provoke a tragedy. I couldn't break it off with him, because I adored him; not me exactly, but my body, and sometimes it's the body that calls the shots, who decides and executes. And I couldn't get an abortion, I just couldn't. What to do? The chilling question remained on the table, and the time to make a decision kept getting shorter. Even if Moisés didn't have one of his rages and kick me and liquidate the little person he was unaware of, sooner or later there would come the moment when I couldn't hide the pregnancy anymore. And then . . . Oh God, what could I do?

For an instant, I considered asking Linda for help. Contrary to me, she assures me, she uses her head for something other than hair, and always comes up with the most creative solutions for the most twisted puzzles. But back then she was furious with me for having taken in Alix, and I didn't dare call her. That flight reflex, which kicked in a little early perhaps, has earned me innumerable reproaches from her lately. What strange conclusion had I come to about her character? Do I think she's cold, hard, cruel, and vengeful? Her enemies (other writers, of course) see her that way, like a fox, always crouching, always ready to pounce, but me too? Or do I think she doesn't love me? Is it possible that after so many years I still don't know her at all? She would have helped me. Yes, of course she would have. In spite of my unforgivable betrayal, she tells me, she would have helped me. I believe her. I believe her now. In fact, I look back and wonder how I didn't call her. I dunno, maybe by then I'd already started to lose control.

I don't read a lot of poetry, it doesn't do much for me. But there's one poet I love: Charles Baudelaire. A very anguished and passionate guy. His existence is one of the few reasons I've ever regretted dropping out of the Alliance Française. But that's what translations are for. In one of his books, *Artificial Paradises* (I'm not sure, I don't have it on hand), he exhorts people to get drunk on wine, on poetry or virtue, because it doesn't matter, the important thing is to get drunk in order to escape the vertigo of time. It's a very elegant way, I think, to express the doctrine of the sorry carcasses. My memory of the time just before I realized that all the doors had closed, that I had no way out, are pretty fragmented and probably distorted, like Father Ignacio, Dr. Frumento, and Linda all say. That's due to the fact that I followed Baudelaire's advice to the letter. I got rigorously drunk. Not with wine and much less with poetry or virtue. With rum. Puddles, lakes, rivers, cascades of rum. An authentic Niagara Falls. So I could forget Moisés, who was more or less in the same condition, my confessor who didn't understand me, Alix who I couldn't convince to go back to Pinar del Río, Linda who was absent, Poliéster so present with his cornet and his percussion instruments, W. too old to get involved in such complicated and earthly conflicts, and the shameless megatherium who wouldn't stop barking. To forget about myself, my lack of skills and my faults and my contradictory wishes. So that I could go on dragging myself through the disgusting and remote roads our miserable lives have taken us down. It may seem like irresponsible behavior and it probably was, plus very selfish given the little person, the little six-, seven-, eight-, nine-and-a-half-week-old person, who almost drowned in liquor, but the vertigo of time was killing me.

It was a helluva party, continuous, action-packed, crazy. Day after day, from very early to very late. Sometimes at home, sometimes out in bars and clubs, always with Alix in tow. I would have preferred to be alone, but I have to admit that her dogged persistence in accompanying me wasn't altogether bad. The girl with the black hair could really hold her liquor; she drank like a veteran, like a professional Kurd, like those who bat .500 and then compete to see who's the toughest, the most macho, who can kill more bottles without killing themselves. She never went down. Me neither. Even though we barely ate. I'd get up every morning with a monstrous hangover and, to take care it, drink some rum. An effective therapy. Luckily, I had plenty of money (I've come to believe Moisés made it on a little machine; too bad he never showed me), and I never had to resort to Pancholo's rat-killing potion. Although I wouldn't have minded. Nor Coumadin, nor rubbing alcohol, nor head lice medicine—none of it would have turned me off. No way. Come hither, unhealthy potions. Come hither, that I will drink thee to the last drop. Because it wasn't about the taste or the burning in my throat, or the bombs that exploded in my stomach, but about oblivion, forgetting, escaping. To get so drunk, I'd be transported to another time and place. The eighteenth century, for instance.

With that as my backdrop, I did all sorts of things I'd never done before. Among other misdeeds, I stopped going to confession and, of course, I stopped taking communion and going to Mass. With my flip-flop, I squashed three cockroaches, two dark ones and an albino, because I'm phobic about them. A couple of times, I joined the chorus on the porch to sing the anthem of all Cuban drunks, the one that goes like this: "Even though you . . . / have abandoned me . . . / even though . . . / all my dreams have died . . . / instead . . . / of cursing you with righteous anger . . . / in my dreams I lavish you . . . / in my dreams I lavish you . . . / with blessings . . ." I stuck my tongue out at a cop, who didn't give a damn. I pulled the megatherium's tail with the intention of fleeing immediately afterward, even though I knew he would catch me and eat me, because he has four legs and I only have two. But I didn't have to take a single step. When the bastard turned around, indignant because of the disrespect and ready to bite my head off, it found Alix. She made no indication of movement, didn't move a muscle on her face or say a thing. She simply *looked* at it. Right in the eye. What an impact. The poor beast, because that's what it was reduced to, cowered on the floor and went crawling away, whining as if it were hurt, as if it had recognized the angel of death in that taciturn, thin, and black-garbed figure. If I'd been told about it, I wouldn't believe it. But I saw it. I swear I saw it. And Usnavy saw it too. And she was dumbfounded. What kind of freak, she must have asked herself, was I hanging out with? An angry ape, a gunslinger, a witch . . . I could put a circus together. The Bewitched Tent. Now I think animals smell danger in the literal sense, that they perceive certain dark clouds with much greater clarity than us.

But the most sensational thing, my greatest feat, was stealing the flower van. I remember it in a haze, as if it happened through a cloud of a foggy glass. It happened one morning when the angel of death and I were strolling along Colón cemetery, around the main entrance where there's a sign that says IANUA SVM PACIS, or something like that. In spite of the traffic, it's easy to see the last block on 12th Street from there. A bar, a liquor store, a few shops. The flower shop. There was a van stopped right in front of the flower shop. You walk up to it, without the slightest intentions, just to see, and you notice how the driver parks and goes into the shop with some papers and a clipboard in his hand. Guided as if by instinct, a heartbeat, you get closer and discover, surprise, the van, full of gladiolas, has the motor running and the door unlocked. Oh, how beautiful. Maybe the guy's in a hurry or this is a parking place after all . . . whatever. The guy's a jerk. Poor man. Without hesitation, you jump in the van and take off, with Alix as a copilot (you would have preferred she didn't meddle but this isn't the time to argue the point) and you don't stop until you get to Marianao, where you sell the gladiolas on your own to another flower shop and earn a nice piece of change. Then you dump the van somewhere where it's not too conspicuous, and that's that. Heh heh! You're the best!

Now it scares me to death, though it didn't scare me at all at the time, to think about the risk we took. And the risk wasn't driving the van. No way. With the exception of trains, I can drive anything that's ground transportation, from a velocipede to a truck. I've never had an accident. I've never run over a cat. I'm not boasting, it's a skill. One of those habits that turns into second nature. But I learned it on the sly with Pancholo Quincatrece and other rustlers in my city and I don't have a license to drive vans or buses or cranes or camellos or any of that. Only cars and that's enough. If I'd been stopped by the police for blowing a red light or something like that, I'd have been in a tight spot. Without a license, with alcohol on my breath, in a van that wasn't mine and with a bunch of gladiolas that weren't mine . . . I think they would have given me sixty to seventy years in jail for that. Crazy. Thankfully, everything went according to plan. Although I wasn't thinking about the risk while I was driving. I wasn't thinking about anything. My mind was blank, I was singing that song: "Ali Baba . . . / I'm the king of the snakes . . . / I ride a burrito . . . / I eat bananas." Whatta trip.

My copilot laughed because of the beauty of the whole thing. Though at first, when she lived in the penthouse, she'd looked at me with hate, later with fear on the porch at La Pelota, then with gratitude and later still with pity, now it was with admiration. At the end of the adventure, while we were celebrating Ali Baba's victory with a bottle of moonshine at the Malecón, she made one enigmatic comment.

"So you don't depend on him to live, you manage on your own . . ."

I didn't pay much attention to her. And then, three days later, the night of December 18, the eve of the end.

Whatta night. Alix and I had been drinking at a dive next to the Corners. I don't remember what we were talking about, if in fact we talked. Generally speaking, we didn't talk much. Although there was never anything uncomfortable about our silence, nor anxious nor tedious, nor was there ever that discomfiting emptiness that sometimes exists between people who stay together without having anything to say to each other. With Alix Oyster, it was as if we lived in the deepest seas, as if the silence was a natural human state. By that point, I'd stopped trying to convince her of the convenience of going back to Pinar del Río. To be honest, I didn't care anymore if she left or if she stayed until the end of time.

We went back to the Corners around midnight. We could hear hammering in the distance. The air conditioner was softly purring in rhythm. I tiptoed into the bathroom. My boo, who'd returned from one of his escapades that afternoon, was sleeping peacefully in the tub. As I quietly peed, I amused myself by watching him. He only had on a pair of denim shorts. Just like Alix, he loved the cold, to freeze, to pretend to be a polar bear. He said that our climate, with its humidity, hurricanes, scorching heat, and perpetually green trees, was for insects and, he added, that explained why there were so many people around us with insect brains. I never let on that he might be talking about me. As I looked at him, in spite of our routines and all the hassles, I was fascinated. He was so beautiful. So solid, so majestic, so perfect. How was he at twenty—long before I was even born? At fifty, the years still hadn't caught up with him. At least not on the outside. I've only seen (in person, I mean) one other man in my life who could compare with him physically: Cheo Piculín, the basketball star from Puerto Rico. Why hadn't Moisés, with that splendid physique of his, ever taken up sports? Maybe he would have been less unhappy. I know he boxed for a while, when he was very young, but then he switched to philosophy, penal law, oratory, the Napoleonic Code, the ancient Romans, and that foolishness. Life lays its traps. If it weren't that way, I thought as I left the bathroom, it wouldn't be worth living.

Tired, but at peace, I got in bed, where a drowsy Alix was waiting. I said good night and fell asleep, free of guilt and fears, disinfected by all the alcohol. I think I dreamt about a homeless kitty, a tiny thing left without a mom or dad, which whimpered the whole time. I would stroke him and say, "Kitty . . . kitty . . . kitty . . ." to no avail. The luckless creature continued crying. Then I woke up. I was still hearing the whimpering and for a moment thought there was, in fact, a cat in the apartment. But no. Of course not. It was Alix, whimpering in her dreams, very softly but right next to my ear. I got up and turned on the bamboo lamp with the red silk shade. Hugging herself, the girl with the black hair looked like she was really suffering. I turned and tried to wake her up as delicately as possible.

"Alix . . . Alix . . . girlee . . . it's a nightmare . . . Alix . . ." All along, I caressed her as if she were a kitty.

But, as Father Ignacio says, there is a great difference between a person and a cat. Still dreaming, Alix turned to me and hugged me and kissed my cheeks, my chin, my mouth . . . holy mother of God! This is all I needed! That the writer's ex-lover should want to get romantic with me! More than anything, I was shocked. Even in the moments when alcohol was running freest in her veins, Alix had never so much as insinuated anything with me, had never made the most insignificant untoward gesture. And now she was passionately kissing me, with her eyes closed, so boldly. Between kisses she said that she loved me, yes, like no one else, that we would never be apart again, because she was mine and I was hers, forever, eternal love, and all that extravagance. I was stiff as a board. And scared too, I won't deny it. Why did this have to happen to me? Why? I didn't dare try to get her off me or scramble away or anything. I got nauseous when she promised to leave N. Cohen alone and read all my novels. I would have preferred that she leave *me* alone. And that's what she did, and rather abruptly, when she touched my tits over my t-shirt and something in her head went "click," like a warning, and she realized her mistake. Linda may have many virtues, but her chest is practically flat.

The somnambulist opened her eyes and looked at me with terror, as if she'd just committed a crime. It was the same face I imagine she had when that supposedly unloaded gun went off and there was blood all over my friend's face. She took her hands off me immediately, as if they were burning. She mumbled some nonsense in the form of apology, but without much conviction, with the resignation of someone who believes they're doomed and has no right to appeal. Maybe she thought I'd make a big deal out of it, or something like that, poor girl. I felt sorry for her.

"Hey, hey, it's not so bad," I said while trying to keep the look of astonishment on my face in check so she wouldn't think I was icked out by her or some such atrocity. "Don't get that look. It's not the first time I've been mistaken for Linda. If you only knew . . . I mean, she and I look so much alike . . ."

She raised an eyebrow. Then she cocked her head, the way a dog does when it hears a strange noise. I think she thought I was making fun of her. People love to think I do that, I dunno why. I shortened the distance that had suddenly grown between us.

"Listen, Alix, nothing happened. Do you understand? Nothing. If I was Linda for a moment, fine. Linda's extraordinary in many ways. She's lucid, talented, brave, strong, pretty, and, though it may not always appear to be the case, a good person. Why would I get offended if you confused me with her?

The only thing I regret, and I say this with total honesty, is not really being her. At least right here and now, for you."

Her eyes got teary. I hugged her before she started crying, like before, very softly. I stroked her back. "It's okay, it's okay . . . calm down . . . calm down now." She whispered in my ear, choking, that I was the kindest person she'd ever met, that I didn't deserve what was happening to me, and that she was going to take care of my problem once and for all, that she had it all figured out and was ready to go. I didn't understand a word she said. What problem was she talking about? What did she have figured out? I didn't ask her right there and then because I was exhausted, nauseous, and dizzy. I asked her to please turn off the lamp, to see if we could catch a few winks. She could tell me all about what she'd figured out and what she was ready to do tomorrow.

But there was no tomorrow. There were no more days with Alix. She simply disappeared. I haven't seen her again, and I like to think she went back to the little farm. Me, I'm off liquor, grass, and even cigarettes. It won't be long before the baby's born; it'll be a boy and he'll be named Luis Enrique, after my dad. Linda asked me to go live with her, because Happy Hammer Corners is no place for a baby. I'm thinking about it. Father Ignacio doesn't think it's a bad idea, but I'm not sure it'll happen. We'll see. For the moment, I'm trying to forget, though I fear that image of the angel of death—a taciturn, svelte, black-garbed figure slipping in and out of the shadows to approach me and warn me that the window's open—will never leave me.

CPSIA information can be obtained
at www.ICGtesting.com
Printed in the USA
JSHW032155220322
24149JS00001B/90